PRASE FOR

By Fire, By Water

"A grand novel that shows not only Kaplan's knack for storytelling, but also his eye for details." —*Pittsburgh Tribune-Review*

"Debut novelist Kaplan depicts a turbulent period in fifteenth-century Spain, focusing on the story of Aragon's royal chancellor . . . Deftly moves through a complex web of personal relationships, religious zeal, and political fervor." —*Kirkus Reviews*

"Blending artistry with intense drama and violence, *By Fire, By Water* takes readers on a picturesque tour of the Iberian Peninsula of the mid-1400s . . . *By Fire, By Water* is a finely crafted novel . . . It's rare to find historical fiction this intense and exquisite." —Bookreporter.com

"A must-read." —*Pittsburgh Jewish Chronicle*

"Kaplan's greatest success is in his ability to portray the inner lives of his characters." —*Washington Jewish Week*

"Mitchell James Kaplan's *By Fire, By Water* must take its place as one of the most important contemporary historical novels with a Jewish theme." —*Haaretz*

"Beautifully written, *By Fire, By Water* is a powerful story of religion, love, and violence—timeless themes honed by Kaplan into an enthralling narrative that doesn't let up until the last sentence." —Simon Read, author of *War of Words*

By Fire, By Water

By Fire, By Water

. . . .

a novel

MITCHELL JAMES KAPLAN

OTHER PRESS · *New York*

2023 Edition
ISBN 978-1-63542-400-3

Production Editor: *Yvonne E. Cárdenas*
Text Designer: *Simon M. Sullivan*
This book was set in 10.75pt Garamond by Alpha Design &
Composition of Pittsfield, NH.

10 9 8 7 6 5 4 3 2 1

LIBRARY OF CONGRESS CATALOGING-IN-PUBLICATION DATA
Kaplan, Mitchell James.
By fire, by water / by Mitchell James Kaplan.
p. cm.
ISBN 978-1-59051-352-1 (acid-free paper)—ISBN 978-1-59051-357-6
(e-book) 1. Inquisition—Spain—Fiction. 2. Spain—History
—711-1516—Fiction. I. Title.
ps3611.a656b9 2010
813'.6—dc22 2009041068

For Annie

The world owes all its onward impulses to men ill at ease.

—NATHANIEL HAWTHORNE,
The House of the Seven Gables

By Fire, By Water

Kingdom of Navarre

Kingdom of Aragon

Zaragoza

Barcelona

asterio de
anta Cruz

Teruel

Castellon
de la Plana

Valencia

Murcia

om of
anada
nada

Almeria

ubreña
laga

Middle Sea

Darkness in Zaragoza
July 1487

NDER A SLIVER MOON, Luis de Santángel, royal chancellor of Aragon, trudged down a narrow street toward the center of the capital, his high boots softly clopping against the cobblestones. A silk surcoat covered most of his tunic and hose. Abundant chestnut hair, tinged with gray, fell to the top of his back. Beside him shuffled Abram Serero, shorter than Santángel, with rounded shoulders, a thick chest, and a close copper-red beard.

They stopped before a stone building. Santángel pulled open the massive door. Fumes wafted out, cold, musty, rancid. Overwhelmed, Serero stumbled backward.

At the bottom of the stairwell, the chancellor clanked a metal ring. A man coughed. A key rattled. The door grated as it swung open.

The warden of the ecclesiastical jail, a dwarf in a formless robe, held a fat candle. Santángel handed him a pouch. "This is for your discretion. Show us to his cell."

The warden counted the coins. He raised his eyes and peered at the chancellor as if to discern his features.

"Please refrain from gazing at me."

"Certainly, my lord. I meant no harm."

The two visitors lowered their heads and descended into the dwarf's bedchamber. A jug of wine sat on the beaten-earth floor. A blanket dangled from the bed, a niche in the wall.

The warden led them through another archway and down narrow corridors. He opened a door into a cramped cell where Luis de

Santángel's brother Estefan—his brother who was not, in truth, his brother—lay on the dirt floor, a gaunt and squalid heap. The chancellor fell to his knees. Estefan's eyes, beneath their lids, twitched.

"He is a brave man," said the dwarf. "He didn't give in."

"When did he last eat?"

"I leave what I can. A piece of cheese. A crust of bread. But the rats finish it before he gets to it."

"Thank you." Santángel glanced at Serero. "What are we to do? He can't ask God for forgiveness."

"He need not ask for forgiveness. We can still pray. Perhaps he will hear."

Abram Serero began chanting softly, in a rich baritone, a prayer recited every year on the Day of Atonement. *Ashamnu, bagadnu, gazalnu, dibarnu dofi, hevinu.* We have been guilty, we have betrayed, we have stolen, we have spoken falsely, we have caused others to sin.

Luis de Santángel watched his brother's face. Estefan, more than any other man, had witnessed the chancellor's struggle, taken pride in his precarious triumphs, cringed before the demons that haunted both their lives. He had cautioned Luis about the perils of their secret identity. Yet he was the one held captive in this place. Luis de Santángel gathered his reeking, emaciated brother into his arms and rocked him gently.

CHAPTER ONE

Rome, Six Years Earlier

A TURKISH SLAVE ESCORTED Luis de Santángel and his translator, Cristóbal Colón, through the wide marble hallways of the papal palace. "First, endeavor to put him at ease," said the chancellor. "Speak of all you know and share. Then, as soon as he's comfortable . . ."

"I shall disappear behind the mask of my purpose." As he walked, Colón pushed his wavy mane, the color of wheat mixed with ashes, back from his forehead. His face, lined and tanned, appeared to be a few years older than Santángel's. At thirty, he was in fact two years younger.

Their Turkish escort stopped at the door of the pope's bedroom. Cluttered with candelabras, tapestries from Arras, sculptures of saints and angels by Luigi Capponi and Andrea Bregno, paintings of the Annunciation and the Nativity by Perugino, and a large gold birdcage filled with canaries and finches, this single chamber served as the pope's throne room, dining room, and washroom. A food taster stood by his bedside to check each plate and cup for poison. A clerk sat at the desk, jotting notes on every word uttered. Two guards watched the door. Although the palace boasted more than a thousand rooms, the pope received cardinals, kings, princes, and their most influential advisors without rising from bed.

"Luis de Santángel, chancellor of Aragon, and Cristóbal Colón, a ship's captain, who will translate for him."

"Show them in."

Under a velour blanket, magenta and cream, the pope's stomach protruded like a rat in a snake's belly. His face, with its small eyes, long aquiline nose, and recessed chin, reminded Santángel of a falcon. The chancellor and the ship's captain knelt at the pope's bedside.

"You have voyaged a great distance," remarked the pope.

"Tell him about yourself," Santángel encouraged Colón, in Castilian. "We'll have plenty of time to talk about me."

Colón turned back to the pope. "Voyaging great distances is my life. But my heart remains in Liguria, where I grew up, and where Your Holiness spent so much of his youth. My uncle Nicolo, he knew you, many years ago."

The pope frowned, searching his memory. "Colón . . ."

"In Castile, yes, I'm Colón," explained the captain. "But in Genoa, I'm Christoffa Colombo, son of Domenico, the weaver." The two names, though similar in sound, were vastly different in meaning, as both men knew. *Colón* meant "colonizer," while *Colombo* meant "dove."

"Ah, yes. Nicolo Colombo, the cloth merchant. A talented man. And honest, or so it seemed."

"Talented, yes," confirmed the captain.

"But not so honest, perhaps?" The pope's eyebrows swam into his forehead.

Colón glanced at the chancellor. "My uncle, he cheated nearly everyone. He borrowed my father's inheritance, then lost it. The magistrate Giambattista Fregoso—"

"Yes, yes, I knew his brother," rasped the pope.

"My uncle sold him wool for a coat. Fregoso found the same fabric down the street for a third of what he paid. But the magistrate, he was no fool, Your Holiness. He got his revenge."

The pope smiled, savoring the gossip. "How?"

"In those days, the two men were seeing the same prostitute."

"Who?"

"Donna Sofia, in the Gobbe."

"Yes, yes."

"Let us say Fregoso paid her well. She gave my uncle a moment he never forgot."

The pope laughed heartily, his double chin wiggling. His face turned scarlet. Luis de Santángel was pleased to witness the warm feelings developing between the two.

"And how is your father?" the pope resumed, to Colón. "I believe I met him once."

"I have no idea," replied the captain. "Haven't spoken with him in years."

"Why not?"

"If you'll pardon the expression, Your Holiness, he's a goatish, addle-pated lout."

The pontiff's laughter degenerated into a fit of coughing.

"How can I help you, Chancellor?" The pope recovered, turning his eyes to Santángel.

"Most Holy Father," began the chancellor in Castilian with as much confidence as he could muster. "I hesitate . . . I hesitate to impugn an institution that was created by, or with, the sanction of the Holy Church." He inhaled deeply, steeling himself.

Colón translated fluidly. Glibly, perhaps, reflected Santángel.

"And which institution might that be?"

"The New Inquisition," replied Santángel, "which Father Tomás de Torquemada has established in Castile, and which he hopes to import to Aragon."

"He hopes to?"

"We have our *cortes*. Our legal councils. So far, we have prevailed. But without the support of Rome, we won't prevail for long."

"Please, continue."

Santángel noted the pope's interest. He suspected the pontiff held little enthusiasm for Torquemada's enterprise. Unlike the traditional Inquisition, the New Inquisition in Castile refused to divide its spoils with Rome, instead sharing them exclusively with Queen Ysabel.

"As you well know, Your Holiness, this New Inquisition ignores almost all forms of heresy, except one—'judaizing.' And that one it pursues with a zeal we've never before seen."

The pope coughed into his fist.

"Your Holiness," resumed Santángel, "in Madrid, Segovia, and Cordoba, friends spy on friends, neighbors on neighbors, children on their parents. Even criminals lodge accusations."

He paused to allow his translator to catch up.

"There's no punishment," pursued the chancellor, "despite the Ninth Commandment of our holy book, for bringing false accusations. If two men claim they heard another express heretical thoughts, that man's conviction is assured. He'll have to confess and pay penance, often everything he possesses, whether he be guilty or not. The man's accusers will receive a portion of the spoils—a rich temptation, especially for criminals."

He swallowed to slow his speech, but the rush of thoughts and emotions propelled him forward. "And even after the suspect confesses, it won't be enough. He'll have to name other secret heretics, whether or not he knows any."

In the huge birdcage, one of the canaries warbled. The chancellor stopped. He had hardly begun to enumerate his grievances, but did not wish to tax his gracious listener.

When Colón, in turn, ceased speaking, the pope nodded. "I sympathize with your confusion and pain. But I'm not sure I fully understand your reasoning."

"What can I clarify, Your Holiness?"

"Do you deny that we must fight to preserve the integrity of our faith? Or do you feel that every man should feel free to think and act as he wishes?"

Santángel stiffened. "That is not what I'm advocating."

"Let me ask you a question. Are you, yourself, a *converso*?" The pope knew the Spanish term, which designated one whose parents or grandparents had abandoned the Jewish faith and embraced the faith of Christ, usually under duress.

"I am a Christian, Your Holiness."

The pope nodded slightly. "And how did you come to work so closely with the king and queen, in the conjoined courts of Aragon and Castile?"

"My father was chief tax farmer of Valencia." The chancellor spoke more cautiously. "Even as a boy, I was on familiar terms with royalty. Not only in Castile, but in Aragon as well. As you surely know, Holy Father, the project of marrying the realms of Castile and Aragon was the work of many minds."

The pope's lips curled into a half-repressed grin. "And now, you feel trapped, serving a regime whose interest—particularly, whose zeal to confiscate the property of rich *conversos*—no longer corresponds with yours." Again, he coughed. His taster handed him a glass of almond liquor.

The pope resumed: "You can't walk away from the coveted position you've created for yourself. You'd lose not only the power you wield over your subordinates, and perhaps a great deal of your wealth, but more importantly, you would lose your precious influence over the Crowns. Is that not so?"

Still kneeling, Santángel gripped the bedrail.

"You see," added the pope, "in this corrupt world of ours, everyone must make compromises." He glanced at his guards.

Appreciating the pope's honesty, Santángel followed his eyes. The two guards turned. It was a cue whose meaning was not lost on the chancellor. "Holy Father, thank you for hearing me."

From his pocket, he removed a leather box filled with gold coins. Upon the pope's gesture, Santángel placed the box on the bedside table.

. . .

Though owned by the Church, Civitavecchia bustled as brassily as any other port town. Standing in the open doorways of their brick-and-stone two- and three-story homes, merchants called out their wares.

"Mussels, clams, sardines, still wiggling in their juices!"

"Candles for your bedside! Iron fixtures I have, hinges, rods, door locks!"

"From Perugia, the finest soap!"

"Hot brew, step inside! Come, come!"

In the heavy air, victuals, old urine, and spices blended into one pungent stench. Drunks loitered outside taverns. A child, brandishing a stick, chased a barking mutt down the street. Prostitutes in garish dresses competed for the gentleman's eye. Santángel and Colón ignored them as they plodded toward the harbor.

"Are we ready to sail, then?"

"Just chasing a few stragglers," replied the captain. "We'll be off before long."

"We haven't got a full crew?"

"Don't worry, Chancellor. These louts, when they're not pouring ale down their gullets, they're wasting their vigor in brothels. But we'll find enough men. This town is full of sailors. They all get hungry sooner or later."

At the end of a narrow, dark alley, the sky and sea opened before them like an immense gate. Galleys and caravels, encrusted with barnacles, rigged with blackened, swaying ropes, their sails yellow-brown and patched, clustered about the docks like pigs at a feeding trough. Carpenters, blacksmiths, and caulkers hammered and sawed on the worn bulwarks. Sailors hauled crates up long gangways. Gulls circled and called in the tar-scented morning air.

A square-rigged caravel had come in. Crewmen lowered its jib sail and reamed its scuppers, the drains that channeled water off the main deck. On the quay, a grizzled merchant-sailor harangued a motley crowd of shopkeepers, guildsmen, farmers, and loiterers. Portly, with tight leggings, a laced linen shirt that must once have looked extravagant, sagging jowls, and wet hair the hue of charred driftwood, he injected every word with a ragged, grim earnestness. His human cargo slouched and slumped behind him, a sorry assortment of outlanders exuding sweat, fear, and defiance, chained together at the ankles. Their bruises testified to a harrowing voyage.

As Santángel and Colón approached, the slave merchant pulled forward a captive. "This miscreant, his wife, poor thing, passed on during the crossing. What a feisty, wild animal she was. Her husband's eyes, as you see, gentlemen, they're still brimming with tears."

The slave was a burly man with a thick moustache and curly, shoulder-length hair the color of mud. The raw, red stripes of a recent lashing streaked his chest and arms. He directed his murky regard somewhere in the distance.

"But his boy, here," the merchant tugged a child forward, "not more than ten, and as pliant as clay. He'll grow big, like his father. Raise him right, you'll have a sturdy laborer."

The boy's father drew his son to his chest, shouting something incomprehensible. The crowd answered with hoots, yelps, and laughter. Luis de Santángel found no humor in it. He, too, had lost his wife and had been left raising a son alone.

"Six silver lire," a man in a hair tunic called to the slave merchant. The merchant ignored this insulting offer. "Let me tell you another secret about this fellow. We put him to work on our caravel. Yes, we did." He turned to a member of his crew. "How good a sailor was he, Giovanni?"

The sailor spat and answered, "Real good."

The child was now sobbing, his bare stomach contracting in spasms.

"Why don't we bid on them?" Santángel asked Colón. "We need sailors, don't we? The boy can be our steward. Purchase them both."

Colón called out an offer. Others began increasing their bids. In the end, Colón won the father and the boy. The price Santángel paid for them, the captain found not merely excessive but outrageous. How any man could blithely cast away so many of the same gold pieces that Colón labored and sweated endlessly for, on stormy seas and in freezing ports, he could not fathom. Luis de Santángel, the royal chancellor of Aragon, was reputed to be astute, haughty, and guileful; but these epithets, Colón sensed, hardly sufficed to define him.

. . .

Santángel's eyes drank in the immensity of the *Giustizia*, a resplendent man-of-war, a hundred and thirty feet long, twenty-eight across, its carved hull painted in ocher and gold leaf, radiant under the cobalt sky. For Santángel, the procurement of this warship represented a triumph. With Colón's assistance, he had transformed a perilous investment, silver and ivory from the Southern Continent, into a windfall not only for himself, but also for the Crown of Aragon.

"All fitted-out to meet your king's desires." Colón stopped, pulled tight the cord around his linen smock, and corrected himself: "*Our* king's desires."

At present, Colón was living in Lisbon, where his brother was a mapmaker, but he intended to resettle in Spain. He wanted those close to the king and queen, and especially Santángel, to think of him as a Spaniard.

Santángel stepped back to view the ship better. He ran his palm over his cheek. "She is splendid."

"Let me show you." Placing a hand on Santángel's back, Colón guided him to the main deck, past rope cages that held pigs, chicken, and sheep. He led him up narrow stairwells to the fore-castle and the poop castle, fitted with swivel guns and cannons. He escorted Santángel down to the galley and the hold, where barrels stacked three-high contained gunpowder and ammunition, extra sails, pickled beef, olive oil, diluted wine, and fresh water. He ush-ered Santángel into a small room below the gun deck all the way aft, dimly lit through a narrow, rectangular porthole.

"A stateroom to yourself, Chancellor."

The chancellor grabbed hold of a post, adjusting to the ship's slow up-and-down motion, and glanced about the tight, oaken chamber. Tar-filled floor planks, a hay mattress, covered with a dusky linen cloth, two candles in a wrought-iron lantern. "And the sailors, where do they sleep?"

"On the deck, in the hold, anywhere. If they can't find a spot, they stay awake. Most likely, they'll keep you awake, too, with their shouting, their singing, their quarrels. A bunch of brawlers, the lot of them. Some wine?"

"Please."

Colón had taken the trouble to place a ceramic decanter and two tin cups on the writing table. He filled one and handed it to Santángel. "To the *Giustizia*, and to the holy war against Granada, which she'll help win for our king and queen."

. . .

That night, as the *Giustizia* groaned and swayed, the two men slid roughly carved knights and pawns across the crude squares of a chessboard painted on the lid of Colón's trunk. Being the more voluble of the two, the captain entertained the man who controlled King Fernando's finances, relating tales of trading and the sea.

"Near Lisbon, pirates attacked us," he reminisced. "They set my ship ablaze. I had to swim ashore. Lost everything. Had to start all over in a foreign land. To learn a new language. To scrabble for bread." He sipped his wine. "Eventually, I befriended a cartographer close to the court. My brother now works for him. I've stayed in Lisbon six years, now. More than ready for another move."

"Where will you go?"

"Andalusia. Medina-Celi and I, we have plans."

Santángel nodded. His sometime business associate Luis de la Cerda, the duke of Medina-Celi, owned a shipping enterprise near Cadiz. He had helped finance the *Giustizia* and had introduced the chancellor to Colón.

"I married the most beautiful, loving woman in existence," resumed the captain. "To believe in a hapless dreamer like me, she had to be an angel sent by God. She died. You, too, lost your wife, did you not, Chancellor?"

"Yes." Santángel glanced into Colón's pearly eyes. "I only regret God didn't give me more time with her." He remembered his departed wife's laugh, her lively voice, her love for their son, whom she had carried with so much pain and whom she had held only once.

His thoughts wandered to the fruit of their love. He had left Gabriel, now eight, in the care of his brother Estefan. "No wine, no women, I promise," Estefan had assured him. Eager to let Estefan prove himself, Santángel had accepted the arrangement.

"And today?" asked Colón. "Is there a woman close to your heart?" He inched one of his pawns forward.

"No." Santángel pushed a knight toward the center of the board.

"I'm always riding the sea, and what a skittish stallion she is, from port to port," said the captain. "From one wench's arms to another. Haven't found another lady like my wife." The boat heaved. He held onto the trunk, which was nailed to the floor.

"Our wives die," said Santángel, "to give birth to our sons. And we go on through life, pursuing our vain ambitions." He shook his head.

"Life's cruelty surely must lead to some reward."

"What reward?" Santángel shot back. "Wealth? Prestige? Titles? Do you believe God cares about our rank?"

"No. God cares about one thing. Jerusalem."

"How so?" Santángel moved a bishop. If he had sentiments about Jerusalem, he was not about to reveal them. Not even here, so far from home.

"God wants Jerusalem liberated. He needs our help." Colón quaffed his wine and wiped his mouth on his sleeve. "I would think you, of all people, would appreciate that, Chancellor."

Santángel ignored the insinuation. "Why would God want us to shed blood over a few stones in a desolate, faraway desert?"

Colón peered at him skeptically.

"There's so much strife in our own land, Señor Colón. In Aragon, in Castile. No, there are certainly more worthy quests than the liberation of Jerusalem."

"I cannot think of any." Colón slid his king one square to the right.

Santángel was not about to list the worthier pursuits. To speak of such things would be to reveal his private hopes and disappointments. "Why don't we stop for now? We'll resume tomorrow."

Colón's eyes met the chancellor's. "Quite the lazy wretch, that pope of ours, eh?" he spat out, apropos of nothing.

Santángel decided not to accept this bait, either. "Good evening, Captain." As he rose, the ship tossed. He almost fell.

Colón caught him. "Are you all right, Chancellor?"

"Just a little queasy, thank you."

The captain held on to him until the chancellor steadied himself.

. . .

Santángel retreated to his cabin, where he relived his meeting with the pope, searching through the pontiff's words and expressions for encouraging signs—signs that he, his friends, and his associates would prevail in the struggle of their lives, the struggle *for* their lives. He closed his eyes and covered his ears to muffle the hollering, pounding, and cursing of the sailors, the creaking of the ship. Occasionally he nibbled on the salted, dried cod and hard bread, or sipped the wine that his steward, the child whose freedom he had purchased, delivered to his room.

Santángel attempted to teach this boy a few words of Castilian. He learned his name, Dumitru, and his father's name, Iancu. He sent a short note to Colón: "Please permit Dumitru to sleep with his father."

On the third morning, Santángel ventured out for a taste of the crisp, salty air. The ship squawked as a stiff breeze shoved it westward. Cristóbal Colón greeted him with a lopsided grin. "Ah, Chancellor, finding our sea legs at last, are we?"

"I'm feeling somewhat better, thank you."

He glanced down the deck at a group of sailors entertaining each other with a fight. A seagull called out and dove toward the water, then soared upward again, a small mackerel squirming in its beak.

"If you would follow me, Chancellor. I have something that may interest you." Colón gently took his guest's arm.

From his battered wooden chest, the captain removed a variety of texts, some hand-copied, others mechanically printed. Onto many of these pages, Colón had scribbled his own comments.

"Aristotle. *Treatise on Heaven and Earth*. Look here." The captain found a page in the thin octavo and read not from the Latin itself, but from the notes he had written in the margin: "The Ocean, it is not immeasurable." He looked up. "You see, Chancellor? One can sail from Castile to Cipangu."

"Cipangu?"

"The great island-state of the Indias, where gold and pearls can be had for next to nothing." His large, chafed hands dug further into the chest until he found a ragged copy of Marco Polo's *Description of the World*. "Ah." He leafed delicately through this book, once again examining his notes.

He closed the volume and searched for another. "Ptolemy. He proved that of the three hundred and sixty degrees of the globe, only one hundred and thirty-five are water." The captain recited this fact, and others, in the manner of a student preparing for an examination.

"That's quite a collection, Captain. And your knowledge is hardly less impressive. But what is it that . . ."

Colón interrupted, eyes gleaming. "If we sailed west, Chancellor, if we just sailed due west, a few weeks, not more, we could reach the Indias directly. We wouldn't have to trade with the Saracens."

"Señor Colón, if you're asking me . . . If what you're asking me is to finance a voyage of exploration . . ."

The captain plunged forward. "And if we continued westward from there . . . the Garden of Eden. Paradise. A land so abundant with spices, gold, and every fruit and animal you can imagine, it puts even Cipangu to shame. And beyond that," he added in a reverential tone, almost a whisper, "Jerusalem."

Santángel sat down on Colón's berth. "Suppose we were to go there, Señor Colón. Suppose we were to retake Jerusalem from the east, as you suggest. Then what?"

"Then . . . this world would be a different place. A very different place."

"Perhaps. But if such a voyage could truly be done, surely someone would have gone there and come back to tell of it."

Colón removed a worn leather envelope from his trunk. "That is the right question, Chancellor. I have other texts, rare texts, that just may answer it."

From the pouch he extracted small pamphlets, a rolled-up parchment, single leaves—some torn, some printed, and some in manuscript. He closed the trunk, lay several pages on its lid, and gazed at their characters like a child peering into a cloudy pond, trying to discern the forms of wriggling fish.

"What are they?" Santángel gawped at the strange calligraphy.

"I don't know. I was hoping you could tell me. I know you speak many tongues."

"Castilian, Aragonese, Arabic, a smattering of Italian. No others."

"I got these," Colón explained, "from Señor José Vizinho. Perhaps you've heard of him. The great cartographer, in Lisbon. A Jew."

"I'm afraid I know little of that science."

"These texts, they're quite rare. And the secrets in them, they're invaluable, from what I was told." He began replacing the texts in their pouch. "Perhaps you know someone who could translate them." Colón attempted to place the leather envelope in Santángel's hands.

"I'm sorry, Señor Colón, but I cannot accept this." The chancellor was not a fearful man, but the thought of harboring Hebrew documents filled his heart with a black dread.

"That is unfortunate." Colón dropped the pouch on his berth and clapped Santángel on the shoulder. "But I understand, Chancellor. I understand."

The chancellor doubted Colón could possibly understand. The New Inquisition was a war. For Luis de Santángel to possess a Hebrew text would amount to suicide.

Despite that war, and in part because of it, Santángel longed to return to Zaragoza—to his son, his brother, his home.

. . .

At the port of Barcelona, he took leave of Cristóbal Colón. On unsteady legs, he proceeded to the Braying Goat, a small portside inn. He paid the innkeeper for feeding and watering his horse Béatriz while he was away, and commissioned him to forward his trunk to the royal palace of Zaragoza.

Béatriz measured only fourteen hands, but she was strong and alert. Her silky mane fell to one side of a graceful, arched neck. Her shoulders gently sloped. A narrow stripe, nearly black in color, stretched along the top of her roan coat from her mane to her tail. While the innkeeper saddled her, Santángel sipped a bowl of well water and asked for news from the royal court. The innkeeper claimed to have heard Queen Ysabel's name spoken, more than once, as well as King Fernando's, but could not say whether troops were massing in the south or whether the plague had struck Sevilla. "I can quote you the price of a barrel of wine or a bucket of fish. But news from the court . . ." He rubbed his neck. "The high and lofty don't pass this way often. Except you, my lord." He handed Santángel the reins, accepting with a bow the coins offered.

The chancellor rode for five days, savoring the foretaste of his reunion with those dear to him, attempting to put out of his mind the challenges ahead. He traversed long valleys where peasants harvested wheat and fruit. He crossed hills covered with oak and scrub. Clouds filled the sky. The autumn air grew chill. On the fourth day, a storm broke. Santángel persisted through the rain.

Having traveled these muddy roads before, he knew where to find a good cup and where to lay his head.

. . .

When he reached the hills south of Zaragoza, the sun was sinking through bloated yellow clouds, washing the region in a golden light. He pulled back on his horse's reins and contemplated the view, this oasis in a parched land, irrigated by the softly meandering, teal-colored River Ebro.

The almond and peach trees beside the river had shed most of their leaves. Beyond them, peasants wearing dun-brown smocks bent over fields of wheat, wielding scythes. Roman walls, which the army of Caesar Augustus had built centuries earlier, separated these orchards and fields from the cluster of tile-roofed dwellings.

The city's name, as well as its architecture, told the story of its long-contested territory. The Romans had named the settlement after their emperor. The Visigoths captured "Caesaraugusta" from the Romans, and the Moors from the Visigoths. The syllables of its name melted together, as if in the North African sun, into the more Arabic-sounding "Saraqusta." After the Christians retook the city in 1118, their tongues rounded the sharp edges of "Saraqusta" to "Zaragoza," much as the River Ebro smoothed the stones of its bed.

To the west lay the crenellations of the monumental citadel the Moors had built, the *aljaferia*, now King Fernando's palace. Near the center of the city, the towers of La Seo Cathedral, once an Islamic mosque, cast long shadows toward the river. The seven-arched stone bridge, the *puente de piedra*, stretched across the river behind the cathedral.

Zaragoza. This small, isolated, land-locked village, home of Aragonese rulers for so many generations. Santángel's refuge, and his battleground.

. . .

That morning, residents of the town had celebrated the Fiesta del Pilar, commemorating the day when the Virgin Mary appeared atop a pillar in the center of Zaragoza, ushering Christianity into the Iberian Peninsula. Parades had wound through the cobblestone streets. Peasants and guildsmen had danced together in the plazas. In many homes, festivities would continue into the night.

In honor of the holiday, celebrants had festooned La Seo with ribbons, clay figurines of the Virgin, crudely painted wooden icons, and field flowers. At this hour, late in the afternoon, the worshipers had gone home but their offerings remained. A few churchmen hovered in the corners, muttering.

Santángel strode to the back of the cathedral and knelt facing the bloody crucifix. He wanted not only to attempt sincere, wholehearted prayer, but also to be seen praying. "Dear Lord," he closed his eyes, "thank you for protecting me and bringing me home safely. Please bestow your blessings and protection on my only child, Gabriel. I pray that my late wife is watching him from a place of repose. Please also protect King Fernando and Queen Ysabel. Open their hearts to the sufferings of those worthy of their compassion. Bring us success in our war against the kingdom of Granada. Let us be victorious, but let us not abuse our victory." He waited for more such earnest thoughts. "Bring us clear sight, Lord," he concluded, "of what is good and what is evil."

He opened his eyes and peered at the wounded, twisted statue of Christ. He tried to visualize the real Christ standing before him, the God made flesh and blood who came to die for man's sins, the God of forgiveness and redemption. Try as he might, he could not see God. He could only see a man. He had seen those same eyes, that gaunt face a year previously, at an *auto-da-fé* in Sevilla. On that day, in the name of the Lord, the Inquisition had burned fifteen heretics, fifteen *conversos*. Among them, four women and three boys barely out of childhood.

When those poor souls, who had endured starvation and torture, stared down at the spellbound crowd, it struck Santángel with the force of a nightmare that one of them looked just like the Lord Jesus Messiah. He remembered a painting he had seen in Barcelona, a depiction of Jesus reaching out to help as Saint Peter attempted to walk upon water. That pale, absent, *undone* expression. The chancellor, shocked, had crossed himself. The others around him, entranced by the spectacle of human agony, seemed not to notice.

He examined the statue again, hoping to perceive something of its divine mystery. To his chagrin, another prayer came silently to his lips, a prayer his mother had taught him when he was nine years old, a secret heritage. He thought he had forgotten. He should have forgotten, for his own sake and for that of his son.

Shema Yisrael . . . "Hear, Israel: the Lord, our God. The Lord. One."

One. Abstract, impalpable, unseeable, even unknowable. The God of Santángel's grandparents, so distant, so silent, so inaccessible. Santángel crossed himself, lonelier than ever, and rose to leave.

As he walked back through the nave, he caught sight of Pedro de Arbués, the canon of La Seo Cathedral, speaking in the shadows with Pedro de Monterubio, the monsignor of Zaragoza. A mountain of a man, swathed in white and gold vestments, the canon listened with his fleshy face slightly lowered, looking up at Monterubio.

"With your new responsibilities, Father, surely you won't have time to lead the Mass or take confession."

"On the contrary," insisted Arbués, "Even as Chief Inquisitor of Zaragoza, I remain the humble shepherd of my flock." Hearing Santángel's footsteps, he glanced down the nave, then back at the monsignor.

Santángel slowed his pace.

Monsignor Pedro de Monterubio, thin, gray, and frail with age, pleaded with the canon as though he ranked lower in the hierarchy. "Father Arbués, I beseech you. Please avail yourself of our assistance."

Perhaps the monsignor, too, feared the encroachment of the Inquisition, reflected Santángel, and wished to plant eyes and ears within Arbués's office.

Arbués turned again to face the chancellor. The two churchmen ceased speaking.

His heart pounding, Santángel stepped into the plaza. Dusk was approaching. A wood seller, pushing a cart, saw him and spat onto the cobblestones.

Santángel grabbed him by the shoulders. "Wood seller, why did you spit?"

"My lord, forgive me. I meant nothing."

The chancellor held him. "You saw me. You spat. Why?"

The woodsman coughed and swallowed. Santángel released him and climbed onto his horse.

. . .

He dismounted at his stable, entered the courtyard, and paused. Beyond the high windows on either side, candles and a hearth fire lit the front rooms. Music stung Santángel's ears, staccato, droning, sinuously melodic. He peered inside and felt his face grow warm.

A young, round-faced woman with pale skin, curly black hair, and dark, mournful eyes stood by the stone fireplace, singing in a high-pitched voice. A few scruffy town-dwellers accompanied her on organistrum, rebec, pipe, tambourine, and castanets. Others— some just emerging from youth, some ragged with age—danced with their arms stretched skyward, stomping their feet, clapping their hands, punctuating the lively pastorale with chirps and yelps. Santángel recognized among them his cook, his stable boy, even his son's tutors. Señora Gómez, a blowzy peasant's daughter who worked in the kitchen, pranced around the middle of the room, a bright red scarf over her shoulders, reaching out as she jiggled and swayed. The greatest affront of all was a bull of a man, in a luxurious cobalt blue doublet, fitted pants, and calfskin boots that looked too dainty to support his prominent gut, who strutted through a raucous *jota* with her, holding one hand behind his back and spinning the servant with the other. Estefan.

Estefan was the son of Santángel's uncle and a sturdy, strong-willed, blond-haired peasant whom Santángel's parents had regarded as an *extranjera*, a "foreigner" to the family, its social class, its traditions. The girl had died while Estefan was still an infant. Estefan's father had remarried. His well-bred, haughty second wife had resented the child, so Luis de Santángel's parents had taken Estefan into their home and raised him as Luis's brother. Estefan's thinning, sand-colored hair and heavy-set build belied his *diferencia*.

By allowing commoners into the chancellor's residence, Santángel feared, Estefan had also invited inquisitiveness and envy. By celebrating the miracle of Mary's apparition in such an ostentatious manner, Estefan was calling attention to questions of faith. Perhaps, too, he was exposing Santángel's son to similar scrutiny.

The chancellor threw the door open. "What in God's name is going on?"

The clapping, stomping, and swaying ceased. Señora Gómez stopped dancing. The musicians quit their plucking and banging. Estefan slowly turned to face the man who had always called him brother. "It's the Fiesta del Pilar, Luis. A day of revelry, debauchery, and God-fearing zeal, honored by all good Zaragozans since time immemorial. Why don't you join us?" He reached out a hand.

Luis stared. He had to distance himself from Estefan's behavior, if only in the minds of his staff.

"What harm is there in celebrating?" Estefan challenged him.

"Need I justify myself?" returned the chancellor frostily. "This is over."

After the last of the revelers shuffled out, Estefan approached his brother. "Luis, you wear your importance, your position, your affluence, like . . ."

"You're drunk, Estefan."

". . . like a mask. A mask so snug it prevents you from smiling." He tied his coat. "A mask that has become your jail."

"And you, your conviviality, your . . . vulgarity," Luis shot back. "Is that not a disguise, as well? A prison of some sort?"

Estefan responded with a wistful smile.

The chancellor shook his head. "I know there's more to you than that, Estefan, far more. But you don't know it, yourself."

The two men glared at each other like wrestlers, each searching for an advantageous grip. Estefan started to leave.

Luis gently took his forearm. "Stay. Another moment, please."

Taking note of his brother's changed tone, Estefan turned back. As quickly as the tensions had arisen between them, they both let their choler slip away. The love and trust they shared, with their parents and wives long gone, flowed deeper than their differences. "Your voyage. Rome. You didn't . . . ?"

"I bought a warship. Magnificent. The *Giustizia*. King Fernando will be pleased." Luis sat down astride a sturdy oak chair, backward, his hands clutching the top of the chair's back as if holding on to a rail in a storm.

Searching Luis's face, Estefan took a chair. "You didn't achieve all you hoped for."

Luis shook his head. "The pope made no commitment."

"He refused your gift?"

"He took the gift, but questioned the arguments. And in my absence, they made inroads. They appointed an inquisitor for Zaragoza. Pedro de Arbués, the canon of La Seo."

Estefan knew of his brother's obsession with the New Inquisition. He leaned forward and placed a comforting hand on Luis's shoulder. "Of course, *they* made inroads. And they'll continue making inroads. Our only hope is to proclaim loud and clear that those old traditions hold no water for us. That is why I dance and sing with the common folk, Luis. If I drink with them, if I carouse with them, I'm a good Christian. It's as simple as that. And if they love me, if they feel I'm *of their kind*, then Torquemada loses his power over me. Don't you see?"

Luis shook his head. "No, I don't. Drinking doesn't make you a good Christian. Drinking, drinking to excess, only makes you a pitiful *converso*."

"A *converso*? I don't even know what that means." Estefan snickered scornfully. "A few words of a language that's all but forgotten. A few rituals whose meaning was lost generations ago. Why should such things weigh us down? Our parents, wherever they are, would rather see us survive."

Although Estefan presented a face of gaiety to the world, the chancellor perceived sadness in his soft, slightly crossed acorn-brown eyes, in his small, down-turned mouth. "Why hold these worn-out, hand-me-down traditions in our hearts?" Luis replied. "Because . . ." But he found himself unable to complete the sentence.

"No one cares a straw what you believe, Luis." Estefan sat back into his chair. "No one cares what I believe, in the black dungeon of my heart. That's the outrageous joke behind this madness. They care about your estate, your powerful friends, your elegant mistresses, your fine horses. They care about your power, or the power they *think* you wield over *their* king. They care about your . . . your remoteness. They care about the conspiracy they see, or believe they see, between you and all the other New Christians, and all the Jews you may or may not consort with. But if you're *one of them*, ostentatiously, deliriously, and, yes, hedonistically, *one of them* . . ."

Luis shook his head. "You think you're one of them, Estefan. But neither you nor I shall ever be one of them, no matter how much we drink or dance or take confession." He drummed his fingers on the back of the chair. "What they call arrogance is nothing but caution. And a well-earned caution, I might add. Where they see a conspiracy of New Christians, I see . . ." He paused to find the word. "History. Shared history. And history, memories, how can you escape them?"

"It's late, Luis. You've been away four months. Nothing is going to happen tonight. Get yourself a goblet of wine. I'll fetch you one."

. . .

Upstairs, Santángel crept into his son's bedroom. Gabriel's unblemished face lay on the pillow, wild strands of long black hair sweeping over delicate features like rivulets of water streaming across an unperturbed beach. Startled by the flickering light of his father's candle, Gabriel bolted upright, brandishing the foil he kept at his bedside. "Who goes there? Are you an evil sorcerer?"

"I am but a humble pilgrim," replied Luis under his breath.

"Go no further, or I'll hack you to pieces with my faithful sword, Elsamere."

"I seek not the thrill of battle," said Luis. "Only a safe place to lay my head."

Gabriel peered at his father past the candle flame. "I've seen you before, humble pilgrim."

Luis bowed. "At your service."

"I said I've seen you. I didn't say I trust you. You're known as a deserter in this kingdom. Flee at once," he added in a voice as deep and menacing as an eight-year-old could muster. "My half-wolf, half-dragon friend, Accalia, is getting hungry."

The chancellor heard the note of resentment in his son's warning. He sat down on the bed. "You couldn't be more wrong, bold *caballero*. If you reside in these realms, you should know that my dwelling place is here, as well. I have traveled far and wide, but not by any choice of my own." He modulated his voice. "Now, scoot down under your blanket."

In the air of Gabriel's room lingered the sharp odor of a recently extinguished candle. A book, one of the romances in which his son delighted, lay open beside Gabriel's head. Gabriel put down his sword and snuggled. Luis reached to stroke his hair. "You weren't sleeping, ruffian, were you."

"I was reading, Father. Isn't that what you want?"

"Did your uncle's stomping keep you awake?"

The child shook his head.

"Did Uncle Estefan take good care of you?"

"He always does."

"And your Latin? Your fencing? Your chess? Did you keep them up while your father was away?"

"At chess, I can beat Uncle Estefan. And he's good."

"I'll bet you could even beat me, now."

"I'll bet I could."

This was the first pleasant news Santángel had heard in some time. "In the morning, we'll share a bowl of hot broth and battle it out on the chessboard. Now, go to sleep."

"I'm not tired." Gabriel yawned.

"Oh yes, you are. We'll have plenty of time to talk."

Gabriel reached up and hugged his father. Luis held him fast. "Can I go with you, next time?"

"We'll try." He started to rise, but his son held him.

"Tell me one of your stories."

"It's late."

"Please."

Santángel cherished the moments, too few and far between, when no worldly events intruded upon the fictional universes he created for his son. And so he began, "There once was a man who possessed a very great treasure. So great, in fact, that he was afraid to speak of it with anyone."

"Why?"

"Because if anyone else knew, they would envy him. And if they envied him, they might kill him."

"Was he a knight, like the Cid?"

"No. His parents weren't landowners, but they were quite wealthy. In fact, they were wealthier than the king himself."

"How could that be?"

"Many said it shouldn't be. But it was so. And being a decent man, he used this wealth to help the king. The king rewarded him with the greatest prize of all, his friendship. But there was one thing the king could not do for this man."

"What?"

"The king couldn't protect him from those who envied him. He tried to."

"If he kept his treasure secret, how could they envy him?"

"They didn't know, but they suspected. And that was enough."

"And what did this man do with his treasure, Papa?"

"He couldn't do much with it, except keep it safe." He combed his son's hair with his fingers. "He didn't even allow himself to look at his treasure, because he might be found out. But the more he forbade himself to look at it, the more he longed to . . . to run his fingers through it, to use it for some purpose, even though he had forgotten what purpose his treasure was meant for."

Gabriel waited for more. "Is that the whole story, Papa?"

"That's all I know of it." He kissed his son on the forehead. "Good night."

"If I were that man," declared the boy, "I'd get rid of that treasure. What good does it do him? It only brings him trouble."

. . .

In his bedchamber down the hall, Santángel threw open the trunk he had forwarded from the port of Barcelona. On top of his night-clothes sat a leather pouch. Hardly able to believe the gall of the

Genoese sea captain, he locked his door and removed the few items from the pouch. A rolled-up sheet of parchment, obviously quite old, caught his attention. He sat on his bed to examine its Hebrew letters. In some places, they danced, in others, they wept—the effect of candlelight flickering on the faded, smudged figures.

What was the meaning of this? Why would Colón, who coveted Santángel's friendship, have risked offending him with a gift he neither desired nor could use? He would not keep these documents in his home, especially now that Zaragoza had an inquisitor, legitimate or not. Someone might discover them and mention their existence during confession.

As he lay down to sleep, he could not help thinking about the parchment. The letters flowed off the page and filled the air above him, fluttering and floating, enticing him to a place he dared not enter. He closed his eyes. He covered his face with his arm. There they were, still, burning brightly, mocking him.

"Are you a blessing, or a curse?" He thought he should know the answer. Like a boy trying to catch a firefly, he reached for its glow, but it eluded him.

CHAPTER TWO

*I*N THE SOUTHERNMOST REGION of Iberia, set off from Christendom by the Sierra Nevada mountain range, lay the remnant
of a once-great Islamic emirate. Nestled within the capital of this
small state, in the shadow of the Alhambra castle, the narrow streets
of Granada's Jewish quarter twisted and climbed over a few small
hills. Whitewashed walls isolated the houses' courtyards from the
clatter of carts, donkeys' hooves, and foot traffic outside. Jasmine
tumbled over the tops of the walls. Where the alley grew steep it
formed a stairway, which opened onto a triangular plaza. Water
splashed softly in a fountain.

Most of the residents' families had dwelled in Granada, and
other territories of Moorish Andalusia, for centuries; some for a
millennium or more. A smaller group, which occupied the homes
near the synagogue, had fled more recently from Castile and Aragon, seeking temporary refuge among the Muslims. They gathered for holidays. Their sons married one another's daughters.
They conversed in Arabic and prayed in Hebrew, but still practiced their beloved, slowly decaying Spanish dialects when they
met together.

Judith Migdal occasionally counted herself in this group.
Never more so than for the celebration of Purim, when costumed
children chased each other, blew horns, shouted, and devoured
"Haman's ears," fried twists of dough flavored with lemon rind
and sugar. The adults took turns reciting in Hebrew and Spanish
the story of Queen Esther, which Judith loved. It was the story

of a beautiful woman in a land not her own, who had acquired status among a people not her own, but refused to turn her back on her kinsmen.

This year, however, Judith sat alone, preoccupied with the fate of her brother and his wife. It had been seven weeks since Yossi and Naomi had departed for the port of Malaga with their gray-spotted mule and a satchel of silver ornaments. Seven weeks without a word. Judith had been praying, with increasing urgency, that no harm had come to them.

Yossi, a silversmith, had been the sole wage earner in the household. He and Naomi had been given only one son, Levi, now eleven years old. Naomi's aging father, Baba Shlomo, lived with them. Judith asked God for direction. Should she admit to herself that her brother and sister-in-law had probably perished, and recite *Kaddish*? The mere thought brought tears to her eyes.

As she walked through the narrow, twisting streets following the Purim celebration, she saw the physician Isaac Azoulay slowly approaching. Even with his slight stoop, he was much taller than Judith. "What is it, Isaac?"

"I know of no manner in which to convey to you my sorrow." He regarded her amber eyes, the splash of freckles across her nose, her glistening night-black hair, as if poring over a treatise on the medicinal qualities of an exotic flower. "I correspond with an apothecary in Malaga, so naturally I inquired about your brother."

"Please," Judith urged him. Isaac almost always spoke in a cautious, measured way. Widely respected for his erudition and humility, he counted among his clients the famous general, recently named vizier of the realm, Ibrahim al-Hakim. But his very brilliance, and his habit of thinking everything through more than once, could be exasperating.

"My herbalist asked at the synagogue." He rubbed his close-cropped, gray-flecked beard. "Yossi never attended services there."

"He never . . . But Isaac, that doesn't mean a thing." She smiled. Azoulay's eyebrows met above his nose.

"What if Yossi and Naomi traveled past Malaga? Maybe there was no reason to stop."

They resumed walking. "If only that were all," said Isaac.

Judith clutched her white dress with a perspiring hand. "What else?"

"Two bodies, by the road. Near the sea. A man's and a woman's. Their bags emptied. Everything stolen."

"It can't be." She stopped. "How would they . . . How would they know?"

"They don't know, Judith. They don't know. On my suggestion, the synagogue in Malaga has acquired the remains. They're sending them here. Until then, we can only pray."

Judith closed her eyes.

"I have some ginger root. I'll make you an infusion. You'll feel better."

She stood outside his door while he went in to fetch the savory root that cost more by weight than gold, then accepted his offer to accompany her home. Passing the moss-covered fountain in her courtyard, they entered the main room of her dwelling.

Judith had installed the floor herself, colored tiles in complex geometrical patterns—polygons interlaced with circles, surrounded by rectangles, with abstract, leaf- and tear-like shapes scattered throughout. A rug, woven in the Atlas Mountains, lay near the brass table. She had painted the low beams of her ceiling in ocher, asparagus green, and pear yellow. She fell onto a round leather cushion at the low brass table where Isaac prepared the infusion.

"Judith, with an old man and a young boy to care for, and no one to help you . . . Anything you need. Anything."

She smiled and placed her hand on top of Azoulay's. They heard Levi leading his grandfather into the courtyard, and removed their hands from the table.

"Is someone visiting?" asked Baba Shlomo as Levi guided him into the house. His eyes no longer perceived distinct forms, but he sensed a presence.

"Azoulay, the doctor," said Levi.

Levi had not yet removed his Purim costume, the rough cotton windings, turban, and charcoal smudges of a Barbary pirate. He was beautiful, thought Judith. She waved Levi over for a hug. He ignored her.

"Is someone ill?" Baba Shlomo, a frail, small man, looked every bit his age, with his shaggy white beard and creased visage. He spoke with an accent, a relic from his distant childhood. He held on to Levi's forearm with a weak grip.

"Judith isn't feeling well," explained Isaac.

"What is it?"

"Just an upset stomach," said Judith. "I'll be fine, Baba Shlomo."

. . .

Two days later, a mule-drawn cart clopped to the gates of Granada. The *Khevra Kaddisha*, the burial committee of the synagogue, waited, as did several other curious souls, Jewish and Islamic. Death fascinated so many.

The driver was an emaciated peasant from the borderlands who spoke both Castilian and Arabic, but neither with ease. Despite her preoccupation with the cart and its contents, Judith felt pity for this man. Who but the most desperate of mortals would accept an occupation like this, which involved handling that most upsetting of all things, decaying human bodies?

He swung his leg over his mule, dismounted, and opened the lid of his wagon. Before Judith lay two human corpses thrown haphazardly one atop the other, covered with flies and worms, vulture-pecked, sickeningly malodorous, largely decomposed except for their hair, fingernails, and parts of their noses and ears. On an intact portion of one thigh, Judith recognized an ancient scar.

She covered her mouth as a shriek burst from deep within. Staggering from the corpses, sobbing, she felt a tentative hand on her back and turned to see Isaac Azoulay.

"Allow me to walk with you."

Judith shook her head.

Walking home alone, she had to make decisions, many of them, and quickly. She had no idea how to tell Levi and Baba Shlomo. Nor did she know how they would live. Most women in her position, she knew, would hope to find a suitor. Judith had survived other losses. She had learned the virtue of patience. What she desired from marriage was more than mere survival, or even friendship.

At present, she needed to sit in Yossi's workshop, to bathe in his presence, mourn his absence, and await an answer. She picked up some of his silver-working instruments and glanced at his account books, reflecting upon his life and hers.

When Judith was Levi's age and Yossi was eight, they had slipped out of the Jewish quarter together, into the Arab city, so contrastingly alive with horses, jugglers, water bearers, blue-veiled women, and wealthy foreigners in plum- and saffron-colored robes. They peeked inside a mosque, where prostrate men prayed. They listened to the ballad of a troubadour who claimed to have sailed to the far edge of the world, a place utterly magical. They lost each other in the crowd at the souk, where a Malagan farmer proudly encouraged Judith to taste his dried fruits, nuts, and breads.

When she turned around, Yossi was gone. She ran the length of the street, between donkeys and goats, bags of dried beans and jars of honey, calling his name. At last she found him sitting on the ground, crying, his clothes torn and wet with blood. He refused to tell her what had happened.

The scar on his thigh never disappeared. To this day, Judith felt responsible for that injury, which now branded an inanimate chunk of flesh.

Yossi never distinguished himself in learning or business, but always maintained an attitude at once stoic and affable. The order from the Great Synagogue of Cairo, the very transaction that had led to his demise, had been a beacon of hope. He had spent weeks in this smoky, lonely chamber, twisting silver wire into intricate arabesques with the tiny pliers Judith now held in her hand, marrying these wires to cones and cylinders of silver, bending the edges into smooth lips, buffing, polishing. Judith knew that his exquisite work had been Yossi's answer to the world's chaos.

If only for the sake of Yossi's memory, she had to keep his shop alive. She would nurture his legacy and offer the same quality of merchandise that her brother had produced. She would begin by filling, once again, the order from the Great Synagogue of Cairo.

And then she shook her head at her own folly. To acquire the necessary skills, not only silver-working, but adding and subtracting, reading and writing, and all that was required to transact business, would involve intensive training. To master the craft, as her brother had, would require more than training—a gift. She put down his tools and went out, shutting the door firmly.

. . .

However, five days into their period of mourning, she asked Baba Shlomo for instruction in silver crafting. They were alone in Yossi's workshop, where she replaced pincers and hammers in their cubbies.

"That's impossible," replied the old man.

"Is it because I'm too old to learn, or because I'm a woman?"

"It's because I have no desire to teach you."

"I've watched Yossi for years. I've assisted him." She knelt to remove ashes from the smelting oven. "We don't have many choices. We can live on handouts, we can starve to death, or we can try to resurrect Yossi's shop."

"How do you think it feels?" Baba Shlomo muttered. "Losing not just my only child, and my son-in-law, but also the shop I created with these two hands? What do I have to live for, now?"

"What do you have to live for? Your grandson, Levi. That is what you have to live for. Who knows what will become of him? He's our future, Baba Shlomo. Our hope."

"To teach you everything . . . There's so much more to it than pretty necklaces." He wiped his face with a trembling hand. "Even putting aside your lack of qualifications, what about *my* lack of qualifications? I'm blind. There are few in Granada who know how to do what I once knew how to do."

"All the more reason you should pass it on."

Baba Shlomo turned his head slightly, as if to hear the sound of

Judith breathing, of her heart beating. Judith knew that beyond his crippling grief, he understood how delicate and fragile their precious little world was.

. . .

The flowers, creeping vines, and fruit trees of Granada bloomed, a riot of yellows, whites, greens, and reds. In the workshop attached to Judith Migdal's home, Baba Shlomo taught her to transform black stones of raw metal into finished, gleaming objects of beauty and value. He guided Judith as she fashioned a beaker, beginning with the melting of ore and the separation of molten silver, through hammering, cutting and shaping disks and wires, filing, buffing and polishing.

To purify the lumps of raw silver, Judith placed them, together with a few grains of lead, over a layer of ash in a white crucible. Baba Shlomo pumped the oven coals with bellows until they glowed brightly. Holding the crucible with tongs, Judith set it inside. The impurities and lead floated to the top of the molten silver. Judith skimmed them off with a stick. When the silver was pure, she removed the crucible, sprinkled a pinch of salt into it, and poured its contents into a hot, circular mold.

When this circle of silver cooled, she removed it from the mold, centered it on the end of an anvil, and folded it away from herself, over the anvil. She beat the metal with a round-headed hammer, striking it in soft concentric circles to an even thinness, until it took the form of a cup, then filed it inside and out and around the lip to smooth it.

"All the beauty," Baba Shlomo told her, "will be in the details. But you can't master the art of filigree until you learn to write."

The waves and curls of silver that had adorned Yossi's pieces were characters of the alphabet, spelling words like jewelry spilling over the edges of a bowl or serving dish. When the filigree did not represent letters, it resembled the distilled essence of Arabic writing. Judith longed to receive that essence, like a potion of knowledge, but it eluded her.

Although Baba Shlomo was unable to see her creations, he measured her progress by running his fingers over her work, or feeling it with his cheek.

"It's lopsided."

"How can I fix it?"

"If you hammer it, you'll destroy the filigree. You'll have to re-melt it and start all over."

Judith took the beaker from Baba Shlomo and turned it lovingly in her hands. She dutifully picked up the mallet and began crushing the beaker, folding its sides over each other so it would fit into the crucible.

Again, Baba Shlomo stoked the flames while she held the crucible in place with long iron tongs. Because the oven was low, she had to stoop, causing her back to ache. The heat brought beads of sweat to her face. Removing the tongs from the fire, she burned her arm.

Again, she poured the liquefied silver into molds, hammered them to an even thinness, cut and twisted wires, poured molten silver into seams.

Four days later, the second beaker was finished. Baba Shlomo held it to his cheek.

"The filigree doesn't seem right." He felt it with his fingers. "The slope of these wires. Too wide. It's not symmetrical." He handed it back to her.

Judith pushed the beaker to the side, lowered her head onto her arms, and wept silently.

. . .

Dina Benatar, the mother of Levi's friend Sara, was the only woman of Judith's acquaintance who knew how to read and write. She had grown up in Fez, where her father exported cinnamon, ginger, pepper, "dragon's blood," and other spices. Like Dina, her father spoke Arabic, but when he wrote to Jewish vendors in other lands, he used a stylized Hebrew alphabet. After his brother, who was his business partner, died, he taught his daughter to write in Arabic using either Arabic or cursive Hebrew letters.

Judith offered to pay for lessons, but Dina refused compensation, saying she would relish the opportunity to spend more time with the fruit merchant's daughter. "It will be an honor to get to know you."

Judith laughed. "An honor?"

"You're raising a child, taking care of an old man, learning a difficult craft. And all without a husband to provide for you."

Stout and ungainly, wearing an elegant robe the color of robins' eggs, she led Judith into her scriptorium to show her the work of well-known Arabic and Jewish calligraphers. "Since you'll have both Arab and Jewish clients, you'll have to learn both alphabets. But we'll start with Hebrew."

In some of her precious texts, the letters bent into each other, over each other, and through each other, forming complex geometries. In others, the words rippled, ebbed, shivered, and flowed across the page like water. For Dina, these writings were a pure, rarefied art not of the body but of the mind.

"Calligraphy is the highest art form," Dina told Judith. "There are so many styles of writing, you can't hope to master even a small fraction. Look at the proportions, the balance, the firm grace of the writer's hand. The shape of the letters says almost as much as the words. They are blades of grass, bending under a spiritual breeze."

Dina showed Judith the tools they would use: a reed pen, a knife for shaping the pen, an ink bowl. "Is this an acceptable *daleth*?" Judith asked, trying her best to copy Dina's model.

"That's good, but write from top to bottom, like this, or you'll get in trouble later."

At the end of every lesson, the two shared a cup of lemon water, almond milk, or pomegranate juice and spoke of matters neither broached to others. Dina's husband, Yonatan, a spice merchant like her father, traveled almost all the time. He communicated with her as much in writing as face-to-face. Dina spoke of the frustration of raising her daughter alone. Judith talked about the unanticipated duties that had fallen upon her, her responsibility for a heartbroken child and a defeated, helpless old man, and how unprepared she felt.

. . .

After eight months of training, Judith sat beside Baba Shlomo, proudly holding a decorated silver alms box. "I'm ready."

"You're not ready," the old man told her. "Ready for what?"

"To fill the order from the Great Synagogue in Cairo."

"Too much time has passed."

"But they deserve an explanation, and a gift."

"How would we pay for the materials? The transportation? You'd be better off selling trays and cups in the marketplace."

"I'll borrow the money."

Baba Shlomo shook his head. "Getting further into debt, just when you're starting a new enterprise, is not good business. That's why I said: This is not a job for a woman. Business sense, women are not known for."

"Nevertheless," insisted Judith, "we do owe them an explanation. And a gift."

· · ·

She borrowed three thousand dirhams from Isaac Azoulay. "My money is as safe in your hands," the physician assured her, "as in my cabinet. Perhaps safer, since no one knows it's there."

"I owe you nothing, then, but the principal?" Judith wanted to establish that this loan did not imply anything beyond mere friendship.

"That is perfectly correct."

She set about procuring the silver ore and fashioning each of the nine pieces, one at a time, comparing her models with the best she could find and adding touches to improve on them. She refashioned many of the pieces several times. Three weeks into the ordeal, exhausted, coughing, her hands chafed, she considered taking a few days off to recover her strength, then dismissed the thought.

All the while, she shopped, prepared meals, and accompanied Levi and Baba Shlomo to synagogue. More than once she asked Levi for help, but he ignored her. One battle at a time, she reflected.

With Dina she spent a week composing the letter that would accompany her gift to the Great Synagogue of Cairo. She began by describing what had happened to the previous order, what had befallen her brother and his wife, and went on to explain her decision to honor the contract again. She conveyed the respects of her rabbi to the rabbi of the Great Synagogue. Finally, she provided a brief summary of the situation in Granada. "The rattling of sabers near our borders," she concluded, "as well as the brutal rivalry between our emir, here in Granada, and his nephew in Malaga, has all of us, Jew and Muslim alike, lying awake at night in fear."

Dina suggested they celebrate the completion of this missive. "For once, we're all together," she said, glancing at the doorway. "Stay for dinner. We'll have carrot salad, lamb, and dates stuffed with almond paste."

"A most delicious suggestion," came the sonorous, booming voice of Dina's husband, Yonatan, from behind Judith. She turned to see him filling the doorway. He waved her over and hugged her, practically lifting her off the ground.

"Tell Levi and Baba Shlomo to join us," insisted Dina. "There's plenty for everyone."

"All right, then. I'll fetch them." Judith turned to go.

"Can I walk with you?" asked Sara, Dina's daughter, appearing from behind her father.

Exquisite, with sparkling green eyes, Sara was every bit as vivacious as Judith had been at twelve. As they walked the two blocks to Judith's house, the girl noticed the slipper-shaped filigree pin on Judith's dress. "Oh, I love that."

Judith touched the slipper-pin. It had belonged to Yossi's wife, Naomi. "Thank you. You know what's inside?"

"There's something inside?"

"A tiny Hebrew scroll. It has the *Shema* written on it."

"How could anyone write that small?"

"Not many people can. They're specially trained scribes. All they do is make tiny scrolls like this."

"Does it bring luck?"

"I don't know," said Judith. "When I'm wearing it, there's no way to know how lucky or unlucky I'd be if I weren't wearing it. I'd have to live the same day twice, once without it and once with it, to really know for sure."

Sara giggled.

. . .

Fourteen months after her brother was murdered, almost two years after the Great Synagogue of Cairo placed the order, Judith sent off her work and letter in the care of Yonatan Benatar. Unlike Judith's late brother, Yonatan possessed not an iota of naïveté. When he traveled, he hired armed Islamic guards for protection. "Jews are good at many things," Yonatan explained, "but wielding sabers is not one of them."

Following so many months of study and feverish production, Judith bade good-bye to the nine pieces of silver into which she had poured her heart and her labor. She went up to her bedroom and lay down, although it was not yet evening.

The silver objects she had fashioned for the Great Synagogue of Cairo refused to leave Judith's mind. In her imagination, she continued turning them over and upside down, running her fingertips across their surfaces. She told herself the whole project had been a wager on the direction of the wind. Yet she could not prevent herself from feeling, by turns, worried, hopeful, disappointed, and proud.

. . .

She awoke before dawn to the sound of a child softly whimpering, or a cat mewling under the floorboards. She knew that spirits roamed the world at night. Perhaps they wanted to frighten her. She would show them she was not daunted.

Her warped door neither closed nor opened all the way. It creaked loudly as she pushed it. She followed the noise to Baba Shlomo's room. The old man lay on his mattress, his lips slightly parted, uttering muffled, at times almost inaudible howls. Judith shook him. He opened his eyes and stared.

"Were you having a nightmare?"

He answered in the Aragonese dialect of his childhood. "A nightmare, no."

Judith responded in the same tongue. "I could hear you from my room."

"It was nothing. Go back to bed."

"I won't go back to bed," she reverted to Arabic, "until you tell me what you were dreaming."

"It isn't of any importance."

He turned onto his side. Judith waited. Finally, Baba Shlomo rolled onto his back. "My parents, of blessed memory. They were standing before me, here in this room."

"What did they tell you?" She took his hand.

"Strange things. Things beyond my comprehension. The wind blowing over the *aljama* of Zaragoza, after the riots. After they died. The world beyond."

"What about the world beyond?" She squeezed his hand.

He shook his head. "It was gibberish. Incomprehensible. Frightening."

"It isn't good, then," said Judith, as if Baba Shlomo's dream were the final word on the afterlife.

"That, I can't say, since I couldn't understand what they were saying." Baba Shlomo sighed. "But I would like to visit their graves. I've never seen them. It's all that's left."

"Go back to sleep, Baba Shlomo. We have to attend the military procession in the morning."

"Another military procession? What is it this time?"

Judith frowned. "Yonatan spoke of it over dinner. You were sitting right there."

"Perhaps I was dozing."

"It's the emir's nephew. He claims he can defend Granada against the Christians better than his uncle. He marched with his army from Malaga, but General al-Hakim met them halfway and sent them running."

Baba Shlomo shook his head. "What good is a parade to a blind man? Let the emir arrest me for missing it. But I doubt he'll care much. He may not even notice." He closed his eyes.

. . .

Early the next morning, Judith and Levi hurried to Dina's home. Excited about the morning's festivities, Sara took Levi by the arm. The two ran off together.

"Levi, Sara, stay with us," Judith called after them.

"We'll meet you there," Sara called back.

The residents of Granada thronged the streets, plazas, and balconies of the capital. As morning shadows grew shorter, the citizens heard a steady, insistent beating of drums, the winding melodies of rasping reed instruments, and the rattling of shields and swords—at first far away, but slowly growing louder.

The massive wooden doors of the city, on wheels thick as logs, rumbled open. Into the capital strutted three huge birds, each nearly as tall as a man, perched unsteadily atop long, spindly legs. Great feathery wings flanked their wide bodies, yet they did not fly. Their big eyes, set in heads almost as narrow as their long, S-shaped necks, blinked at the onlookers.

No one had ever seen creatures like these. That their emir could possess them proved his wealth and power. Some children pointed. Others hid behind their parents' legs as the otherworldly creatures strolled slowly past, urged forward by soldiers with sticks.

Behind them strutted birds whose bright blue and vivid green tail feathers opened into enormous fans, filled with eyes; strange antelopes with horns like oxen and long, tufted tails; dromedaries saddled in silver, their humps and long necks shifting as they walked; bejeweled monkeys who screeched as they ran and jumped between the other animals; and two rare elephants wearing colorful headdresses, shipped for the occasion from the Southern Continent. Suspended between the two elephants, on a litter hung with silk and rugs from Persia, sat the vizier himself, Ibrahim al-Hakim, looking dignified but pleased with his victory and the crowd's adulation. From the ornate sheath on his hip, the sapphire-encrusted handle of a large saber peeked out like a shy kitten from a bag.

Behind the vizier, on elegant Arabian horses, rode hundreds of dirty and weary archers in ornamented, conical helmets and mail shirts, clutching disk-shaped shields. On long poles, some held aloft the heads of their fallen enemies, whose features, drained of blood, sagged dreadfully like masks of white putty.

The parade slowly wound into the Jewish quarter. Judith and Dina watched, fascinated, as the vizier's elephants plodded toward them.

An infant started bawling. One of the smaller monkeys, hardly bigger than a human baby, jumped onto someone in the crowd, screeching. Perched on his elephantine throne, the vizier waved his arms. "Stop the procession!"

The drumming ceased, and the reed instruments' whining, and the rattling of swords and shields. Silence fell upon the Jewish quarter as the vizier turned his head, frowned, and broke into a peal of laughter so loud it echoed off the face of the synagogue.

He climbed down from his litter, aided by two lieutenants, and proceeded forward, cutting a path between the peacocks, the oxen, and the ostriches. He stood on the street at eye-level, a citizen among other citizens, as he waved someone forward.

Sheepishly lowering her chin, much of her chest covered by the terrified simian, a girl shuffled into the street and looked up, wearing a brave smile. The crowd saw the girl, and the monkey grasping her like a baby clutching its mother. The monkey turned its head this way and that as if trying to make sense of the sudden calm. Many of the onlookers laughed together with the vizier. Their laughter conveyed as much about the humor of the situation as about their nervousness to have the vizier standing in their midst, no taller than the rest of them.

Gently, General Al-Hakim urged the girl forward, peeled the monkey off her chest, and handed it to his assistant. Placing his index finger under the girl's chin, he raised her scratched face to look into her dark green eyes. The crowd fell silent.

"What is your name?" he asked her in his gentlest tone.

Mustering her courage, the girl replied in a small voice: "Sara. Sara Benatar."

. . .

From where they were standing, Judith and Dina did not see Sara's exchange with the vizier. The silver merchant caught herself glancing through the crowd, searching for Isaac Azoulay. At almost every event, he sought her out and exchanged a few words: comments on the weather, reassurances about Levi's studies, inquiries about Baba Shlomo's health. After the soldiers, court attendants, and musicians had left, after most of the residents had deserted the little plaza and all that remained were ostrich droppings and a few stragglers, Judith decided to pay him a visit.

Fragrant honeysuckle and passion vines crept over the white wall around Isaac's garden. She had never before knocked at his door. Her motives might be misread, but she told herself: Why worry about the gossipers? They had chattered before. She had survived. She opened the gate, walked through the garden, and knocked.

Isaac wore his customary indigo robes, but his feet were bare. He smiled warmly.

"I was expecting to see you at the procession," said Judith.

"I had a special dispensation. The vizier asked me to do some research."

"Is he ill? He seemed well enough."

"It isn't too serious. Please, come in."

The room appeared to be a blend of living room, apothecary's office, and alchemist's retreat. Rugs and cushions lay haphazardly across the tile floors. A tall lantern, with stars and crescent moons cut out of its copper sides, hung from the ceiling. Incense perfumed the air. Shelves of vials, flacons, mortars with pestles, rolled parchments, and books in several languages lined the walls. On a low wooden table lay a large, open tome.

"What a nice, spacious home."

"Perhaps too spacious." He poured her a cup of partially fermented quince juice spiced with cloves.

"You're wondering why I'm here."

"I'm enjoying the surprise. But please, tell me." He handed her the cup.

"I'm concerned about Baba Shlomo."

"What about Baba Shlomo?" Isaac poured himself a cup and sat on a cushion across from her.

"He sleeps all the time. He no longer seems interested in anything. He has dreams. Perturbing dreams. He forgets things."

"What sorts of things?" He sipped his concoction.

"Simple things, like the parade this morning."

Isaac nodded. "Sometimes, when a person survives long enough, his memory starts to weaken. It's quite rare, presumably because few manage to live as long as Baba Shlomo." He sipped again. "How old is he, exactly?"

"He himself has no idea. Can anything be done?"

"Let me tell you how memory works," said the physician. "Our memories are images of the things we see and hear and touch, stamped into the tissue of our hearts."

"Stamped?"

"Like a seal into wax. And just as wax receives a stamp best when it's warm, so our hearts receive our memories best when our blood is warm."

Judith noticed the open book he had been reading, but was unable to make sense of its Latin characters. "What is this?"

For the briefest moment, Isaac seemed at a loss. "That pertains to the vizier. To his . . . his illness."

"What is it?" Judith insisted.

"*De Amore.* A commentary on Plato's *Symposium*, by a brilliant Florentine, Ficino."

"*De Amore*," repeated Judith.

"General Al-Hakim is . . . well, he's hot-blooded, of course. And lonely."

Judith wondered how the vizier, with all his concubines and servants, could be wanting. She sipped more of her beverage. "Speaking of hot blood, this potion of yours is making me feel warm. Lightheaded."

"That's because alcohol is thinner than blood. Thinner than water, too. Thin liquids, like warm liquids, rise above the level of our physical bodies, toward the level of our souls. And thus, they affect cognition."

Judith rested her head on a couple of fingers, considering this.

"There's no other animal that walks upright, as we do," pursued the physician. "Why do you think that is?"

"Isaac, we were talking about memory, and now you're asking why we walk upright. What does this have to do with that?"

"Everything. We walk upright because our blood is so warm, the warmest of all animals. And again, warm things rise. Our warm blood, by rising in our bodies, causes us to walk upright."

"I never thought of that."

This beverage, she thought, was making her sound slightly ridiculous. She removed the two fingers from her chin.

"But as we age," continued Isaac, "our blood cools, and we begin to stoop. Like Baba Shlomo. And our hearts become less soft, like wax as it cools. As a result, our ability to remember begins to fade."

Judith put down her cup. "Isaac, that's all very interesting, but is there anything I can do?"

"Try to keep Baba Shlomo warm. And upright, on his feet, as much as possible. But don't think you can reverse Time, or even slow it down."

"Ah, that I know." She nodded wistfully.

"You're still young and beautiful, Judith." Isaac blushed.

Judith smiled. "Thank you."

. . .

Ten years earlier, she had fallen in love with an apothecary's apprentice named David Corcos. Despite the long hours he spent mixing herbal potions and searching through ancient texts, David had found the time to meet with her, late at night or before dawn, at their clandestine corner near the gate of the Jewish Quarter. There, they talked, sometimes for hours on end. His reasoning was subtle and his knowledge, deep, but what mattered most was the quiet sound of his voice and the glints of light playing on his onyx eyes.

He gave her precious gifts, an ivory bangle, a delicate porcelain pot of kohl, a silk dress from Venice. Marriage, and freedom from her parents' domicile, was in the offing. Judith was sure her father would approve, but David wanted to complete his apprenticeship first. This perturbed the seventeen-year-old Judith. Many girls her age were already mothers. She told herself to be patient. Life reserved its most precious gifts for those who knew how to wait.

One night, Judith and David forgot how to wait. In a fever of exploration, discovery, and abandonment, they allowed each other the gratification their hearts and bodies craved. Though she knew carnal relations were proscribed for those who were not wed, she convinced herself that in this particular case, where betrothal was certain, the most intimate expressions of love were excusable. Their moment of shared passion would cement their union and ensure their future together. It was the ultimate expression of trust.

A mere two weeks later, when she went to their meeting place, David was not there. Thinking he was delayed, she waited until dawn, half-sleeping with her back to a wall. Nor did he show up the next night. The following day, she inquired of his mentor and found him as bewildered as she. His gifted young scholar had vanished.

Several months later, Judith learned what had happened. David had been courting another young woman even before he and Judith began their sensual explorations. She was the daughter of a high-ranking official in the employ of the Alhambra, and was reputed to be flirtatious and rebellious. If the apothecary's apprentice had been found out before the two of them took flight, he would most certainly have been killed. Word-of-mouth placed them in Alexandria, where David claimed not only to adhere to the Islamic faith, but to be descended from an illustrious family originating in Mecca.

Isaac Azoulay and the other inhabitants of Granada's Jewish quarter knew this story, or at least parts of it, in various forms. For the physician, it compromised neither Judith's attractiveness nor her integrity. In her own heart, however, she had never transcended the shame.

. . .

Three weeks after Yonatan left for Cairo, Judith felt lost and directionless, as if she had been following a road not to her destination but to a field overgrown with weeds, into which her path dissolved. It seemed that creating the nine pieces for the Great Synagogue, and the letter that accompanied them, had simply been a way to convince herself that her new profession was viable, her prospects real.

She searched through her brother's account books. She met with his clients. Few needed more silver. Others had found new suppliers. Isaac Azoulay suggested she pay a visit to the under-undersecretary of the minister of finances, who had recently acquired eight horses and would be needing silver harnesses. Judith hastened to his stables, located near the majestic Alhambra castle.

"I would love to transact such business with you," said Khalil, keeper of horses for the under-undersecretary. "But the work is gone. We have already ordered the new harnesses. I am sorry. Perhaps next time."

Judith trudged home, discouraged. Eight silver harnesses! She could have paid off part of her debt. If her clients were pleased with her work, they might have spoken to others among the ruling families.

She had no choice, after all, but to peddle trinkets in the little marketplace of the Jewish quarter. Levi would have to assist her when he was not studying or praying. They might eke out enough to feed themselves, but not enough to begin paying their debts.

. . .

"God must be testing me," she confided to Dina. The two still shared a cup of sage tea or pear juice once or twice every week. Although Judith now knew how to read and write, they continued reading together, and not just for practice. The written word had become the medium of their friendship. They took pleasure in the works of Jewish-Arab poets, Ibn Gabirol, Yehuda Halevy, Todros Abulafia, and others.

"Of course God is testing you," Dina agreed. "God tests all of us." She poured more tea.

They turned back to the book at hand, a folio of verse by Abraham Ibn Ezra, who had lived near Zaragoza when that region was under Muslim rule, centuries earlier. Judith read the Judeo-Arabic cursive aloud.

> I have a cloak that's a lot like a sieve
> for sifting wheat and barley:
> at night I stretch it taut like a tent,
> and light from the stars shines on me.
> Through it I see the crescent moon,
> Orion and the Pleiades.
> I weary, though, of counting its holes,
> which look like a saw's sharp teeth.

Judith laughed. "Yes, that's how life is, isn't it. We stretch out our tattered cloaks and peer through the holes, looking toward the stars."

CHAPTER THREE

S THE CHANCELLOR SAT WORKING, his aide knocked to announce a caller. A hefty fellow with short hair and a close-cropped beard, the visitor did not bow. "Your Excellency," he said in a deep baritone, "forgive me for intruding. Abram Serero, a scribe by trade, and a teacher. I've come to deliver our community's contribution."

"Your community?"

"The Jewish community. A small offering, I admit. But as you know, Chancellor, we're not as prosperous as in the time of our grandfathers." He waved the paper in his hand. "It's all accounted for."

Santángel looked up from his books. "Señor Serero, have a seat." He turned to his aide. "Señor de Almazón, stay with us. Close the door." If the chancellor was going to receive a Jew in his office, he wanted a witness.

Serero reached into his satchel and produced a purse of gold coins, which he handed to Santángel along with the accounting sheet. Santángel counted the coins and noted their value. "Normally, these deliveries are not made to my office."

"I wanted to meet you."

"Why?"

"I'm new at this."

Santángel nodded, glancing at the accounting sheet. "Do you read Hebrew?"

"When I said I was a scribe," Serero explained, "what I meant was, I am a Hebrew scribe. I copy our holy books in the holy tongue. If I did not read and understand Hebrew, I would be going through the motions without experiencing every word. And if I copied the Torah that way . . ." He shook his head.

The chancellor looked up from the accounting sheet. "What would happen?"

"There's a traditional way of doing these things. I learned the craft from my father. He learned it from his."

"Your family," asked Santángel. "You've lived in Zaragoza for some time?"

"My family has lived in Zaragoza and also Valencia for as long as anyone remembers. But others make such claims." Serero scratched his beard. "Perhaps, Señor Santángel, you've heard of the Zinillo family."

Santángel's face registered nothing. Being a Christian, and a close collaborator of the king, he did not appreciate Serero's reminding him of his ancestry.

"They say my forbears have enjoyed the generosity of this land ever since the time of King Solomon," boasted the scribe.

"Señor Serero, please express to your community His Highness's gratitude."

"Thank you." After a moment, Serero added, "May all your endeavors, and the king's, be crowned with righteousness."

On Santángel's nod, his aide showed Serero the door. The Jew again turned to the chancellor. "If you should need anything further, please, come visit me. I live in the house next to the synagogue, one door to the left."

"What could I possibly need from a Jew, other than taxes, my good man?" Santángel smiled with deliberate condescension and waved the scribe away.

Serero glanced at him once more, then shuffled out of the office.

"The fellow has no tact," Santángel muttered, loudly enough so that his aide could hear. Felipe de Almazón stared at the door.

. . .

The *judería*, the Jewish quarter of Zaragoza, lay adjacent to its royal palace, not far from Santángel's home. He almost never ventured there. Enveloped in a dark surcoat, he entered the neighborhood on a chill winter night, scarcely more noticeable than the shadow of a cloud passing under the moon.

He rapped lightly at the door of Abram Serero's narrow, decrepit, two-story habitation. After a pause, he knocked again. He heard loose shoes shuffling across the floorboards.

Dressed in a long nightshirt, holding a candle, the scribe pulled the door open a crack, then all the way. "Chancellor. What an honor."

Santángel faced a cramped room with low beams, small windows, a dwindling hearth fire, unvarnished wood floors, and piles of books on a pine table. Serero pulled a coarse, bark-colored curtain to close off the area where his wife and children were sleeping, and led Santángel to his worktable. "What brings so illustrious a visitor to our modest home?" he asked, low.

"It's your accounts," replied the chancellor, mindful not to wake the children. "You owe the king seventeen *maravedís*. Look here."

He produced Serero's accounting sheet and showed him his own. As he studied them, Serero placed his hand on the table, beside Santángel's. The chancellor observed the scribe's hand, ink-stained and raw, and his own beside it, gloved in the finest calfskin.

Serero looked up. "Is that all?"

He did not address Santángel by his title. This scribe clearly had a great deal to learn about the standards of hierarchy and proper behavior.

"Is there anything else?" repeated Serero.

"Why, yes. You mentioned the Zinillo family."

The scribe gestured for him to sit down and took the chair opposite. "What about them?"

"What do you know about them?"

"Of course, you're curious. To be cut off from your history, your family, your roots. Not to know where you come from." He shook his head.

"If you please, Señor Serero."

"The Zinillos were cloth merchants, lawyers, and moneylenders. Most of them lived not here, but in Valencia. Surely you know that. A respectable enough family, until . . . until one of them, the most ambitious, some would say—but others would argue, the least courageous—decided that his world, the world of the judería, was too small."

"The least courageous?" echoed the chancellor. "Do you not mean, perhaps, the one who cared most about his wife, his children, grandchildren? The least selfish, perhaps? The one with the strength to elevate himself, to flee this . . . this . . . ." He waved his hand at the pocked, stained old table, the shabby curtains, the disjointed floor planks.

"If you already know all you need to know, Chancellor, why did you come here?"

No one, certainly no commoner, dared speak to the chancellor with such effrontery. "Why, indeed?" Santángel crossed the room, stopped short of the door, and turned around. He had not found what he had been seeking. He would leave when he was ready to leave. "One more question."

"As many as you'd like." Serero smiled.

"Were they devout in their faith?"

"When a man turns his back on his people, Señor de Santángel, there will always be those who wonder how sincere he ever was."

"Perhaps, but *before* his conversion?"

Serero finally joined his guest at the threshold. "Before, I'm sure no one thought much about your grandfather's—my great uncle's—beliefs."

Santángel crossed his arms. He scrutinized the man's face, looking for a resemblance and finding none. "You claim, then, Señor Serero, that you and I are cousins?"

"I do not merely claim it. The synagogue in Valencia has records."

Santángel could hardly fathom Serero's recklessness. "Now I understand why they sent you. What do you intend to do about those seventeen maravedís?"

"I shall do what's expected of me."

"I appreciate that, and so will the king. Good night."

"Good night, Chancellor." Serero opened the door. A cold breeze blew in.

. . .

Holding a candle, Abram Serero climbed the tiny, twisted staircase to his refuge, a work nook on the second floor. He sat at his desk. A collection of rare books, some dating from the time of his great-great-grandfather, clothed the plaster walls around him.

He resumed copying the words of a Hebrew Bible letter by letter, using the special inks and instruments prescribed in ancient times. His writing tool was a quill. No Hebrew copyist used iron, copper, gold, or silver in this work for fear that someone might later melt such bits of metal into instruments of death.

As Serero wrote each word, he pronounced it aloud. Each letter, with all its extensions, was a holy, living being. If a scribe erred, the rabbis taught, an entire world would be destroyed. Precisely what this meant, no one knew.

When thoughts of his conversation with the chancellor intruded, he pronounced the Hebrew word a second time. This technique, he found, did not dispel the perturbing thoughts. He wiped his quill and closed the inkpot.

We live in two different worlds, he told himself. One world honors tradition. The other tramples upon it. Serero doubted he or anyone else could build a bridge between them. And yet, the survival of the Jewish community in Zaragoza required that such bridges be built, rebuilt, and maintained.

. . .

Two weeks later, Santángel again visited the Hebrew scribe. He handed Serero the leather pouch Cristóbal Colón had placed in his trunk. "An acquaintance of mine, a ship's captain—I hardly know him, mind you—but he placed this in my possession. I have no use for it. Nor do I have any idea what it represents. According to this gentleman, its contents are of some value. Especially to a Jew like you, one would imagine."

Abram Serero studied the documents, sliding his fingers under certain phrases, sometimes reading them aloud. Finally, he looked up. "Where did you say you obtained these?"

"A sailor. He placed them in my trunk even though I had no use for them and, indeed, refused them."

Serero nodded slowly. "Did he tell you where he acquired them?"

"He mentioned Lisbon. A mapmaker, I believe. A Jew."

The scribe lowered his expert eyes and allowed them once again to wander across the fragments and pamphlets until they stopped on the most aged of them, the stained and ragged parchment.

The chancellor, leaning over the parchment next to the scribe, scrutinized the characters as if facing natives on a foreign shore. "What is it? What does it say?"

In a slight shifting of Serero's eyes, he perceived a tinge of concern, perhaps dread.

"I would need to spend more time with them," said the scribe.

"Do you want to keep them, then?"

"Some of them, perhaps. Others," he rolled up the ancient parchment, "no one would want lying around." He tried to hand it back to Santángel.

"Please. Consider it yours."

"This particular document, I could never consider mine."

"Nevertheless, it's surely safer in your care."

Serero relented, placing the parchment back on the table. "Is there anything else I can do for you?" His face eased into a smile.

"There is one more thing."

Serero waited.

"Señor Serero," Santángel began again. "Suppose I wished to learn more about . . . about the faith of my grandparents."

"Why?"

"Not in the interest of conversion, mind you, but so I can understand what it is I'm rejecting."

"You're asking whether I would teach you? I would not," said Serero.

"And why not?"

"You said your objective would be to find fault with the tradition. What teacher would want such a student?"

"Suppose we were to make a financial arrangement. Not between you and me, but between the kingdom and the Jewish community of Zaragoza. I understand what a burden these war taxes represent. Perhaps we can find a way to offset them."

An ember crackled in the fireplace. Serero knelt and pushed the logs with an iron poker.

The First Meetings

WITH ABRAM SERERO, Luis de Santángel explored ideas that had intrigued him all his life. He argued about the nature of truth, God's role in history, justice, love. He came to feel an intellectual enfranchisement he had never felt before, invigorating and empowering. The freedom to navigate between the great ideas and sentiments of his own faith and that of his grandfather was a rare privilege.

Late at night, sometimes once a month, sometimes more frequently, the two men entered a concealed, arbored passageway behind the castle and walked to a private entrance that defied surveillance. Santángel let Serero into the apartments where King Fernando carried on his amorous escapades when in town. They sat amidst brocade curtains, oak trestle tables, large, painted crucifixes, canvases by Bartolomé Bermejo abounding in bright color and detail.

The king and his chancellor jointly owned the dwelling, and the neighboring residences as well. No one would ask what was taking place within these walls. Other than Fernando and Santángel, only the king's steward possessed keys.

To their first session, Serero brought a small bag containing the seventeen maravedis his community owed the king. Santángel placed the pouch on the table. Late the next morning, realizing he had left the coin bag behind, he went back to retrieve it. The pouch was no longer there. To ask the king's steward about it would be to raise uncomfortable questions. The seventeen maravedis were lost. Santángel cursed himself for his lack of vigilance and replaced them with coins from his own purse.

. . .

Jorge Bargos-Saucedo, steward of the royal palace of Zaragoza, wore his gray-streaked hair short, his moustache and beard full. During his ten years in King Fernando's service, his belly had ripened like a melon. He balanced himself by throwing his head back and walking with his nose pointing upward, a hand behind his back, black robes hanging to his ankles. Thus he toured the palace and adjacent properties every morning, checking that chairs and books had not strayed from their places, that mice had not chewed into larders, that no brigand had violated the king's privacy.

On a bright summer morning, in the great room of the Bermejo suite, Jorge discovered a small leather pouch. He loosened the cords of its mouth and poured silver pieces into his hand.

The door and its jamb were intact. Jorge knew that only two other men possessed the key. The king was away. The pouch must belong to Luis de Santángel.

Jorge found his way to the tiny office of Felipe de Almazón, the chancellor's aide, who sat stiffly at his desk, writing with his left hand in a careful, deliberate manner. Usually left-handedness was a sign of deviousness. Felipe's left-handedness, the steward knew, was different. His aristocratic family had raised him to fight on the battlefield, but an accident had injured his back and right arm, his javelin arm. The king, eager to strengthen the allegiance of Felipe's father, had offered the young man a position in the chancellery.

"Good day, Señor de Almazón. Is your back acting up?"

The chancellor's aide turned his head, as if unable to adjust his body. "It's bearable. What brings you here, Jorge?"

"A small matter. I believe this belongs to Señor de Santángel." Jorge held out the pouch.

"Where did you find it?"

"In the Bermejo suite."

While Felipe de Almazón counted the coins, the king's steward contemplated the wooden creatures that jostled for space on the walls. Haloed countenances of lions, oxen, eagles, and men, some with six wings, some with fewer. Some with multiple eyes. Some painted in gold leaf, lapis blue, yellow, red, or silver. Others, bare walnut, ebony, or gall wood.

"Thank you," said Felipe.

The steward bowed.

"Please pull the door closed as you leave."

Felipe spilled the coins into their sac. Seventeen maravedis. A familiar number. A note he had jotted two or three weeks earlier. He leafed back through his ledger books, hoping to refresh his memory.

. . .

Luis de Santángel sat at his desk, reading correspondence. His aide requested permission to enter. "Yes, yes. Come in, Felipe."

Felipe closed the door and sat down. The chancellor turned from his work to see his aide staring at the ground, hands clasped in his lap.

"What is it?"

"May I speak honestly?"

"I wouldn't ask less of you."

"I know of your meetings."

"What meetings?"

Felipe raised his eyes. "Your meetings with the Jew."

Santángel regarded him blankly. He had always thought Felipe worthy of trust. His aide had long ago mastered the twin arts of discretion and respect for authority, requirements for any position in the chancellery.

"No one else knows," he reassured Santángel.

"What, precisely, did you wish to discuss, Felipe?"

"I want to attend them with you. The meetings."

"Why?"

"Because I don't think they'd be working so hard to suppress it—Torquemada, Pedro de Arbués—if it didn't hold some truth. Some power."

The chancellor forced himself to smile. "I'm afraid these meetings aren't what you think. They're nothing but philosophical discussions. If you're looking for religious instruction, you'll have to search elsewhere, although I would not recommend it."

"Whatever they are, Chancellor, I'd like to participate."

Santángel saw determination in Felipe's clenched jaw. For the first time, his aide was challenging him.

"That is all," concluded Felipe. He rose, bowed, and turned to leave.

Santángel stopped him. "How did you learn?"

Felipe reached into his pocket and produced Abram Serero's coin bag. "This was found in the Bermejo suite."

He handed the pouch to Santángel, who looked inside. Seventeen maravedis.

"Who else knows?"

"Jorge found it, but he knows nothing about the Jew."

"Thank you." Santángel waved his apprentice out and tried to return to work, but preoccupations hindered him.

He had either to end his meetings with the scribe or invite Felipe to participate. To continue holding the meetings without including him would be to invite disloyalty. His aide would feel shunned, perhaps resentful. Such sentiments made spies even of close associates.

. . .

After several days of deliberation, Santángel stepped into Felipe's office. "Those meetings you referred to. If they ever took place in the king's apartments, they will cease."

Felipe's lips tightened. A small crease formed above his chin.

Remaining in his aide's office, the chancellor closed the door. He fished in a pocket and lowered his voice. "This is a key to the back door of my house. Come by tomorrow evening if I can't persuade you otherwise. Just after Compline. Climb the stairs to my private study, the first door on the left."

The crease above Felipe's chin vanished as he broke into a grin. "Thank you. Not just for inviting me. For having the courage."

"Courage? There's nothing wrong with these meetings," said the chancellor. "They're entirely legal. We're permitted to discuss ideas, even with Jews. It's the New Inquisition that is illegal, here in Aragon."

"Unfortunately, Tomás de Torquemada doesn't agree."

"Let him confront us, then, in our *cortes*. I would welcome the opportunity." Santángel handed Felipe the key.

The Sixth Meeting

FELIPE DE ALMAZÓN PROVED AS EAGER in the ad hoc classroom as he was in King Fernando's treasury. "Father Serero," he began on more than one occasion.

"Please don't call me 'Father.' I'm not a rabbi. And even if I were, I wouldn't be your father."

"Forgive me, Señor Serero."

"What is it you wanted to know?"

"Angels."

"Why?"

"Nine years ago," said Felipe, "I was thrown from a horse. They say I appeared dead, but they didn't bury me. I was breathing. It lasted three days. Then I woke."

"Did you dream of angels?" asked Santángel.

"I felt a presence. In my cousin's castle, near Tarazona. In my very room."

"A presence?" asked Serero. "A warmth? A breath? Voices?"

"I just know it was there. And it still is there. Here. In this room. As we speak."

"Do you believe angels saved you?"

"I don't know if angels saved me. But I do think they're guiding me. Not just me. All of us. I've done some reading."

"What have you read?"

"St. Dionysius, the Areopagite."

"I've never heard of him," said Serero. "But I find it strange that a Christian saint would have the name of a pagan god."

"It's just a name," said Felipe.

"A man's name," said Serero, "is important. Take for example our chancellor. Santángel. *Holy angel.*"

Santángel smiled.

"Much of Dionysius's thought derives, or so he says, from the Hebrew Bible," said Felipe.

"Tell us, then, what you've gleaned from this pagan Christian expert on Judaism."

"He describes the celestial choir," said Felipe. "Nine species of angels. Seraphim, cherubim, seven others. Some have six wings, some have four, some two. Some have eyes all over their wings. Some have the faces of oxen, lions, or eagles. Some burn as they sing. He goes into great detail."

"The sculptures in your office," remarked Luis de Santángel.

"Yes, Chancellor. For me, carving angels is like praying."

Santángel thought of those busts and faces. Some looked menacing. Others, scheming or mocking. Grim prayers, he reflected.

"Regarding angels," said Serero, "There are many traditions. The Torah tradition, the prophetic tradition, the Talmudic tradition, the Kabalistic tradition. They don't necessarily agree."

"But what, if I may," asked Felipe, "is the official position of the Jewish Church?"

"There is no official position. On angels or any other matter."

"How can that be? It is a religion, no? Not just a collection of opinions."

"There's the Pentateuch," conceded Serero. "What you Christians call the books of Genesis, Exodus, Leviticus, Numbers, and Deuteronomy. That is certainly official, if you want to use that term. But in many ways its meaning is not clear. So there's the Talmud, a guide to help us interpret the Torah. But the Talmud itself is full of disagreement. Rabbis do their best to make sense of it all. But where you have three rabbis, you have five opinions. And sometimes, in those rare instances when the majority of rabbis do agree on something, it turns out they're all wrong."

"I came here to get answers," Felipe told Serero. "And all I'm getting are more questions."

"If you want answers, don't look to Judaism. The entire edifice, beautiful and convoluted as it is, is built not of answers, but of questions. That, in any case, is my opinion. Others would disagree." Serero smiled.

Felipe insisted: "Is there anything at all you can tell me about angels?"

"Of course. You have the angel that wrestles with Jacob. The two angels Lot invites into his home. The three angels who announce the birth of Isaac to Abraham. None have eyes on their wings. None even has wings. As far as we know, none sings in a choir."

"Then what makes them angels?"

"They're messengers from heaven. But they look like men. Like you. Like me."

"So angels look like people?"

"Some of them. But there are other angels. The cherubim who guard Eden. The 'messenger' who appears to Moses in a burning bush. Ezekiel's vision. These angels, if you want to call them that, don't resemble us at all."

"If I wasn't utterly confused before," said Felipe, "I am now."

"What makes them angels isn't their appearance. It isn't any magical powers they may or may not possess. It's the role they play in people's lives."

Felipe leaned forward. "What, then, is their role? How do they perform their mission?"

"Let me tell you one of these stories. The story of Jacob, a man whose memory we cherish. One of the fathers of our people. But until he wrestles with that angel, the Torah is quite clear, he's not a good person. At his birth, he grabs his brother Esau's heel, trying to pull himself into the world before him. Later, he tricks his father into giving him a blessing meant for his brother. He steals his brother's birthright. Why do we revere such a man?"

"Why, indeed?" asked Felipe.

"We certainly don't revere him for his moral failures," said Serero. "We revere him for whatever good he did, despite his moral failures. The same applies to King David, and even to Moses."

"If you compare any of them to Jesus," said Santángel, "it's hard to see them as great leaders, let alone as founders of an ethical religion."

Serero turned to him. "Only if you believe Jesus was morally perfect. The Jewish view is, we're all flawed. What matters is the struggle. That's what the story of Jacob wrestling with the angel tells us. The struggle transforms Jacob. The angel gives him a new name, Israel, which means, 'one who struggles with God.'"

"That transformation, that struggle," said Felipe. "I want to understand it."

"That is why we're here, Señor de Almazón," said the scribe. "That is why we're all here."

The Ninth Meeting

ABRAM SERERO MADE A REQUEST. "A friend of mine, a learned Jew, has cordial relations with Monsignor Pedro de Monterubio."

Felipe de Almazón frowned. "How is that possible?"

"It hardly surprises me," said Luis de Santángel, remembering the frail old churchman he had seen speaking with Pedro de Arbués on the day of his return from Rome. He asked Serero, "But why are you mentioning this?"

"A priest in the monsignor's office asked my friend for instruction. My friend has too many students."

"A priest?"

"Not just any priest. The monsignor's personal secretary. This man studied Hebrew in the seminary. And Jewish mysticism, which is not my specialty."

Felipe de Almazón shook his head. "We needn't take more risks."

"This particular risk, I don't think is so serious," said the scribe.

Both looked to Santángel for a decision. "To have a churchman in our midst," the chancellor reflected. "Someone close to the monsignor, no less. It might bring a certain legitimacy to our group. To our pursuit. Pedro de Arbués would hesitate before pursuing the monsignor's personal secretary. But we need more information."

. . .

Luis de Santángel spent two weeks discreetly inquiring after the priest's background. Raimundo Díaz de Cáceres had studied at the University of Salamanca, a community of intellects famous for casting a wide net, encompassing the great thinkers of all faiths, in their pursuit of Truth. His teacher at Salamanca had been none other than Hernando de Talavera, a cleric renowned for his knowledge of Judaism and Islam. Many observers of the Church in Castile regarded Talavera as Tomás de Torquemada's ideological adversary.

Father Cáceres made his first appearance the week after Santángel consented. He wore not the habiliments of his calling, but a simple gray smock. His queries challenged; his manner bristled with perplexity. During those first meetings, he posed a number of questions about that most forbidden of topics, the Jewish understanding of Jesus Christ's messianic mission.

"Christ's mission, Father Cáceres, is beyond our scope," explained the scribe.

"I understand," conceded the priest in his reedy voice. "But what about the concept of the messiah in general? The divinity of the messiah. His purpose."

"Suppose Señor Serero were to explain his people's position on this subject," asked Felipe. "Suppose he were to defend that position to a Christian, and in a secret meeting, no less. It would amount to a capital crime."

"Forgive me," said the priest. "I intend no disrespect." He ran his hand over his bald pate.

Serero nodded.

Cáceres challenged him again. "What about His disciples? What does Judaism say about them? Were they liars?"

"Please, Father," Felipe protested.

"I am not going to claim these subjects are never broached," the scribe admitted. "But those texts—the most ancient of them, the most authoritative—don't get circulated much."

"Why not?"

"They could be seen as provocative. You know that, Father."

"All of them?" asked the priest.

"Some of them," said Serero.

Cáceres pushed relentlessly. "What about the Jewish God? The God of justice and wrath. Why do some people find the Jewish God more to their liking than the Christian God, the God of mercy and love?"

For once, Serero seemed flustered. "Father Cáceres, the Christian understanding of my faith is like a blind man's description of a beautiful valley, from the edge of a cliff: all darkness and danger."

The priest took a deep breath.

Luis de Santángel intervened. "Please. This discussion is over."

Even Santángel could not help wondering whether this priest was not, after all, one of Pedro de Arbués's spies, attempting to collect damning evidence of heretical thought, of clandestine conversions. Why was Abram Serero deliberately ignoring this danger?

After the meeting, Felipe lingered. "Chancellor, my wife and I would like to invite you and your son for dinner."

The invitation surprised Santángel. None of his subordinates had ever violated the social distance between them in this manner. But neither had Santángel discussed the nature of angels with them, or entertained the notion that Jesus Christ was not morally perfect.

"Please thank your wife, Señor de Almazón. I shall be happy to accept your invitation."

"Friday evening, then. At sunset."

The chancellor nodded, placed a hand on his aide's back, and ushered him outside.

. . .

Felipe de Almazón and his family dwelled two streets from Santángel, in a stone house slightly less impressive than the chancellor's. His wife, Catalina, with a pale complexion, umber hair, and hazel eyes, greeted Luis and Gabriel warmly—an elegant, vivacious woman clearly at ease entertaining men of wealth and distinction.

"Chancellor. What an honor. In more ways than you know, you've been like a father to my husband."

Gabriel glanced at his father. Santángel answered him with his eyes, then turned back to his hostess. "It is my privilege, madam," he told Catalina.

"We've sent the servants away," Catalina ushered them down a hallway, "so we can spend the evening alone together, just your family and ours."

The chancellor thought this peculiar. When they entered the next room, he understood.

Before them stood a long table, clothed in white linen. Two brass candlesticks and a jug of wine rose from a jumble of silver plates and goblets. A loaf of bread sat beside the wine, braided in the unmistakable manner of the Jews.

To celebrate the Jewish Sabbath openly, to engage in Jewish ritual in one's home, with one's family, was a far riskier and less ambiguous undertaking than merely to discuss the fine points of theology with friends in one's private study. The chancellor's instinct was to walk out at once, and perhaps find a way to distance himself from his aide, but to do so would serve no purpose. Felipe de Almazón knew too much.

Once again an image from his past, liquid and turbid, seeped into Santángel's mind. As a child, in his parents' home, on rare but resonant occasions, he had seen this very room, this tablecloth, these candles, this bread, this wine, these pulled curtains.

Despite his better judgment and muted irritation, he stayed. Felipe clapped his hands together. Two young children, a boy and a girl, both fair haired, dutifully took their places. Gabriel stood rigidly beside his father, pressing his eyes closed. Felipe uttered prayers, carefully enunciating each syllable of transliterated Hebrew from a battered leather book. He broke the bread and sipped the wine, then sent the children upstairs to eat and play. The three adults sat down to share an elaborate meal.

"I appreciate your cordiality," said Santángel. "But this," he glanced at the candlesticks, the loaf, the goblet, "is perhaps overdoing it."

"How so?" asked Felipe.

"In weighing any proposition, one must consider the risks."

"Chancellor," his aide assured him. "I would never endanger you or your son."

"You may already have done so."

"Zaragoza is not Sevilla," insisted Felipe. "The New Inquisition hasn't made a single arrest in our kingdom."

"Why tempt them?"

"That is not our intent."

"What is your intent, then?" It was all Santángel could do not to raise his voice.

Felipe took the battered Hebrew prayer book from the table, leafed through a few pages, read something to himself, and placed it back on the table. He looked the chancellor in the eye and replied, "I should have thought you'd guessed."

. . .

Upstairs, Gabriel half-heartedly played hide-and-seek with Felipe's children. Midway through their game, he found himself in Felipe's woodworking studio. In the trembling brown light of his small candle, the faces of incomplete seraphim and cherubim scowled, leered, and glared. Certainly a frightening place, but like most frightening places, also magical.

At the rear of the room, Gabriel discovered a closet with a key in its door, full of trinkets and books. He crept inside.

He saw volumes in Latin, a silver cross dangling on a chain, rosaries made of gold and rubies. Tucked behind them, other books, with strange writing on their spines. Scattered on the shelves, brass stars, silver hands and eyes, candelabras. An oval wooden spice box, adorned with miniature carved lions. Gabriel gazed at these anomalous objects, disturbed and transfixed. The giggle of Felipe's daughter broke the spell.

"I'm going to find you! I know you're here."

Breathing audibly, Gabriel reached out and took hold of a small, silver *hamsa* hand. An amulet, terrifying and beguiling, in the shape of a flat upturned palm, with a lapis eye in its center. He wondered, was this the work of the devil? Of an angel? He felt an icy coldness.

"I can *smell* you," said Felipe's daughter, just outside. She giggled again.

Gabriel could not remain in this place, holding this strange object. He knew he should put it back.

He had heard of amulets that could make a man wealthy, a field fertile, or a knight courageous. He did not know whether this was such a talisman, but he was sure it had special powers. There were so many strange objects in this room. He doubted anyone would notice, or care, if this one disappeared. He slipped it into the pocket of his jerkin.

"Here I am!" he announced, throwing open the door, wearing a smile to hide the turmoil in his heart.

"I got you!" The dimpled, blue-eyed little girl grabbed his arm and pushed the door closed behind him. Its lock made a small clicking sound as it fell into place.

. . .

As his father tucked him into bed that night, Gabriel asked, "What was that about, Papa? That . . . that gibberish before dinner, that book, those prayers. Was that . . . Are they . . . ?"

"Just a tradition in their family." Santángel stroked his son's hair. "Señor de Almazón may come from a distant land, with different customs."

"What if they're heretics?"

"Who spoke to you of heresy?"

"Brother Pablo." One of Gabriel's tutors. "He said we're all guards in the lookout tower of our faith."

"And what are we watching for?"

"Secret prayers. Strange foods. Statues. Magical rings, necklaces, cups." He frowned, remembering the *hamsa* hand he had pocketed, worried but also excited to possess such an object. "Were those people heretics, Father?"

Luis let out a forced laugh. "Felipe? He's as Catholic as any of us. Now go to sleep." Santángel kissed his son on the forehead.

Gabriel closed his eyes, shuddering inwardly. His father seemed not to take his concerns seriously. He found something troubling, frightening, dishonest in that dismissive chuckle. After Luis left his bedroom, Gabriel silently uttered a prayer. Having been raised as much by his seminarian tutors as by his father, having absorbed more of their conviction than of his father's confusion, Gabriel prayed as he had never prayed before. He asked God whether contact with these unusual people and their frightful customs had tainted him or his father, and begged Him to cleanse their hearts if it had.

The Tenth Meeting

ABRAM SERERO BROUGHT the leather envelope that Cristóbal Colón had foisted upon Santángel. The chancellor was about to object, but

Serero stopped him. "Please, Chancellor. There's no cause for concern." This confused Santángel, but he allowed Serero to continue.

The scribe addressed Father Cáceres. "You wanted to see texts that discuss the Messiah. Some of these texts do just that. Others deal with travel to places like the Garden of Eden and the Holy Land."

Now the chancellor understood Colón's interest in these documents. As Serero spread the leaves upon the table, Santángel leaned forward to steal another glimpse at the ancient, precious writings.

Serero described each document. The first was a commentary on Abraham's passage from the city of Ur to the Holy Land. "But it wasn't only a journey through those lands. This is the point." Serero's finger came to rest on one of the Hebrew phrases: "It was a journey of Abraham's soul, from a state of unholiness toward a state of holiness."

Cáceres, who had studied Hebrew, leaned over the text, his bald head reflecting the candle flame.

Serero showed them another. "This one . . . This concerns the journey of the Jews back to the Holy Land, after the coming of the Messiah." And another: "This describes some of the conditions surrounding his coming."

"What are those conditions?" asked Cáceres.

"Let me ask you something, Father," returned Serero. "Why do we have rainbows?"

"To remind us of the Flood. Of God's agreement with Noah. That He'll never again destroy most of the life on earth."

"Well, according to this text, when the Messiah comes, the rainbow will be fresh again, as fresh as a woman just married, entering the bridal chamber." Serero smiled mischievously. "Of course, Father, that's something you may not have had the good fortune to experience firsthand."

The priest, usually so somber, responded to the jab with a chuckle.

"And on that day," Serero concluded, "God's promise to man will be renewed."

Cáceres examined the text, stopping at one of the words. "What is this? Is this not *Roma*?"

Serero looked where he was pointing. "So it is."

"And the city of Rome will crumble," Cáceres translated. Clearly, if his reading was correct, these words amounted to a warning, an evil slur against the Holy Church.

"That is what it is saying, Father," admitted Serero, following his index.

"Rome will grow dissolute." The priest's voice dipped as he continued. "And will collapse."

"It is happening," observed Santángel, "in our day."

"How so?" asked Cáceres, raising his eyes from the text.

"Graft, harlotry, illegal commerce. The usual signs of decay."

"How do you know this?"

"I spent a month there. I saw enough."

Cáceres read on: "There will be a war against the people of Israel. But in the end, they will be delivered."

"Where will this Messiah come from?" asked Felipe.

"Some say his soul resides in the Garden of Eden," said Serero.

"Where is that?" asked Santángel, again thinking of his conversation with Colón.

"If I knew where paradise was," answered the scribe, "would I be sitting here with you?"

. . .

After Father Cáceres left, Santángel posed another question to the scribe. "But what of that other document? The rolled-up parchment, very ancient." He remembered its letters floating in the air.

"Ah, yes." Serero nodded slowly. "I've placed it elsewhere. For safe keeping."

"What is it? What does it say?"

"That parchment would be better left alone."

"The sailor who gave me these," insisted Santángel, "urged me to report back to him. It wouldn't be decent for me, or you, to hoard this knowledge."

"The parchment." Serero nodded, scratching his ear. "I knew of this document long before I had the privilege of setting my eyes on it. I was under the impression not one copy remained. Because of this text, many Jews have been massacred. The Christians searched out every copy and burned them in auto-da-fés, along with their owners."

The Thirteenth Meeting

AS SERERO AND CÁCERES ENTERED Santángel's study, Felipe set a pine box on the table. "I have spent many, many hours struggling with this."

"What is it?" asked Santángel.

Felipe opened the box and removed a sculpture, about a foot high. Two men wrestling, mirror reflections of each other. Delicate curves of cherry wood formed their hair, mouths, hands, calves, feet. Their facial muscles and eyes conveyed not only intense concentration, but also awe, as if both figures were astonished to find themselves embracing in combat.

"Jacob wrestling with the angel."

"Please put that away," said Serero.

"Why?" asked the chancellor's aide.

"It is a graven image."

Felipe frowned. "But it doesn't claim to be a representation of God."

"I don't want to see that. Please take it out of here."

"You showed us a book, a Passover Haggadah, with people drinking, talking, eating. Were those graven images?"

"An illuminated Haggadah," explained the scribe, "is not the same as a depiction of people and scenes from the Bible. I know how proud the Christians are of their statues. But I don't have to look at them."

"Why not?" asked Raimundo de Cáceres.

Felipe de Almazón slowly, deliberately replaced the statue in its box, then carried the box to another room.

"The Bible," explained Serero, "is made of words. Words exist in the same realm as ideas. A physical form is another matter. Images and words affect the soul differently. The Muslims understand this. The Christians don't."

"I do," said the priest. "And I am a Christian. You're talking about Neoplatonism."

"I am not talking about that," said Serero, "whatever that means."

Felipe de Almazón returned, but hardly said a word the rest of that evening. His lips tight, a small crease above his chin, he listened.

After the others left, Santángel again detained Serero. "Did you not say, life is more sacred than ritual? That if a life is at risk, a Jew should even violate the Sabbath?"

"Without a doubt," replied Serero. "That is the principle of *pikuach nefesh*."

"I'm afraid that principle escapes Felipe."

"His statue," said the scribe, "is not a danger to anyone's life. And Felipe is not a Jew."

"I'm not speaking of the statue."

The chancellor told Serero about the Sabbath invitation, the elaborate meal, Felipe's clumsy attempt at Hebrew prayer. "I fear he believes that these meetings . . . that we're trying to convert him."

"We have been clear," said Serero. "We're discussing ideas. We're not telling anyone what to believe or not to believe. That is our agreement."

"But why this Sabbath invitation?"

"Felipe seems to . . ." Serero searched for the words. "He seems to cherish the secret. The common ground he shares with you. You're like a father to him."

"What common ground? Neither of us is a Jew. He doesn't even understand the purpose of these rituals."

"Chancellor, I agree. Señor de Almazón is not a Jew. But according to Jewish law, you *are* a Jew."

"Yes, yes, of course," said the chancellor irritably, ushering the scribe outside and locking the door.

. . .

Over the next few days, Felipe removed every unfinished angel from his workshop and every sculpture from his office. He placed them carefully in a pine box. On top, he nested Jacob and the angel. He buried this coffin in his courtyard, vowing to himself never again to make or even regard an image of holy beings. He would survive as well without their protection.

The Nineteenth Meeting

SERERO SHOWED THEM another ancient text, a bulky tome with a well-worn leather binding and ornate Hebrew lettering on its spine, in gold. "The *Zohar*," he explained, opening the volume on the table. "The Book of Splendor. Tell me if this doesn't have something to do with what we're witnessing, in this terrible time." He translated from the Hebrew: *"The gazelle of the morning star . . . that most compassionate of animals . . . goes to find food for others . . . and in the darkness before dawn . . . feels the pain of exile. Like one who's giving birth . . . she cries out in pain."* He read silently a moment longer.

"What does this mean?" whispered Santángel.

"More than I can say," answered the scribe. "But this much even I, with my limited understanding, can tell you. The gazelle is the people of Israel, as it's written in Psalm 42: *As the gazelle thirsts for the brook, so my soul thirsts for you, O God.*"

"And this gazelle," asked Father Cáceres. "This people, what is the text telling us about her?"

"She goes out into the world."

"Out into the world. Into exile. The people of Israel. Yes." This, the priest understood. The Jews had been a wandering, stateless people for centuries.

"Exile, yes, but not forever. In the darkness of the morning. By the light of the morning star." Serero placed a hand on the priest's arm. "Which is to say, daybreak is surely coming. But for now, this gazelle, this people, is crying out in pain. *Like one giving birth.*"

"Who's she giving birth to?" asked Felipe.

"What we are talking about," said Serero, "are the birth pangs of the messianic age. The time when Israel will return from exile and all the nations will be at peace. The time of the true Messiah."

He closed the massive volume with a thud. "That is what I wanted to show you. We're living in strife, darkness, and exile. But it won't last forever." He turned back to Santángel. "You, of all people, Chancellor, must hold that in your heart. If anyone is in a position to help bring this about, you are."

"How so?"

"You are one of the few who can change this world. You are a messenger. That is the meaning of your name."

"If I ever had that kind of influence, and I'm not sure I ever did, I fear I no longer do."

"You can change this world," Serero repeated. "And God knows, it needs to be changed. Utterly. That is our hope. Please, whatever happens, don't forget all we have learned together. Don't forget the purity of our intentions. I know I won't."

The Twentieth Meeting

FELIPE ARRIVED LATE. He probably would not have come at all, he explained, had he known what was best for him. That morning, two constables of the *Santa Hermandad*, "Holy Brothers," had appeared at his door. They carried lances and wore long white tunics with black crosses emblazoned across their chests. With a hand that Luis de Santángel saw quake, Felipe produced the summons the constables had delivered.

In it, the Reverend Pedro de Arbués, canon of La Seo Cathedral and Inquisitor of Aragon, demanded that Felipe de Almazón appear for questioning. Santángel studied the document. Who had denounced Felipe? Was it one of their group? A suspicious servant who wondered why she had been given time off on a Friday? A neighbor who had witnessed Catalina preparing the Sabbath dinner? And beneath these questions, a slithering heap of half-formulated worries: When would the Hermandad come for the rest of them? Would their high positions and powerful associates be of any avail? What would become of their wives, their children, their friends? He thought of Gabriel, already wanting a mother—the shame he would bear if Santángel were publicly implicated in heresy. He handed the summons to Father Cáceres in silence.

"I wouldn't despair," Raimundo de Cáceres advised Felipe when he finished reading. "Remember, all they want from you is confession. And repentance. Tell them the devil tempted you. You looked for truth in Judaism, but now you know better."

"Father Cáceres, I'm no fool," Felipe answered. "I've seen what has gone on in Cordoba and Sevilla."

The priest held up his hand. "I'm not saying there aren't abuses. Egregious abuses. Horrifying abuses. I'm as angry as any of you. Perhaps more angry." He shook his head in frustration and concluded, "Just confess. Repent and be done with it. They'll jail you for a time, then they'll release you. I shall do all I can to ensure that."

"As will I," added Santángel.

Felipe turned to Santángel. "With all the esteem and affection I hold for you, Chancellor, I beg you, do not attempt to defend me, or we'll all end up dead."

"None of us will die," insisted Father Cáceres. "Just confess and repent. Ask Christ for forgiveness. They'll spare you."

"How can I ask Christ for forgiveness," asked Felipe, "when I don't believe in him?"

Luis de Santángel had been puzzled when Felipe de Almazón asked to join their group. He had been disconcerted when Felipe invited him for a Sabbath dinner. Now he was utterly bewildered. There was more to this man's behavior than courage, or foolishness, but he did not understand what was driving the young aristocrat to behave in this manner. He prayed it was not his own example.

Abram Serero finally spoke up. "Don't speak nonsense. Your life is holy. Created in the image of God. I wouldn't want to feel responsible if you lost it."

Felipe turned to Santángel. "Chancellor, I hope you understand."

"I do not. Tell them what they want to hear," Santángel advised him. "Submit to the Church's authority. To the Church's love. Do penance. I, for my part, vow to you I shall do my best to put an end to this madness."

. . .

Night after night, week after week, Luis de Santángel prayed fervently that the Inquisition treat Felipe de Almazón with the mercy due an aristocrat and an associate of the king's court. That even under torture, Felipe de Almazón never accuse Father Cáceres. That he never breathe a word about the ancient, dangerous manuscript

Abram Serero possessed. That he never allude to secret meetings. He trusted Felipe as much as he trusted anyone. He also knew what his former aide was facing.

Despite Felipe's warning not to intervene on his behalf, the chancellor worked hard to free him from the ecclesiastical jail, and thus to advance the longer-term project of crippling the New Inquisition in Aragon. He discussed the matter with others among the king's advisors, some of whom tried to help in subtle ways, always anonymously. He visited Felipe's wife, the beautiful Catalina de Almazón, assuring her no harm would come to her husband. But as the weeks passed, it grew more difficult to appear confident. Silences punctuated their conversations. The pauses grew longer, the words fewer.

Four months after his arrest, Felipe de Almazón was dead, reportedly having succumbed to an illness that made his teeth chatter and his mouth foam.

. . .

Felipe's confession, according to the ecclesiastical authorities, had been incomplete. To make the point, a half-dozen constables of the Santa Hermandad dragged his corpse into the Plaza de la Seo, where, before Sunday Mass and the entire city, they hacked it to pieces and fed it to dogs.

To ensure that Felipe's soul would rise to heaven despite his perfidy, Pedro de Arbués presided over a postmortem "reconciliation ceremony" on a platform before the cathedral, even as the hounds growled and yapped over their supper below.

The sight of these jackals, sinewy, coated in hues of streaked and mottled mud, chewing off the face of the aide who had become the chancellor's trusted friend, pulling at the tendons of his shoulders, ripping the flesh of his ears and nose, rooting in his entrails, caused the floodgates of revulsion, contempt, and rage to swing wide open in Luis de Santángel's heart. Standing with other dignitaries at the front of the crowd, his cheeks wet with tears, he closed his eyes to distance himself from the event. The Latin sacrament falling from the canon's mouth beat upon his eardrums like an enemy army thumping at the city gates.

When he opened his eyes again, he observed the expression on Canon Arbués's fleshy face. A look of contentedness and serenity.

Across the immense divide between them, the canon's gaze met the chancellor's. Pedro de Arbués's composure dissolved. In the set of his jaw, Luis de Santángel now saw ardor, determination, and accusal.

. . .

Late that night, Father Cáceres entered the chancellor's house through the back door. He found Santángel sitting on his bed, lost in thought.

"Please be assured," the priest told him, "I loved Señor de Almazón. His thirst for knowledge. His sincerity. His search for God."

"I . . . I should never . . . have allowed him . . ."

Cáceres placed a hand on the chancellor's shoulder. "He would have found a way, with Abram Serero or someone else."

The chancellor swallowed, his shoulder tensing under Cáceres's grasp. "Father, I and many others have fought battles in the cortes. I've pleaded with the king. Others have pleaded with the queen. I've even appealed to the pope, personally."

"I too have tried, Chancellor. I've written to my university master, Hernando de Talavera, who shares our sympathies. For now, we're powerless against . . . against *him*." It seemed to Santángel the young priest did not wish to pronounce Torquemada's name, for fear it might contaminate his faith.

"Talavera, yes, the scholar. Please, Father, sit down."

Cáceres sat in a chair before him. "The records of Señor de Almazón's testimony, Pedro de Arbués is guarding them like holy relics. Keeping them, as far as we can determine, in his private chambers. I have that from the canon's servants."

"But do we know if there's anything in them? Anything that . . ."

". . . that might incriminate us? Señor Santángel, how could there not be?"

Indeed, Santángel himself had never heard of anyone who failed to provide names under torture. "These records, these logs of Felipe's deposition . . ."

"It's all in one log," the priest corrected him. "And soon, sooner than you think, if we don't act, this book will find its way to Torquemada."

The chancellor looked at the window. It was as black as the Strait of Gibraltar at midnight, separating two continents in his life—all that had come before, and all that would come after this day.

"We must recover that book. The log of his testimony." Turning back to the priest, he affirmed aloud what they both knew. "And the canon, he must die. Pedro de Arbués," he nodded slowly, "must die before he destroys you, me, and our associates."

Cáceres lowered his voice. "I know the man to do it. A horseman. A Basque. A skilled assassin."

They looked into each other's eyes. It occurred to Santángel that if he had ever felt anything akin to Christian love, it was in this moment, in their shared hatred.

CHAPTER FOUR

RETURNING FROM THE MARKETPLACE on a bright, cool afternoon, Judith found her home deserted. She began preparing supper.

An hour later, the meal was almost ready. Baba Shlomo and Levi still had not appeared. She searched through the streets of the quarter until she discovered the old man sitting on a stone bench near the synagogue.

"Where's Levi?"

Baba Shlomo shook his head. "This is what happens when women run a business. You ignore the children, soon they don't need you."

For religious purposes, having passed the age of bar mitzvah, Levi was a man. For practical purposes, he was still a boy. When his studies prevented him from working in the shop or accompanying Judith to the marketplace, Judith expected him home for dinner.

She wandered out of the Jewish quarter to the vast Arab marketplace, where children sometimes made mischief running between the stalls or stealing fruit. She remembered her brother Yossi and the mysterious gash on his thigh, incurred here all those years ago. Panicking, she visited all the vendors.

She paused at a fountain, telling herself there was no cause for alarm. "The wind that blew on the Red Sea will never blow on the Middle Sea." History never repeated itself. Whatever had happened to her brother would surely not happen to Levi. She sat down,

A young Muslim woman sat down beside her, placing her sack of vegetables on the ground. A scarf covered her hair, but her exposed face, with its refined features and pale skin, brightened in a warm smile. "It is a lovely day, isn't it?"

The sky was azure, the air crisp and clear. The sun, nearing the horizon, cast long shadows as shopkeepers packed up. "I suppose it is."

"What are you searching for?" asked the Arab woman.

"What makes you think I'm searching for something?"

The Arab woman laughed. "Why else would a Jewish woman be running from stall to stall in the Arab marketplace, as if possessed by a djinn?"

"My nephew," said Judith.

"Don't worry: If you lost him here in the marketplace, no harm will come to him."

Judith turned to her and smiled, appreciating her intent. No Muslim, she knew, could understand the feelings of gratitude and fear that mingled in the soul of a subjugated people.

"Go home," the woman told her. "A child's journey, you'll never fathom."

. . .

Earlier in the day, Sara Benatar had found Levi in the silver workshop. "My father is coming home," she told him. "He'll have a gift. Want to come?"

"Come where?"

"He always takes the same path through the Arab city. Come!"

Levi put down his tools.

She led him down the hill into an opulent neighborhood of sprawling villas and gardens. They passed women wearing silk veils and men in fine wool robes. Three boys bounced a small ball to one another off the wall of a residence. A courtyard gate yawned open. Sounds of drums and conversation wafted out. Sara peeked inside.

A woman in a dark silk robe with gold embroidery was dancing—swaying and dipping, her arms bobbing, her finger cymbals accenting the beats. Sara watched, fascinated. "Isn't that beautiful?"

Levi swallowed, uneasy. In the crowd of men, he noticed a pair of dark eyes. They wandered toward Sara and halted. Levi recognized the man.

"Let's go. We have no place here." Levi took Sara's arm and pulled her away.

The man left the group and met them outside. He looked down into Sara's eyes and smiled warmly. "I have seen you before, have I not?"

Sara lowered her face, remembering the day of the parade and the vizier who had peeled the monkey off her chest.

"How old are you now?"

"Fourteen, Your Excellency."

The vizier nodded.

. . .

When Judith finally returned home, the sun was setting. Her nephew was sitting in the courtyard playing Quirkat, a board game, with Sara.

"Levi!" Judith exclaimed. "You gave me such a fright. Don't ever do that again!"

"I'm no longer a child," he told her.

"I know, I know. Where were you? I looked everywhere."

"Sara's father had something for you."

"What did Yonatan have for me?"

"Look in your bedroom."

Judith gazed at him, bewildered, and turned to go into the house.

On her brass table sat a box of intricately carved olivewood, with inlaid ivory, gold, and silver.

"Open it," Levi urged her, standing in the doorway. Sara stood beside him, watching curiously with her striking green eyes.

As carefully as if she were opening a precious book, Judith lifted the cover. Inside, several small jars with corks in their mouths gaped at the sky like mackerels in a fisherman's crate. She took one and removed the cork. A fragrance of orange blossoms crept out. She touched the cork with her finger and rubbed it on her palm. A body oil. The most delicate, beguiling essence she had ever breathed. She recorked the vial and opened a second. Roses. And a third. Jasmine.

"Read the note," said Sara impatiently.

Beneath the main body of the perfume box, she pulled out a small drawer. In it, she found a missive addressed to her in a delicate Hebrew cursive. Never had anyone sent her such a note.

The congregation of the Great Synagogue of Cairo told her of their joy upon receiving the silver ornaments, and their regret upon learning of her brother's fate. This box and the perfumes in it were a small expression of their appreciation and condolences. Although the synagogue had no further need of silver ornaments, for now, several members of the congregation wanted to commission mezuzot, beakers, bracelets, and necklaces.

The next page listed their orders, line after line of bracelets, menorahs, cups. Judith read all of it, pronouncing each word like a prayer.

"Levi, we have work. A lot of work. You, me, and maybe another silversmith or two, if we're going to fill these orders promptly." In her visits to the silver shops of Granada, she had come to know some of the workers. More than a few were barely eking out a living and would welcome the opportunity. "Come here, both of you."

She took Levi and Sara in her arms. They hugged her back.

. . .

The clinking of tweezers, the clatter of chasing hammers, and the rasp of files once again filled Yossi's atelier. Odors of sweat and sulfur pervaded the cramped, musty workshop. Levi hummed as he worked.

Ten weeks into this labor, Dina Benatar shuffled in, her hair unbrushed, her robe loosely thrown together, her eyes rimmed with red. She leaned down and placed her palms on Judith's worktable.

"I know you're busy."

Judith, who had never seen her friend in such a state, put down her tools. "Come. I have mint and orange-blossom tea."

They crossed the courtyard.

"They took my Sara."

"Sara?" asked Judith. "Someone took Sara? Who?"

"The vizier's guard. They promised her . . . they promised her jewels, clothes, everything, except freedom."

Judith ushered Dina inside. "When?"

"Two soldiers of the royal guard." Dina dropped onto a cushion. "In the middle of the night, they knocked. I served them fig liquor. They spoke about the vizier, his kindness, his generosity, his . . . his interest in my Sara." She sniffled, trying to hold back her tears.

"The vizier." Judith sank onto a cushion beside Dina, forgetting the tea.

The soldiers had assured Sara, Dina continued, that Ibrahim al-Hakim would provide her with comfort the rest of her days. She would enjoy the honor befitting a member of the emir's court.

What they chose not to say was just as telling. Dina and Judith understood that Sara would dwell in a harem with the vizier's concubines. Al-Hakim would compel her to accept the truth of Islam. He would forbid her to communicate with her family or her community.

"She chose to go with them. I tried to stop her. She did it to protect me. To protect us. With Yonatan away again . . ." Dina could no longer hold back her tears.

"What could Yonatan do?" asked Judith. He was a wealthy man, but his wealth would mean little to the vizier. Judith held Dina in her arms until she stopped crying.

"I walked to the Alhambra. At sunrise. The guards turned me away." Dina swallowed. "So I went to the rabbi's house. I talked with his wife. Maybe he'll put in a complaint."

"He won't. He can't. If he offends the vizier, our whole community will pay."

Dina wiped her eye. "Then my last hopes were false hopes."

"Hope can't be true or false." Judith stroked Dina's arm. "Hope is hope."

. . .

Judith hired another silversmith, and with Sara in mind, began work on a new project. She created an exquisite teapot with curves suggesting a young maiden, and a matching cup. She labored three weeks designing, crafting, and buffing these two items, pouring more feeling and care into their fabrication than into any previous work. She also composed a note for the vizier.

Your Excellency,

We, your loyal subjects among the Hebrew residents of the capital, honored that you have chosen one from our midst to love and gratify, humbly offer you this drinking vessel from the workshop of Yossi Migdal, Master Silversmith, in honor of your choice. Long may the emir of Granada, his vizier, and his kingdom thrive!

Her work finished, Judith slipped the note, the teapot, and the cup into a box and set out for Dina's house.

Dina had lost weight. Her complexion was sallow. She wore a simple white gown, as if in mourning.

"Look." Judith removed the lid from the box. The teapot and its cup lay glistening on a bed of silk, a mother sleeping beside her child.

Dina gasped. She dared not touch them, for fear of dulling the silver with fingerprints. Judith showed her the note.

"To love and gratify?" asked Dina, outraged. "He seized her. He's raping her."

"We need to be cautious."

"Why only one cup? Do you imagine the vizier, that animal, drinks tea alone?"

"That's the point," said Judith. "Now slip on your nicest dress. We're going for a walk."

The two women set out through quarters they hardly knew, where roosters, dogs, and children playing with marbles shared the streets with merchants, who stood outside their shops watching them pass.

They left the city streets behind. Vines, hedges, and fruit trees filled the sides of the road. Judith and Dina approached the base of the hill where the magnificent Alhambra castle stood, a great eagle watching the still valley.

They continued along a path through these gardens, toward the top of the hill. The castle complex presented high, windowless walls, broken with lookout towers and topped with the square teeth of crenellation. The view from these walls embraced the entire region of Granada. Two black slaves with sabers guarded the hoof-shaped archway of an enormous square tower.

"We're here to meet with the vizier," Judith told them.

"Is he expecting you?"

"We have a gift."

The two guards conferred. "Wait here." One of them went through the gate.

"He'll have us thrown out," said Dina. "I already tried this."

"He won't meet with us," agreed Judith.

"Then why are we here?"

The guard returned, cordially explaining, "Unfortunately, the vizier is occupied. But he sends greetings."

"Please tell the vizier we are honored. Give him this on our behalf." Judith handed the wooden box to the guard.

. . .

Six days later, Judith sat working in her shop, alone. Ever since Sara's abduction, Levi had been spending a great deal of time in the synagogue, or in Baba Shlomo's room, studying and praying.

She heard men talking, coughing, and chuckling outside. The clink of a sword, a stirrup, or a chain. One man's voice, louder. "Wait here."

Ibrahim al-Hakim, the vizier of Granada, entered, stooping to avoid hitting his head against the low beams.

Seeing him, close-bearded, big-bellied, in a scarlet and saffron silk *juba*, Judith felt her stomach turn, but rose to greet him. "How may we be of service to you, Your Excellency?"

"Quite a teapot, that gift of yours," said Ibrahim al-Hakim. "But tell me, do you imagine the vizier of Granada takes tea by himself?"

Judith smiled. "It was a personal gift, Your Excellency. Nothing more."

"Nothing more?" He arched one eyebrow. "My physician, Isaac Azoulay, perhaps you know of him."

"We are a small community. He's a famous physician."

"He insists I drink from silver. Indeed, he insists the emir and all the court take hot beverages only in silver vessels."

"Why?"

"He says silver promotes health."

"That is true."

"Yes, of course."

Al-Hakim noticed an inlaid-turquoise brooch on a small shelf amongst other jewels. "This is a lovely piece, is it not? Do you think it would please a fourteen-year-old girl," he picked up the brooch, "with eyes of emerald?"

"That particular piece would please any girl. But it might look better on one of your older slaves. I mean, concubines, of course."

The vizier nodded slowly. "Feisty and beautiful," he quipped. "A shame you're not younger."

Judith thanked God she was twenty-nine, far too old for the vizier.

"What do you have for my Sariya?"

Judith's smile vanished. *Sariya* was the Arabic form of *Sara*. That Levi's friend had been forced to convert to Islam went without saying, but to hear the vizier refer to her by a new name broke Judith's heart.

"Maybe this." Judith unpinned the filigree slipper from her dress. Al-Hakim grasped it between his thumb and forefinger and brought it to his face. He could not know that the slipper-pin contained a Hebrew prayer, rolled up on a tiny parchment inside. Perhaps, thought Judith, it would be of some comfort to Sara.

"Sara will look exquisite with it, Your Excellency."

"Exquisite Sariya looks, with or without any adornment." Al-Hakim sighed. "I'll take both. Your slipper pin and the brooch." He dropped them in his leather satchel. "As well as twenty more cups to match the one you offered."

For a moment, Judith said nothing. Then she cleared her throat. "If you'll forgive my impertinence, Your Excellency, I have a small request of my own."

"You have my ear."

"Please, follow me."

Ignoring his armed guards, who stood outside, she led him out of her workshop and into her home.

"I know I'm being presumptuous. I'm sure you don't often visit the homes of humble citizens."

"It's not often they invite me," he replied politely.

She served him mint tea. As they sat and sipped, she explained all that Dina Benatar had done for her. Ibrahim al-Hakim listened attentively.

"Dina misses her daughter terribly. She is alone," Judith concluded.

"I'll allow my Sariya's mother private visits with her daughter, once a month," the vizier offered. "But the visits must take place in a guarded room, and each will last no more than half an hour. The subject of religion must never be discussed." He rose to leave. "Will that be all?"

Inwardly exulting, Judith nodded. "Thank you, Your Excellency."

He smiled and turned to leave. "When should we expect the teacups?"

"Four months. Maybe five."

"Four months, then. I'll expect a visit from you." Al-Hakim retrieved a few gold coins from his satchel and placed them on the table. "This is for the brooch and the pin." He had decided on their value without consulting her. The price he paid was far in excess of what Judith would have asked.

CHAPTER FIVE

DEVOTIONAL CANDLES FLICKERED on La Seo's altar, a small island of light in the dark cathedral. Luis de Santángel knelt near the back of the pews as if praying.

In the shadows before the transept stood the Basque horseman, tall and lean, with straight hair to his shoulders and an elegant quilted doublet. He acknowledged Santángel with a terse nod.

Pedro de Arbués knelt at a wooden altar, seemingly oblivious to the world, an egg-shaped lump of flesh swathed in a white tunic and a black, hooded scapular. Wheezing inhalations punctuated the canon's barely audible prayer. As Santángel watched him from behind, he remembered the jackals chewing Felipe de Almazón's shoulder and the look of satisfaction on Arbués's face.

"It will all be over soon," Santángel prayed.

. . .

The Basque horseman had been observing the monk for weeks. Pedro de Arbués rarely went anywhere without armed guards, except when he prayed late at night.

As the horseman slid out from the shadows, he knew that Arbués's conversation with God would continue another sixty or seventy heartbeats. If the canon rose sooner than usual, then something was amiss, and the horseman would have to abandon tonight's meticulous plans.

He dug in his pocket and pulled the leather strap from the handle of his dagger, freeing it from its sheath. His fingers caressed the dagger's braided-ivory hilt. He grasped it firmly.

He discerned a slight ridge under the shoulder of the inquisitor's gown. That would be the edge of his coat of mail. Despite his
faith in a better afterlife, the horseman reflected, this man of God
seemed in no hurry to shed his corporeal envelope.

As the horseman slid closer, he watched Arbués's high-arched
nostrils and buttery hands for signs of disquiet. He heard the canon's
labored breathing, his mumbled prayer. Arbués was undoubtedly
aware of his presence, but did not appear alarmed.

He came so close that despite the dimness of the candlelight, he
perceived the canon's eyelashes twitching. Arbués's right hand rose
to his forehead, then touched his breastbone and shoulders. He
started to rise.

The horseman drew the dagger, lifted it above his shoulder, and
brought it forcefully down to the base of Arbués's neck. He fell
forward, clasping Arbués's head and pushing him to the ground.
The knife tore through muscle; the horseman wedged it between
bones, twisting. The inquisitor's arms flailed outward. He screamed
ineffectively. His attacker's forearm was in his mouth.

The horseman continued torquing and shoving his knife into
the monk's sinewy nape, aiming for a particular spot that, he knew
from long experience, would deliver the canon's rapid death. When
he found that spot, thick, hot blood burbled through the wound
onto his victim's shoulder.

The horseman left the knife in the monk's flesh. He jerked his
other arm free of Arbués's teeth. The canon fell to the floor, writh-
ing and gurgling.

His doublet and hose spattered with blood, the horseman turned
down the central aisle as Luis de Santángel rose in the pew. They
heard the clatter of hoofbeats on the cobblestones outside. Few
other than Pedro de Arbués visited the cathedral this late. An ecclesiastical messenger, however, might be arriving with an urgent note
for the local hierarchy.

"Go, now," Luis de Santángel instructed the horseman. "I'll find
the book."

"I fear we should both leave, or search together." The horseman's voice was guttural, accented. "You must not search alone.
Too dangerous."

Observing the man's blood-splashed clothing and hands, Santángel caught his breath. "No. Leave now. I'll finish our task."

"Are you certain?"

"Tomorrow morning," Santángel heard himself instructing him. "At the Bull's Head."

The horseman turned, hurried down a side aisle, and walked out through the transept door. The chancellor retreated into the shadows, attentive to the hoofbeats, no louder in his ears than the pounding of his heart. Slowly, the clattering diminished as horse and rider continued on their way.

Santángel proceeded to the back of the nave, trying to avoid the spreading pool of blood, but stopped as he approached the agonizing canon. He had not predicted how it would feel to witness his victim in death-throes.

The Inquisitor of Zaragoza writhed on the floor, gasping, reaching with his left hand for the spike in his neck. His fingers found the ivory handle, crawled around it, tugged on it. He pulled it out. Lips of flesh spewed blood onto the marble floor stones like the liquid words of a final prayer.

The sight of Arbués, defenseless and irredeemable, appalled the chancellor. His throat constricted. A cold sweat coursed his spine. He clutched a bench to steady himself. The expression on the expiring canon's face, a look that combined ice and embers, yearning and revulsion, defiance and resignation, shook Santángel to the depths of his soul. Even as the canon's regard grew vacant, Luis de Santángel knew he would never forget that ardent gaze, that foreboding of measureless despair.

. . .

Although he had never before penetrated into the cathedral's entrails, Santángel knew where he was going. He had studied Father Cáceres's sketches. He had lain awake imagining every detail of his path: the wrought-iron candleholders clutching the walls like great insects terrified of the dark, the walnut door of Pedro de Arbués's chambers, his elevated bed clothed in purple velour and ocher damask. If a sleepless cleric appeared, the chancellor would have to flee or, worse, murder him. Such a circumstance, he reminded himself, was unlikely.

Once inside the canon's chambers, he glanced quickly around to ensure he was alone and locked the door. A small entrance adjoined the canon's messy, musty sleeping quarters. A few thick candles burned in the iron chandelier. The carved walnut trunk gaped open. A stained, ivory-colored silken chasuble lay on the floor. Papers and a pewter bowl of leftover stew littered Arbués's writing table. And there, set in the wall four feet above the stone floor, were the leaded-glass windows that Santángel was prepared to smash, if necessary, in order to flee.

His gaze stopped at the bookshelves, filled with leather-bound journals. Santángel took a candle, placed it on the desk, and carefully, almost reverently, removed the first volume.

At least two people had heard Felipe's confessions. The first lay dead on the marble tiles of La Seo. The other was the scribe who had recorded every utterance of the canon and his confessor. The name of that scribe, Santángel hoped, would appear at the opening of the volume he sought.

He studied the handwritten Latin text. It recorded financial transactions and directives from hierarchs. He pulled out the second volume, an account of ecclesiastical proceedings of various sorts.

As he turned pages, his heart rapping against the walls of his chest like a moth trapped in a box, he listened for sounds from the cathedral. Had some sleepless monk discovered the corpse? The only noise was the hiss of wind under the doors of the church and through the interstices of its windows.

The third tome, at last, recorded witnesses' testimonies and a penitent's confessions. He searched for Felipe de Almazón's name, in its Latin form, but found it nowhere. A fourth tome of endless, precisely transcribed dialogues. A fifth. Surely, Felipe's confessions were here. Otherwise, this assassination and all the wrath it would surely engender were for naught.

. . .

The night was hot and damp, the air tangy with scents of wild mint, sage, open sewers, fried lard, and warm ale. Santángel passed through alleys where drunks, minstrels, and harlots loitered. Beggars solicited alms. A door creaked somewhere. Santángel's mind was still in the nave of La Seo and the canon's sleeping quarters.

Just the day before, a palace employee had reported that Felipe de Almazón's wife, Catalina, had been seen in this neighborhood of taverns and beggars. Santángel had not believed him. Now he found her, sitting on the ground across the way.

In the glow of candlelight from a nearby house, he saw she was thinner. Her loose umber hair seemed too wild and full for her slender face. Her embroidered dress was soiled.

"Catalina?"

"Chancellor."

Despite the nearness of a gutter that reeked of filth, he sat down beside her. "Why are you sitting here, alone in the dark? Your house. Your lands."

A dog barked somewhere. A man cursed and slammed his window shutters.

She looked not at him, but past him, as if afraid to show the sadness in her eyes. "They took it all."

That was how Pedro de Arbués conducted his business, the chancellor told himself. The inquisitor's purpose was not merely to seek out heretics, but to collect funds from them so others could be found. The Inquisition was not an achievement, but a process. It had to be self-sustaining.

"And your children?"

"They took them, too," she replied, her voice breaking. "I . . . I understand they're well."

Santángel's eyes sought hers. She swallowed.

Her children were alive. For this, Santángel inwardly thanked God. The Church, with its vast resources, was caring for them. The offspring of convicted heretics often rose through the ecclesiastical hierarchy. The monks and nuns seemed to make a point of not blaming them for their parents' errors.

"Where do you live, now?"

She simply smiled.

"Have you no family?"

"No family that wants me."

"I understand." To associate with the widow of a heretic, or of a suspected heretic, especially if she was one's relative, was to contaminate one's soul, or worse, arouse suspicion. "Are you hungry?"

"Nearly always."

"Please, come. We cannot linger here." He would not leave her exposed to the elements and brutality of the street. He wished he could risk telling her that the man responsible for her husband's death, and for her present circumstances, was now dead himself, and that he, Luis de Santángel, had sponsored the deed.

"You are the chancellor of Aragon. You can't be seen with a wretch like me. Give me a piece of silver, if you will, and go on your way."

He rose and held out his hand. She ignored it at first, but finally allowed him to help her to her feet.

In the chancellor's courtyard, Catalina rinsed herself at the well. Santángel proceeded inside. Dismayed to discover blood on the soles of his boots, he shoved them into the fireplace and kindled a flame.

Catalina entered. She still looked gaunt and untidy, but showed off her clean hands and scrubbed face with a sweet smile. It was not the clear, ingenuous smile Santángel had seen before her husband's arrest. He knew he would never see that face again.

She glanced at his stockinged feet and at the smoky hearth. He led her through the kitchen to a small rotunda where no one would overhear them and offered stuffed olives, a garlic sausage, a handful of bread, a cup of Rioja wine. "My majordomo's sister, in Sevilla," said Santángel, "has come down with the plague. He went home to care for her, and ended up ill, himself."

Her chewing slowed as she searched his face.

"The queen has called me to Cordoba. I need someone to watch the house, the servants. Someone I trust."

"You want me to stay here, in your home? To replace your majordomo? Is that what you're asking, Chancellor?"

"No," replied Santángel, embarrassed. "That wouldn't be consistent with your station. Your husband served the king well. You're no maidservant. You could be like a visiting relative, if you will."

"And they say you're cynical and sly."

"People say many things, especially about those they envy."

"I'll gladly keep an eye on your home, if you, in turn, will do one thing for me."

He was surprised to hear her haggling about terms. The wine, he imagined, had gone to her head. "And what is that?"

"I would politely request," she said, correcting her tone, "that you not address me as an equal. We never were equals. I would be honored to serve you as your maidservant. Nothing more."

Luis de Santángel laughed. Her blend of pluck, humility, and wisdom amused him. Naturally, no one could care for his home and remain his equal. "As you like."

"And from this moment, I'll cease to be Catalina de Almazón. That name could only bring you trouble. Call me Leonor. She was a childhood friend."

"Good night, then, Leonor. You'll find an empty room at the end of the hallway. Consider it yours. In the morning, I'll be gone."

"Good night, my lord."

He rose and left. Leonor finished her simple meal by the flickering light of one small candle.

. . .

Shortly before dawn, Luis de Santángel entered his son's bedroom. "Remember my promise? I'm leaving soon. And you, my valorous knight, are traveling with me."

Gabriel squinted. "Where are we going?"

"I'm taking you to Valencia. Your uncle's house. I'll be continuing south from there to meet with the queen. We don't have much time."

"Why so early?" Gabriel rubbed his eyes.

"Get ready."

Gabriel drew himself out of bed and began dressing. Sleepily he pulled on a laced tunic, embroidered at the neck and hems and belted at the waist, black woolen leggings, and his striped jerkin, oxblood and blue, with silver buttons.

. . .

Beside the road to Daroca sat a small inn, alone and neglected but not abandoned. The weathered sign showed a cut-off bull's head bellowing in agony.

In the kitchen, Conchita Gutiérrez leaned over a table tearing the ends off white bean pods, dropping their seeds into a wooden bowl. A lanky woman with limp black hair, spindly fingers, and sunken eyes, she looked older than her thirty-three years.

Little light sifted through the soiled wool sheet that covered the room's single, glassless window. A crucifix hung on the wall. Beside it, a crude painting on a rough board depicted the Virgin mourning her not-yet-resurrected son. From her blue tears, daffodils sprouted.

Conchita heard her husband's feet clump against the floor upstairs. Bits of red and green paint flaked from the low beams. A fruit beetle flew up from the pile of unshelled husks on the table. She brushed it away. Lying on the floor, the mule Juanita, faded brown, with patches of hair missing, let out a throbbing breath and shook her ears.

"Even Juanita is awake before my husband," the innkeeper's wife complained, louder than if she had been talking to herself. Her husband was thumping down the narrow stairway.

Miguel Gutiérrez appeared at the base of the stairs wearing a brown blanket with a hole for his head and a cord for a belt. A corpulent, clumsy man with an unkempt beard, he glanced at the mule. "When Juanita is awake, she looks like she's sleeping. It's easy to be awake, when that is how it is."

He kicked Juanita lightly. The mule snorted and shook her head. Miguel leaned his full weight over the beast and pulled her up by the neck. His wife had shelled fourteen beans by the time he succeeded. The innkeeper pulled the door open and led the mule outside.

While her husband was tying Juanita to a post and throwing oats and barley onto the ground under her nose, Señora Gutiérrez heard hoofbeats in the distance, at first faint, then more distinct.

The horse slowed and came to a stop before the Bull's Head. "How may I help you, my lord?" she heard her husband call out. "If a bowl of hot soup is what you long for, or a glass of warm ale, you have indeed come to the right house." It was his standard greeting, from which any semblance of enthusiasm had long ago drained like wine from a worn-out pig's bladder.

Conchita heard the stranger dismount. "Three ales, then," answered the rider. "I'll be joined by two others. And a bowl of broth for my son." A cultivated voice, tinged with smugness and contempt, Conchita thought. The voice of a wealthy man.

She lifted the soiled sheet and looked out the window. The visitor wore simple clothes, a black shirt with laced-up sleeves, knee-length black pants, stockings, and riding boots. None of this fooled her. His bearing and voice were anything but common.

Another man arrived in a simple gray cloak. Miguel Gutiérrez showed the two travelers inside. The boy remained outside, tethering their horses and then, seated on the ground, whittling a stick.

Santángel pulled out a chair before the fireplace. Cáceres sat across from him.

"Well, it's done."

"Yes, I know. Did you find the log?"

"I found a number of logs. But Felipe's testimony . . . Nowhere. I've been summoned to the king's camp, outside Cordoba."

The priest frowned. "Go, then. I shall continue our search."

While they conversed, the horseman stepped in. "Good morning, gentlemen," he muttered, hanging his hat on a peg.

Miguel Gutiérrez, balancing a jug and three earthen cups, approached from the kitchen. He slammed the pitcher down, causing some of the frothy beverage to spill. More carefully, he placed the bowl of broth on the table. Santángel handed it back to him. "My son is outside."

"As you like, my lord."

Gutiérrez brought the soup to Gabriel.

"Put it on the ground," the boy commanded him without looking up from his whittling.

The innkeeper wondered why he was so grumpy. "Is there anything else you'd like?"

"That will be all."

When Gutiérrez returned to the kitchen, he crossed himself, muttering.

"Maybe the men need something else. What kind of host are you?" The innkeeper's wife did not bother looking up from her bowl of white beans. Since her husband had begun fooling around with that young bawd from the village, she had lost respect for him. She made sure he felt her resentment at every occasion.

"They want to be left alone," Miguel whispered. "These aren't the kind of men who come back."

Señora Gutiérrez glanced at her husband's sad blanket, shaking her head at his ineptitude, pitying herself for ever having crawled into bed with him.

Miguel Gutiérrez opened the kitchen door a crack and peeked out.

The chancellor and Cáceres each handed a purse to the horseman, who untied the string of one and looked inside. He opened his jacket and attached the purses to a cord.

"If I can be of further service—" he began again.

"The best you can do, now," Luis cut him off, "would be to leave Zaragoza as quickly as possible."

"I will," agreed the horseman, securing his jacket over his reward.

"Then our work here is settled," observed Luis de Santángel. "There's no need to linger. Let us pray this is all over."

All three raised their glasses and drank deeply.

"Let us pray we have saved lives," offered Cáceres.

Santángel closed his eyes to meditate upon such a prayer.

The horseman left. Santángel placed a silver coin on the table and went out with Father Cáceres. Miguel Gutiérrez was untying Father Cáceres's horse when it reared and the innkeeper fell to the ground, losing his grip. The horse galloped into the surrounding fields. While the innkeeper sputtered excuses and apologies, Luis de Santángel climbed onto Gabriel's horse, Ynés, and gave Cáceres's horse chase. He failed to capture it.

"If he is in this valley, I shall find him, señor," stammered the innkeeper. He untethered his mule.

"I doubt it," said Santángel. "Take my horse," he told Cáceres. "Leave her at my home, in the care of my maidservant. I'll ride with Gabriel."

Father Cáceres mounted Béatriz. Gabriel climbed onto Ynés, behind his father. The two horses and their riders rode off in opposite directions.

CHAPTER SIX

*T*OMÁS DE TORQUEMADA, Inquisitor General of Castile and Aragon, sat at his desk in the monastery of Santa Cruz, examining plans for a new Dominican abbey. He wore a brown habit, the hood lowered on his back. A thin circle of hair surrounded the shaved dome of his head. His eye sockets and cheeks appeared hollow.

One of Torquemada's penitents had recently died, leaving enough wealth to build a spiritual refuge in Avila, specifying in his will that the prior of Santa Cruz was to supervise its design. Additional funds would come from the Inquisition itself, money pried from the clutches of heretics. Although alchemy was associated with doctrinal divergence, and unquestionably evil, this sort of reverse alchemy, beating ill-gotten gold into the stones of an edifice dedicated to the service of the Lord, was a pursuit worthy of the monk's most diligent efforts.

Indeed, Torquemada preferred architecture to all other arts. So much was unstable and transitory in this world. To serve as midwife in the birth of something both functional and durable was to help import a measure of the Eternal into mankind's ephemeral life. Just as God was the greatest architect, so it behooved man to follow His example.

The inquisitor general loved the sharp, rough, solid feel of skillfully hewn stones, joined together with or without mortar. They yielded to the will of man only with difficulty, but once shaped, did not budge. They stayed where one placed them. They performed their humble tasks without grumbling or questioning, holding up a building, providing shelter through storms, giving townsfolk a place to gather and pray. Of course, they were not alive, but they were part of God's creation, and thus worthy of man's respect. Aye, of man's wonderment.

The widow of the deceased penitent was one of Queen Ysabel's preferred ladies-in-waiting. Eight years ago, she and her husband had recommended Torquemada as confessor to the queen. The monk and the headstrong, vigorous sovereign had discovered they shared a vision for Castile. The New Inquisition and this little monastery at Avila were among the first fruits of that friendship. The monastery was therefore doubly worthy of Torquemada's earnest attentions.

Outside, a horse's hooves thumped to the gate and stopped. The guard exchanged words with a visitor. Any disturbance so late at night was not only unusual, but also frowned upon, as the monks rose early for matinal prayers.

The visitor ran to the door of the prior's office and rapped. "Fray Tomás, a frightful thing has happened!"

Torquemada crossed the small room and unlatched the door. He recognized the tall man with a scar on his forehead under a shock of persimmon-colored hair, who stood there panting. "You were Fray Gaspar Juglar's aide, were you not?"

The man caught his breath. "Yes, I was. But now I'm a constable of the Inquisition." He reminded Torquemada of his name: "Juan Rodríguez."

"Yes, yes. Rodríguez. And before you began with Fray Juglar?" Torquemada had heard rumors about this man.

"Before I dedicated my life to the service of the Church," replied Rodríguez, "I was not a good man, Father."

Torquemada nodded compassionately. "Come in, Señor Rodríguez. What's all this fuss?" He closed the door.

"It's Maestre Arbués, Father. He's dead."

"Pedro de Arbués? Dead? What happened?"

"Murder. A deed too evil to contemplate."

Was the constable lying? The inquisitor general had seen too much of the blackness in men's hearts to take anyone at his word, especially someone who had just admitted to his dark past. He asked himself what a constable of the Inquisition could have to gain by dissembling about such a matter. "Murder? And the perpetrators, were they apprehended?"

"Not yet. But soon after Father Arbués died, the cathedral bells started ringing on their own. They haven't stopped since."

Torquemada did not believe in such pint-sized miracles, but he was convinced most people needed them as anchors for their faith. He noticed the constable eyeing the cauldron of lamb broth that hung from a wrought-iron stand in the fireplace. "Are you hungry, Rodríguez?"

"Yes, Father."

He rolled up the plans for the monastery at Avila, reflecting that unlike the buildings in Madrid or Barcelona, those in Zaragoza were constructed not of stone but of adobe, crumbling, impermanent clay mixed with straw and held in place with beams of wood. Clay, the very substance from which God had fashioned man, his fickle, rebellious child.

He fetched a bowl and filled it with the steaming broth. "Our earthly lives are fleeting," he comforted the constable. He placed the bowl on the table and pulled out a chair for him. "Father Arbués has gone to a better place. And to those followers of Satan who perpetrated this evil act, Jesus will make his wrath known. I can assure you of that."

The Jesus of compassion and love mattered greatly to the faithful, who knew they could depend on His affection and support. At present, however, they desperately needed the help of the other Jesus, the messiah of righteous anger, the incarnate God who commanded obedience and instilled terror, the Jesus who promised eternal fire and wailing for sinners and for those who refused to recognize His divinity.

Torquemada would demonstrate his fealty to that Jesus. By murdering an officer of His Church, the perpetrators of this crime had pounded yet another nail into Christ's wrists and ankles. The pain thus inflicted upon the Lord was not His alone to carry. Mankind's duty, and especially the duty of Christ's servants, was to undergo the torment with Him.

"Jesus will make his wrath known," echoed the constable, "in the next world, yes. But in this one?"

"Those who committed this unspeakable act will be found, I assure you."

Finding comfort in the words of this wise potentate of the Church, Juan Rodríguez sipped the steaming brew.

Torquemada took the chair across from him and lowered his head into his hands. In his mind's eye he saw the powerful face and large, commanding body of Pedro de Arbués, clothed in the finery of his station, leading Mass. The man Torquemada had chosen to be Inquisitor of Zaragoza had never been a friend. Torquemada did not approve of his carnal appetites, but the canon of La Seo had been a tireless servant of the Lord, struggling as all righteous men must to better himself and extirpate sin and temptation from the world. What more could God's Church require of its frail, hidebound servants? For no matter what his enemies imagined, Torquemada was not a man who lacked compassion. Not to feel pity for a sinner who sincerely repented, he felt, was not to be Christian.

As he watched Pedro de Arbués officiating in his mind, tears came to the inquisitor's eyes—tears not only for the man whose murder was an affront to God, but for all mankind, who knew not from one moment to the next what destiny awaited them.

. . .

Torquemada rode hard for two days to the city where Pedro de Arbués had resided and died. He set up quarters in the rooms formerly occupied by the canon of La Seo.

The *cierzo*, a brusque southeasterly, blew over Zaragoza. The inquisitor general found the chambers drafty. Small echoing sounds, unfamiliar and occasionally disturbing, leaked from the nave at night. Doors and windows creaked, sometimes so loudly the Dominican could hardly keep his eyes closed.

He read all of Arbués's logs and journals. He noticed that not all the confessions and depositions from his inquisitorial proceedings were among them. Had the canon misplaced one or more volumes? Was there some meaning to their absence?

Four nights after he arrived, a repetitive whine and clap awoke him. Unable to fall back to sleep, he rose. In his rough woolen habit, holding a small candle, he clomped down a narrow corridor to locate the door or window that was blowing open, then slapping closed.

As he peered into each room, he found only latched doors, until he came at last to the dark nave. The main entrance was wide open and a terrible wind was howling through. It blew so strong the inquisitor had to struggle to push the heavy door closed and latch it. When he turned around again, what he saw startled him. The candle fell from his hands.

Kneeling in front of the cross was the canon himself. Torquemada knelt to pick up the candle, which was still burning, and moved closer. "Make me as a branch of the willow, Lord," he prayed, "bending before the gale of your volition, that I may better serve you. If this be a demon that ye have placed here to test me, give me the strength to wrestle with it and banish it from Your house."

When he approached close enough to observe Arbués's skin and vestments in the candlelight, he saw the bloodstains. The canon rose and turned to him. His plump face showed no horrific traces of martyrdom. What Torquemada saw in that face was an image of serenity, the kind of serenity Torquemada himself had been striving for over the years, through fasting and meditation. Drained of color, reflecting the candlelight, Arbués's countenance glowed. As if touched by celestial radiance, Torquemada felt his fears slip away.

"Fray Pedro! Why have you returned?"

The canon smiled in death precisely as he had so many times in life, an expression that blended condescension with love. Now, however, his air of superiority seemed justified. In it, Torquemada saw the patronizing affection of one who knew firsthand the inexpressible comforts of Elysium.

"Let me tell you something about our Lord Jesus Christ, the sacrificial lamb," Arbués pontificated. "His torment didn't cease when they hauled his body from the cross. It is ongoing, Fray Tomás, and it will continue. It will continue for as long as the Jews keep denying Him."

Torquemada stood before him unflinching. "But how can we change the Jews? You know as well as I, they are stiff-necked. You know how they despise our Lord."

"You cannot save those who serve Satan," the ghostly messenger concurred. "But those who have turned toward the Light, only to be frightened by its brilliance, and who wish to crawl back into the shadows, those weak, indecisive souls can and must be helped."

"Are we not doing all we can?"

Arbués responded in a commandeering tone he would never have dared employ with Torquemada during his life. "Eliminate the darkness from their world, and they will have nowhere else to turn. Then, and only then, will their eyes fully open to the divine effulgence, which is love."

Before Torquemada had a chance to question the canon further, the door of the cathedral, though firmly latched, blew open again. The wind extinguished the candle in his hand. The monk from Segovia reached out to grasp Pedro de Arbués's bloodstained robes, as if to clutch one last, precious fragment of a missive from heaven. He fell to his knees, sweating and dizzy.

CHAPTER SEVEN

ACH NIGHT, Luis de Santángel and his son Gabriel slept in a different bed, in a different town: Teruel, Castellón de la Plana, Sagunto. Each night, as the chancellor closed his eyes to sleep, Pedro de Arbués's last cold stare greeted him, reminding him that wherever he traveled, his deeds traveled with him.

He took comfort in his distance from Zaragoza, but distance was no substitute for peace of mind. The eyes and ears of the Inquisition were as plentiful as the marigolds, periwinkles, and peonies that bloomed in the fields of La Mancha. Tomás de Torquemada and his cohorts would soon be seeking every accomplice in the murder of Pedro de Arbués, finding some and inventing others, if they were not doing so already.

Estefan Santángel's house in Valencia, tall, built of stone, with a sloping tile roof and small windows, stood behind walls and wooden gates on the outskirts of town. His son following, Luis de Santángel walked Ynés into the courtyard.

Alerted by his guard, holding his hand behind his back, Estefan came out to greet them. "Still tempting the devil, eh?" he asked his brother cryptically. "But, thank God, still with us." He swung around to his nephew. "And you, Gabriel, how quickly you shoot up—an indubitable weed! Still fencing like a madman?"

Gabriel reached into his saddlebag and whipped out the stick he had fashioned for this purpose. "See for yourself, scalawag!" he shouted. He swung the stick and lunged.

Estefan was prepared. In the hand behind his back, he held a similar stick, whittled into the rough shape of a fencing iron.

He expertly parried Gabriel's thrusts. He roared with laughter as he ducked and darted to evade the boy's reckless *coups lancés* and launched deft counterattacks. Luis stood to the side, watching patiently, vaguely smiling. Estefan's servants carried in the visitors' bags.

Finally, Gabriel pinned his uncle to the wall, his "sword" across Estefan's chest.

"Have mercy on me, worthy Christian," begged the portly tax farmer.

"I shall allow you to live, infidel," his nephew warned him, "but only this once. If I should catch you praying to your heathen gods again, within my realms, I shall scatter your guts like fertilizer across my fields."

Estefan and Luis exchanged a glance. "You are indeed the valorous knight they say you are, sir." Estefan bowed floridly as Gabriel removed his sword.

"Gabriel," the chancellor directed his son as this game wound to a conclusion, "take Ynés back to the stables."

Panting, Gabriel led his horse away.

"He's too smart by half for a twelve-year-old." Estefan led his brother toward the door. "Let's talk inside."

He ushered Luis upstairs to a small room lined with benches and bookshelves, closed the door, and addressed his brother quietly. "Tongues are wagging. Pedro de Arbués . . ."

"The canon of La Seo? What about him?"

"But surely you know. He's been killed. Right in the cathedral. While praying."

"I've been traveling," answered Luis. "I'm sorry to hear about it. But I must admit, I felt little fondness for the man, as you well know."

"They say the crime was perpetrated by a 'cabal' of New Christians."

"Who is making outlandish statements like that?"

"Oh, just . . . everybody."

"And how would they know, this 'everybody' that has no name and no face, but whose authority is absolute?"

"Brother, let us be calm."

"I am calm."

Estefan leaned backward and peered at Luis. He changed the subject. "For how long will you be entrusting me with your off-spring? I promise not to dance on the tables or otherwise corrupt the poor, impressionable thing."

"The queen has summoned me to Cordoba. A two-week ride each way. Beyond that, I have no idea what she wants, or how long it will take. While I'm in the south, I also intend to pay a visit to my associate, the duke of Medina-Celi."

"Two months, then? Three? I only hope Gabriel isn't bored."

"Perhaps more."

"You know, when I'm here at home, I actually work."

The two brothers did not again broach the subject of the murder or the Inquisition.

. . .

That night, Luis de Santángel lay beside his son on their bed, a heavy wooden frame with leather latticework supporting a bag of feathers. They talked quietly, listening to the falling rain and oc-casional claps of thunder.

"Papa, is it true there's going to be a war against the kingdom of Granada?"

"Who told you that?"

"García, my tutor. He said King Fernando and Queen Ysabel are finally going to rid our land of the infidels."

"It is true, Gabriel. But it may not happen quickly."

"So there will still be war when I'm old enough to fight?"

"Perhaps. But you're not a knight, and you're not a knight's page either. You're going to serve your king in other ways, like your father."

"Counting money?"

"Counting money is the least of it. Deciding how the kingdom should use its revenues—that is important. And because your func-tion will be so important, you'll have the king's ear. You'll even ne-gotiate with foreign powers on his behalf."

"And who will be the king? Prince Juan?" The prince, Ysabel and Fernando's only male child, was seven years old.

"Yes. Juan will rule over Castile and Aragon—and Granada, too, after the war. That will make you a very powerful man, if you prove your loyalty to him."

"He's so annoying."

"How so?"

"When we fence, I'm not allowed to score any points. He makes me say I lost, even if I didn't."

Luis chuckled. "You have time."

"Time for what?"

"To learn to like him." The chancellor kissed his son.

CHAPTER EIGHT

A CATHEDRAL, by virtue of its dimensions, was meant to inspire awe, but awe was only the means to an end. The end was the complete, unconditional, limitless subservience of the individual will to God, as conveyed to man through His Savior and His Church.

When awe alone did not suffice, the purveyors of God's graces in this world occasionally had to use a different instrument: fear. Mortification of the flesh was in itself beneficial, for how else was man, sullied by temptation and corruption, to aspire to purity? The Inquisition's machines of torture, though, were not primarily intended to cause suffering. They were meant to arouse in the sinner an awareness of his powerlessness, to lead him to repent and be reconciled with the divine will.

For certain purposes, a third set of tools, compassion and the profound intimacy of confession, were more effective than awe or fear. When meeting with a good-willed informant, it seemed fitting to Torquemada that they should sit together not within a vast, echoing hall or a dismal, fetid dungeon, but in the cool, commodious confines of La Seo's rectory.

The tonsured Dominican sat at a table, studying Tomás Aquinas's *Summa Theologica* and jotting notes in the book's margins. Torquemada greatly admired the subtle, probing intellect of the hallowed saint, who had proven to the world that reason and faith, both emanations from God, not only were compatible but also fulfilled each other. His own mission, Torquemada believed, while infinitely less meritorious than that of the great theologian, would also demonstrate that reason, the patient exploration of sinners' minds and the effort to turn them toward Truth, would always prevail over ignorance, superstition, and heresy, except when impeded by Satan.

Rodríguez ushered in the innkeeper Miguel Gutiérrez, who glanced by turns at the inquisitor, at the leaded windows, and at the wooden chandeliers. It did not take long for the prior to evaluate him. Gutiérrez was a large, uncouth man with a wild beard and rotten teeth. Sweaty and malodorous, he seemed ill at ease even in the relative comfort of the rectory. Did he have something to hide? Surely something, but probably nothing too heinous. Those whose consciences were burdened with the most terrible sins were usually far more practiced at concealing their discomfort.

"Please, Señor Gutiérrez, have a seat. Would you like some water? Rodríguez, you may leave us."

The innkeeper sat down heavily while Torquemada filled a cup. The constable closed the door behind himself. "Father," Gutiérrez spluttered, "I am not a man who's used to talking, face-to-face, with the great and powerful of this world. I am but a humble innkeeper."

"And what is the name of your inn?" Torquemada smiled, hoping to put him at ease.

Gutiérrez drank half his cup of water, practically in one gulp, and wiped his mouth with his shirtsleeve. "The Bull's Head."

"The Bull's Head," repeated the inquisitor.

The innkeeper wondered whether this was a question. "A mad bull got loose . . ."

"When was this?"

"Fifty years ago. Maybe forty. I'm not sure, exactly."

"A mad bull got loose, and . . . ?"

"It was my grandfather who trapped him, and . . . and chopped off his head. Ever since then . . ." Rather than finish the thought, Gutiérrez finished his water.

"Many Spaniards," remarked the friar, "dwell in the shadows of their grandfathers. You're fortunate yours was a hero."

The innkeeper had no idea what he meant. "He was no hero, Father. But he was a good wrestler of bulls. And when he was angry enough, he knew how to hack them to bits and simmer their brains into a tasty stew."

"Do you still serve that stew?"

"As I said, we are very poor."

Torquemada refilled his cup. "As you may know, Señor Gutiérrez, when a man sins against the Lord through perversity of belief, if his heresy is sufficiently evil, it's sometimes necessary to confiscate his property. The purpose of such confiscations is to reduce the sinner's worldly pride and to help reconcile him with God."

"Father, I know I have sinned. But if I confess . . . ?"

"I'm not referring to you, Señor Gutiérrez. I'm talking about men who betray Christ deliberately, who take malicious actions against His Church, who want to see His reign on this earth destroyed."

Gutiérrez crossed himself, frightened. Although he could be a raucous drinker and reveler when the occasion presented itself, he felt like a boy in this place, in the presence of this man.

"For example," continued Torquemada, gazing into the courtyard, "whoever was behind the murder of our sainted canon, Pedro de Arbués. Probably several people." He looked back at the innkeeper. "I don't believe it could have been the work of one man. Do you?"

"No, Father. No, I don't."

"All those involved will most certainly lose their property, at the very least. And those who help us find them will naturally be entitled to a share of whatever is confiscated. If there were a number of conspirators, that portion could be quite considerable."

Gutiérrez swallowed. He had not come here with a hope of reward, but he appreciated the wisdom in the monk's proposal. If Mother Church took away people's goods when they sinned, it made sense she should reward them when they were virtuous. "I understand."

"Please go ahead. I can hear your confession right here."

Gutiérrez was not accustomed to receiving absolution face-to-face with his priest, in broad daylight; even less so, with the queen's confessor. He steeled himself and began, "Forgive me, Father, for I have sinned. I lusted after a girl, and we . . . we . . ."

"Fornicated?"

"Yes." The innkeeper was not sure what the word meant, but it sounded right enough.

"Are you married, Señor Gutiérrez?"

"Yes."

"And I take it this girl, she was not married, at the time this was going on?"

"No. As I said, she was . . . she was young."

"How young?"

"Thirteen."

Leaning back into his chair, Torquemada examined his fingernails. "How many times did you fornicate with her?"

"I don't know. Fifteen, twenty times. But she got, she became . . . heavy with child, and . . . and she died giving birth. She never told a soul." Gutiérrez took a deep breath, avoiding Torquemada's eyes.

"Not even her priest?"

The innkeeper shook his head.

"And the baby?"

"The baby?"

Torquemada nodded, urging him on.

"The baby was born dead."

"This girl whom you loved, she died without confessing her sins?"

"Yes."

"And when did all this happen?"

"It started a little more than a year ago. She died, she passed away, a few days after Ash Wednesday."

"And you? All this time, you haven't sought absolution, either?"

"I was ashamed, Father."

"And the eternal well-being of your soul, you weren't worried about that?"

"I thought my soul was lost." The innkeeper lowered his head into his hands. "When I heard she was dying, I wasn't strong enough to visit her."

"I see."

Gutiérrez wiped his sweating palms on his knees and lifted his face, looking directly at his confessor. "Is her soul rotting in hell, Father? I hear her screams, sometimes, at night. Is that real, or is it a dream?"

"It's too late for you to concern yourself with her soul, Señor Gutiérrez, or with that of the baby you helped conceive. You should be worried about your own. But this you could have confessed to any priest. Why are you here? Why did you want to speak with me?"

"There is something else."

"What is it, my son? You have my full attention."

"Some men. The morning after the canon's assassination. Only, I didn't know. I didn't yet know."

"Some men?"

"At the inn. The Bull's Head."

"How many?"

"Three. And a child. You don't often see a mere boy wearing an expensive suede jerkin."

"No, you don't. What color was this jerkin?"

"Stripes of leather. Red, blue. With silver buttons."

"There are many shades of red, Señor Gutiérrez. The color of wine? Of bricks?"

"More like wine. And blue like the sky here in Aragon on a warm day."

"With silver buttons."

The innkeeper nodded.

"How old was he?"

"Eleven, maybe twelve."

"These men, do you know their names?"

The innkeeper shook his head. "You could tell they were educated. And wealthy."

"What did they look like? Did they have accents? How did they get to the Bull's Head?"

"They rode beautiful horses. Not together. Separately. One of them, yes, had an accent. A tall man. Thin. Straight hair, the color of wheat, down to his shoulders."

"And the others? What did they look like?"

Gutiérrez did his best to describe them. The beauty of their horses, especially, had impressed him: a roan mare, a chestnut stallion, a dun stallion, all clothed in expensive blankets and silver fittings. He remembered, in particular, the black stripe on the back of the roan mare. The man who arrived on this horse, it seemed, was their leader. Another of the horses, white with large black spots, had run off.

"Did it come back?"

Gutiérrez shook his head.

"Did they come back for their horse?"

"No."

Torquemada searched the innkeeper's face.

"What aroused your suspicions, Señor Gutiérrez? Did these men refuse to eat or drink the food from your kitchen? Did they say something?"

"They didn't say much. *Did you find it? No, it wasn't there.* The exact words, I'm sorry, Father, I can't remember."

"They were looking for something?"

"Something, yes. At the time, I had no idea what to make of it."

"At the time?"

"This was before I heard about Father Arbués."

Torquemada pressed his fingertips together and applied them to his pursed lips. "And then you thought . . ."

"The whole thing was . . . What is the word, Father?"

"Unusual?"

"More than that, I'd say. They gave the foreigner two purses."

Three men, wealthy men, reflected Torquemada, going out of their way to gather in an obscure, neglected tavern outside of town, the morning after the assassination. One of them foreign. A valuable horse that in the urgency of the moment they were willing to abandon. Two purses. What of the boy? Why was a child present?

"These men were not Jews, but Christian?"

"I didn't see horns."

Torquemada nodded understandingly. If only life were that simple. If only the acolytes of Satan were so easily identified.

"And you told no one?"

"I wanted to talk with someone. But as I said, Father, with . . . with all that was going on with *her* . . . and then, when she died . . ."

"Your conscience was overburdened."

"Besides, I was thinking: If their business was so secret, why would they meet in the Bull's Head? Why not in their homes?"

"They couldn't risk that, Señor Gutiérrez. These are crafty, worldly men. They mustn't be seen together, not immediately following their evil work. It could raise suspicions. The Bull's Head is some distance from Zaragoza. No one knows them there. In their homes, they have servants. Their servants go to church. Unlike you, their servants confess."

"I am confessing, Father."

"Yes, but that won't suffice. You'll have to do penance."

"Please," Gutiérrez begged, leaning forward. "That is what my soul longs for."

"For all the ruin engendered by your impure and sinful relations, eat nothing from dawn until dusk the first two days of every month, for one year. And if you can, try to ease the suffering of her family. The deceased girl's family."

"I shall, Father. Gladly." Tears welled in the innkeeper's eyes.

Tomás de Torquemada contemplated the fate of that innocent girl who would dwell for so long, at least until the Return, in unthinkable distress. The act of reparation he had assigned was not commensurate with the evil Miguel Gutiérrez had done. But in his effort to represent the will of the Eternal in this world, Torquemada had also considered the good that Gutiérrez was now accomplishing. The innkeeper had unburdened himself of what was most shameful. He had helped the Inquisition redeem other souls.

"You may leave now."

"Thank you, Father." The innkeeper rose clumsily, almost knocking over his chair, and stumbled across the room.

. . .

After Miguel Gutiérrez left, Torquemada searched for Juan Rodrí-guez in the cloisters, the garden, the cellar. He finally found him in a small chapel intended for individual prayer at the back of the monastery. The constable knelt naked before a carved wooden altar to the Holy Mother of God. A phallus as rigid as an oak branch rose from his lap.

Torquemada found Rodríguez's posture as insulting to his faith as it was abhorrent to his eyes. He reminded himself, however, that all humans were victims of carnality. Besides, this man was not trained for the priesthood. To judge him by the standards of that calling would be unfair.

Rodríguez turned to see him, blushing, and reached for his tunic. Torquemada decided not to comment on what he had witnessed, feeling that his presence alone had shamed the man sufficiently. "We need to locate a roan courser with a bridle of black leather and silver, and a black stripe down its back. Is that feasible, constable?"

"Would that be . . . Would that be for your personal conveyance, Father?" Rodríguez clumsily tightened his belt.

"No. You might start by looking among the wealthy *conversos* in this area."

"I'll attend to that at once." He stood up and straightened his tunic, avoiding the inquisitor's eyes.

"And one other thing. A boy of twelve or so, wearing an expensive waistcoat, maroon and light blue, with silver buttons. Get word out to the Hermandad. Let's keep an eye out for this boy."

Torquemada went out, closing the door softly.

. . .

That night, as Tomás de Torquemada lay in the deceased canon's chambers, Miguel Gutiérrez's utterances echoed in his mind. *Did you find it? . . . It wasn't there . . . Something, yes . . .*

Affliction and sin filled his days, the confessions of corrupt men and, worse, their reluctance to confess. Nights, the inquisitor meditated upon timeless things: the sky, the earth, man's humble efforts to bring the two together by raising stones from the ground and dedicating them to the service of God.

His architectural plans for the Avila monastery had progressed. He imagined buttresses supporting high walls, gargoyles spouting rainwater, gothic arched doorways carved with figures of saints and demons. He heard monks chanting in the chapel and smelled the fertile earth as they irrigated and planted the fields.

The voice of that coarse penitent broke in again and disturbed his reverie: *Did you find it? . . . It wasn't there . . . Something, yes . . .*

The inquisitor's eyes fluttered open. Nothing was moving. Torquemada's gaze wandered to the gothic bookshelves where Pedro de Arbués had stored his logs.

CHAPTER NINE

ALKING HIS BAY STALLION, King Fernando surveyed a sea of canvas lodgings, festooned with yellow and red ribbons, coats of arms, and banners in vermilion, emerald, and royal blue. Twenty-five thousand troops had gathered from all over Iberia, and others from as far as England and Helvetia. Scents of charred suckling pigs, goats, and rosemary filled the air. Quails and apples roasted over firepots. In a clearing, a bearded lutenist sang of love and war.

A man of average height with a high forehead and slanted eyes, Fernando wore breeches of yellow satin, a crimson doublet, and a mantle of rich brocade. Behind him rode a half-dozen equestrian heroes with their brightly liveried pages. Wherever Fernando passed, wealthy barons and their servants cheered. When the king and his attendants came to a stop in the center of the encampment, a trumpet blasted. The lutenist ceased singing. The tent-builders stopped hammering.

"Brave knights of Christ," shouted Fernando, "our most hearty thanks to you for assisting in this holy endeavor." The soldiers cheered. "The battle in which we shall soon be engaged will bring to an end, once and for all, the presence of an infidel nation on this continent." Again, the crowd roared. Halberds and shields clanged. "It will be grueling. It may take years. Many of you will spill blood for God and your land." The clamor grew deafening. King Fernando held up his palm. "But in the end," he bellowed, "we will prevail!" He continued over the din, "Europe will be united, once again, under the banner of Christ!"

While the king rallied his troops, Luis de Santángel walked his horse to the royal tents. He introduced himself to the queen's guards and produced a letter of summons. Her majesty's sentries, though illiterate, recognized the official stamp. One of them ushered him inside.

Fine silk-and-wool rugs from Tabriz covered the dirt floor. Sumptuous tapestries from Bruges enlivened the walls, keeping the noise and, at night, the cool autumn air outside. Rosewood partitions separated the large volume into distinct spaces. A servant showed Santángel into the tight, dignified receiving chamber. The room smelled musty, as if the stale air inside had been transported along with the heavy fabrics of the shelter.

When Queen Ysabel finally entered, she smiled to Santángel as if offering him a precious gift, her friendship. He knew it was not truly a gift at all but a loan to be paid back with usurious interest. Like the debtor with a pocket of gold coins, Santángel enjoyed the illusion of possessing the queen's affection.

Despite the contrary opinion of courtiers and the citizenry, she was not beautiful. Small in stature, with round arms, puffy cheeks, small eyes, and lazy lips, she could have passed for a peasant working in the onion fields near Sevilla. What she lacked in pulchritude, she made up for in mystique. Her gold-flecked eyes and thick, rust-blond hair infused her artful demeanor with a touch of wildness.

She greeted him not in an elegant robe but in an ornate dressing gown, its high collar half-concealing a goiter the size of a mouse. Like her smile, the choice of attire was meant to convey that she considered Santángel an intimate acquaintance rather than merely an administrative counselor.

"Señor de Santángel, you must have some hot mulled wine. You've been riding for days." With a wave of her hand, she commanded a lady-in-waiting to serve him.

"Thank you, Your Highness. What a sight, the army you and King Fernando have raised."

"We've set up a tent for you nearby," the queen replied. "I hope you find it to your liking."

"I have no doubt but that I shall, Your Highness. Your consideration in such matters has never disappointed me." He sipped his beverage, a precious melange of local wine with spices imported on the backs of camels and on trading ships from the Indias. "But tell me, how may I be of service to you?"

"You have relations in Granada, do you not?" The queen drank from a silver goblet filled with sweetened orange blossom water.

"Would the emir, or his vizier, remember me? I suspect they would." Santángel had visited Granada more than once on diplomatic missions, but wished to dispel any suggestion that he casually consorted with the infidel.

"You do speak their tongue, do you not?"

"My father tax-farmed the Arabic-speaking community of Valencia. He made sure I was thoroughly trained to take up his mantle."

"But your brother, as I understand, took up the mantle instead. Estefan." The queen took pride in her ability to call to mind such details about her highest-ranking attendants, and her husband's.

"Absolutely correct, as always, my lady," replied the courtier between sips of wine.

"We want you to travel to Granada. Warn him that his nephew, Abu Abdullah, is fomenting rebellion in Malaga. In the interest of stability, we would like to help protect the emir and his kingdom."

"How?"

The queen smiled, fingering her dress. "That ship you procured for us. The *Giustizia*. It could be quite useful against a rebellious coastal city."

Santángel smiled—a forced, ironic, bitter smile. He knew the emir's nephew had raised an army in Malaga. He doubted, however, that the emir would allow a Christian battleship into his waters.

"He has no choice," said Ysabel. "He is vulnerable. We're offering protection."

Santángel felt he understood Ysabel's true intent, and that she was asking him to destroy a bond of confidence he had worked hard to fashion. What was in it for him? An opportunity, once again, to prove his allegiance.

"Can you accomplish that, señor?"

"I would be honored, Your Majesty."

Ysabel turned to a maidservant. "Elena, please show our guest to his quarters." To Santángel, she added, "You'll need rest if you're going to join us in the parade this evening."

Luis de Santángel bowed and followed the pretty, young attendant out of the royal tent.

. . .

Watching him leave, Ysabel found the *converso*'s dignified manner vaguely discomfiting. True, as an advocate of the Crown, the man was redoubtable. True, her husband Fernando greatly appreciated him. Santángel had helped smooth the way financially and politically for his ascension to the throne of Aragon. Was not that, paradoxically, the problem with people like Luis de Santángel? Was it right that a king should depend so openly on the support of families that, two or three generations earlier, had dwelt among the moral and social dregs of society, families that had built their fortunes through the base occupations of trading, tax collecting, and usury? Had Luis de Santángel not himself added the "de" between his first and last names to suggest a patrician lineage? To the queen's aristocratic mind, where noble blood carried with it an imponderable measure of responsibility and purpose, the very existence of powerful upstart families like that of Luis de Santángel was menacing. What propelled such men through life was neither love of their land nor personal conviction, but an inordinate lust for self-promotion. Such men delighted in shattering the social barriers that had held her society together for uncounted generations.

Ysabel withdrew to her private quarters to prepare for public appearances with her husband. She loathed dressing up in jeweled gowns and fancy boots, but her soldiers believed they were fighting on behalf of a beautiful, benevolent, imperiously remote queen. One of her royal duties was to nourish those convictions.

CHAPTER TEN

*J*UAN RODRÍGUEZ TOLD HIMSELF to concentrate on the task at hand, the assignment the inquisitor general had so generously entrusted to him. He would make it a mission of expiation.

On a chilly autumn morning, he mobilized the constables of the Holy Office in Zaragoza. He instructed them to search the houses and stables of New Christians. "If there's any doubt as to their ancestry, or the beliefs of their grandparents," Rodríguez told his little army in the cathedral plaza, his breath visible in the air, "investigate anyway." Their mission was to look for a roan mare with a black stripe along its spine.

They fanned out through the city. Rodríguez visited the highest officials, those who dwelt in sprawling houses near the palace. When he arrived at the wrought-iron gates of Luis de Santángel's manor, at the end of the second day, Leonor was washing her master's roan mare. She looked well fed and comely. Pouring a bucket of water over the horse's back, she saw the officer approaching and called out, "What can we do for you, constable?"

"You can begin by opening these gates."

"And what business, if I may, brings you here?"

"I'm an officer of the Holy Inquisition of Zaragoza. I come here on orders of Tomás de Torquemada."

Leonor smiled awkwardly, a wet towel in her hand. "I am most sorry, constable, but I know of no one by that name."

"Do you refuse to let me enter, then?"

As Rodríguez pronounced these words, louder than he intended,

Santángel's horse lurched backward and to the side. From its mane to its tail stretched a long black stripe.

"I haven't refused you anything," protested Leonor. "But how am I to know you're really who you say you are? These days, anyone can strap on a short sword and call himself an enforcer of the law."

"Enough of this. I'll return with plenty of proof." Rodríguez kicked his horse and rode away.

. . .

When Juan Rodríguez returned several hours later with Torquemada and two soldiers of the Holy Brotherhood, they found the gates open and the front door unlocked. They wandered through the house's deserted rooms until they happened upon Gabriel's tutors, García and Pablo, playing a card game in their compact, unadorned quarters. When the two seminarians saw the inquisitor, they stiffened, embarrassed to be caught at such a frivolous pastime.

"Where is the chancellor?" Torquemada demanded.

"He's gone, Father," answered Pablo. "On an errand for the Crown."

The inquisitor felt a knot tightening in his chest. He reminded himself not to let his passions rule him. "And when did he leave?"

"More than a week ago."

"What, if I may, is the nature of your concern, Father?" asked García.

Torquemada ignored the question. "How long have you been in Señor Santángel's employ?"

"He hired us when his son was five. Now his son is twelve."

"Have you heard or seen any heresy?"

"Heavens, no."

"We would have brought such a matter to the tribunal," said Pablo.

"The night of Canon Arbués's assassination, were you aware of it?"

Pablo crossed himself. "The next morning, we heard the bells."

"We went to La Seo," added García.

"Was Señor Santángel home that night?" pursued Torquemada. "Did you know where he was?"

Pablo and García exchanged a glance. Before either had a chance to provide further information, the voice of Leonor, tentative but urgent, emerged from the doorway behind the inquisitor general: "Father?"

Torquemada slowly turned. "Yes, my daughter?"

"Father, that night . . ."

"And you are . . . ?"

"Leonor." She curtsied. "The daughter of Béatriz and Enrique Domínguez y Blanco, of Tortosa." The girl who went by that name, whom she had known as a child, had disappeared one day, probably eaten by wolves.

Torquemada noticed his constable staring at her. "Rodríguez, enter her name in the record."

The constable obeyed.

"Father." Leonor looked down in apparent shame. "I was with the chancellor."

"That night? The night of the assassination?"

"Yes."

"Where?"

"Here, Father. In this house."

"And what were you doing with him, my daughter?"

"I served him supper."

"And?"

"And it was late."

"How late?"

"Very late, Father."

"Yes, but no one eats supper *that* late. After supper, did you see where he went?"

Again, she cast down her eyes. "We were together all night."

Torquemada placed two fingers over his lips. If she was lying, she was clever, for there would likely be no witness to an act of fornication—at least not in the spacious house of a wealthy man. Not wishing to antagonize or embarrass her unnecessarily, he turned to his constable. "Rodríguez, why don't you question the señorita in private?"

Rodríguez assented. Two soldiers took hold of Leonor.

She took a deep breath and swallowed. "I can walk unassisted, thank you."

Torquemada signaled for them to release her. The soldiers clamorously followed her and Rodríguez out of the room.

For the moment, it mattered little whether this woman was telling the truth or not, reflected Torquemada. Either way, it would be necessary to apprehend and question the *converso* Luis de Santángel.

He turned to leave. Speed, now, was of the essence. Too many judaizers slipped out of the Holy Office's grasp into foreign lands. To be sure, they were burned in effigy, but such measures were of doubtful advantage for their souls, and ineffective as a deterrent vis-à-vis the public. If the Santa Hermandad was alerted throughout Castile and Aragon, Santángel would be found. Before ordering the arrest of one of the king's highest-ranking servants, however, Torquemada needed to notify the king personally.

. . .

Leonor's room was a tiny chamber with a trunk and a hay-filled mattress. She had sewn together scraps of silk and velour to form a colorful bedspread. A torn sheepskin covered the unfinished floor. Absent was a crucifix or any sign of religion. She felt no need to demonstrate a false religiosity. Her life had already ended. But if she could help protect Luis de Santángel, she would do her utmost. Juan Rodríguez pulled the clothes trunk alongside her bed and sat on it, facing her.

"How long have you been living here?"

"Since . . . since that night. The night of the murder."

Rodríguez raised an eyebrow. "Late that night? Early the next morning? Please, señorita, we need details."

"The sun had barely gone down."

"Shortly after sundown? Did you not say you served him dinner quite late?"

"Yes. I served him dinner quite late. But he brought me here much earlier."

"And where were you living before?"

"On the street."

"How did this come about?"

"I can't explain it."

"Why not? There is nothing to fear, señorita. Father Torquemada could have had you arrested." He leaned forward and lowered his voice. "We could be having this conversation in the ecclesiastical jail, rather than in the privacy of your room. But he chose not to."

Leonor forced herself to smile.

Rodríguez leaned back again. "So, you were living on the street. And now you are living in a wealthy man's home." He waved his hand. "Your own room. Let me ask again: How, exactly, did this come about?"

"How do these things ever come about? He saw me. I smiled at him. We spoke very little. That first time, he offered me two hundred maravedis."

The constable pretended not to understand. "Two hundred maravedis? For what purpose?"

"To come home with him."

Her avowal of sin elicited no sympathy in Rodríguez. He felt himself growing hot and, momentarily at a loss, contented himself with repeating her words, once again. "To come home with him."

She assented with a small jerk of her chin.

"And did you go home with him?"

"As you see." A vein pulsed in her graceful neck.

"A man you did not know?"

"All men are the same."

"What do you mean by that?"

"Of course they are. Even men of religion. They say it's a sin, but they're no different." She inhaled deeply, her well-defined breasts rising under her dress.

"And you, do you not believe it's a sin?"

"That's not what I said."

Under Rodríguez's cloak, the part of his anatomy that seemed to function independently of his will, the part he hated, asserted itself. To compound the insult, the chancellor's maidservant lowered her eyes. They stopped upon the bulge there, like a snail hindered by a rock. The persimmon-haired constable allowed himself to do something he feared he would regret the rest of his life. He placed his hand on her leg.

She gasped. Rodríguez wondered why. She was a tramp, was she not? She was used to men who placed their hands on her—indeed, all over her. Was this strumpet being coy?

He could not risk being overheard. He slapped his hand over her mouth, pulled her up, and turned her around. He pushed himself against her from behind.

She struggled, trying to scream—pretending, for reasons he could not fathom, to be a woman of virtue. He held her mouth firmly. In the intoxication of the moment, he pushed harder against her, simultaneously pulling up her robe.

Her naked skin felt soft, warm. As Leonor squirmed and squealed, the constable loosened his tunic so his flesh could make contact with hers. She tried to bite his hand. He pulled her head back, clutching her mouth and nose, as he thrust from behind.

She continued twisting and lurching, trying to shout. It astonished Rodríguez, how strong she was. As he strained against her, he jerked her head back again, as hard as he could—until he heard a crack and her shrieks stopped.

Juan Rodríguez released her. She fell limply upon the bed. He closed his tunic and tried to catch his breath.

As he looked down at her, suddenly immobile, the enormity of his sin filled his lungs, making it difficult to draw air. He sat down, closed his eyes, and instructed his heart to calm.

CHAPTER ELEVEN

*O*N A CLEAR WINTER MORNING in the year of the prophet 890, which was the Hebrew year 5246 and the Julian year 1485, Judith set out on foot for the Alhambra. Under each arm, she carried a crate wrapped in green silk.

Sara met her at the gate. Sara looked more lovely than ever, gracefully proportioned, with green eyes, ivory skin, and long auburn locks peeking out from under her partial veil. The slipper-pin clasped her blush silk robe.

"If you please, my lady." She led Judith through a dark, winding corridor and another gate, into the gardens.

"Sara," Judith whispered. "Are you well?"

"Oh, yes," Sara answered quietly. "At first, this was all so different. But now, there is so much to do. The women in the harem are kind. They are teaching me many things."

Judith found Sara's diction uncharacteristically formal. "What are they teaching you?"

"My favorite subject? Dancing. I practice every chance."

"Dancing?" Judith had heard about the belly dancing practiced in the private homes of wealthy Arabs. "And your mother's visits?"

"There's a beautiful verse in the Koran." Sara quoted, "*We command you to be dutiful and good to your parents. Your mother bore you in weakness and hardship upon weakness and hardship.*"

As they passed out of the entranceway, the castle grounds opened before them. "Is this not the loveliest home you could imagine?" asked Sara. "These gardens, are they not splendid?"

Splendid they were, beyond anything Judith had ever seen. The contrast between the building's stark exterior and the lacelike carved walls, thick vegetation, and gurgling fountains inside enhanced the beauty and serenity of the palace. Stone canals adorned the gardens, fragrant orange trees and myrtles flanking their edges. Arcades, on slender, intricately carved columns of white marble, surrounded reflecting pools and opened into private rooms and halls, which in turn gave access to other gardens and chambers. Small geometric tiles in white, blue, orange, black, and yellow covered the walls.

They passed through an enclosed garden. Thin, intertwined plaster tendrils, like lace, formed the rear wall. Through an archway, they entered the small, rectangular room where Ibrahim al-Hakim sat on a cushion, before a brass table, placing his stamp on a document. Two bare-chested guards stood at the back of the room. Sara prostrated herself and introduced Judith.

"Ah, yes, my silver goblets. Come! I'm eager to see them."

The palace's blend of exquisite luxury and fortified strength impressed Judith more than she had expected. She replied simply, "It is an honor, Your Excellency," and placed the silk-wrapped box on the floor.

Al-Hakim took one of the cups in his hand and turned it over. "Beautiful. Beautiful. I can hardly wait to drink from these." He held up the tumbler for Sara to admire. "What do you think, my gazelle?" The word for gazelle, *rejalla*, also meant "beautiful."

"They are lovely," confirmed Sara.

"Will that be all, Your Excellency?" asked Judith.

"Please, sit down. Have some candied almonds." He placed the goblet on the table.

Judith understood the man's hospitality to be neither more nor less than polite repayment for the mint tea she had offered him. She sat on a leather cushion and took a dried fruit from the brass tray.

"Tell me," the vizier asked Judith, "how are your people faring, here in the capital? We know there have been troubles, but that's over, is it not?" He glanced toward the courtyard as if expecting someone. "The Muslims and the Jews, we are brothers. We must never forget that."

Judith savored the date in her mouth. Sensing Sara's gaze on her, she turned again to look at her. She wondered what Sara's eyes were trying to tell her.

Upon a nod from al-Hakim, Sara turned and strolled away. The vizier watched her until she disappeared.

"Your Excellency," Judith tried, "yes, there have been troubles. Nevertheless, we thank God we're comfortable and prosperous, for the most part, these days."

Al-Hakim nodded, satisfied. "As they say, a ruler who can't protect his Jews will bring calamity upon his realm. It happened to the Babylonians. It happened to the Egyptians. It happened to the Romans. And so many others."

Judith could not ignore his graciousness. She smiled.

Al-Hakim glanced at the doorway where a guard had appeared. At the guard's side stood an opulently attired foreigner.

"My lord, the chancellor of Aragon."

Familiar with the mores of the place, Luis de Santángel bowed low, placing his right palm on his forehead. "Peace be with you, Your Excellency. The queen of Castile and the king of Aragon send their greetings. May you and your emir enjoy prosperity and health."

Ibrahim al-Hakim gestured for him to rise. "*Sidi* Luis de Santángel. We were told you were coming. We remember your last visit fondly, though it was too long ago. Come in. Look at this lovely goblet."

The chancellor took the ornate silver cup. "What does the inscription mean?"

Rather than answer him, the vizier directed his gaze at Judith.

She felt unsure of herself. How was one, in the home of the vizier, to address an advisor to enemy crowns? She assessed the newcomer. He looked wealthy, self-important, and Christian. In her lifetime, she had met only a handful of Christians. She had not trusted any of them.

"Allah alone conquers," she replied quietly in Santángel's own language.

The chancellor's eyes lingered on hers. She shifted her regard toward the vizier.

Ibrahim al-Hakim nodded, impressed, "Not only a master silversmith, but also a linguist. How could one woman be so talented?"

"For me to explain that," said Judith, "would tax your patience."

"We have time." The vizier smiled.

"My family came here from Aragon. On the Sabbath, Baba Shlomo, my late brother's father-in-law, insists we speak Aragonese."

"And what brought your Baba Shlomo to the kingdom of Granada?" asked Santángel.

"Riots," said Judith. "Uprisings . . . against the Jews of Zaragoza. His parents died, like many others."

"If he lost his parents there," pursued the chancellor, "and fled to Granada, one wonders why he would insist on speaking Aragonese."

"It was their language. It's his way of honoring them."

"Surely there's more to it than that. One can honor one's parents in many ways."

Taken aback, Judith allowed her composure to slip. "And why would that concern you?"

"For many reasons."

She frowned. Why was this foreign dignitary addressing her in this direct, familiar manner? Surely he had not traveled all the way from the kingdom of Aragon to discuss her family's linguistic practice. Nevertheless, she straightened her dress and tried to explain. "We are a community, the Jewish exiles from Christian Spain. We share memories, foods." She smiled and turned back to the vizier, who had been observing their tense exchange. "Your Excellency, if you will forgive me, I'm expected at the shop."

The vizier dismissed Judith good-naturedly. Santángel again turned to her and bowed from the waist. "A great pleasure and a rare honor, madam." He kissed her hand.

No one had ever kissed her hand before. Of course, Christians had different customs. Surely, for the chancellor of Aragon, this exceedingly intimate act meant nothing at all. For the Jewish silver merchant, the touch of a man's lips was inappropriate and undeniably sensual. She turned to leave.

. . .

That evening, amidst the flowers and fountains in the Garden of the Generals, the chancellor of Aragon sat with Mohammed bin Sa'ad al-Zagal, the emir of Granada. Beside the emir sat his vizier, sipping a fig liquor, eating crisp pastries stuffed with squab, cinnamon, and almonds, watching a young girl called Sariya perform a dance she had learned in the harem. Musicians plucked and scraped their bows across stringed gourds, blew on wooden flutes and the *sabbaba*, a reed instrument. They struck the skin of a tambour with their fingertips and the heels of their palms.

Kneeling, partially hidden behind a silk curtain, Sariya at first moved only her hands in graceful, flowing undulations, parabolic flourishes, and sudden sweeps. As the music grew faster and louder, she slowly rose from her knees, her head loosely swaying, her shoulders and chest twitching with the drumbeats, her hands floating through the air on either side, in front of her face, behind her head, like birds lost in flight. The veils seemed to fall of their own accord from her long hair and shoulders. Her belly and hips burst into life, swiveling and thrusting, and then her legs and feet, pivoting, skipping, whirling. Her body bobbed and shuddered, translating the instruments' twisting melody into one long, delirious gesture. Finally, as the music climaxed and ebbed, Sariya collapsed and disappeared behind the low curtain.

"She is like no other woman, your Sariya," the emir complimented Ibrahim al-Hakim.

"Indeed, I've not seen another like her," agreed the chancellor, who had found her performance not only refreshingly exotic, but also sensual beyond anything he had seen, or could imagine seeing, in the court of Queen Ysabel.

The emir turned to Santángel. "The women of Andalusia please you."

"From what I have seen, Your Royal Highness," confirmed the chancellor, "they constitute a most exquisite breed."

"And what have you seen, other than Sariya?"

The flutist and tambour player resumed a quiet *taqsim*.

"This afternoon, the lady who delivered these goblets." Santángel held aloft his cup.

"Yes," said the vizier, pouring more liquor for his guest. "Stunning, but headstrong, as only Jewish women can be. Migdal. Judith. She has a workshop in their quarter."

The chancellor nodded, imbibing another mouthful of the fruity, intoxicating beverage. Al-Zagal examined his cup, as if noticing its exquisite craftsmanship for the first time. He was not tall, but at the venerable age of forty-three, he was still muscular and fit, with short, graying hair and coal-black eyes.

"Now, if you will," he turned back to the chancellor, "explain why you have traveled into the heart of an enemy kingdom, with all the danger that entails, to warn us of a threat from my nephew."

"Your Royal Highness," said Santángel. "We hardly need more instability on our borders. Abu Abdullah is, to us, an unknown entity and a greater threat."

Bringing his hands together under his chin, al-Zagal peered at the chancellor, nodding slightly. The flute music swelled to its conclusion. Al-Hakim leaned close to the emir and whispered a few words.

"Tell me something," al-Zagal challenged Santángel. "You Christians possess virtually all the land from the Sierra Nevadas to the Balkans. Why are you so preoccupied with the tiny Moslem emirate of Granada, a narrow swath of land in an isolated corner of the continent? Why is it more acceptable for your armies to be stopped by seas than by mountains?"

"Your Highness," replied the chancellor, "I am hardly qualified to comment on such matters."

"For the last several years," resumed the emir, "you have availed yourselves of every opportunity to spoliate our farmlands just south of your border. Your purpose is not merely to harass and demoralize the local populations, but to destroy our economy."

"These border raids have been going on for centuries," Santángel objected calmly, "in both directions."

"It is not the same. Those were small-scale incursions. These are invasions. Tens of thousands of Christian peasants have participated. Granada's most fertile fields have been laid waste. Your famous knight, Rodrigo Ponce de León, attacked our town of Al-hama and took it, separating the two great cities of our emirate, Granada and Malaga, and accentuating the strife between me and my nephew. And now you come warning me of his intentions—as if I were not well aware of them."

"Neither the king of Aragon nor the queen of Castile authorized Don Rodrigo's attack."

"Not openly."

"Your Highness, if you do not wish to avail yourself of our assistance, that is, of course, entirely your decision. My only purpose is to convey the offer."

Al-Zagal peered over the hills of his kingdom, toward the sea that divided Europe from the Southern Continent. Santángel knew better than to say anything further, unless asked.

. . .

The door of Santángel's intricately tiled room, deep within the Alhambra castle complex, creaked open. A girl with long, champagne-colored hair, small breasts, and fawn-colored eyes slipped in.

"Carlina," she introduced herself while disrobing. "A gift from the emir, for one night."

"And how is it you speak Spanish so well?"

"Before I came here, I was Christian. From Murcia." She slipped into bed beside the chancellor.

Carlina offered her pleasures graciously, even ardently. Her smile, thought Santángel, revealed a surprising softness; her voice, a certain sweetness.

Later, as he allowed his head to sink into the feather pillow, watching candlelight play upon the ornate, carved ceiling, the chancellor of Aragon reflected upon his inability to find contentment in the fresh-gardenia embrace of a young lover.

He allowed his mind to wander, again, to his departed wife: her laughter, her voice, her hopeful smile. Unlike most women of her station, she had accompanied her husband on many of his journeys, including to Granada, years ago. Her passing had torn a hole in Luis de Santángel's life. Into this hole, much of the satisfaction he took in ordinary things had flowed, like water down a drain.

For the first time in many years, another woman entered these thoughts. The silversmith he had met at the Alhambra. Migdal, the vizier had later told him, Judith. Something about her had captured his fancy. He had known many beautiful ladies. This Carlina, lying next to him, was hardly less striking, and certainly younger.

In Judith's regard, he had seen a hint of resilience. In her voice, a resonance of compassion and experience. She had seemed determined not to appear impressed with his finery and station. Her words about Zaragoza and riots had implied a subtle reproach. She remained with him—her amber eyes, the splash of freckles across her nose, her proud bearing.

. . .

Late the next morning, as a donkey brayed down the street and a small wagon clattered past, Luis de Santángel dismissed his guide at the gate of Judith Migdal's home. He noticed the mezuzah on the threshold and contemplated its simple olivewood case, covered with silver branches and leaves so brightly burnished they glistened in the morning sunlight. He had never seen such a lustrous, assertive ornament outside a Jewish home. Then again, he reminded himself, he had rarely visited a Jewish home in the broad light of day.

The door of Judith's workshop stood ajar. Inside, she was linking a clasp to a bracelet. Her black hair loosely tied, strands of it falling into her face, she wore a work dress and leather mules.

He paused at the doorway, his hands clasped behind his back. "My lady."

Judith smiled. "Chancellor. Please." She gestured for him to enter, hiding whatever surprise she may have felt at his sudden appearance.

The chancellor stepped into the room.

Judith rose. "I'm sorry it isn't more comfortable, here."

"This is your workplace," said the chancellor. "I wasn't expecting a royal palace."

She smiled vaguely. "Are you enjoying your stay in our city? It may seem foreign to you. Even strange."

"Not terribly. I've had the pleasure of traveling here before. The people I've met, your vizier, your emir, have all been most gracious."

"Your talks with the vizier, were they satisfactory? Did you accomplish what you wanted?"

"Time will tell."

She seemed to notice he was being evasive, and changed the subject. "May I ask what brings you to my workshop?"

"I was most impressed with what I saw, yesterday. With what I heard. Your silverwork. Your mastery of my language." Hoping to put her at ease, he added, "The vizier himself seemed quite satisfied."

"Then perhaps my fortunes are improving."

"You don't seem so very unfortunate."

The chancellor glanced around the dim chamber—the rough beams, the tiled floor and whitewashed walls. A disagreeable, smoky scent hung in the air.

"Were you looking for something?" asked Judith.

"I suppose I was. I am." The chancellor glanced at the trays and religious ornaments on the table. "Something to take back to Castile. Perhaps a gift. For my queen."

"What did you have in mind?"

"Something she would cherish. A pendant, perhaps. A clasp. A cross. Elaborate, in your arabesque manner, and large. She would like that."

"How long will you be staying in Granada?"

"Perhaps another night."

"One night?" She shook her head. "It won't be possible, Chancellor. The Sabbath starts tonight and lasts through the day tomorrow. We Jews don't work on the Sabbath. As a matter of fact, I should stop, now." She began organizing the silver, stones, and tools.

"I'll send for it, then."

She smiled. "From Zaragoza? That would cost you a fortune."

Santángel tapped his fingers on the table. He watched her as she prepared to leave. "Perhaps something more substantial, then, to justify the cost of the messenger. A sword-hilt for my king. As well as a cross for my queen. Two items. Perhaps more in the future."

"Why?" she breathed.

"You are—your work is—exquisite." There, he had said it, if inadvertently. Judith glanced away. She had heard it.

She wrapped the bracelet in its polishing cloth and dropped it in the pocket of her smock. "Chancellor, I have to go to the market."

"Perhaps I could accompany you."

"Accompany me?" She frowned.

"I may need to purchase a few gifts."

"Here? In the Jewish quarter?" She let out a little laugh. "I'm afraid, Chancellor, there isn't much to see just now. It's getting late."

He followed her out. She locked the door of her workshop.

"And my scimitar? My cross?"

She shook her head. "If you wanted a cup or a bangle, I might be able to oblige. But a sword, a cross, the very emblems of your war?" She shook her head. "Thank you for visiting me."

She walked out of her courtyard. Santángel watched her another moment, then turned to leave.

. . .

The synagogue, a small two-story building, stood at the side of a misshapen plaza, neither a triangle nor quite a rectangle. Inside, the Jews of Granada prayed individually and together. Some mumbled, others loudly declaimed Hebrew blessings, supplications, and psalms. Still others exchanged news, in Arabic, about events in far-off lands. A foreign sea captain had recently discovered a great river, perhaps the longest in the world. The king of Portugal had executed some eighty noblemen at once. The great Jewish philosopher, Isaac Abravanel, had narrowly escaped their fate.

Young boys played tag or hide-and-seek. Wives and daughters, in the balconies, looked on, reciting the liturgy. Judith stood among them, as always, glancing at the people around her, mumbling the prayers.

Near the wall, in his foreign, close-fitting vest and pants, stood the last person she would have expected to find here, the chancellor of Aragon. He watched the men blessing and beseeching God in their jumble of Levantine cadences as if studying an unintelligible map.

Luis de Santángel had surprised her earlier, when he came to her shop, but his presence in the synagogue was incomprehensible. Had he followed her? As she glanced again at the elegant courtier, he must have sensed her thoughts, for he turned and looked directly at her.

Again, as she guided Baba Shlomo out of the synagogue, Judith met the chancellor by the door.

"Madam." He bowed.

"Good evening, Chancellor."

Santángel turned to the small, white-bearded man beside her. "You must be Baba Shlomo," he said in the Aragonese dialect.

"I am, indeed." The old man beamed, clearly delighted to meet a stranger who spoke the language of his youth. "With whom do I have the pleasure of speaking?"

Judith turned to Baba Shlomo and carefully adjusted his robe. "This is the gentleman I told you about. The diplomat from Zaragoza."

"Ah. And what brings you to our house of worship?"

"The romance of the exotic, I suppose," replied Santángel.

"Would you find a Sabbath supper sufficiently exotic?" Baba Shlomo looked blindly at the chancellor. "We'd love to have you for the night."

Santángel knew that custom, here, dictated that hosts house their guests from evening until morning. "That is very kind, but entirely unmerited."

Baba Shlomo reached for the chancellor's shoulder. "Nonsense," he insisted. "Come, join us. I have many questions."

Santángel turned back to Judith. She was looking askance, her amber eyes impenetrable.

. . .

After washing their hands, lighting the candles, and pronouncing the blessings over bread and wine, Judith and Baba Shlomo invited

Santángel to join them at the low brass table, where they sat with Levi on leather cushions. She had prepared a spicy fish stew. They drank from silver cups and ate from glazed clay pots.

Judith had rarely seen Baba Shlomo so animated. Questions spilled from his lips like tea from a deep pitcher. Were there still Jews in Zaragoza? The old man seemed relieved to learn that there were, and that Santángel personally knew one or two members of the community. How were the Israelites of Aragon faring? What about the holidays Baba Shlomo remembered from his youth, the day of Rejoicing in the Torah, the Festival of the Harvest, when the followers of Moses would exit their quarter, parading around the city with their scrolls or their palm fronds, and the followers of Jesus would join them, and for a brief time it would seem there had never been strife between them? Were there still enough Jews in Zaragoza to bring life to such festivities? Did the Christians allow it?

Santángel hated to disappoint the old man by not responding. At the same time, he represented the courts of Castile and Aragon, even in a private home. He answered with a challenge. "Do you have it so much better in Granada? Because of your faith, you have to pay a special 'Jew Tax,' no?"

"Yes, of course, just as in Christian lands."

"And you're not permitted to build houses taller than those of your neighbors, or to pray in public."

"Such regulations," said Baba Shlomo, "hardly affect our daily lives."

"From what I understand," pursued Santángel, ignoring his objection, "your graves have to lie flat upon the ground, so the Mohammedans can walk upon them. And if a Muslim wants to marry your daughter, you can't refuse him. In what way do you fare better than the Jews of Aragon, or Castile?"

"We may disagree with our neighbors," remarked Judith, unsettled by all the chancellor was suggesting, "but they don't kill us for it."

Santángel smiled, pleased she had decided to join the conversation.

"Usually, they don't," Baba Shlomo corrected her.

As she turned to Baba Shlomo, her expression softened.

"The same can be said of the Jews in Zaragoza and Toledo," asserted Santángel, "and the other Christian lands." Even as he uttered the words, he knew that while literally true, they were meant to disguise his unease about the state of Jewish life in Zaragoza.

"But you, yourself, sir," asked Judith. "Why did you come to our services? Are you Jewish or Christian?"

Santángel sipped his wine. "My lady, what is the advantage of knowing, with absolute certainty, what one believes? There's much to be said for doubt."

"All people suffer," said Judith. "But if you don't know what you believe, you suffer alone."

"I'm Christian, madam. Third generation." He said it as though he meant it, meeting her gaze.

Judith had invited gentiles into her home before, but the Sabbath dinner was a religious observance. Christians, she knew, sometimes studied Jewish rituals with the sole aim of finding fault in them.

On the other hand, this chancellor appeared to be a man of great distinction. Was it not an honor to entertain such a gentleman at one's dinner table? Again, her eyes caught his. This time, she did not look away.

What she saw surprised her. For a moment, he was not a foreign dignitary, but a man. Christians, she had heard, rarely revealed their vulnerability. "Third generation," she repeated.

"They say the errors of past generations are erased," the chancellor explained, "when one accepts Christ." He smiled tenuously and sipped his wine again.

Judith returned his smile, resting her chin lightly upon the back of her hand, a loose strand of hair sweeping her cheek. Luis de Santángel made no effort to hide his fascination.

"I have a question." Levi, now fourteen, asserted his right to participate as an adult. "If you are Christian, that means you believe in Yehoshua ben Yosef—Jesus Christ, as you say. No?"

Santángel peered at him. He was two years older than Gabriel. Had Gabriel been raised in the traditions of his ancestors, would he resemble this young man, at least in his bearing and manner?

The differences were immediately apparent. Levi's posture, slightly hunched, conveyed humility and a familiarity with life's disappointments, but his warm expression communicated trust and confidence. He seemed to feel no shame about wearing a skull cap at dinnertime. While Gabriel fancied himself a knight or a crusader, courageous and proud, conquering infidels, Levi thought of himself as a Jew, content to remain in his small, confined neighborhood.

"Yes, of course," the chancellor replied. "The Christians believe in Jesus."

"He was a magician, right? He knew how to turn loaves of bread into fish, how to bring dead people back. That's what my rabbi told me."

"I wouldn't want to contradict your rabbi, but the Christians don't characterize Him as a magician, any more than Moses was a magician when he threw down his rod and it turned into snakes."

"But Moses didn't do that. God did that."

The chancellor smiled. "Well, I suppose you could say God was responsible for Jesus's miracles, too."

"Then why do you pray to Jesus?"

"Levi, stop this," Judith reprimanded her nephew.

"I just want to understand."

"Your nephew is unusually intelligent" the chancellor told Judith.

His words reassured Judith, who agreed with his assessment but knew others often thought Levi bold.

Santángel turned back to the boy. "I'm sorry I can't answer all your questions. I'm simply not the right person."

He glanced back at Judith, who offered him the hint of a smile, evidently pleased that he had cut short her nephew's inquiry.

. . .

Santángel lay on the tree-shaded terrace atop Judith's home. Under a wedge of moon and a splash of stars, a warm breeze washed over him. He relived the evening: Judith's eyes, lingering on her nephew and Baba Shlomo; the way she tilted her head to the side as she listened; her high cheekbones; her jet-black hair. He was struck by her manner, anxious to please but challenging nonetheless, and the way she unsettled him. He had not found a woman so beguiling since he had first set eyes upon his departed wife.

The warm air of Granada and the spicy dinner made his throat feel dry, keeping him awake. He heard a few quiet footsteps somewhere in the house. He rose to slake his thirst. As he padded down the stairwell, he passed Judith's room, with its warped door that did not quite close. He saw his hostess preparing for bed. He told himself not to stare at her milky ivory skin, untouched by the sun; her graceful legs; her taut, full breasts; the half-shadowed curve of her back. He caught his breath.

Downstairs, Santángel filled a silver goblet and drained it in one gulp. Water trickled down his chin onto his nightshirt.

For once, as he reluctantly crossed between the waking world into the many worlds of dreams, imagery of blood and horror did not flood his mind. Nor did he frantically search Pedro de Arbués's apartments, once again, for the book that could damn him and those he loved. Instead, he revisited the evening's dinner conversation, the synagogue, the glimpse of Judith's skin, the Alhambra, lulled by the half-remembered refrains of ancient prayers.

CHAPTER TWELVE

O_{N THE FOURTH NIGHT} of the siege, Tomás de Torquemada rode to the king's encampment outside Velez-Malaga. The city was ablaze. Acting in part on Luis de Santángel's misinformation, the emir had prepared to defend Malaga itself, not from the Christian forces but from those of Abu Abdullah. The Christians had pounded Velez-Malaga, about twenty miles distant from Malaga, by sea and land, bringing it to its knees well before the Muslim forces arrived.

As Torquemada approached the king's tent on foot, he heard a woman's half-suppressed cries. The voice was not Queen Ysabel's. This came as no surprise to the monk. In her rambling, intimate confessions, the queen had complained about her husband's lecherous ways. Torquemada turned back with his horses and men for a monastery a half hour's ride away.

He rode back at dawn. The king's guard announced him and Torquemada entered alone.

Unlike the palatial accommodations outside Cordoba, where Luis de Santángel had visited the queen, the king's tent was a one-room affair. The wench was a lean Moorish girl of about fifteen years with long, henna-tinted hair and black almond-shaped eyes, captured by the Christian forces on the road from Cordoba. When the king was finished with her, probably within a few nights, he would hand her over for his soldiers' enjoyment. She hid under the blanket, shivering, while the king shamelessly dressed in front of the inquisitor.

"Your Majesty," began Torquemada, "we have learned certain things."

"Regarding?"

"The assassination, Your Majesty."

Pulling up his breeches, King Fernando peered at the tonsured monk, with his hollow cheekbones and full, dark brows. "What have you learned?" The king slipped his arms through the sleeves of his blousy shirt.

"It is not only what we have learned. It's also what we have not learned."

"We're speaking in riddles, now." The king found a rapier belt at the foot of his bed and attached it at his waist.

Torquemada ignored the sarcasm. "Your Highness, the records of Father Arbués's last deposition are missing."

Indeed, a thorough search of Luis de Santángel's home had failed to retrieve not only those registers, but any inculpating evidence against the chancellor. Torquemada attributed this failure not to Santángel's innocence, but to his cunning.

"We believe Father Arbués was murdered for those records, and for his recollection of their content. And we believe . . . We believe the chancellor of Aragon was involved. Luis de Santángel."

King Fernando did not flinch. "What leads you to think that?"

"He was seen paying the killer."

"Seen? By whom? And what precisely do you intend, Father?" The king picked up his sword and stuffed it into the scabbard on his hip.

"His horse was identified, Your Majesty. A roan courser with a black stripe down its spine. A very particular horse." Aware that this evidence might not convince Fernando, he quickly changed the topic. "We know Santángel is here in the south. We intend to place the Holy Brotherhood on high alert, throughout Castile and Aragon."

"His *horse*?" The king sat down in a chair and shoved his feet into his boots. "Father Torquemada, I've known Señor de Santángel for decades. He helped arrange my wedding with the queen. He *paid* for it. This battle we're fighting—not just for Castile or

Aragon, mind you, but for the whole of Christendom—we're going to win it. Thanks to whom? To Luis de Santángel, who procured the *Giustizia* for us, our most important battleship. And as everyone knows but doesn't dare say, he is a better Christian—a far better Christian—than I."

Torquemada felt his heart pounding. "Your Majesty," he tried again, "the best way to demonstrate the innocence of your chancellor, if innocent he is, would be to interrogate him, and let him show those who suspect him of wrongdoing, of wrong thinking, how wrong *they* are. Good Christians, as you know, my liege, have nothing to fear. But if we fail to give him that opportunity, a cloud of suspicion will hang over him for the rest of his life. And by extension, if you will permit me, over *you*."

"Father Torquemada," spat King Fernando with imperious finality, "don't threaten me. Now I have a war to fight."

"So do I, Your Majesty." He said it softly, but the message was clear. The inquisitor was not daunted.

The king glared at him, astonished. "Allow me to show you something, Father." He found a letterbox in his trunk and fished out a large envelope with a florid scarlet stamp. Torquemada recognized it as a missive from the pope himself. Fernando shoved it into the inquisitor's hands.

While Torquemada read the Latin, the king summarized. "The Holy Father asks that the New Inquisition be realigned with the interests of Rome. What does that mean for you? It means this war of yours may no longer be yours at all."

As he read, Torquemada contemplated the implications of the pope's letter. If the New Inquisition, which he had been working so hard, for so long, to establish throughout Castile and Aragon, were to be softened and corrupted until it resembled the creaky, lumbering machinery of the traditional Inquisition, all would be lost. Christianity itself might become so sullied, so defiled in these territories as to become an instrument of the devil.

His fingertips, as he clutched the page, were white. He looked up. "Someone has been quite generous with the Holy Father, I would imagine."

"Perhaps," said Fernando, throwing the letter onto his bed. "All the same, it doesn't serve our interests to be in disagreement with him. Unless the New Inquisition is willing to take our needs and our present situation into account, it may not be worth it."

He moved to exit, but Torquemada interrupted one last time. "I understand, Your Majesty, the chancellor is not to be arrested, for now. But can we question his relatives? His associates? As witnesses, they have nothing to fear. The Inquisition has always protected its sources."

"That is a matter for your judgment."

Fernando left Tomás de Torquemada in the company of the Moorish girl, who remained half hidden under the blanket. Most likely, she had not understood a word. The monk, furious and indignant, hardly noticed her.

. . .

Riding away with his guard, Torquemada told himself that his meeting with the king had not been futile. Fernando had authorized him to investigate Santángel's cohorts and kin, throughout the realms of Aragon and Castile. They might provide valuable information. They might also be used to pressure the chancellor. He would prioritize the search for the boy with the striped jerkin. He would begin by finding out every detail about the boy's departure from Zaragoza.

As Torquemada and his men galloped across Andalusia's wild, mountainous terrain, the inquisitor's displeasure slowly turned to hope, not only for the soul of Luis de Santángel, but also for the alliance of Church and Crown in Castile and Aragon. Tomás de Torquemada never permitted himself to dwell in despair. Those who loved the Lord must have confidence in His divine plan.

. . .

Walking from his tent to greet the soldiers, King Fernando tripped on a small rock and cursed under his breath. His morning conversation with Tomás de Torquemada had brought to mind events he would rather have forgotten.

Seventeen years before, Luis de Santángel had escorted Fernando on a secret mission to meet and betroth Ysabel. The young financier and the prince rode together, ate together, and talked late into the night in their guarded tent, laying out the future king's aspirations and strategies.

At that time, King Enrique IV still reigned over Castile. Enrique and his half-sister Ysabel despised each other. The king insisted that upon his death his only offspring, Princess Juana, be crowned Queen of Castile. Ysabel countered that Enrique was a sodomizer, that Princess Juana's birth was surely illegitimate, and that Ysabel was next in line for the throne.

With Santángel, Fernando traveled incognito, dressed as a peasant. En route they stayed with friends of Santángel's family, New Christians who secretly swore to support their ambitions. Had Juana's champions, including the king himself, learned that the prince of Aragon intended to marry Ysabel, they would have guessed his intention—to help her usurp the throne of Castile.

The prince hoped, through his marriage, to acquire sovereignty over Castile. He never intended to share power with his wife-to-be. Ysabel insisted they jointly wear the twin crowns of Aragon and Castile. Fernando grudgingly agreed, privately considering it a provisional arrangement.

In the town of Calatayud, Prince Fernando and his small entourage met a dark-skinned soothsayer with a strange accent, a deep voice, and only two teeth. "I tell you only what you must know," she promised, "by reading words, mystery patterns, leaves in the bottom of the teacup." Although Luis de Santángel scoffed at the idea, the prince welcomed her offer.

While preparing a brew of strong, hot tea, she spoke with both gentlemen about their travels, the weather, and the land where she was born, "a place far in the east with no name." She asked the prince to drink as much as he could in one gulp. After he drank, she poured what remained of the liquid onto the ground, replaced the cup on her table, and spun it three times. She studied the small leaves that clung to the sides and bottom of the cup. In some places, they clumped together. In others, they formed dancing strings.

Looking up from the cone-shaped cup, the woman rapidly proved her genius. "You are . . . you are man of power. Great power."

Fernando glanced triumphantly at Santángel, seated next to him, then turned back to her. "Tell me what the future holds."

"Ah," she told him, holding up a finger. "When I learned secret arts, I made promises. I keep them. God creates man with eyes in the back of his head. He cannot see the path before. I will not cross God. But this much I can tell you." Again, she pondered the pattern of leaves, then raised her gray eyes, clouded with apprehension. "You will achieve many dreams. But when your wife dies, the door of dreams may close."

For years following this chance meeting, Fernando tried to make sense of her obscure prognostication. When Ysabel finally fell pregnant, its meaning dawned on him. If the queen were to die before the king, their child would inherit Castile. Fernando would find his royal powers diminished, once again, to the periphery of Aragon.

He spoke of the matter with Luis de Santángel, the only other person who had heard the tea-leaf reader's strange prediction. To his steward, Fernando entrusted the mission of consulting with an herbalist to discover what might be done to prevent such an outcome.

Fernando's steward acquired a small quantity of *aquae serpentis*, an exceedingly costly brew made from rare mushrooms, python's blood, cow's dung, and other ingredients. The ingestion of a very small quantity of this blend by a pregnant woman would ensure that her child, upon reaching maturity, would lose control of his or her faculties, and thus be rendered unfit to rule. King Fernando, then, would continue to control Castile as the child's regent.

In what appeared a normal delivery, Queen Ysabel brought into the light of day a girl, whom the king named after the niece Ysabel despised—Juana. To the world, this princess was the future queen of Castile. Only King Fernando and his steward knew the truth. If anyone else learned it, the queen would certainly have taken all necessary steps to dissolve her legal bonds with Fernando of Aragon.

The king's steward died five weeks later, in circumstances mysterious to all but the king himself, leaving no one the wiser regarding Princess Juana's destiny. Fernando, however, began to wonder whether Luis de Santángel did not have knowledge of their dark transaction. The payment of the apothecary had come out of funds the chancellor controlled. Santángel reviewed all such disbursements in detail with the king's steward.

If Santángel knew about the *aquae serpentis*, he could be trusted to keep their secret. If, however, the relentless Torquemada were to interrogate the chancellor of Aragon, who could predict what might be said, and how the future of Castile and Aragon might be altered?

CHAPTER THIRTEEN

VERY EVENING, Cristóbal Colón rode alone from the port of Santa Maria to the estate of Luis de la Cerda, the duke of Medina-Celi, outside Cadiz. Medina-Celi owned the ships Colón sailed, but their partnership now extended far deeper than mere business. Colón had become the duke's dearest friend.

Colón took what pleasure he could in the solitude, the calm of the brush-covered hills, the scents of rosemary and heather, the occasional glimpses of ocean below, and, most of all, the time to contemplate the world and his life.

Some men blithely stroll through their lives, accepting what Destiny offers, like farmers gathering fruit in their orchards, not looking off into neighboring properties or envying their yield. Others view Destiny with suspicion, as an adversary. What she freely offers, they value little, while what she withholds, they covet. To satisfy this desire, they will fight Destiny with ardor. Occasionally they succeed; more often they die disenchanted.

Colón viewed his entire existence as a struggle with Destiny. While his peers may have marveled at his ability to ingratiate himself with the powerful of this world, including the duke of Medina-Celi and the chancellor of Aragon, such accomplishments meant little to him. The business of negotiating with buyers and sellers of exotic commodities, hiring sailors, trying to keep them in line, earning and disbursing wages—all this was nothing but a dissipation of the brief, invaluable allotment of days given him to accomplish God's work. Indeed, every moment he devoted to such pursuits was nothing more than a digression.

Nonetheless, during these long rambles he occasionally allowed himself to doubt. So many learned men had seen no value in Colón's scheme. Even if the Indias could be reached by sailing westward, how could he be certain he would accomplish what none had before him?

. . .

Dressed in black, with a small, pointed beard, piercing blue eyes, and long, slender fingers, the duke of Medina-Celi preferred to break his colts himself. As he sometimes remarked, they were his only children. This particular horse, with its long neck, white socks, and spindly legs, was likely to become a favorite.

In the corral, he placed a saddle on the ground and allowed his colt to draw nearer to it, to examine it, to smell its leather. Leaning against the fence, the duke was watching his colt bemusedly when Colón arrived.

"What news from the harbor, my good captain?"

"The ocean's still breathing, Your Lordship, her tides rising and falling like a beautiful woman stretched out on a bed of silt."

The duke delighted in the contrast between Colón's rough, powerful build—his bulbous nose, his deep chest—and his poetic mind. The Genoese captain was the opposite of the duke himself, whose features and manners were finely sculpted and whose mind was practical.

"By day," Colón added, "men never cease filling some ships with freight, and unloading others."

Quick-witted and sensitive when he cared to be, Medina-Celi seized the innuendo. "But one seaman has had his fill of all this mundane commotion. A Genoese-Spanish seaman. No?"

"Indeed," Colón confirmed, noting the sarcastic inflection.

Medina-Celi picked up the training saddle and raised it over his colt's back. The horse backed off nervously, its ears flattened. "He's not ready," he declared as he replaced the saddle on the ground. He tried to stroke the animal's nose, but the horse broke loose and galloped around the corral, its mane blowing. Luis de la Cerda walked back to join Colón by the gate. "He's of little value to me, running around freely," he remarked. "But of course, I'll keep feeding him. He'll accept the saddle and the bit sooner or later. They all do."

The sailor was aware that despite the life of privilege Medina-Celi enjoyed, he often felt lonely and dejected. "It is my private melancholy," the duke sometimes complained. "I was born with it." He shared his home with the Genoese sailor to distract himself from his aching solitude.

"Yes, they all do take the saddle, sooner or later," agreed Colón. "He's a beast of burden, after all."

"Are horses so very different from you and me, my dear Cristóbal?"

"No, not so very different. You'll ride him ten, fifteen years, then he'll die, or Your Lordship will die, but nothing much will have changed in this sorry world."

"And suppose I never did saddle him? Suppose I let him canter off into the hills? What good do you imagine would come of that?"

"A horse doesn't ask why God put him in this world," replied Colón. "The good Lord didn't endow animals with the faculty to pose such questions. A horse's life has no purpose, other than the purpose we give it."

Before Medina-Celi had a chance to respond, his eunuch rode up to the corral.

"What is it, Fadrique?"

"The table is set, my lord. The players are here. The chancellor of Aragon has arrived."

"Thank you." The duke called out to one of his stable hands: "Gonçalo, put him back in his pen, will you? He isn't ready." He began walking toward the house. Colón followed. Neither said another word until they reached the door, but Colón was fuming inside. It seemed the duke thought of him the way he thought of his favorite horses: as palliatives, to reduce the anguish of his spiritual isolation.

They found Santángel in the front room of the duke's manor house. "Ah, Chancellor, such a pleasure." Medina-Celi bowed. "I see Chronos has been ignoring you, you handsome bastard. If I'm not mistaken there's even a new spark of youth about you. What's your little secret?"

"I have no little secrets, Medina-Celi, as you well know."

"Of course not, only monumental ones. Little people have little secrets."

"You haven't aged, either, my dear friend."

"You're well versed in the art of deception," riposted the duke. "But I'm no fool. Look at these crow's feet." Medina-Celi sighed. "Ah, well. Our time here is fleeting. Perhaps it's just as well."

Santángel turned to Colón. "And you, Captain. Still carousing in Rome?"

"I'm afraid not." Colón bowed. "Chancellor, if you don't mind," he added breathlessly, "do you recall a certain leather pouch?"

"Ah, your little gift. How can I thank you?"

"You have it, then." Colón broke into a smile of relief. "God heard my prayers."

"Perhaps we should ask God who put it in my trunk."

"Dumitru packed your trunk as well as mine. He must have thought it belonged to you."

The chancellor doubted Colón's explanation, but decided not to challenge him.

"Did you find out what those documents meant?"

Santángel glanced at the door. Medina-Celi, always alert, pulled it closed. The chancellor cleared his throat. "I'll try to summarize." He told Colón what Serero had taught him about the texts: that Abraham's passage from Ur to the Holy Land was a spiritual journey, as well as a geographical one; that before the People of Israel returned to the Holy Land, corruption and decay would infect Rome. He spoke of the war against the Jews and the great rainbow, as fresh as a bride. He stopped himself, however, before mentioning the other manuscript, the ancient rolled-up parchment that Abram Serero had refused to discuss—the text that, according to the scribe, had caused so many Jews to be murdered.

"Is all that of some use to you?"

"It is, most certainly. I cannot thank you enough," replied Colón. "The decay of Rome. The great rainbow. The war against the Jews. Now I know what to look for."

"When you go to Jerusalem, Señor Colón, you won't need to know what to look for. You'll see it before your eyes."

Colón beamed. "Thank you, Chancellor. Thank you."

"Cristóbal," interjected Medina-Celi. "We are being somewhat earnest, are we not? You know how exhausted he must be, our friend, the chancellor." He turned to Santángel. "We've prepared an evening of entertainment in your honor."

As the sun went down, he escorted the chancellor and the captain to his great room. A fire crackled in the stone hearth. A wide array of foods, artfully displayed, awaited them—pheasant, turnip soup, an apricot pie, a salad of boletes, milk cap, and Judas Ear mushrooms.

The duke's eunuch bowed. "A troupe of players, en route to Madrid, for your amusement and instruction." The troupe entered. The duke raised his hands and applauded with the tips of his fingers against his open palm.

While the duke, the captain, and the chancellor dined, the itinerant troupe performed a suite of songs arranged around a loose story. The characters had names like "Fortune," "Charity," and "Desire." Their silk raiment, in gold, white, and burgundy, reflected these identities. They sang of love, patience, and suffering. In their passions, they resembled real people rather than figures of allegory. Their melodies were woven together and bridged with rhyming narration, almost forming a unified drama. A eunuch played the young woman. A handsome tenor portrayed the male suitor. This type of theater, drawn from the emotions of common men and women rather than from Bible stories, was a new and bold experiment. Luis de Santángel, charmed, rewarded them with a few coins. The tenor pulled off his pointed cap, releasing long hair, and picked up his lute. He slid closer to Santángel and crooned a ballad for him, the tale of a lonely falconer.

That night, as he drifted off to sleep, Luis de Santángel thought again of the woman he had met in Granada—her pensive expression as she listened to Baba Shlomo, the way she held her wine cup, the graceful unrobed body Santángel had glimpsed. He closed his eyes and once again smelled the sweet, heady scent of jasmine growing in her garden.

Judith was no noblewoman, he reminded himself. She seemed simple, straightforward, touchingly provincial. Yet, despite himself, Santángel wondered whether she was not precisely the kind of woman he would marry if he were living in another time, another world. She was clearly as compassionate as she was intelligent and strong-willed. She had taken responsibility for another woman's child and elderly father.

But she was a Jewess. Even if she accepted baptism, the choice of such a companion would cast a cloud over the sincerity of Santángel's faith and destroy everything his grandfather, his father, and he had achieved. His beloved son's future would be compromised.

As his mind glided downward over the darkening slope of somnolence, just when it could fight his heart no longer, he admitted to himself he had to see her again.

. . .

In a dining nook adorned with hunting-scene frescoes, Santángel, Colón, and Medina-Celi enjoyed a midday meal of dried sardines, fresh grilled prawns, flat bread, and wine. Santángel thanked the duke for his hospitality. "As always, my dear Medina-Celi, you've shown me unmerited warmth and generosity."

"In that case," replied the duke, eyeing a sardine that he held up by its tail, "perhaps you can help our friend Colón, here. He desires an audience with the Crowns." He dropped the sardine into his mouth.

"For what purpose?" asked Santángel, taken aback.

Medina-Celi looked at the captain.

"The chancellor well knows," said Colón in his most dignified manner, "how my ambitions could bring glory to the conjoined kingdoms of Castile and Aragon."

"Your route to India? Jerusalem?"

"Indeed."

"I'm afraid my captain will never become a landlubber," said the duke. "It was all a vain dream." He looked at Colón questioningly. Colón shook his head, laughing.

Santángel dipped a grilled prawn in spicy sauce. "The king and queen are quite busy with this war of theirs."

"They're always busy with one thing or another, aren't they," said Medina-Celi.

"I suppose something could be arranged," said Santángel.

"Thank you," replied the duke. "Now we have a gift for you." He opened the door and waved someone in.

The man who entered, a large fellow dressed in the sober livery of a high-ranking servant, bowed. Santángel recognized the full moustache, the murky eyes of the slave whose freedom he had purchased in Civitavecchia.

"Iancu."

The Moldavian's arms, legs, and neck had thickened. His curly hair was now short; his face weathered.

"You're no longer a sailor?"

"A sailor I still am, my lord," Iancu replied mysteriously. "But I live now on firm land."

"And your little boy, Dumitru?"

"Little, he is not. A boy, he is not even. He is taller than me."

"Is he living on firm land, as well?"

"He doesn't like the sea. But it is his salt and bread."

"I understand your majordomo passed on," Medina-Celi told Santángel. "The plague, no? Sevilla?"

"Yes."

"We've trained Iancu. He's quite good."

The chancellor shook his head in disbelief and gratitude. He had thought he would never find someone to replace his majordomo, a man of rare loyalty and discretion. Iancu, who owed the chancellor his freedom, as well as his son's, was as good a bet as any.

CHAPTER FOURTEEN

AR FROM HIS TUTORS, his servants, and his games, Gabriel de Santángel grew bored and restless. Before departing for Cordoba, his father had taken his hands: "This will be a respite. No tutors, no assignments. But don't let your mind rot. Read Aristotle. *The Nicomachean Ethics*. You haven't read it, have you?"

"Too boring."

"Well, I can't claim I have, either. That's why I need you to write a summary. It will sharpen your understanding—and mine. Will you do that, my trusted knight?"

"I prefer the arena to the library."

"A great knight," Santángel instructed his son, "knows how to fight with his mind as well as his sword." He kissed Gabriel and left.

Two months passed without word from Gabriel's father. Despondent, Gabriel sat on the stairs inside Estefan's house. Gabriel had read a few sentences of *The Nicomachean Ethics*, then given up, finding the material impenetrable. Uncle Estefan had been too busy to play chess. Gabriel felt weary and confined. "If I can't be with my father in Cordoba, I'd rather be back in Zaragoza."

"Knights have to learn patience, Gabriel," answered Estefan.

"Knights don't stay cooped up. Besides, I'm not a knight."

"To go back to Zaragoza . . . It wouldn't be safe, just now."

"Why not?"

"You'll just have to believe me."

"Can I go out for just a few hours? I want to explore Valencia."

Estefan shook his head. "I'm sorry."

"You're sorry," Gabriel echoed resentfully. He stood and walked out, pulling the front door loudly closed.

The tax farmer cherished the boy's impertinence. Growing up as the putative younger brother of Luis de Santángel, he had displayed plenty of impertinence himself.

His parents had tried to enforce rules that made no sense. Before every meal, if the meal was taken inside their home, adults and children were required to wash their hands with fresh water. But if they dined in another's home, they ignored this rule. On a certain day every fall, a day whose exact date changed from year to year, one was not to eat—unless one was invited by a nonrelative. It was acceptable to eat pork outside the home, but not in the house, except for servants, who were allowed to eat pork anywhere. All this the young Estefan Santángel found confusing and incomprehensible, and when he came to understand as an adult, he remained perplexed by the risks his parents had taken.

When Estefan was thirteen, just months older than Gabriel, Luis discovered him sitting in the garden with a servant, chewing on hog jowls. The older brother said nothing, but there was no mistaking his powerful contempt.

Gabriel needed to go out from time to time, Estefan decided. He needed to make mistakes, too. If Gabriel made a mistake, he would learn important lessons about the world, far better than through any instruction.

. . .

Béatriz responded to Gabriel's gentlest cues, communicating with movements of her head and changes in her gait. On the muddy road into town, with open fields on either side and no one to slow him, Gabriel rode as he had not in many months: fast, his hair blowing in the cold wind. The unfamiliarity of his surroundings combined with the wild scent of the horse's sweat made him feel unfettered, free, invigorated.

In Valencia, it was the day of the monthly fair. Farmers, craftsmen, merchants, musicians, jugglers, beggars, ragged dogs, pickpockets, goats, chickens, and pigs crowded the center of town.

Gabriel tethered his horse outside the market square. On his hip he carried the pouch of coins his father had given him. While purchasing a thick slice of headcheese and a rye-bread roll, he decided his stay with his uncle could still be an adventure, after all.

A group of children danced in a circle to music played on panpipes, a tambour, a Jew's harp, and a zither. As Gabriel approached, swallowing his last bit of bread, a girl—whirling, with a flowered wreath in her hair and long chestnut locks—reached out for him. Gabriel took her hand and joined in the revelry, spinning, running to the center of the circle, clapping hands, tripping, laughing. He lost the girl, rejoined her, lost her again.

When he finally returned to his horse, exhausted and elated, two monks with brown tunics and short swords crossed the street to stop him.

"Excuse me, young man. Where did you get that jacket?"

Gabriel glanced down at his oxblood-and-blue striped jerkin. "Why do you ask?"

"We have our reasons."

"What kinds of reasons?"

"Important reasons. If you don't tell us where you got it, we'll have to arrest you, and then you'll have to confess to someone else."

Gabriel de Santángel stared at the monks with contempt. Who did they think they were, speaking to him in this manner? He was the son of the chancellor of Aragon! Ignoring their threat, he began mounting his horse. They pulled him down roughly and wrapped ropes around his wrists.

"Let go of me! Put me down, you donkeys! My father will have you whipped!" He struggled, kicked, tried to bite them.

. . .

Estefan Santángel asked his servants to arrange the boy's belongings and straighten his room. He directed his cook to prepare a meal for two: leek soup, a chicken-breast cake with crushed almonds, Majorcan cheese, and quince pie.

As midday approached, he worked in his study. When Gabriel failed to return, he hoped the boy was being capricious. As afternoon stretched into evening, he grew worried.

He rode into town, where he walked his horse through alleys and squares, asking whether anyone had seen Gabriel. He stopped at the small inn where Ferran Soto, the local chief of the Santa Hermandad, often drank with friends.

"Ferran, my good man, have you heard anything about a boy, so high, wearing a striped leather jerkin?"

"Do you know him?"

"It's my nephew. He's disappeared."

Ferran Soto furrowed his brow. "I've heard about him, Estefan, and so has everyone else. It wasn't our doing." The official was so drunk he could hardly stand. "The Holy Inquisition. They're the ones who took the child and his horse. What a pity."

"Took him? Where? Why would they seize a child?"

Ferran Soto shrugged. "He probably witnessed something."

"What could he have seen? The boy went to the fair! And why did no one notify me?"

"I don't know, Estefan. This is a crazy world. You might ask at Santo Juanes."

. . .

The church of Santo Juanes was quiet and empty. The priest emerged, a tall, wiry man just five years out of the seminary, with whom Estefan had taken confession many a Sunday morning.

"Father Muñoz, the Inquisition took my nephew. My brother, Luis de Santángel, the royal chancellor of Aragon, entrusted the boy to my care."

"You needn't worry, Estefan," the priest assured him. "No harm will come to the child."

"Allow me to visit with him."

"That I cannot do."

Estefan pushed past him to an inner door and shouted, "Gabriel, can you hear me?"

"Please, Estefan. In times like these, one must rely on one's faith."

"What does my faith have to do with this? This is about my nephew."

Two constables entered.

"Please, Estefan," the priest urged him. "God will answer your prayers. And mine."

"Gabriel," the tax collector shouted. "We'll get you out of here!"

The constables took him out.

. . .

Estefan could hardly work or eat. He drank himself to sleep, then woke hours later, terrified. He had betrayed his brother's trust. His nephew, a spirited and intelligent child, was in danger. He returned to the church every day for a week, pleading with Father Muñoz, calling to the boy. He hoped Gabriel would find courage in his uncle's voice.

At the Iglesia Mayor, the cathedral of Valencia, he asked to speak with the priest, Rodrigo de Borja, a man widely admired for his compassion and wisdom. Like Father Muñoz, Father de Borja listened, nodding sympathetically. "In the realm of Castile, today, as you know," this priest told him, "the Inquisition . . . How shall I put this? The Inquisition doesn't take orders from priests like me. But I shall inquire. I shall see what I can do."

Estefan called upon some of the most important men in the region, the masters of the stone-makers' and carpenters' guilds, the city treasurer. Some confided they had nothing to do with the Inquisition and wanted nothing to do with it. Others, more cautiously, assured him they trusted the inquisitors to do what was right—and that he should, as well.

He returned to Santo Juanes to plead with Father Muñoz. The priest informed him that "the boy" had been transferred to Zaragoza. Gabriel was in good health, he assured him.

Luis had been vague about his plans. Estefan dispatched a messenger to his brother, in the care of the king, but received no reply.

. . .

Two Dominican monks carted Gabriel de Santángel to La Seo Cathedral in Zaragoza. They locked him in a bare room in the rectory. He slept on a hard bench as often as he could, day and night, if only to erase his present circumstances from the slate of his mind.

"My child, sit up."

The air was fresh with the scent of morning. Gabriel heard a bird chirping. He opened his eyes. A man in a brown habit stood in front of him.

"It pains us grievously," the man said, "to see a well-born boy like you reduced to this condition."

He knelt before Gabriel. He took Gabriel's hands in his.

"We know you've been judaizing," Tomás de Torquemada said gently. "And we would like nothing more than to lead you back to the one true path. You're still so young. You have so much to see and do in this world before moving on to the next. The best thing for you right now would be to unburden your heart."

"Your words. What you're doing to me." Gabriel, his throat parched, spoke in a raw whisper. "I can't make sense of it." Why were they treating him like an infidel?

Torquemada repeated Gabriel's words, turning them over in his mouth like a sweetmeat. "You can't make sense of what we're doing. Perhaps you can help me, though." He reached into the pocket of his habit and produced the small, intricately adorned, silver hamsa hand that the monks had found in Gabriel's jerkin.

Gabriel looked at the hamsa hand he had stolen from Felipe de Almazón's home. He still had no idea what this object was or what it meant, but the queasy sensation he had felt in that closet of treasures returned when he saw the regretful look on the priest's face.

"Why don't you tell us who gave it to you? Was it your father? An uncle? An aunt?"

The boy shook his head. His mind turned, as so often since his arrest, to thoughts of his father. He was sure the powerful, universally admired Luis de Santángel would soon appear, fighting off his captors at the point of a sword, if need be.

"Who gave it to you?"

Gabriel turned his eyes back to him. "You're a monk. You have a special relationship with God, no?"

"Each of us has a special relationship with God."

"Do you talk to Him?"

"All the time."

"Does He listen to you?"

"He certainly does."

"Does He answer you?"

"Yes."

"Then why don't you ask Him where I got it?"

"God doesn't need to save His soul through the purifying act of confession," explained Torquemada patiently. "You do."

"I'm hungry," said Gabriel. "And cold."

Torquemada smiled. "Do you like pear cake?"

The thought of pear cake appealed so much to Gabriel, it caused his stomach to twinge. "Please."

"We'll give you some, fresh and warm, with almond milk. And a robe. You and I shall talk in the morning."

Gabriel watched Torquemada rise. He loomed above him like a demon or an angel, then swept out of the room, closing the door softly and locking it.

. . .

"You must keep in mind," observed Torquemada as he led Gabriel de Santángel to the ecclesiastical prison of Zaragoza, "this jail isn't administered by the Inquisition, but by the Kingdom of Aragon. And that is a most important distinction. The Holy Church never bloodies her hands with torture or death."

In showing the prison to the chancellor's son, he was not giving him special consideration; most prisoners of the Inquisition were granted a preliminary round through the facilities as a means of "moistening their lips."

Torquemada pulled open the heavy door of the unremarkable stone building. "We are a Church of compassion," he continued as he ushered Gabriel down the tight stairwell. "All we ask is that those who have erred confess and atone. Only if we cannot succeed do we send them here to the State. Even then, we do so with regret."

The warden met them at the bottom of the stairs. "Spiritual Father." He knelt to kiss the inquisitor's robe. Torquemada lowered his head and continued through the small arch. Gabriel followed.

The excremental stench made the boy dizzy. His eyes adjusted to the obscurity. Filthy, long-bearded men and half-naked women slouched upon the dirt floor, some of them groaning, others sleeping. A man with a gouged-out eye reached toward him, mumbling. A small one-legged woman, her hands chained to the wall, her hair twice as voluminous as her head, implored Gabriel with mad eyes.

"This," the inquisitor explained to the child, "is the fate we want you and your father to avoid."

The inquisitor opened a small door. Gabriel crossed himself and followed him inside the torture chamber. This room was cleaner, unoccupied except for the machines of torment positioned around its walls. Torquemada explained how they worked.

There was the scourge, a whip with multiple lashes, "like the ones the Jews used upon our Lord," Torquemada explained, "as He stumbled to his crucifixion." There was the rack, a wooden bed with gears and attachments at either end, for pulling a man's limbs apart. Torquemada demonstrated how it could be adjusted for a person of any height. There was the brazier for coals and the pincer, which, when glowing red-hot, warmed the soles of the feet, burned off hands, and tore flesh. There was the strappado, a pulley that suspended sinners mid-air and jerked them downward, with weights attached to their feet.

"All this, my son, I'm showing you in the hope that you and your father will avoid it. Because all the torments around you are nothing compared to the eternal agony of Hell."

That word *father* resounded in Gabriel's mind. Where was his father?

He looked up at the inquisitor and, despite himself, began weeping. Torquemada patted him on the back, pleased to see that young Gabriel understood the seriousness of his predicament. He was growing more and more confident the boy would be spared all but the mildest forms of torture—sleep deprivation and questioning.

"Come," offered the monk. He turned to go, but Gabriel's sobs seemed to prevent him from moving. Torquemada lifted him and carried him out of the chamber. As he continued up the stairs, Gabriel lowered his head onto the monk's shoulder.

. . .

Estefan Santángel lay awake on his bed, his wool jerkin wrinkled, his hair a tangled skein. He had rounds to make through the countryside, but found himself unable. He had not risen in days. His head throbbed. Casting his eyes about the room, he spied a half-empty jug of wine on the floor.

He sat up, leaned against the wall, and drank deeply. "I'm not riding into those stinking fields," he told himself, "to wrestle with angry peasants. Not today, and not tomorrow." He drank again.

Hours later, still rumpled and unwashed, Estefan trudged to the inn he had visited on the day of Gabriel's arrest. The room was dusky and clamorous. The air stank of beer and sweat. A fire blazed on the hearth.

A group of his drinking companions waved him to their table. Horacio, a rat catcher by trade, beckoned the innkeeper. "Another ale for our friend!"

Estefan plodded over and fell onto the bench.

Horacio noticed his unkempt appearance, dark orbits, and unbrushed hair. "Where have you been dragging that beefy rump of yours, Estefan?" Although Horacio earned his keep in the company of vermin, he was a prosperous and respected citizen.

The innkeeper plonked a mug of thick, black brew onto the table. Estefan grabbed it and thirstily quaffed.

He had not eaten, and the spirits affected him at once. "My beefy rump, as you so poetically put it," he told Horacio, "has been loath to raise itself from a horizontal bearing. Which is to say, I've been lying abed and would indeed still be there, had I not consumed all the wine on hand."

"Lying abed?" asked a stonemason, "at the height of tax season? Hardly sounds like you, Estefan."

"I am hardly myself these days."

"And the taxpayers thank you for it," bellowed Gustavo, the blacksmith's son.

Estefan turned to him. He had never much liked Gustavo, but he agreed. "It is a despicable, loathsome, and thoroughly deplorable way to earn one's beer, is it not?"

"What else can you do?" Gustavo comforted him. "You came into it honestly enough."

Estefan reared his head back and peered down his nose at him. "Just what do you mean by that, my good man?"

"Your father was a farmer of taxes, was he not? It's not like you inherited a blacksmith's shop."

"And what are you implying?"

"Why, nothing. What is the matter with you?"

The tax farmer drew a deep breath. "I'll tell you what's the matter. They took my nephew. A mere boy. God knows what they're doing to him."

"They? Who?" asked Horacio.

"The so-called Holy Inquisition. A bunch of louts."

The innkeeper refreshed mugs all around. "As you know, Señor Santángel, I hold you in high esteem. But I'll have none of that talk in my establishment."

"Then stay away from my table. You have other guests." Estefan closed his eyes, leaned back in his seat, and gulped more ale.

Across the room, Sancho Morales, an officer of the Santa Hermandad, picked up his lute and began plucking. What he lacked in skill, he made up for in vigor. A few others joined in, banging on mugs and tables. Juliana Méndez, the sultry young widow of a cobbler, known about town as a hussy, danced gaily. Others clapped, whistled, and stomped. The ruckus drowned Estefan's conversation, providing him with an excuse not to talk. He attacked his third mug.

A few young men danced by turns with Juliana. As she whirled past, she reached for Estefan's hand. He ignored her. Juliana insisted, calling him with her fingertips. Estefan closed his eyes and leaned back into the wall.

"You're not going to dance, Estefan?" Horacio seemed baffled.

Estefan ignored him, too.

"It's a Jewish holiday," Gustavo remarked.

The tax farmer half-opened his eyes. "And what do you mean by *that*, Gustavo? Must I dance, to be a good Christian?"

"Gustavo was jesting," said Horacio. "You've had too much drink, Estefan."

"You should know, you incorrigible souse." Estefan drained his mug.

"What was your nephew up to? Why did they take him?" Gustavo vigorously cleaned his ear with his little finger.

"They took him," Estefan raised his voice. "They took him because, as I said, they're nothing but a pack of rabid mongrels."

"Enough of this. I'm taking you home." Horacio had never seen Estefan in such a foul mood. He rose and tried to pull him up. The tax farmer resisted.

Sancho Morales ceased picking on his lute. Juliana Méndez stopped dancing. Estefan barely noticed.

"No one is taking me home, Horacio. And I'm not going to pretend," he was speaking to the entire room, now, "that I retain a shred of admiration for those splenetic choirboys, Torquemada and his minions. Not that I ever had much in the first place."

"What are you trying to do, señor?" asked Ferran Soto, seated at the table with Sancho Morales. "Why would you insult a venerable Christian institution? Without it, this land would fall into chaos. Is that what you want?"

"All I want is for your friends to free my nephew," muttered Estefan. "Whatever it costs."

"If the Inquisition took your nephew," said Soto, "they had their reasons. And your money won't save him. Nor will it save you, if you don't watch your tongue."

"You don't threaten me, Ferran."

"They say Jews can't hold a pint," the stonemason put in.

Estefan turned to him. "If I am a Jew, then you are the son of a storm-beaten trollop."

"Aye, a Jew tax farmer," added a peasant Estefan had never before seen. "And a flayer of honest Christians."

"Don't listen to them, Estefan," urged Horacio. "They're just as besotted as you. Let's go home."

"They're saying aloud what many think." Estefan glanced around. "I'm a Jew," he sneered. "And to think, I didn't know!"

"As long as you believe in the virgin birth," Ferran assured him, "and that Jesus Christ was the Son of God, let them say what they want."

"*Marrano*," someone muttered, the double *r*'s scurrying from his mouth like cockroaches. The word, derived from "swine," signified a *converso* who practiced Judaism in secret.

Estefan looked in the direction of the voice. A peasant sat drinking in the shadows. "I know you," said the tax farmer. "I've flayed you once or twice, haven't I."

"Aye, so you did, and told me you didn't believe."

"Didn't believe what?" asked Ferran.

"He said the Holy Mother of God was not a virgin."

The tavern erupted in indignant mutterings.

"I said that?" Estefan challenged him. "Since when do I discuss theology with illiterate peasants?"

"I know you believe in the virgin birth," Horacio urged the tax farmer. "Why don't you tell them?"

Estefan turned to him and opened his mouth. No words came out.

"And that Jesus Christ was the Son of God, too. You always said it. Just tell them." Horacio nodded encouragingly.

"You're a good man, Horacio," Estefan said finally.

Ferran Soto and Sancho Morales exchanged glances. "Horacio is right," said Ferran. "Go home, Estefan. I don't want to arrest you. I don't want to work tonight."

"Ah, threatening me again. Don't you see? I no longer care about your lances—or your pyres."

"You will care when you feel them."

"Ah, so I shall feel them."

"Yes, you will, if you don't stop insulting the Holy Inquisition."

"I don't need to insult her," said Estefan. "She insults herself, every time she arrests an innocent boy. Every time she murders men like me."

"She does so to protect the Holy Church," Ferran insisted.

"The Holy Church." Estefan snickered.

"That's enough."

Estefan drew a deep breath and quietly confessed, as if talking to himself, "I used to believe it. At least, I tried my damnedest. But now, with what's being done in His name . . ."

The fire crackled in the hearth. A mug softly smacked a table.

"Where's the mercy?" Estefan asked, looking around. "Where's the other cheek? *Where is He?*"

Ferran reluctantly nodded to Sancho Morales. Two Hermandad soldiers lumbered over to Estefan's table, stretched his arms around their shoulders, and pulled him out of the inn.

CHAPTER FIFTEEN

*B*ABA SHLOMO REACHED UP from his bed and squeezed Judith's arm: "That diplomat from Zaragoza, what was his name?"

"Santángel." Judith was surprised to learn that Baba Shlomo had been thinking of the chancellor as well.

"Yes, yes, Santángel. He showed up here for a reason."

"Why do you think he came?"

"First, give me some tea."

Judith held a cup to his lips. When he finished sipping, she dabbed his chin with a towel.

"I'd like to visit my parents' graves."

"In Zaragoza?" Judith could hardly imagine such a journey.

"It will be a pilgrimage."

"How long a pilgrimage? A month? Two? With no income?"

"Maybe two months," Baba Shlomo agreed, "at a leisurely pace. You've had little work, lately."

Although Judith had not spoken with him, recently, about her work, she could hardly deny that ever since the Christians had captured Velez-Malaga, commerce between Granada and the rest of the world had all but halted. Local residents, too, were spending less.

"Zaragoza still has a Jewish quarter," said Baba Shlomo. "We may find new clients. What other hope do we have?"

Judith offered him another sip of tea. "It would be dangerous."

"I survived it. I was a child, fleeing, with nothing. Things here are becoming impossible, anyway."

Judith heard the clop of a man's mules. She looked up. Isaac Azoulay, in his indigo silk robes, stopped at the doorway.

"We were waiting for you," said Judith.

Isaac knelt at Baba Shlomo's bedside. "We've missed you in synagogue," he told him. "We've been praying for your health." He examined the color of the old man's skin.

"And what went on that was different from any other week?"

"There was a heated discussion."

"On what subject?" asked Baba Shlomo.

"Granada's destiny. Our destiny."

"What did they conclude?" asked Judith.

The physician turned to her. "Our rulers will fight valiantly, but our kingdom will fall. Maybe next year, maybe in ten years. As for us, it's anyone's guess. They say Fernando and Ysabel have been protective of their Jews."

Judith put down Baba Shlomo's cup. "Would you care for some tea?"

"No, thank you." Isaac pulled down the lower lids of Baba Shlomo's eye, looked at his sclera, felt his pulse.

Most illnesses involved a disproportionate blend of the four humors, the vital liquids that flowed through human bodies. While conversing with Judith and Baba Shlomo, Isaac tried to determine whether the old man felt slow and indolent, due to an excess of phlegm, or melancholic, with too much black bile. In making his diagnosis, the physician also took into account Baba Shlomo's eye color and skin temperature.

He asked Judith out to the courtyard. "Let's not be naive. Baba Shlomo has lived a long life. I'll prescribe an infusion of verbena and peony, which, if properly mixed and depending on astrological conditions, may cause his symptoms to subside. It's also important that he walk or at least sit up every day. To lie down is to welcome Death. And make sure he eats meat."

"Thank you, Isaac."

He nodded and turned to leave.

Judith stopped him. "He wants to travel. He can't get out of bed, but he's talking about journeying all the way to Zaragoza. A pilgrimage, he calls it."

Isaac smiled at the folly of it, but then said, perhaps in jest, "If it gives him a reason to rise from his bed, it might be of benefit."

Judith watched Isaac exit her courtyard. She wondered whether the streets of Zaragoza resembled the narrow, steep alleys of Granada. Her own great-grandparents, on her mother's side, had lived there. She wondered how far the chancellor resided from the Jewish quarter.

"Third generation," he had said. The grandson of an apostate. He carried himself like a nobleman, with all the impassivity and smugness the highest titles can bestow. She remembered his glances, that evening, his unflinching eyes.

CHAPTER SIXTEEN

A LIGHT RAIN FELL on Valencia. Returning to his brother's home with Iancu, after an absence of almost four months, Santángel saw from a distance that the gates were closed. He rode closer and noticed the heavy chains. Slowing his horse, he tried to quiet his racing mind. He dismounted, pounded on the doors, and rattled the metal links.

"Estefan!"

Only the wind answered.

"Gabriel!" He shook the gates a second time. He leaned against them, breathing hard, his eyes darting about for clues.

A peasant hummed a simple tune as he drove his mule up the street. Santángel hailed him: "My good man. This property, do you know anything about it?"

The peasant stopped and bowed. "My lord?"

"This gate, why is it chained? Does no one live here?"

"No one lives there," confirmed the peasant.

"Are you familiar with the goings-on in this street? Or do you rarely come this way?"

"I walk down this street every morning, and up it every evening, my lord."

"The owner of this house," insisted Santángel. "Do you know him?"

"Know him? Me? Oh, no, señor." The peasant laughed, shaking his head. "But I have seen him."

"How long has the house been empty? How long has this gate been chained?"

"Maybe a month."

"They moved out?"

"They moved out."

"They moved out, or they were taken out?"

"People say they took him to Zaragoza," he said at last. "I don't know more." He waved a fly from his head.

The peasant continued on his way.

Iancu came closer, searching the chancellor's crumpled face. He waited, then began in a quiet voice, "On the ocean crossing, my wife. They . . . they insulted. They raped. They laughed. Like an old rug, they threw her overboard." He stopped, his face twisted. "They tied us—me, Dumitru—in hold. No light. But we heard. We heard her screams. My boy. He heard his mother's screams." He clenched his jaw and stared beyond Santángel. "If I may." The former captive spread his arms and hugged the chancellor tightly.

No one unrelated to Santángel had ever ventured such intimacy. Finding consolation in their shared misery, the chancellor allowed the burly foreigner to hold him.

. . .

Since relocating to Zaragoza, Tomás de Torquemada had discovered he preferred the calm of La Veruela Monastery to the noise and bustle of La Seo Cathedral. Tonight, however, all was not quiet. Waking well before matins, he heard voices and rose from bed.

"Señor Santángel," one of the inquisitor's guards was saying, "allow me to remind you that this edifice belongs to God. The Holy Church is obligated to protect it. We have the power to arrest noblemen, as well as servants of the court, even in Aragon."

"No, my good man," came the voice of Luis de Santángel. "You do not have that power."

Torquemada was pleased that the chancellor had finally deigned to pay him a visit, but he did not approve of his sentry's tone. Now that he had the chancellor in his territory, Torquemada saw no reason to insult him.

"And what is it," asked the guard, "that you are seeking?"

"I'm here to speak with Father Torquemada."

"At this hour?"

"Indeed."

The inquisitor general, now fully clothed, pulled the door open to face the chancellor. "Light the candles in my front room," Torquemada commanded his sentry. He turned to Santángel. "We have much to discuss." He ushered him into his private chambers.

"Where is my son?" Santángel's voice hardly masked his desperation and fear. "Where is my brother? Four days ago, in Valencia, I found his home empty, the gates chained. And where is my maidservant, Leonor? My home, too, is empty. Surely you haven't seized them all."

Torquemada smiled graciously. "I'll try to answer your questions, Señor Santángel. We're taking good care of your son, right here in this building. We had no plans to arrest your brother. That was his own doing. He'll soon join us here."

A servant lit the candles. "And my maidservant?" demanded Santángel. "What do you hope to accomplish?"

"I know nothing about your maidservant." Torquemada sat down at the table. He gestured for the chancellor to do the same. "You've been traveling. I travel, too. I know how it wearies the flesh."

"Yes, I've been traveling," said Santángel, "on business for the Crown. My son, Gabriel, what have you done to him?"

"You have your expectations of this meeting, Señor Santángel. We have ours."

The chancellor understood the friar's expectations all too well: to entrap him, seize his wealth, and make an example of him, happily destroying his family in the process. Yet, if he did not treat Torquemada with respect, or at least restraint, he risked increasing the danger to Gabriel and Estefan.

"And what are your expectations?"

"I want to understand why Christians—*conversos*, in particular—are drawn to heresy, even when they know how much they have to lose, not just in this temporal world, but in the world beyond."

"Why are *conversos* attracted to heresy?" asked Santángel. "I'm afraid I can't shed any light on that."

"Allow me to think more highly of you."

"Where is my son?"

"I wouldn't think of depriving Gabriel of a visit with his father. But first, let me glean what advantage I can from the honor of your visit with me."

Santángel waited for more.

"You see," the Dominican continued, folding his hands on the table, "I could preach to New Christians forever. The proof that Christ is the Messiah, that He came in fulfillment of the Jews' own prophecies, is visible to all who want to see. The proof that the Jews lost favor with God when they rejected Him is no less obvious. Did Jesus not say to them, 'Ye are of your father the devil, and the lusts of your father ye will do'?"

"I can't argue theology with you, Father. You would surely win."

"So then," the monk pursued, "one has to ask, are the Jews, and the judaizing *conversos*, incapable of seeing and comprehending this irrefutable proof? Are they 'invincibly ignorant,' to use Augustine's term? Or do they actually *know* they're wrong, but persist in their pernicious beliefs out of a perverse, sick willfulness? Did they murder our Lord in the full knowledge that he was their Messiah, as Thomas Aquinas maintains? These questions, Señor Santángel, they haunt me."

"So I see."

"I believe you know the answers. Your help could be invaluable."

"Why do you believe that?"

"For example, there was a certain dinner, at the residence of Señor Felipe de Almazón."

"He was my aide. He invited me to meet his wife and children. It was only proper that I accept. Why should that interest you?"

"Any heretical behavior, in any context, is of interest to the Church."

The chancellor drummed his fingers on the table, then stopped himself. "A dinner with one's aide is heresy?"

"The prayers that were uttered at that dinner. For that alone, Señor Santángel, I could have you burned at the stake."

Santángel was not surprised that his son had betrayed him. How could a mere boy be expected to hold out against all the machinery of the Inquisition? "I didn't utter any prayers at that dinner. But I am praying now."

Torquemada lowered his face and looked up at him.

Santángel swallowed, a knot in his throat. "I'm praying you haven't been torturing my son."

"There's also the log of Señor de Almazón's confessions. It disappeared from the canon's chambers the night of the murder. Hardly a coincidence, one would think."

Santángel wondered what Torquemada expected him to say. Did he know the log had disappeared *before* the night of the murder? Had it *ever* been kept in the canon's chambers with the other logs?

"Please, Father, allow me to see my son."

"Be my guest." Torquemada rose to usher the chancellor out of the room.

. . .

Gabriel occupied a private cell with a trunk, a bed, and a small window set high in the wall. Luis found him sitting at his desk, parsing the Latin words of a large book. Hearing the door open, the boy looked up and saw his father enter with the inquisitor, looking harried and undone.

Santángel inwardly thanked God that Gabriel was alive, that the Inquisition was treating him in a manner befitting a thirteen-year-old of his station. He rushed to embrace his son.

Gabriel swallowed and blinked, but did not rise. "Where were you?"

"On a mission for the Crown. You know that. Come, Gabriel, my young knight."

Gabriel remained seated. "Every day, I prayed you'd come."

"I am so sorry. If only I had known . . ." He yearned to take his son in his arms, but Gabriel turned back to his reading.

"Gabriel, show respect for your father," said Torquemada.

"Yes, Father," replied the boy as he rose.

"What are you reading?" Luis de Santángel sought his son's eyes. Gabriel kept them fixed on the inquisitor. Santángel placed a hand on the boy's shoulder. Gabriel shrugged it off.

"Father Torquemada wanted me to learn more about my . . . my grandparents' faith."

"And what, precisely, are you learning?"

Finally, Gabriel turned to his father. "I've learned how the Jews stab the flesh of Christ, the host wafer used in our Mass, until it bleeds, as part of their ritual. I found out how they poison wells to spread the plague, and why they kill Christian babies."

"And why do the Jews kill Christian babies?"

"They need their blood for the unleavened bread they eat on Easter."

Santángel stood and leaned over Gabriel's desk. *Fortalitium Fidei* had been manufactured cheaply on a printing press, in only two colors, red and black. He flipped backward, his hands shaking, to the title page. "Who is this Alfonso de Espina?"

"An itinerant monk," answered Torquemada. "A skilled orator, they say. The people are drawn to him, from Sevilla to Nuremberg."

Santángel closed the book. "And what does he suggest we do about this stubborn, hateful people?"

"He proposes we eliminate them," said Torquemada. "Them and all their descendents." He placed a hand on the boy's back. "I, however," continued the inquisitor, "do not share his opinion. Those who truly repent, those who humbly prostrate themselves before the Lord to ask His forgiveness and guidance, must be welcomed into His flock."

"But how do you know," probed Santángel, "what someone thinks or feels in the private depths of his heart?"

"You are quite right, Chancellor," said Torquemada. "There's no substitute for constant vigilance. Even the most sincere will sometimes relapse."

"Perhaps. Regardless, it's time my son came home."

"Why don't we leave that decision to him?" Torquemada turned to the boy. "You may leave this monastery whenever you like, Gabriel. However, whatever you decide, as penitence for the improper thoughts to which you've confessed, you'll have to participate in an auto-da-fé, to make your confession public, and to be judged."

"When?"

"I cannot say. The investigation may take years. But however long it takes, if you stay with us, we'll offer you peace, study, and reconciliation with God. We shall prepare you well, and the outcome will reflect your newfound faith."

Gabriel eased himself back into his chair, looking down, and folded his arms on his chest. "I shall stay, Father."

"Are you certain of that?"

Gabriel nodded.

"Why?" Santángel asked in a whisper.

Gabriel stared at his hands. "All those years, when I pretended to be a knight, we both knew it would never happen. My father was away and I was just a scared child waving his sword at the darkness. But now . . ." He raised his eyes. "Now I have a cause worth fighting for."

The chancellor stiffened and turned back to Torquemada. "Regardless of what my son wants," he insisted, "I still have authority over him."

"So you do," agreed the inquisitor. "And I have the authority to arrest and try you for judaizing. I have, however, chosen not to exercise that authority for the time being. We're quite pleased with your son's progress, but he still needs our support and love."

Santángel looked at Gabriel, who was trying to find his place in the book. He took Gabriel's head in his hands and kissed it, his lips lingering on his son's hair.

⋅ ⋅ ⋅

Torquemada wondered what Juan Rodríguez had failed to tell him about his interview with the chancellor's maidservant. With Santángel complaining about Leonor's disappearance, Torquemada remembered the way Rodríguez had stared at her in the seminarians' room. He recalled Rodríguez's unspeakable act before the Holy Virgin and the rumors he had heard about Rodríguez's criminal past. The inquisitor had prayed for his constable. He hoped that Rodríguez's devotion to Christ and His Church was transforming him.

Although Rodríguez was not a monk himself, Torquemada found him the next morning in the crypt of La Seo, far beneath the cathedral's nave, participating in a mortification exercise with a small congregation of Dominicans.

Rather than interrupt the religious observance of the monks downstairs, the inquisitor waited until his constable climbed out of the crypt. His tunic stained with sweat and blood, Rodríguez saw him and turned. He knelt beside Torquemada as if asking forgiveness.

"What is it, my son? What is troubling you? Raise your eyes." He placed his palm under the constable's chin and elevated his face.

"You know, don't you."

"I know what, my son?"

"I murdered her, Father. I fornicated with her, and then I killed her, although I didn't mean to."

"The chancellor's maidservant?"

"I believe she was a witch."

"Why do you believe that?"

"From the moment I saw her, my heart was filled with lust. I've heard that witches use spells to make you their captive, to take away your powers of reason."

Torquemada's voice remained calm and low. "Even so, my son, even if this woman was a disciple of Satan, that would have been for the Holy Inquisition to determine. We can't have laymen conducting their own private inquisitions, can we? They—you—have neither the skills nor the sanction of the Church."

"No, of course not. I have sinned, Father. Send me to the ecclesiastical jail, I beg you."

"Does anyone else know?"

"Only the two constables who were with us. They've sworn not to speak of it."

"What did you do with her body?"

"They helped me carry it into the forest and bury it."

"How did you pay them?"

"With the money I inherited from my uncle, who raised me. He was a candle maker. I now have nothing, Father, other than what the Church provides."

Torquemada nodded. "That will be all."

Tentatively, Rodríguez posed one further question: "Am I forgiven?"

"No. Go to the jail, as your heart dictates. Sit among other sinners and meditate upon your failures."

"And then, shall I be forgiven?" the constable was unable to hold back his tears.

"All who genuinely seek the Lord's compassion," Torquemada replied gently, "if they're willing to pay the price, will receive it."

The constable accepted the sentence gratefully. He had hardly dared imagine that the portals of heaven could open for him. Now God's representative was promising that absolution was possible even for one so depraved.

He kissed the hem of the inquisitor general's habit, then slowly stood. Torquemada did not turn to watch him leave the church but knelt in prayer. Despite Juan Rodríguez's despicable weakness, Torquemada trusted that he knew good from evil. Rodríguez would walk to the ecclesiastical jail without an escort. His period of penance, the inquisitor general decided, should not be long.

. . .

Estefan Santángel sat in a dark, dirt-floored cell in the ecclesiastical jail of Valencia. Chained to the wall, he could hardly ignore the other prisoners' groans and vile utterances. The guards woke him for water and bread at random hours. Sometimes they poured a jug of cold water over his head to rouse him. Other times they prodded him with a hot iron. In the unending twilight, Estefan lost his sense of time: how long he had been there, how much longer he might remain.

He conjured every detail of his drunken behavior in the tavern. "I was soused! Do they hold you to everything that comes out of your mouth, or fails to come out of your mouth, when you're wet as a frog? What do I know about Judaism? What do I care?"

No inquisitor came to query him about his remembrance, or his excuses. No one asked for penitence or offered absolution. Estefan's belly was shrinking. His beard was growing tangled.

After uncounted months, two constables entered his cell, bundled him in a blanket, and hauled him out to a cart. The cart barreled and bumped over rugged highways for three days. They threw him like a sack of grain into another dank, penumbral cell.

In moments of lucidity, he wondered whether there was not a meaning to his incarceration, a reason for the events occurring around him. He found himself meditating upon the nature of belief and belonging, upon the unrequited love his adoptive parents had shown him and their loyalty to the half-digested, minimal Judaism they had tried to instill in him. He thought about death, how death might bring fulfillment to his life. His soreness slowly grew familiar.

He tried to conjure from memory the Sabbath blessings. He wondered what function those blessings could provide in a place like this, where time no longer existed. He concluded that time was what the Sabbath was about, marking and dignifying the separation of the weeks. Although he could not know whether today was Saturday or Wednesday, he would reconstruct the Sabbath prayers in his mind, piece by piece, and recite what he remembered, if only in protest, to remind himself he was human.

. . .

The rack occupied the place of honor in the center of the torture room. The subject lay on its wooden plate, feet and hands tied to the frame. When the torturer turned a handle, the roller advanced one notch. Each notch pulled the subject's limbs slowly apart. Muscles stretched, ligaments popped. The pain was excruciating. A full course of torture upon the rack would prevent a man from ever walking again. Few required such extreme measures. Confessions spilled out much sooner than that.

No one could pretend to be courageous for very long. Estefan Santángel was no exception. He groaned, his face drenched in tears, his teeth clattering, his body trembling and sweating. He mouthed to himself, "It will soon be over."

"I'm sorry. What did you say?" asked Torquemada, sitting near him.

At a table in the corner, a small Latin scribe, tonsured, copied every word.

"I was praying," Estefan whispered.

"In Hebrew, or in Latin?"

"In His language," Estefan replied with as much force as he could muster. It came out as a croak.

The inquisitor waited. The tax farmer was sealing his own fate. "I need a confession, Señor Santángel. For your own sake."

Estefan said something. Torquemada leaned toward the *converso*, his ear close to his mouth.

"What do you need?"

"I need you to tell me about your secret practice of the Jewish faith. Who taught you? With whom did you pray? Why did you abandon the Christianity that was offered to you, a precious gift, in the holy sacrament of baptism?"

Estefan seemed half-conscious. Torquemada waited. Finally, his eyes closed, Estefan muttered, "The God of the Jews, the God of the Christians, they're the same God. If Jesus could pray to Him, why can't I?"

Torquemada shook his head. In his most soothing, pedantic tone, the inquisitor explained, "There are many things you cannot possibly do that our Lord Jesus Christ could do. Can you walk on water? Can you raise someone from the dead? Can you cause a tree to wither?"

The tax farmer did not respond.

"So what makes you think that you, Señor Santángel, of all people, can approach the Father directly, without going through the Son? What makes you so special?"

Estefan closed his eyes. It seemed to him that no amount of torture, no explanation he could come up with, could satisfy his tormentor. It almost seemed, bizarrely and perversely, that Torquemada needed him to come around, to admit that he saw things as the Inquisition did, in order to justify Torquemada's own convictions.

Estefan tried again. "Please, Father, give me my body back, and I shall gladly expose to you my soul."

"Who killed Pedro de Arbués? Who stole Felipe de Almazón's confessions? What was in them that merited such violence?" One of the many techniques in the inquisitor's arsenal was the use of the non sequitur. His aim was to catch his subject off guard.

"No . . . idea . . ."

"The chancellor, your brother, Luis de Santángel. He was surely involved, was he not?"

Estefan swallowed. "No. Luis is no murderer."

Torquemada sighed, discouraged. He nodded to the tall, hooded torturer, who turned the wheel one more notch. Again, Estefan moaned.

The inquisitor general ushered the scribe and the torturer out of the room and blew out the candle on the sconce, leaving Estefan taut on the rack, in the dark.

Outside the torture chamber, the inquisitor turned to the scribe who had been assisting him. "Hernández, where have you been this past year?"

"I have been living in the Monasterio de Piedra. I had much to contemplate, Father."

"Don't we all. But tell me, you worked with Father Arbués, did you not?"

"Yes."

"Do you recall the testimony of an officer in the king's chancellery, Felipe de Almazón?"

"Yes, Father."

"To your knowledge, did Arbués share this with anyone else?"

"Certainly not."

"Did Almazón speak of a plot? Did you hear anything related to the murder?"

The scribe gave this a moment's thought. "Not that I recall. It's all in the log."

"The log is missing. Come with me."

. . .

In his dining room, by the light of a single, fat taper, Luis de Santángel contemplated the pawns and knights on a chess board he had purchased after his son was born. Here, over the years, he had instructed Gabriel when to move boldly and when to devise a subtle strategy, when to surprise and when to challenge. Now he sat alone, trying to play both sides. He pushed rosewood kings and olivewood bishops from square to square, but his mind was elsewhere.

He remembered the expression on his departed wife's face when, thirteen years earlier, she had clasped their newborn to her chest. The physician could not stop her bleeding. She knew she was dying, but she smiled. She turned her eyes to her husband and wordlessly told him she trusted him to nurture their child.

Had she lived, Santángel asked himself, who would Gabriel be today? He would have received a secret Jewish education, as had all the males in her family. He would have prepared and celebrated a secret bar mitzvah, even while attending Mass and studying Aquinas. He would have learned that faith is more about posing questions than receiving answers. This knowledge would have protected him, perhaps, from the lies of an Alfonso de Espina. Santángel could no longer see his wife, but he still felt her eyes upon him. He felt other eyes, too, those of his mother.

He remembered the morning she had roused him and Estefan, well before dawn, two days after his grandfather had died. He was eleven years old.

"Can you keep a secret?"

"Yes, Mother."

"We are going to visit a garden. A very special garden. A garden of death. Your grandfather wanted this. One day you will understand. Wake your brother. Get out of bed. Get dressed. Nothing showy. Linen, not wool. Brown, not crimson."

The two boys, Luis and Estefan, groggily rose and dressed, pulling tight the cords around their brown tunics.

"You must never tell anyone. Or you, too, will surely die."

"Must we go?" the boys whined, practically in unison. At that young age, Estefan sometimes mimicked his older brother.

"We must. You will understand. But never tell anyone."

In a rickety work cart, led by a burro so as not to attract attention, their majordomo Hernán drove them to the cemetery beside the cathedral. Standing on either side of their mother, whose hands rested upon their shoulders, the two boys watched as Hernán unearthed their grandfather's coffin.

"Why is Hernán doing this?" Luis swallowed, hardly able to speak. "Is this not a sin?"

"Hush."

Little Estefan fidgeted.

As his grandfather's coffin cleared the earth, the cathedral bells began ringing, announcing matins. Hastily, Hernán refilled the hole and topped it with sod.

Together, they lifted the coffin into the cart. "Your grandfather wanted this," their mother reminded them in a whisper.

Sitting in the cart with his brother and mother as it rolled through the city, still in darkness, Luis rested his hand on the simple oak box, redolent of mud and worms. How could it contain the silent, insensible body of the man who had kneeled at his bedside so recently, telling him a story about a hidden treasure, a story Luis would repeat to his own son years later?

They transported the coffin to a smaller cemetery in an unknown quarter. A group of men with skullcaps and beards met them. As dawn broke, these men directed them to a part of the cemetery where the grass grew high. Strange signs and symbols adorned the gravestones: gashes and dashes, triangles and circles. The men asked Luis's mother to tear a part of her dress. Luis's mother, usually more comfortable dispensing orders than receiving them, complied with a sniffle, like an obedient child.

They had already dug the hole. The transplantation of Luis's grandfather proceeded rapidly as the bearded men mumbled incantations in a foreign tongue. All this seemed aberrant and perilous. Luis's mind burned with questions.

. . .

As dawn broke, he pushed the chess pieces off the board, found a feather pen and paper, and began writing a heartfelt missive to the king:

> *My Liege,*
> *A terrible scourge has befallen our land. It is a pestilence born not of poison, nor from Divine wrath, but from suspicion, envy, and counterfeit righteousness. Its victims—dare I pen my inmost certitudes?—include not only our most evil, but some of our most*

*noble and more than a few of our most innocent citizens. I know
this well, for my own son, whom Your Highness may recall holding
in his arms when he was but a newborn, must unfortunately be
counted among them, as well as my very brother . . .*

Santángel carefully folded the letter, sealed it with wax, and carried it down to the great room, where he found his majordomo building the morning fire.

"Iancu, see this gets to the king as soon as possible. I want his signature on the delivery log."

"My lord." Iancu took the letter, leaving Santángel alone in the vast, empty hall, trying to warm his hands at the small fire.

. . .

The chancellor attended High Mass in the cathedral. He had not set foot in La Seo since the night of the murder. The gothic demons and horsemen seemed to snarl at him from the arches of the doorways. The very stones of the walls accused him.

As he took his place in the pews, he noticed a small, familiar statue in a dedicated niche, surrounded by candles. Jacob, wrestling with his mirror-image angel. Under torture, Felipe must have mentioned the coffin of angels buried in his courtyard. Soldiers of the Inquisition, in their quest to retrieve the evidence, would immediately have dug it up. Recognizing the beauty of Felipe's sculpture, the care and passion with which he had fashioned it, and fearing Felipe's supposedly heretical intent, they must then have rededicated the statue to the service of Jesus Christ. Tears in his eyes, Santángel turned away from Jacob and the angel.

Monsignor Pedro de Monterubio led the Mass. His adjutant, Raimundo Díaz de Cáceres, administered the Eucharist.

Santángel knelt to receive the wafer of Christ's flesh into his mouth. He and the priest avoided looking at each other.

"We must talk," whispered Cáceres after uttering the benediction in Latin.

"Come tonight," Santángel whispered back.

. . .

Santángel found Cáceres waiting outside his manor.

"I have it." The priest turned his back to the street and removed a large book, similar to the volumes on Pedro de Arbués's bookshelves, from under his cape. He handed it to the chancellor.

"How? Where?"

"We're not alone. We have helpers."

"Have you read it?"

"Not yet."

"Thank you." Santángel clutched it to his chest.

"Do we know who took this down?"

"No."

Pedro de Arbués, that cagey realist, had omitted the name of the scribe. "One other thing. My brother. Has he been transferred to the ecclesiastical jail, here in Zaragoza?"

"I shall find out."

"Please. And if so, let me know what bribe I can use to gain admittance."

. . .

The chancellor spent the night deciphering the sometimes clumsy Latin hand of the late canon's scribe. In the halting, back-and-forth manner of forced confessions, it told of a man who had learned as a child that Jews were not human. They were dogs.

FATHER ARBUÉS: *From whom did you learn this?*
ALMAZÓNUS: *From you, Father. In La Seo. You preached . . .*
FATHER ARBUÉS: *"Beware the dogs, the evil workers, the mutilation."*
ALMAZÓNUS: *Yes.*
FATHER ARBUÉS: *Saint Paul, Philippians three two. Beware the circumcision.*
ALMAZÓNUS: *Yes.*
FATHER ARBUÉS: *Do you recall the rest?*
ALMAZÓNUS: *The rest?*
FATHER ARBUÉS: *Of that sermon.*
ALMAZÓNUS: *Not sure.*

FATHER ARBUÉS: *Saint John Chrysostom?*
ALMAZÓNUS: *No. No, I don't.*
FATHER ARBUÉS: *"Although these beasts, these Jew-dogs, are unfit for nourishment or work, they are fit for killing."*

The interrogation continued along these lines, Arbués probing Felipe de Almazón's understanding of the underlying issues, for several pages. In a later session, the inquisitor took a different tack.

FATHER ARBUÉS: *When did you first learn that you belonged to the species of Jew dogs? When did you . . .*
ALMAZÓNUS: *My cousin's domain. Outside Madrid.*
FATHER ARBUÉS: *His name?*
ALMAZÓNUS: *Antón María Méndez y Flores, the Marquis of Tarazona.*
FATHER ARBUÉS: *How did this happen?*
ALMAZÓNUS: *We jousted, then swam. When he removed his clothes, I saw.*
FATHER ARBUÉS: *You saw?*
ALMAZÓNUS: *His mutilation.*
FATHER ARBUÉS: *He was circumcised? How old were you?*
ALMAZÓNUS: *Seventeen. I remember because . . . because his father died that year.*
FATHER ARBUÉS: *Before this event, or after? His father's death.*
ALMAZÓNUS: *A few months before. And then . . . Antón learned. He learned . . . about his secret past.*
FATHER ARBUÉS: *He mutilated himself, this cousin of yours? Or did someone else . . .*
ALMAZÓNUS: *Yes. Himself.*

At this point, Pedro de Arbués's questions veered away from Felipe de Almazón's narrative into a lengthy effort to catalog every relative of the subject, living and dead, to determine whether each may have secretly met with Antón's father, been exposed to the family secret, espoused heretical doctrines, or otherwise shown signs of deviance. Luis de Santángel thumbed rapidly through these pages, then stopped again.

After he returned from his shattering visit with his cousin, Felipe had attempted to banish any thought that his blood might be impure. He attended Mass more regularly, read the Gospel nightly, meditated with the rosary, confessed his sins.

One afternoon, while rehearsing his lance technique, he fell from his horse and seriously injured his shoulder. The doctor who treated him, Isaac Buendía, an Israelite, prescribed balms and rest. In the privacy of his closed bedroom, during one of this doctor's visits, Felipe related what he had learned from his cousin.

This particular confession took place in Felipe's cell, rather than in the torture room:

FATHER ARBUÉS: *This was when, precisely?*

ALMAZÓNUS: *I met my wife at that time, so it was . . .*

FATHER ARBUÉS: *Eight years ago.*

ALMAZÓNUS: *Yes.*

FATHER ARBUÉS: *What did this physician tell you?*

ALMAZÓNUS: *Nothing, at first.*

FATHER ARBUÉS: *And then?*

ALMAZÓNUS: *I asked many questions.*

FATHER ARBUÉS: *What did you ask him?*

ALMAZÓNUS: *Is Jewishness a matter of blood, or faith? Do Jews believe in salvation? Who gets saved? What about Christ's miracles?*

FATHER ARBUÉS: *What did Dr. Buendía tell you?*

ALMAZÓNUS: *He finally answered some of my questions.*

FATHER ARBUÉS: *Which ones?*

As dawn approached, the chancellor neared the part of the story he already knew. Under torture, Felipe de Almazón spoke of meetings he had attended, some in the homes of high-ranking functionaries including the chancellor himself. To believe his testimony, the court of King Fernando was as surcharged with covert judaizers as a knight's wounded leg with maggots applied by a skilled surgeon. Their fraternity had all the attributes of a classic cabal: a secret language, the promise of special proximity to God, a small number of people deemed worthy of trust.

Felipe also mentioned an ancient parchment. He described Ser-ero's refusal to translate or discuss it: "the Christians" had massacred Jews because of the story it told. This detail, Santángel knew, would have piqued Tomás de Torquemada's curiosity more than any other words in Felipe's story.

Sunrise was breaking in the east. Luis de Santángel could not fall asleep with the inquisitorial log in his arms, or even in his house. He carried it downstairs to the fireplace. He stood watching the flames as they crawled across the pages.

CHAPTER SEVENTEEN

*T*HE CANNON BLASTS and church bells had finally ceased. In place of their infernal noise, the wind howled, a child cried, a door creaked. The city of Almeria was all but destroyed. Here and there, fires still smoldered in the burnt-out shells of homes, mosques, and shops. Cannonballs, stones, and the remains of fallen buildings littered the narrow streets and the small, irregularly shaped plazas. Mothers sat on the ground, their children in their laps, some wearing all that was left to them. Fathers—the proud in silk robes, the humble in tattered tunics—gathered in the squares, wondering what would become of them now that the fighting was over. They would have to wait until dawn to learn of King Fernando's intentions.

. . .

In a tent outside the city, the king consulted with Fray Hernando de Talavera, the prior of Prado. What should he do with the residents of Almeria? Should they be slaughtered? Should they be forcibly converted to Christianity?

A man of great learning, Talavera was known as a rival of Tomás de Torquemada. This was, indeed, why Fernando had invited him. The king had begun, of late, to loathe the inquisitor general, despite the queen's admiration of him.

Father Talavera combed his long, forked beard with his fingers, considering his response to the king's questions. "Sire, your goal should not be to conquer cities; your goal should be to win the hearts of your new subjects. And to accomplish that, you must be generous."

"How so, generous?"

"You mustn't allow your soldiers to plunder Almeria, to rape women and murder children. Offer the people the rights and privileges of your best citizens. After all, that's what you hope they'll become."

Fernando poured wine for himself and his guest. "Plunder. Rape. Murder. You pronounce these words as if you were talking about Satan, Father."

"I am talking about Satan."

Fernando observed Talavera's face. Like caves under a cliff, his dark eyes sat deep within his high forehead. A semicircle of curly gray hair covered the sides and back of his tonsured head, but his forked beard, which reached the top of his chest, was still brown. Overall, the mismatched look of a man who cared little about his appearance but to whom God had given a set of handsome, symmetrical features.

"But isn't it proper to annihilate evil?" inquired Fernando. "Is it not correct to demolish the pride of people who think themselves superior, but who are, in truth, only misguided?"

"To demolish their pride is merely a way of asserting your own pride."

"Take care with your tone, Father. If we don't humble them, and undermine their certainty that God is on their side, Almeria will become a breeding ground for heresy."

"Heresy," countered Talavera, "is not sin; it is error. And it is best corrected not through torture, but through love."

Fernando had never heard a man of the Church speak this way. He wondered whether Hernando de Talavera might not himself be guilty of heresy. Yet he also admired the man's courage. He drained his cup and refilled it.

"They hate us," said the king. "When you're too generous with those who hate, they'll take whatever you give them and use it against you. I can't risk having to quell rebellions while I'm trying to advance my front line."

"Then exile them," suggested the monk. "Separate them. You can't have a mass rebellion when there is no mass. Offer them houses to replace the homes you've destroyed. The good Lord knows, the New Inquisition has seized enough villas and manor houses. Give some to the people of Almeria. Transform your enemies into loyal subjects. Is that not what Your Highness desires?"

Apparently, this man was not going to adjust his views to those of his audience, even if his audience was the king. "Thank you, Fray Talavera. It is late. We have much to accomplish in the morrow."

. . .

The next morning, a crowd gathered behind the city's main gate as King Fernando and two hundred of his troops entered on warhorses. All was silent save the clatter of armor and the clop of hooves as spectators exchanged wary glances with the horse-mounted soldiers.

"Citizens of Almeria," announced the king, "we are not here to destroy what's left of your splendid town. Almeria will remain. Almeria will be rebuilt. Almeria will be more beautiful than ever." A translator shouted his words in Arabic.

"But Almeria, and the entire emirate of Granada," Fernando continued, "will be Christian. We ask that you save your souls by accepting baptism willingly."

The crowd listened. A baby cried. A man coughed.

"After you have accepted the rule of Christ, you will be free to settle elsewhere in the land of Castile. In many cases, we will help to find you homes. In no case will the citizens of Almeria be permitted to keep their homes or shops, or to remain here."

During the night, he had come to admire Fray Talavera's wisdom no less than his fiber. The citizens of Almeria would be spared; they would be free to live elsewhere.

"No Moorish man or woman, however, will be forced to become Christian. Those who refuse the sacrament of baptism will be free to settle in any other kingdom that will have them."

The king ceased speaking. He thought his offer remarkably, even historically, generous. Others might have had every resident of a conquered town, a town of infidels, hewn to pieces and fed to dogs.

The people of Almeria did not thank him. Some spoke quietly to one another. Others silently left the plaza, as if to say: You have destroyed our homes and our places of worship. You offer us exile and a religion we despise. How shall we thank you?

With a gesture, Fernando sent his soldiers into the city. He turned his stallion around and trotted back through the city gates, accompanied only by Hernando de Talavera.

"Victory is sweetest when tempered with compassion, like wine spiced with cloves. Is it not, Father?"

To Hernando de Talavera, it sounded as if the king was trying to convince himself. "Just so, Your Highness. And victory, like wine, can go to one's head."

"I received a letter yesterday," said the king, ignoring the gibe, "from my chancellor, Santángel, in Zaragoza. You know him, do you not?"

"I know of him."

"It seems our friend Torquemada has arrested his brother, a tax farmer whose services are much in need at present. I was wondering whether you could investigate this, Fray Talavera. Discreetly, of course."

"As you wish, Your Highness." Talavera tried not to display his pleasure.

"Please make it your priority. I can't have the workings of my government disrupted. Not during a war."

"Of course."

Fernando kicked his horse into a gallop. There were other battles to fight—Guadix, Baza, ultimately Granada. The plague had broken out in Sevilla. A shattered land cried for direction.

CHAPTER EIGHTEEN

OR JUDITH MIGDAL and her family, life in Granada became arduous. The Christians' advance had eroded support for the emir, Mohammed bin Sa'ad al-Zagal, among the people. The emir's nephew, Abu Abdullah, perceiving another opportunity to seize the throne, attacked not the forces of King Fernando, their common enemy, but those of al-Zagal. For three months, Islamic soldiers on both sides fought in the streets, cousins and brothers, both praying to the same God for victory. Blood flowed in the gutters; stones flew over the city's ramparts. Civilians stayed indoors, their homes closed up like clamshells.

Then came the news that Almeria had fallen. Al-Zagal abdicated in disgrace. Abu Abdullah, known to the Spaniards as Boabdil, took the throne. For three days, on orders of the new emir, soldiers and citizens celebrated in the streets, although there was no legitimate cause for celebration. The Christian onslaught had not subsided.

Orders for wine cups, silver candleholders, mirrors, platters, and mezuzah cases ceased. Burdened with too many unsold wares, not enough revenue, and an ailing Baba Shlomo, Judith made a decision.

Over a breakfast of dried fruit, nuts, and buttermilk, she told Levi about Baba Shlomo's dreams and desires. The old man wanted nothing more than to return to the land of his youth, to see his parents' graves, to bid them farewell in this world before joining them in the next. Levi understood what Judith hesitated to say, that there was little hope for them if they remained, so they might as well try to fulfill an old man's wish. He also knew that Judith and Baba Shlomo would not be able to undertake this journey without the assistance of a capable and curious sixteen-year-old. He nodded, agreeing to accompany them.

They would travel on foot, just as Baba Shlomo had done so many years before, in the opposite direction. They would transport a minimum of supplies, salted meat and other victuals, on the back of one mule. A second mule would carry clothes, silver objects, and Baba Shlomo himself, whenever he became too tired to walk. They would sleep in forests, in fields, and whenever possible, in the homes of Jews.

They would not leave at once. They would wait until spring. There was much to prepare. Not only would they need to purchase two mules and supplies, but Judith wanted to transport a number of silver trays, cups, and other objects, and sell them en route. She knew the Christians prized the Arabic style of silverwork.

. . .

Two months later, Baba Shlomo awoke her well before dawn. Judith dressed and awoke Levi. The mules and bags were ready. Silently, they ate a light meal of fruit and nuts. They snuck out of the city in darkness.

Judith had rarely glimpsed the town of Granada beyond the gates of its Jewish quarter. Now, valleys, mountain passes, plains, villages, and cities lay before her like stars dotting an astrologer's sky after a lifetime of clouds. Scents of grasses and flowers suffused the warming springtime air.

Near Guadix, they spread their blankets on the floor of a musty cave and rested through the day. They would pass into the kingdom of Castile under cover of night. Baba Shlomo told them stories about the world that awaited them.

"You hear those crickets, Judith? Levi? Well, in *Gan Eden*, instead of chirping, the crickets chant very softly, like a choir, in Hebrew."

"But where is this place?" asked Levi. "Where is the Garden of Eden? Is it here in our world, or somewhere in the heavens?"

"You know, my son, it is both. In the Torah, there is the story of the land where Adam and Eve lived. It's still there, in the Far East, guarded by angels and a flaming sword. Some day, when the Messiah comes, we'll be able to go back."

"And what about the other paradise?"

"That one is in the world to come. Only a few have been allowed to go there alive, and return."

"What is it like?" asked Judith.

"When you arrive there, the angels take away your clothes and wrap you in a robe of mist. They lead you to a valley filled with rose and myrtle bushes. They give you a room on the hillside. Outside each room there's a fruit tree. On every branch of this tree, there's a different fruit. When the wind rustles in its leaves, the sound it makes is the sound of words, and the words are more wonderful than anything we can understand, here in Andalusia."

Tall and ungainly, Levi fell asleep with his head on Baba Shlomo's lap, his mind full of images of a place where he would go, one day, where nature and mankind spoke the same language.

It was still dark when Baba Shlomo awakened Levi and Judith for their crossing into the Christian side of Andalusia, the realm of Castile. As they groggily led their donkeys out of the cave, the lush valley before them glowed under a three-quarter moon. Animals and spirits grunted, whistled, and brushed against leaves in the near distance. The three travelers huddled close and talked little, so as not to attract attention. "We're lucky," remarked Baba Shlomo. "These demons hide in the shadows, and the moon is bright. If we stay on the path, out of the shadows of the trees, they won't attack us."

In truth, the old man was no less frightened than his companions. When he heard the almost inaudible flutter of an ethereal being's diaphanous wings, Baba Shlomo was the first to stop. Trembling, he shouted the incantation, "Die and be cursed, you child of mud and clay, like Chamgaz, Merigaz, and Istema!" Only when the noise died, as if withered by his imprecation, did he permit his companions to continue on their way.

The border crossing itself was uneventful. No gate or customs house marked the frontier. At dawn, they met up with a family of farmers pushing carts of produce to the nearest town and noticed they spoke in Castilian. The two small groups of travelers cautiously ignored each other.

In the marketplace of Jaén, for the first time in their lives, Judith and her nephew saw pigs hanging by their feet, to be roasted and eaten. They saw opulently attired merchants and noblemen's pages devouring blood sausages. They saw monks in dark robes and women in showy dresses, their breasts bulging upward like bloated fish gasping for air.

They witnessed a death parade. Musicians playing hurdy-gurdies, bladder pipes, and drums led a procession of black-robed monks swinging incense burners through the town's main square. Black-hooded undertakers pushed a cart heaped with putrescent human corpses, whose stench the sweet odor of the monks' incense hardly masked. Men, women, and children, some wearing crudely painted masks, others bearing flowers, danced wildly behind.

They had indeed entered the realm of the heathen. All they saw confirmed Judith's impression that Christianity was a death cult, with no sense of what was clean and what was unclean. Even Baba Shlomo, who had spent some of his childhood in this other world, felt ill at ease.

That night they prayed in a small synagogue, a room filled with painted arches and candelabras, with a balcony for the women. After the service, the rabbi and his wife invited them home, where they gave them ill-fitting local clothes, showed them how to wear them, and advised them to avoid speaking Arabic in any town.

. . .

Baba Shlomo sometimes felt dizzy and weak. He drank cool lemon water, which provided a measure of relief. Following more weeks of travel, while they were traversing a long path through seemingly endless fields, he slumped forward and fell off his mule. He appeared to be sleeping but when Levi tried to wake him, he discovered his grandfather was not breathing.

Tradition dictated that a corpse be buried as soon as possible.

Judith and Levi found a stand of oak trees, moved the old man's body there, and stretched it upon the ground.

"Take Baba Shlomo's mule into Daroca," Judith instructed Levi. "Sell it for a shovel and a few yards of linen. I'll stay here with Baba . . ." She caught her breath. "With Baba Shlomo."

She tore a small gash in the side of her dress as a sign of mourning, sat on the ground, and pondered the ways their lives would be different. Baba Shlomo had come to occupy a central place in her life, becoming her living connection with the past, with the land she and Levi were nearing.

Her family had come from the north centuries ago. His had emigrated from the east hundreds of years before that. Her mother's ancestors had dwelled in the Jewish quarter of Zaragoza with Baba Shlomo's ancestors, attending the same synagogue, eating the same food. Their paths had surely crossed many times over the centuries. By comparison, Judith's life in Granada, as well as Baba Shlomo's, had been but a moment.

Baba Shlomo had bequeathed to Judith a livelihood, and to Levi a tradition. Although Levi had guided the blind old man almost everywhere, in truth Baba Shlomo had been guiding him. Without Baba Shlomo's gentle, protective presence, Levi would have had no man to look up to following the death of his father. With whom would Levi have discussed, over the Passover seder, the issues of slavery and freedom at the heart of the Jewish tradition? Who would have chanted the prayers in their home, before Levi himself mastered them? Judith still heard Baba Shlomo's voice twisting through those ancient melodies.

After Levi finally returned with a small cart, a shovel, and a length of linen, he began digging without a word. Lovingly, weeping, Judith wrapped Baba Shlomo in the white cloth.

At last the hole was deep enough. Through his tears, Levi began reciting the Aramaic words of the Mourner's Kaddish.

Yitgadal . . . veyitkadash . . . sh'may rabah . . .

The old silversmith, who as a child had witnessed the death of his parents, who had created a new life for himself in a foreign land, was laid to rest much the way he had lived: in exile.

Oseh shalom bimromav, hu berahamav ya'aseh shalom aleinu . . .
"May He who makes peace in heaven, in his mercy make peace for us."

Levi and Judith took turns shoveling dirt onto the coffin.

V'imru, amen. "And let us say, amen."

. . .

Luis de Santángel awoke to the noise of Iancu rapping on his bedroom door. The Moldavian informed him that two foreigners were waiting outside, with a donkey.

"Did you ask their names?"

"Migdal, my lord. A woman, a boy."

"Migdal?" He had not heard the name pronounced in almost two years, except in his own mind. Why would she be here, in the kingdom of Aragon, at his door? Then he reminded himself: it would do no one any good if he were to be seen with her.

"Tell them I'm in Barcelona," he instructed Iancu.

While buttoning his pourpoint, he wondered what purpose could have driven a family of silversmiths all the way from Granada to Zaragoza. He saw them through the window, walking up the narrow street with their overburdened burro. Judith looked leaner, her skin a shade darker. She had lost none of her beauty, but Time, reflected the chancellor, wove a veil of sadness over every mortal's countenance. Or perhaps that veil covered his own eyes, causing him to see the ravages of experience all around him. Despite his better judgment, he finished dressing and hurried through the alley behind his estate. As he emerged to the street, Judith saw him and stopped.

"Chancellor, I thought you were in Barcelona."

"I apologize. I'm eager to learn what brings you to Zaragoza. Unfortunately, I cannot be seen with you. Not here. Not now. I hope you understand."

She looked at him with her familiar, clear regard. "Why? Because I am a foreigner? A Jew? I thought you said the Jews fared as well here as in Granada."

He realized she was observing the gray hairs that had appeared here and there on his head, and that he was slumping, slightly but noticeably. He imagined Judith could perceive the black fog that enveloped his heart. When he had last been with her, his life had been difficult, to be sure. Since then, it had become miserable. He adjusted his posture.

"That night, that evening . . ." The chancellor paused, collecting his thoughts, and continued more deliberately. "I still thought of myself primarily in terms of my function, as a representative of my kingdom."

"You were lying?"

"I was . . . I suppose I was. But that's of little importance now, isn't it?"

She offered him a tentative smile.

Levi spoke to his aunt in Arabic: "He doesn't want us here."

Levi's voice had grown deeper. Santángel turned to him. Levi was a man now, gangly but strong, his chin covered with a wispy beard.

"That isn't true."

Levi blushed. It was the first time he had heard the chancellor speak in Arabic.

"The last time I saw you, you wanted to know whether Jesus was a magician."

"Yes, I remember. Have you found a better answer?"

"Unfortunately, no." Santángel turned back to Judith. "Perhaps we can meet after sunset."

"Where?"

. . .

That night, he led Judith and her mule through the concealed passage to the king's trysting place.

"Where is Levi?"

"We dined in the judería. Baba Shlomo would have been so happy to meet the rabbi. His father was Baba Shlomo's cousin. Levi fell asleep. He wanted to come, but he needs to rest."

"Of course. Is that where you intend to spend the night, in the judería?"

"Yes. They've been so warm to us, like family." She reached

under the burro's belly for the tongue of the saddlebag belt. The bag slipped to the side and might have fallen to the ground had Santángel not caught it.

"Let me take that." As Santángel carried the bag, its contents clinked.

He guided her inside, to the table, where he lit a candle. Judith looked at the paintings and furniture.

"Tell me why you have come here."

She turned her eyes to meet his. The chancellor once again felt she was reading his heart, that she sensed his desolation. She smiled wistfully and began recounting Baba Shlomo's dreams, his desire to travel to the land where his parents had lived and died, to see their graves. She described his sudden demise and burial.

"I'm so sorry."

"The journey here," reflected Judith, "was a kind of fulfillment for Baba Shlomo. We spent so much time talking. He told us the stories he grew up with. I think that was what he wanted."

"After he passed away," observed Santángel, "you continued to Zaragoza."

"With the war, the market for silver in Granada . . ." She finished the sentence with a gesture of defeat. "I was hoping we'd find a buyer here."

"Did you?"

"Not yet."

"Please, let me purchase your silver."

Judith laughed. "You haven't seen it."

"I should like to."

She knelt at the saddlebag and removed an elaborate, large sword hilt and an equally impressive, exotic-looking cross, decorated with vine-like silver rope work. She placed the two objects on the table.

The chancellor picked them up one after the other and turned them over in his hands. "They're exquisite." He knew what it had cost her to fashion these articles. She had set aside her personal ideals, her Jewish pride, to compromise with the great powers of the world. She was not so very different from him after all. "I'll purchase them. What else do you have?"

"Candlesticks, goblets, trays."

"I'll buy it all."

Judith smiled, visibly relieved.

"The palace always needs silver," continued Santángel, "and the king cherishes this kind of ornate 'Arabic' work. That's not the difficulty."

"What is the difficulty?"

"You'll need a way to continue selling your work abroad. Otherwise, you'll find yourself in this position again."

"That would be unfortunate. But I don't believe in miracles."

"You believe in the miracles of the Bible, do you not?"

"That was another era. Another world."

"I know a man who's convinced such worlds are still accessible."

"Who?"

"A ship's captain. He believes he can sail to paradise, the Garden of Eden."

"I wouldn't know," said Judith. "But I'll tell you what Baba Shlomo said about paradise."

"Please do."

She described a place where choirs of crickets sang in Hebrew. To this, Santángel contrasted Cristóbal Colón's paradise of gold and spices.

"In which paradise do you believe?" Judith asked.

"I'm not sure I believe any of it. But I do believe in hell, because my world has come, in so many ways, to resemble it."

"How so?"

He described the Inquisition, the arrests of his brother and his aide, the disappearance of his aide's widow. He described the state in which he had found his only son, with whom he imagined he would never again speak. "They're destroying everyone around me."

Judith listened, horrified and deeply moved. A silence fell between them.

"The captain I mentioned," Santángel offered, regaining his composure. "Perhaps he can help you. He has contacts all around the Middle Sea."

"Where does he live?"

"If you please." The chancellor found a plume, paper, and sealing wax. He wrote a note for Colón. "On your way back to Granada, stop at the port of Santa Maria. Give this to my friend Colón."

"Thank you. I am deeply in your debt."

"Not at all."

The next morning, the chancellor decided, he would have Iancu deliver a gold brooch, with inlaid pearls and rubies, to the rabbi's home in the judería.

CHAPTER NINETEEN

*H*ERNANDO DE TALAVERA rode to Zaragoza, where he met with Monsignor Pedro de Monterubio and the priest Raimundo de Cáceres. Both men, he knew, secretly shared the king's concerns regarding Tomás de Torquemada. They told him a great deal, but not all they knew, about the fierce struggle between the inquisitor general and the chancellor of Aragon.

Talavera proceeded to the ecclesiastical jail. Estefan Santángel slumped in a corner of his cell, his head pressed against his knees, his disheveled hair tumbling over his shoulders in matted ropes, his body contorted in the unnatural dimensions of a man stretched on the rack. Bulky chains needlessly attached his swollen, useless ankles. Despite the grating of the heavy door, he did not look up.

"I have come to console you, my son." Talavera pushed his candle onto a wrought-iron prong on the wall and leaned forward so as not to strike his head against the ribs of the ceiling. "I'm here to help you."

Estefan wearily raised his head. His face was bruised and puffy. His lips hung open.

"And if I have come to console you," resumed Talavera, "it is because I love you, even as the Holy Church loves you, as He who died on the cross loves you."

"Too generous," mumbled the tax farmer.

Kneeling, the monk shook his head. "Not as generous as I'd like. I too am made of flesh." He lifted the prisoner's chin. "It's not too late, Señor Santángel."

A squeaking noise interrupted them. Talavera turned and saw the dwarf-warden's eye and half his craggy nose through a small grill in the door.

"Let him watch," breathed Estefan. "I'm used to it."

Talavera turned back to him and asked in a low voice, almost a whisper, "Señor Santángel, I must know one thing. Have you admitted your guilt?"

"What is the charge?"

"If you were charged with despising the Lord, would you admit your guilt?"

"I never despised Jesus Christ."

The monk felt vaguely optimistic. If he could demonstrate that the inquisitor general had concocted complaints against the chancellor's brother, there was reason for hope. "And the Jews," he pursued, "do they curse the Lord?"

Estefan let his face fall back between his knees.

"Because if they do hate Christ, as Brother Torquemada claims, and if you never did, then clearly, you could not have been judaizing. Is that not so?"

"I wouldn't know," Estefan said softly.

Talavera placed a hand on Estefan's shoulder. "But if, in your despair, you turned to the philosophy of the Hebrews for consolation, that is not a sin, señor. I understand your curiosity, for I share it."

The tax farmer slowly raised his head and peered at the man.

"Nevertheless," added the monk, "I have seen through the arguments of that legalistic and heartless faith. What I'm asking is whether you've done the same. For if you failed to see with your heart as well as your mind, that would indeed be a grave and unhappy error."

Estefan finally answered. "All my life, I strove to be a good Christian. At least, a decent one. But since I've been here . . ."

"You have lost your faith? That would not be surprising, Señor Santángel. Even our Lord was tried by Satan."

Absorbed in his own thoughts, Estefan smiled weakly. "The words of some of the prayers have come back." He began muttering fragments of a Sabbath blessing—haltingly, with long pauses.

Talavera recognized the Hebrew. "Señor Santángel, it is your words, and not the words you were taught, that concern me. Surely every mortal, if he searches his soul honestly, can find sin there and earnestly seek the Lord's forgiveness."

With what little force remained in his arms, Estefan removed the monk's hand from his shoulder. "I shall not repent to a fellow mortal, Father. What is between me and God, I need not share with you. I have no use for your penitence."

The dwarf, at the viewing window, let out a snort.

"You cannot confess?" asked Talavera.

"Not to you, Father."

"And you understand . . . You understand the implications of your words?"

"Yes."

"Then there's nothing I can do for you." Talavera stood up slowly, retrieved his candle, and turned back to the door. The dwarf pulled it open.

Estefan's head fell back to his knees.

In the candlelight, the monk exchanged a glance with the warden. "I was too late," he lamented. "He is lost to us."

. . .

As Talavera walked back down the central aisle of the ecclesiastical jail, one of the common prisoners chained to the wall gestured. "Father, please, one moment. One moment of your time."

The prior of Prado stopped. In the light of the dwarf's candle, he knelt to see the man's persimmon beard, the scar on his forehead, his pitted cheeks.

"I thought . . . I thought if I gave my life to Christ, Father, He would transform me."

"Are you a monk?"

The man shook his head. "A constable of the Inquisition, and a devout Christian. I prayed, Father. I prayed."

"And before you became a constable?"

"I was not a good man."

"Have you confessed to the sins you committed?"

Juan Rodríguez did not answer directly. "I stole. I raped. More than once, I killed."

Talavera placed a hand on his shoulder. "You did so, my son, because you were attached to the pleasures of this world."

"Yes, Father. I tried . . . I begged Christ to help . . . but His help was not forthcoming."

"And who are you to say He didn't provide it?" asked Talavera. "You cannot see what He sees. Your eyes, too, are made of flesh."

Juan Rodríguez lowered his head. Elsewhere in the vast dungeon, a woman laughed quietly at some private fantasy.

. . .

Estefan Santángel sat in the blackness of his damp subterranean cell. His shoulders, hips, and knees ached. The rack had torn the fibers from his bones. The cotton sheath they had given him hardly kept out the cold, but he no longer shivered. Even when he felt, or thought he felt, the warm, trembling body of a rat against his thighs, he did not move. He was prepared. These unmeasured months had changed him more than the twenty previous years. The cathedral's clock tower sounded—once, twice . . . five times. Was it morning or afternoon? The latter, he imagined. Beyond the slit at the top of the wall, children were playing. Their voices floated down through the thick air of his cell. Like motes of dust, they dissolved in obscurity.

"Tell them what they want to hear."

He looked up. The viewing window in the door was open. The dwarf's eye moved away. His mouth appeared.

"Please," he urged him. "Then it will be over."

The dwarf's eye disappeared. The door creaked open and he crept in bearing a candle and a cup of wine.

"You're doing a little better," the dwarf whispered with satisfaction, "since that man—that high official—visited you, with the Jew, two weeks ago. Was that a friend of yours? A relative?"

Estefan continued staring blankly.

"Drink," the dwarf urged him, kneeling before him. "It will ease your suffering." He pressed the cup against Estefan's lip. Wine ran down the prisoner's chin, onto the dirt floor.

CHAPTER TWENTY

ANY OF THE DECKHANDS, thieves, and prostitutes who frequented the port of Santa Maria had worked or consorted with Cristóbal Colón, or at least exchanged sailors' yarns with him over a bowl of mead, but few felt or even feigned affection for him. As a captain, he was reputed to be short-tempered, reclusive, and autocratic. His mastery of navigation was so inadequate that he had led more than one ship astray—though he always found excuses for the delays and never admitted his errors.

None of that mattered much to Luis de la Cerda. Colón possessed skills rare for one of his ilk. He could read, not merely nautical charts but demanding works of literature, including that most subtle and complex of compositions, the Bible itself. He knew how to perform difficult arithmetical operations. He was savvy enough not to betray the trust of his benefactor.

When he was neither at sea nor at the duke's house, Colón's office was a table at the harbor. There, he hired sailors, paid them for a day's work, and double-checked paperwork.

One foggy morning, a woman came to this desk and asked, "Señor Cristóbal Colón?" Like him, she spoke with an accent.

The captain rose. "Señorita, how may I assist you? Is there something you're looking for? In this place, one often encounters seaweed blooms, but rarely such lovely roses."

She smiled. "I have something for you." From under her cloak, she removed Santángel's letter.

Colón gestured toward the empty chair. "Please, my lady."

She sat down. When he finished reading, he looked up at her and nodded. "So the chancellor is well. I'm glad to hear it. And you?" asked the captain. "You and your nephew have been traveling for months, yet you look as fresh as an April morning." He beckoned a sailor. "Dumitru, bring the lady a cup of hot wine, will you?"

Dumitru, the boy Colón and Santángel had saved from slavery, had grown as big as his father. Life on the sea and in rough ports had hardened him. Sucking on a little stick, he approached them. Judith shook her head. "That won't be necessary."

Colón waved Dumitru away. He perused Santángel's note a second time. "Do you have samples?"

"We've sold everything we brought, except this." She showed him the lustrous bracelet on her wrist.

Colón moved his face closer, marveling at its delicacy, its graceful curves. He folded Santángel's letter and placed it on the table. "I can sell your silver. But getting the items to me, from an enemy kingdom…" He waved Dumitru back over. "What are you doing? Counting flies?"

Dumitru knew better than to answer.

"Can you get past the border, into Granada?"

"There are ways," said Dumitru. "But it may not be cheap."

"I want you to accompany this beautiful lady and her nephew back to Granada. You'll be paid regular wages, just like you were rigging the *Santa Juanita*."

Dumitru glanced at Judith, then back at the captain, and nodded without enthusiasm.

"When you get there, she'll give you a box of merchandise." He turned back to Judith. "How much do you have for him?"

Judith smiled. "Right now? Perhaps one small crate."

"Come back with her crate," Colón instructed Dumitru. "And if this works out, it could be a regular job. Land, land, all the way. You hate sailing, don't you?"

Dumitru took the stick out of his mouth and threw it down. "I hate sailing."

"You are very kind," Judith told the captain.

Colón waved Dumitru away. "Anything for a friend of the chancellor," he told Judith. "He arranged my audience with the queen."

"Your audience with the queen?"

"In Cordoba. In a few months, at most. You'll be hearing all about it. Everyone will. But for now, why don't we draw up some sort of agreement, you and I."

He jotted down Judith's name and other information, more for the sake of his records than to protect himself legally. In his letter to Colón, Luis de Santángel had provided all the necessary guarantees.

. . .

Some five hundred years prior to the reign of Ysabel and Fernando, when the Moors ruled a large portion of the Iberian Peninsula, the city of Cordoba was Europe's most important capital. The greatest thinkers of the age, Maimonides and Averroës, were born there. Its alcazar housed the largest library in the world. Cordoba's Great Mosque preserved the holiest relics in the Islamic world, one of Mohammed's arms and the original Koran. Pilgrims, scholars, and diplomats traveled to Cordoba from Damascus and Paris.

Under Ysabel and Fernando, soldiers occupied much of the diminished city. They used the alcazar as a military command post, making it inaccessible to foreigners and scholars. The New Inquisition converted its once-famous baths and towers into torture chambers and burned vast heaps of precious manuscripts from its library in the public squares.

A parade, celebrating the conquests of Malaga and Almeria, wound from the southernmost gate of Cordoba to its alcazar. Twelve trumpeters blew silver horns. Five jesters, with pointed shoes and tight headpieces, danced while juggling painted balls. Several high officials and wealthy merchants rode on steeds draped in silk.

The king and queen, in velour, silk, and ermine, rode rare, high-stepping Andalusians with harnesses of vermeil, nodding and waving at the crowds. Beside Ysabel rode Talavera, draped in his simple Jeronymite habit. Behind the monarchs, their five children sat on ponies. The royal guard followed on foot, shields and spears rattling.

As the procession neared the alcazar, a frenzy possessed the crowd. Craftsmen, farmers, even knights and their squires, seeing in Ysabel and Fernando the saviors of Christianity, longed to touch their robes and hear their voices. They flooded the street, blocking the path, shouting "Hail Ysabel! Hail Fernando! Long live the king and queen!" The procession halted in disarray.

The royal guard began marching forward to disperse the crowd, but the queen held up her hand. "Let us give them what they so ardently desire." She climbed down from her horse, into the throng. The citizens knelt before her, thanking her. She returned the compliment: "It is from you, the common folk, that we derive our courage." Her husband joined her, patting the men on their shoulders and exclaiming, "Good people, let us pass!"

The gates of the royal palace slowly swung open. King Fernando and Talavera walked through, but as the queen followed, a dark-skinned, lanky man emerged from the crowd. "Beware," he warned Ysabel, fixing her with his coal-black eyes.

The feverish intensity in his regard could only denote lunacy, thought the queen. In the ravings of lunatics, she knew, lurked truths inaccessible to ordinary mortals. She decided to hear him out. "Beware of what?"

The lanky man began in an emotionless monotone:

> *Where dazzling flames of conquest are blown,*
> *And in the ravaged fields, sumptuous crops are grown,*
> *There shall madness and death be sown.*

"Let's go, now." A guard pulled him away. Ysabel watched him disappear into the crowd.

. . .

After the queen and her husband settled in the throne room of the alcazar, the duke of Medina-Celi introduced Cristóbal Colón, who laid out his vision of territorial conquest, spiritual redemption, and prosperity.

"Where does all wealth come from?" he began, kneeling before the queen. "Spices—cinnamon, nutmeg, cloves, ginger. Costly dyes—indigo, gallnut, cramoisie. Gold. Where do *all precious things* come from? Where is *paradise* located? Where's the holy city of Jerusalem, which in our wretched age has been so cruelly degraded by the infidel Muslims? The East, Your Royal Highness. The East."

Queen Ysabel found his Genoese accent annoying. It caused him to corrupt the elegant rhythms and soft consonants of her beloved Castilian dialect. His earnest diction, however, and the well-rehearsed ardor of his delivery softened her.

"Please continue, Señor Colón."

"We no longer live in the time of Marco Polo, when a man could cross all the way to the Indies on foot. Today, the Saracens control the routes. But there's a better way."

"A better way, señor?"

"Your Highness, Marco Polo's *Book of Wonders*, Cardinal Pierre d'Ailly's *Imago Mundi*, Pope Pius the Second's *Historia Rerum*, Ptolemy's *Geography*. They all agree on one thing."

The queen smiled graciously. "And what is that?"

"It would be faster to go the other way, from the Canary Islands to the Indias, across the Western Sea."

"If all those authorities," asked the queen, "agreed on such a finding, why has no one tried before?"

"Perhaps some have, but didn't know what to make of what they found. Maybe they chose never to come back, seduced by the pleasures of the East. But I'm ready to do this. In the name of Christendom." He cleared his throat. "All I need, Your Majesty, are four ships."

Although the captain knew every word of this presentation by heart, his enthusiasm sounded as fresh and genuine as that of a child for a promised toy.

"You put forth your views with great conviction," the queen praised, adjusting her lace collar. "If our memory doesn't deceive us, we have previously heard mention of this, or of a similar enterprise."

"Don Enrique de Guzmán," confirmed Colón, pleased. If she recalled her brief and inconclusive meeting with Don Enrique, did that not imply she found merit in Colón's idea?

"And what did Don Enrique report back to you?"

"He told me Your Highness listened attentively."

"Was that *all* he told you?"

"Don Enrique also said that, engaged as Your Highness was in a noble and heroic military struggle, she could not at present devote to this project all the attention it deserved."

"As you surely know, Señor Colón, we are still very much engaged in that endeavor."

"I have been following the conflict with great interest, Your Highness. Velez-Malaga, Malaga itself, Almeria. In nearly every fight, with the help of God, Your Highness's forces overwhelm the unrighteous enemy. And I wholeheartedly pray for the day when not only Andalusia, but the entire world resides in the care of the Christian crowns."

His vehemence surprised the queen. Ordinarily suspicious of sycophants' flattery, Ysabel was equally capable, when she detected something raw and sincere in a man's demeanor, of suspending her natural distrust. Nevertheless, the war and its financial pressures made further consideration of this aging Genoese sailor's proposal difficult. "In that case, señor, you should understand we must have our priorities. Maritime exploration, with no promise of immediate profit, cannot at present stand among them."

"If I may, Your Highness," insisted Colón. "The investment that I propose, it is in no way distinct from your selfless and holy combat."

"How so?" Ysabel asked with the begrudging smile she reserved for her most obstinate petitioners.

Colón glanced at his patron, the stone-faced duke of Medina-Celi, then turned back to Ysabel.

"Both are about defeating the heathen, Your Highness. Both are about advancing Christianity in this world, in the hope of procuring a better world to come." He considered adding, "Both are about retaking Jerusalem," but thought better of it.

"So they are," observed Ysabel. "But if such things were easy to accomplish, our holy struggle would be no struggle at all. As it is, our resources are stretched to the limit."

The sailor pressed on. "Your Highness, my venture would divert almost nothing from the war, while potentially bringing not only a great victory to Christendom, but eternal honor, as well as all the wealth of the Indias, to the Crown."

"Potentially," echoed the queen. "Please, señor, do not try our patience."

In a rare moment of discouragement, Colón cast his eyes downward.

This moment of vulnerability touched Ysabel. What she glimpsed was not only the testing of a man's purpose. She saw something of herself.

Like Colón, Ysabel believed in the rightness of her undertaking with a certainty that ignored others' opinions and even so-called facts. Like him, she took no credit for the authorship of her plan, but believed God Himself had conceived it. Like him, she felt both destitute and desperate. The war against Granada had more than depleted the royal coffers, and her world—even Christendom itself—was still so untidy, sorrowful, fragile.

When Colón looked up, about to take his leave, she stopped him. "Señor Colón, you must never lose faith."

Perplexed, he waited for more.

"Place your ideas on paper. We will ask the learned Talavera to study them." In what seemed a flight of magnanimity, she added, "While you await the outcome, we'll provide you with a stipend to keep you, and your ideas, attached solely to this Court."

This solution seemed pragmatic enough. For a small fee, she would prevent Colón from peddling his theory elsewhere. What the queen did not know, however, was that Colón had already laid out his thinking in every court to which he had gained access, with no regard for concepts dear to her such as allegiance or loyalty. Every one of those courts had failed to find a hint of merit in it.

"And when shall I report to you again?" asked the sailor.

"After the Moors are soundly defeated, we will again take up your proposal, Señor Colón."

   . . .

Elsewhere in the alcazar, servants and retainers of the royal couple shivered on the floor. In the royal bedchamber, a blaze crackled in the fireplace. Ornate tapestries from Flanders hung on the stone walls. Thick Ottoman rugs covered the floors, trapping the fire's warmth. A velour canopy and curtains surrounded the monarchs' bed, ensuring privacy when servants added wood to the fire or removed the chamber pot. Their bed was a flaxen bag of feathers and woolen blankets backed with ermine. Nevertheless, both the king and the queen slept in long nightclothes.

The queen had given the king five children. Only one, Prince Juan, was male. At nine years of age, he was prone to frequent illness. Although Ysabel had proved that a female sovereign could rule as firmly as a male, she hoped to produce at least one more prince to ensure their succession. She had asked her seamstress to sew a hemmed slit into the crotch of her night pants. In a gesture of pride and courtesy rare even for a queen, she always bathed before entering the sleeping chamber.

Fernando never thought of reciprocating. All the unguents and perfumes in the world, Ysabel mused, could not camouflage the robust bouquet of the king's earthbound hide. His shoulder-length hair smelled like the coat of a dog.

"My husband," she said softly, "let us endeavor to produce another heir."

King Fernando, half-asleep, turned toward her and opened his eyes. She was not an ugly woman, but to his mind, she was plain. He had never, even on his wedding day, found his wife attractive. This circumstance was of little importance, however, since in the darkness of their tented bed, he saw little more of her than the glistening of her eyes and teeth.

Without a word, he lowered his pantaloon, pulled her legs apart, and found the hemmed passageway. She wrapped her arms around him, pulling him closer. She did not forgive his grotesque appetites or his faithlessness. Despite her royal attributes, she possessed neither the power to offer forgiveness nor the will to withhold it. That was the function of priests—whom Fernando, unfortunately, seemed to hold in little esteem. She saw no point in allowing the king's slovenliness to rule her passions. When she had married him, she had made a vow to love and serve him, regardless of the vicissitudes of life; regardless, even, of Fernando's deficiencies.

The royal coupling ended nearly as quickly as it began. The queen shuddered as some of her husband's seed trickled out. King Fernando turned onto his side and fell asleep within minutes.

The queen closed her eyes. A stream of images filtered into her mind like fog into a wide valley. She was walking over a barren, parched field, naked, as the sun set. Under a wispy canopy of rippled clouds, orange, yellow, and blue, a dark bevy of songbirds floated toward the horizon, softly whistling. At her feet, she felt a liquid, moist and warm. She looked down and saw blood seeping up from the cracks in the hard earth.

This blood spattered the ankles and calves of her children, Ysabel, Juan, Juana, María, and the two-year-old Catalina. They danced in a circle nearby, shouting and laughing, Ysabel holding Catalina in her arms. The queen called to them, but the children seemed not to hear or see her. Their dance grew wild, their faces, distorted.

"Madness and death." The words of the lanky lunatic echoed in Ysabel's mind as she struggled to open her eyes and emerge from the disturbing reverie. Perhaps this man had been neither a sophist nor a fool, but an utterer of imprecations. Perhaps his words had not been prophecy, but a curse. If so, then by listening to him Ysabel may have doomed her own progeny. The more she reflected upon this possibility, the more she felt convinced, with a shudder of unruly, lawless terror, that she had erred. In the morning, she would make sure the wretched poet was put to death.

CHAPTER TWENTY-ONE

A N AUTO-DA-FÉ WAS GRAND THEATER, and it was costly. In the Plaza de la Seo, carpenters constructed a massive stage, seats for the highest Church officials, tall torches, funeral pyres, barriers to separate the crowd from the clergy, the aristocracy, and the accused. Weavers spun rich brocades for the priests' vestments and cloths of thick flax for banners and canopies. Tailors, guards, and city officials all contributed time and work. To offset the costs, the Inquisition created a contest, inviting each of Zaragoza's largest guilds to donate funds. The organization that raised the most money would lead the procession.

The Coal Merchants' Guild had offered the most impressive gift. Its members wore soot-besmirched smocks and tricornered hats as they solemnly wound through the streets to the main square, stopping at the cathedral where the abominable murder had occurred. In many places, the coal merchants had to knock down onlookers to clear a path for themselves and those who followed: the soldier-priests of Saint Peter Martyr, armed with pikes and harquebusiers, with crosses sewn on their habits; a contingent of altar boys in white, holding high the banner of the Inquisition, an unsheathed sword crossing an olive branch; the aged sexton of La Seo, ringing his bell; Monsignor Pedro de Monterubio, in the red chasuble of martyrs' masses, plodding slowly under a red-and-gold canopy, which four priests held aloft; a troop of soldiers of the Santa Hermandad in steel helmets, carrying lances; Gabriel de Santángel, no longer a boy but a solemn young man, leading the twelve accused, who shuffled forward in cone-shaped hats and yellow sanbenitos, smocks of penitence adorned with flames and devils; on either side of each heretic, Dominican monks, shouting in their ears, "The flames of hell await you! Repent, and be saved!" And, bringing up the rear on black-caped mules, the inquisitors themselves, flanked by knights bearing lances and crosses.

The last of these inquisitors, occupying the place of greatest humility and not riding a mule, but walking, was Tomás de Torquemada. As he passed, the crowds knelt, crossed themselves, and reached to touch his habit. He ignored them, for like every other man, he was a sinner. Only the humble would survive death.

. . .

Estefan Santángel limped forward, supported on either side by monks who shouted in his ears: "The mouth of hell is gaping! Turn your eyes upward, foul creature, or be forever fallen!" Hardly able to support the weight of his own head, the tax farmer stared at the ground.

They had tortured him with water, cords, and whips. He had slept. This morning, they had plunged his ravaged body into an icy bath. They had fed him wheat mush to strengthen him for today's ordeal.

The people spat on him. They shouted curses and shook their fists. The black-draped platform ahead swam above the cobblestones.

They seated him with the other accused judaizers on the platform. Straw effigies of those who had fled before their trials, also wearing sanbenitos, grimaced down at the crowd. A wooden fence and dozens of armed guards surrounded the accused. Estefan searched beyond them, into the mass of faces below.

Pedro de Monterubio, under the red-and-gold canopy, recited Mass. Estefan knew the words by heart. Mixed with the odors of altar incense, they echoed through memories of happier Sundays.

He noticed his hands. They trembled. The skin clung to his smallest bones. His nails were filthy, broken.

He looked down at his red, swollen feet, with open wounds in which white worms twisted, where rats had gnawed his flesh. He brought his fingers to his head. His hair was a filthy mat. He pulled a few strands down before his eyes. Much of it had turned white.

How many days, weeks, months, years had passed?

His eyes, unable to adjust to the blinding light, fell closed. The preacher's words hung in the air, then dissolved like salt in water.

. . .

Luis de Santángel stood in the midst of the rabble, some distance from the stage, dressed in rough linen. Gabriel had grown tall and thin, almost bony. Surely, Torquemada had not deprived his protégé of care or sustenance. Just as surely, he had taught Gabriel a different way of thinking about food, pleasure, and life, the way of the ascetic.

They would never again meet. Gabriel could not risk visiting him, even if he wanted to. If Luis de Santángel happened to pass his son on the street and exchange a nod or a smile, that very act could endanger Gabriel's life. No—Gabriel would pretend not to see him, quickly moving across the street. Although Gabriel's evasive gesture would break Santángel's heart, he could only approve of it. His son had chosen self-preservation. It was a choice the chancellor understood well.

He knew Estefan would not hesitate to exchange a regard with him. But Estefan's eyes were focused on his feet, if they were focused at all. If Luis turned and walked away from this ghastly passion play, Estefan would never know. But he wished to be near his brother and son as long as possible. He told himself to pay no heed to his own agony.

The crowd was crying for vengeance. Vengeance for what crime? For the murder of Pedro de Arbués? In part, but also for the blood of their Savior. For the privileges the *conversos* enjoyed. For the taxes Estefan Santángel had wrested, sometimes with the help of armed accomplices, from their near-empty hands. The taxes that Luis de Santángel had utilized on behalf of their king.

When Mass ended, Dominican monks began the tedious process of dragging one suspect after another to the stage. The new canon of La Seo lectured them, occasionally questioned them, but just as often ignored them, reading lengthy inquisitorial decisions to the crowd. The sun beat down relentlessly. Santa Hermandad soldiers pushed the condemned to their stakes, one after another in a long, slow procession of death.

Gabriel and Estefan were last. Other than those worshipers who stood at the front of the crowd, no one heard the priest's words. They saw him addressing the solemn young man in intimate tones. His air of humility and compassion moved them.

"Gabriel de Santángel," he began in his gravelly, aged voice, "we understand you were led astray, out of the pasture of the faithful, but have repented and elected to return to the flock. Is that not so?"

"That is so, Father."

"And the teachings of the Jews, denying the divinity of our Lord, Christ Jesus—were you exposed to that false and poisonous doctrine?"

"Yes, Father. But I never believed a word of it."

"Have you accepted the Son of God, Christ Jesus, as your Redeemer?"

"Yes."

"And the teachings of the Jews, denying His divinity, have you forever banished them from the territory of your soul?"

"I despise them."

When the new canon offered the young man communion and they saw him taste the wafer of Jesus's body and drink the wine of His blood, some had tears in their eyes. The canon stood again to address them, his voice now strong, "*If another believer sins, rebuke him. Then if he repents, forgive him. Even if he wrongs you seven times a day and each time turns again and asks forgiveness, forgive him.* Those are the words of our Lord. If God himself would forgive the sinner, the frail and fallible mortal who recognizes his error and kneels, begging for absolution, then who are we to judge such a man without mercy?"

Luis de Santángel watched, his overwhelming sense of loss tinged with relief that his son would survive. He tried to be grateful for Gabriel's wisdom. Under his breath, he muttered a prayer that Gabriel remain a devout Christian and live free of suspicion.

The priest turned to the secular authorities, the soldiers of the Santa Hermandad, and pleaded with them to show clemency to Gabriel. "Yes, this young man has wandered from the path of righteousness. Yes, he has been exposed to the most pernicious of sins. And yes, let him wear the sanbenito for two years, in penance." He turned back to Gabriel. "But if you stay away from evil, my son, your soul will be utterly cleansed. And we will do our best to protect you."

Gabriel marched down from the platform, nearly as free as any citizen, his chin up, his posture stiff. He seemed not to notice the Dominican monks behind him, dragging his uncle toward the priest.

. . .

Estefan saw him, however. He, too, thanked God that his nephew had been spared.

"Just as young Gabriel shall be cleansed," the canon of La Seo told the crowd, "so must we, gathered here today, cleanse ourselves of those who would pollute our ears, our minds, and our land. Therefore, let those whose mouths have spoken evil have their tongues stilled, that their wickedness not flow out upon us."

Two guards dropped Estefan to his knees. Others pushed his head back, jerked his mouth open, and pulled out his tongue. They shoved a small wooden board under it and drove a nail through it, lest Estefan utter words of malice or black magic and thus arouse the crowd's sympathy.

The tax farmer did not struggle, but closed his eyes, letting out a guttural cry as his body convulsed. The priest continued, "*He who does not dwell in me is thrown away like a withered branch. The withered branches are heaped together, cast into the fire, and burnt.* Those are the very words of the Holy Apostle John. That is why, Estefan Santángel, in the name of Our Lord Jesus Christ we have urged you, and begged you with all our heart to repent. If you had elected to do so, all the tortures that await you would have been your salvation. But you refused to repent, and therefore the bowels of the earth will vomit your bones, your image will be an abomination in the eyes of God, and your name in the mouths of mortals, forever and ever. Your damnation will be eternal." He allowed his words to linger in the stifling, incense-infused air.

Wearing the yellow smock of shame, his arms tied behind his back, Estefan was not listening. His eyes and mind were elsewhere. Perhaps because he had suffered so long, or because his attempts at prayer had reached God's ears, he perceived a glimpse, or the shadow of a glimpse, of the face of God. He had never imagined it quite this way, for the face of God was simply the world before him, denuded and rehabilitated. The priest in his blood-red vestments, the words falling from his mouth, the rapt crowd below, the guards and the scaffolding, the bright cerulean sky, Estefan's own agony, and so much more—ineffable but utterly real, shimmering in the heat of the summer afternoon. He heard the whispering of angels and the quiet chanting of ancestral scholars. Behind it all, and within it, a warm, amber luminosity, a profound, simple and convincing *reason,* which could not be summed up or expressed in words, flowed through the texture of this world like grain in the parchment of a Torah scroll.

The priest addressed the crowd, "You, Estefan Santángel, whom our Mother Church welcomed into her arms. You, for whom our Lord Jesus Christ suffered and died. You, whom He loved, and whom He favored with gold and all the privileges that befitted your station . . ."

"Death to the heretic!" shouted a man.

"Death to the marranos!" some in the crowd echoed.

The priest raised his arms. "My children, let us be calm. All these sinners' destinies are in the hands of God." He turned back to the tax farmer. "You, Estefan Santángel, who dared insult the servants of our Holy Church during your trial, though they sought only to save you. You, who laughed in their faces when they spoke of your Savior. You, who in the darkness of your cell, and even in the depths of sleep, so tainted was your soul, muttered the diabolical invocations of your people. You, Estefan Santángel, have shunned the love and protection of our Lord. Therefore, you shall know His wrath."

Luis de Santángel tried to advance through the throng, desperate to get close enough to exchange one final look with his brother. When he jostled a big peasant, the man struck him. The royal chancellor, in the garb of a common man, stumbled backward.

"The Church of God can do nothing more for you," the priest was telling Estefan, "Since you have abused His goodness. Therefore, we throw you away like rotten wood, from which no house can be built, and abandon you to the secular justice. And we beg the secular justice to deliver a moderate sentence, without spilling blood."

Indeed, the blood from Estefan's tongue was minimal, and even this, though viewed as necessary, was anathema to the Church. She was forbidden, according to Her own principles and traditions, from spilling blood. Even the secular authorities, in most cases, burned heretics rather than impaling them or cutting them to pieces—except for those, like Felipe de Almazón, who died before their trials.

Three soldiers of the Santa Hermandad seized Estefan Santángel and dragged him down from the platform. The Church had done all She could to save his soul, but had failed. The awed crowd opened for the soldiers as they hauled him to one of several wooden stakes erected the night before, high above the people, far from the altar.

Again, guards forced Estefan to his knees. They applied a torch to his beard, which sizzled and spat small flames, blistering his visage. They raised him up again and lashed him to the stake, his pierced tongue still dangling from his mouth. Using strong ropes attached to a scaffold, they pulled this stake up over a heap of firewood, much of it fresh and green to slow the burning. They touched their torches to the dry twigs at the base.

. . .

If there was a God, Luis de Santángel at that moment hated Him. Estefan had been subjected to unimaginable humiliations and torments. Now he was dying, and the powerful chancellor could do nothing to stop it.

Estefan had believed in the intrinsic goodness of his fellow man. Christian, Jew, Muslim, rich and poor—they had all been the same to him. He had celebrated their common humanity. Luis, in contrast, had survived by trusting no one.

Suspended upon his stake, looming over the crowd, half-obscured by smoke and flames, neither alive nor entirely dead, his features no longer those of a man, he was less and less the Estefan Santángel of Luis's memories. The Inquisition had transformed him into someone or something else. Those memories, however, flowed through Luis's heart like a wide river, as strong and deep as any day before. Estefan holding up a glass in laughter. As a boy, running into the woods, naked. Hugging Luis, his eyes brimming with tears, after Luis lost his wife.

Fumes of human char wafted over the transfixed assembly, blending with the odor of incense from the altar. The chancellor of Aragon felt he should be the one burning on a stake, the smoke of his transfigured body hovering over the people of his city, halfway to the skies, like a soul stranded in purgatory. He knew his proximity to the king had spared him so far, but all the royal friendship in the world could not soften his pain. To lose his son, to watch his brother die, was to lose a part of himself— whatever faith remained, whatever hope he had once held for this life, for this world. Overwhelmed, dizzy, he would have fallen to the ground had a peasant, standing nearby, not caught him in his arms.

Stinking of sweat and onions, unaware that he held in his arms one of the most influential men in the kingdom, the peasant whispered in his ear. "This is impossible to bear, is it not, señor?" He spat upon the ground.

Santángel looked at the man's rough, tanned face, thick eyebrows, and wrinkled, dark eyes.

The peasant noticed Santángel's tears. "You know him, don't you?" He jerked his chin toward the pyre.

Santángel nodded.

"I am truly sorry, señor. This is a terrible thing that is happening. But even this will pass."

Glancing back at the stage through the crowd and clouds of smoke, Santángel caught a fleeting glimpse of Tomás de Torquemada. The prior of Santa Cruz seemed to be looking directly at him.

. . .

As he wandered through the streets of Zaragoza, the chancellor spoke to no one. Those who greeted him, he ignored. In his mind's eye, he watched his son repent, his brother smolder upon the stake. The acrid smell of roasting human flesh still pricked his nostrils. Numb to the world, to the past, and to the future, he looked up at the moonless sky and the bright stars as though seeing them in their distant coldness for the first time.

Inside his home, Iancu removed his coat. He looked around the *zaguán*, the entrance hall—its painted wooden ceiling, hanging candelabra, and tapestry-covered walls—as if this too were now unfamiliar. Sensing his master's distress, Santángel's majordomo dared not breathe a word.

The chancellor contemplated the table where he had shared soup and played chess with his son. For a brief moment, Gabriel was sitting there again, focusing on his knight or bishop, determined to prevail. And there he was, himself, Luis de Santángel, as he must have appeared to his son, swallowing a spoonful of broth, smiling at Gabriel with guarded pride—so controlled, so thoroughly determined to give to the world what it required of him.

The chancellor's vision of himself ripped off its mask, its benign disguise. Underneath, a lonely, weak, frightened Jew cowered, covering his face with his arm.

Luis understood how his son had learned to live two lives. From the public Luis de Santángel, the courtier, Gabriel had learned how to present himself to the world. All the while, Gabriel was also learning how to despise the inner Luis de Santángel, the Jew. In the end, Gabriel had murdered his own daemon, his own inner Jew whose existence had never been recognized or mentioned.

Santángel took the chair in his hands, lifted it over his head, and brought it crashing down upon the table. Heavy and solidly constructed, the chair made a cracking sound but did not break. He hurled it toward the crucifix on the wall. The chair clattered and fell, taking the cross with it. As the ivory Christ hit the floor, it splintered.

Leaning forward, Santángel pressed his hands upon the marred table. He inhaled deeply, then exhaled slowly, as if to expel his rage, his powerlessness. When he looked up again, his eyes met those of Iancu, who stood at the threshold of the dining room.

"You may . . . you may retire to your quarters, Iancu." Santángel's voice was broken.

"As you wish, my lord."

Luis de Santángel pulled out another chair, fell into it, and rested his head on the table.

. . .

Late that night, the chancellor was half-asleep at the table, his head on his arms, when a hooded form entered the room. Santángel awoke with a start and was about to cry out, when the intruder spoke.

"Hush." The man covered the chancellor's mouth with his gloved hand.

As Santángel's eyes adjusted, the trespasser slowly removed his hand and pulled back the hood over his bald head. The chancellor recognized Raimundo de Cáceres.

"I can only imagine how it must feel to be you, Señor de Santángel."

Still groggy, Santángel blinked.

"And that is why, after all this, I hesitate."

What additional evil could be forthcoming?

"Everything is known."

"Everything . . . Please, Father . . ."

"Torquemada is making preparations. He has asked my master, the monsignor, for help. People will be arrested. Up to the highest echelons of government, they say. It is imminent."

"That cannot be," Santángel whispered. "I found the log. I watched it burn."

"The scribe. The scribe who took down Felipe's confessions."

Santángel had feared this possibility. "That would put you in danger, as well," he told the priest.

"I'm leaving tonight. It isn't likely we'll see each other again."

Santángel stood and held the priest by his shoulders. "Where will you go?"

"North. Past the Pyrenees. An old, quiet monastery in a secluded valley. He can't reach me there. And you?"

"There's only one place for me to go. Granada, where the king is handily winning a war, which I financed."

"No one ever accused you of lacking courage," whispered Cáceres after a moment. "But what do you have to gain?"

"Nothing, except to deny Torquemada the satisfaction of exiling me. Of destroying what little I have left."

"That is, indeed, what we've been attempting from the first. But I fear we've failed."

"We have, in many ways. What of Abram Serero?"

"It is he who betrayed Felipe de Almazón."

The chirping of crickets filled the pause. "It cannot be."

"They threatened him," Cáceres explained. "They threatened his entire family. Arbués wanted to make an example of him. He was to be a warning to any Jew who dared teach the *conversos* in Zaragoza."

Santángel thought of all Serero had done for him. The secret meetings. The visit to Estefan's cell, at the risk of his life.

"Someone lied to you, Father."

"He had to give names," Cáceres added. "He decided to sacrifice only one of us. He chose Felipe. Felipe wasn't just talking, he was practicing Jewish ritual. That put us all in jeopardy."

"Serero gave up the only one of us who practiced his faith? How do you know this?"

"Please, Chancellor."

Santángel remembered Serero's words to Felipe. "Your life is holy. Created in the image of God. I wouldn't want to feel responsible if you lost it." The scribe's solicitude now took on another meaning.

"Where is he?"

"He, his wife, his children, all of them have fled. It was part of the arrangement."

. . .

Torquemada did not arrest Luis de Santángel that night. Time, he felt, was on his side. The chancellor's demise was inevitable. All that was required now was to accumulate testimony and evidence, piece by piece, until the weight of proof was irrefutable. The king of Aragon would finally offer his support. The arrest of the chancellor would free Torquemada to carry out the last element in his plan for the theological unification and spiritual redemption of the Iberian Peninsula.

He did, however, order the arrests of many, including Raimundo de Cáceres. It grieved him more than anything else, when a man who had taken vows turned his back on God. Felipe de Almazón's memory, as transmitted through Pedro de Arbués's inquisitorial scribe, clearly indicated that the monsignor's highest-ranking aide had done just that.

Ever since the night Pedro de Arbués had appeared to Torquemada, bloody and imperious in the nave of La Seo, the inquisitor had been meditating upon his words: "Those who have turned toward the Light, and now wish to crawl back into the shadows, must be helped." Clearly, the canon had been speaking of the *conversos*, retreating from the Light of Christianity into the shadows of Judaism. Torquemada understood the deceased canon's message, but he was at a loss to understand exactly what God expected him to do.

"Eliminate the darkness from their world." Was Arbués asking him to erase all vestiges of the ancient Hebraic rite? The inquisitor wondered how this could be accomplished. Even when seeking out traitors within the Church, he encountered resistance. How was he to extend the reach of the Inquisition beyond its native community?

But if the Jews were conspiring to lure *conversos* back to their former, erroneous faith—if the Jews, represented in Felipe's testimony not only by the Hebrew scribe Serero but also by the physician, Buendía, who had treated Felipe's wounded javelin arm—were actively recruiting powerful *conversos* in Aragon and Castile, then action would have to be taken against them. Against their entire community.

. . .

Santa Hermandad soldiers searched the judería for the evidence mentioned in Felipe's confessions. They emptied the synagogue of its Hebrew texts. They carted them to the rectory of La Seo for Torquemada to inspect with the help of three visiting scholars.

Most of the recovered documents were already familiar to the Church and Torquemada: fragments of the Talmud, that maddening compendium of lies and calumny; the Hebrew Bible; the writings of Maimonides, Rashi, and other scholars. Torquemada instructed his monks not to waste time on these tracts, but to search for other documents, secret texts the Jews had managed to hide from the Church through the centuries. Documents that would demonstrate their hatred of Christianity and their devil-inspired schemes to overturn its dominion.

CHAPTER TWENTY-TWO

*T*HROUGH FOUR BLEAK and grueling winters, the Christian sword hacked its way toward the center of the Islamic emirate. The hooves of King Fernando's horses pummeled the wide *vega*, raising vast clouds of dust. Velez-Malaga, Malaga, Almeria, Guadix, and Baza fell.

A sense of helplessness descended upon Granada. Soldiers bolted and chained the gates of the city. Everyone knew that while the citizens' provisions might last a few weeks, the Castilians' assault could continue forever.

A call to arms rose from minarets and battlements. A clamor of metal and horses' hooves violated the peaceful, clear afternoon as troops assembled throughout the capital. They waited.

The Christian king, confident that only haste, now, could defeat him, decided not to launch a frontal attack against the greatest soldiers of the Moors' precious stronghold. Instead, he would starve Granada.

He ordered his soldiers to burn and despoil all the towns and fields within fifty miles. For the Christian fighters, the battle of Granada was a great free-for-all. Gold, silk, spices, precious objects, beautiful women, handsome Moors—they seized them, spent them, discarded them, and impaled them at whim. A spectacular, thrilling conclusion to a long series of grueling battles.

. . .

Behind the walls of Granada, the Alhambra rationed the citizens' food. Horse-mounted soldiers patrolled the streets day and night.

Even the mosques and the synagogue, vital institutions to most, ceased to provide regular services.

Judith Migdal's response, once again, was to immerse herself in her work. She and her workers continued production as if there were no war, as if the enemy were not about to plunder their town. No one, other than she and Levi, knew what she did with the bangles and Torah handles they manufactured. No one knew how Judith procured a seemingly endless supply of silver ore and food for herself and her workers.

The answer lay under the walls of the city, where the river Darro flowed through a tunnel, carrying out effluvia. There, once a month, late at night, Judith and her nephew conveyed a crate of silver goods out of the municipality. They came back with a box of food, raw metal, and coin. As arranged, Cristóbal Colón's courier, Dumitru, acted as their exporter and supplier.

In the underground passage, Judith and Levi often met strangers. Most of them, in fear of imminent catastrophe, were fleeing the city, carrying but a few meager possessions. Others, like Judith, smuggled goods. Judith feared nothing from these fellow lawbreakers. All people, she told herself—Jews and Muslims, thieves and honest citizens—when faced with a shared threat, learn to trust one another.

. . .

Abu Abdullah, the emir who had seized the throne from his uncle to save it from the Christians, finally abdicated and capitulated to the forces of Ysabel and Fernando. He knew that to surrender Muslim lands to the Christians was anathema to his faith, that it would bring dishonor to his name. The lives of his citizens mattered more than his reputation or even his religion. In tears, he begged the Christian Crowns to spare the beauty of his capital city.

Hours later, trumpets blew and town criers called out in public squares, armor-clad Christian soldiers deployed flags emblazoned with the Holy Cross from the walls of the capital and flew the banners of Castile from its towers. Ysabel and Fernando, their soldiers, and many of their advisors began a raucous parade into the heart of their new domain.

A clamor of drums resounded through the narrow streets of Granada. Most residents cowered in their shops and residences. Thousands of freed Christian prisoners cheered and danced in the bright sunlight. When the royal cavalcade reached the Great Mosque of Granada, King Fernando stopped the procession and turned to his ecclesiastical advisor.

"Talavera," he demanded in a voice grown hoarse from shouting battle commands, "It is our fervent desire that the accursed emblems of Mohammedanism be ripped from these walls." His attendants and knights, together with the freed prisoners, let out an exuberant cheer. "Let us replace them with crucifixes, madonnas, icons, and other objects befitting Christian devotions. And we desire that this edifice be reconsecrated in the name of Jesus Christ, that we may take confession and celebrate a Mass of Thanksgiving in the morrow." Fernando's hand, on his hip, clutched the Moorish scimitar his chancellor had sent him, a lovely weapon that symbolized the vast wealth he was acquiring by means of war.

Fernando and Ysabel, their court in tow, progressed up the long, leafy path to the great castle of the Moors, the reputedly impregnable Alhambra. All their lives, they had heard talk of the splendors of this castle. Nevertheless, what they found astonished them: a military fortress, several palaces with fountains and gardens, ceilings painted in gold leaf and lapis-blue, carved partitions, additional housing sufficient for an army of functionaries, all of it utterly deserted.

. . .

When Hernando de Talavera and his aides entered the Great Mosque, they found no emblems or symbols that could be construed as representations of God. Talavera had little to do but to cleanse and christen the mosque and erect a great crucifix upon its eastern wall.

Tomás de Torquemada, arriving in Granada that evening, found Talavera along with several other churchmen, patiently washing every stone with holy water.

"Allow me to assist you, Fray Talavera." Torquemada knelt beside the prior of Prado, took hold of a towel, and began washing the adjacent stones. "I understand you intend to lead Mass here tomorrow morning."

"That is our sovereigns' wish."

"I shall look forward to your homily."

Talavera raised his eyes again and looked into Torquemada's, then resumed wiping the stones, observing the patterns created by the play of torchlight on the wet marble. Sometimes their hands, independently of either man's will, appeared as coordinated as the back-and-forth gestures of dancers executing an elegant carol. At other times, their hands traced inharmonious dashes and jagged vacillations, like the thrusts and parries of swordsmen.

So it is with our lives, reflected Talavera. Each of us has the clear impression that he controls, in some measure, his own small path. The greater patterns lie far beyond any individual's will. It is in the yielding of our will to God's that we become holy.

If in capturing the capital Ysabel and Fernando were doing God's work, they should be careful to continue doing His work in the possession of it. At that moment, Hernando de Talavera conceived the sermon he would deliver the following morning. He would speak not to the people of Granada but to their rulers.

. . .

The queen worried that a newly christened cathedral, in a city that only days before had been an Islamic capital, was unlikely to attract many worshipers for its first Mass. She feared God would be offended. She prayed vigorously, in advance, for His forgiveness. She saw to it that word went out: the king and queen would be hosting an important event in the converted mosque. For all Christians in the capital, attendance was mandatory.

Most of Granada's residents believed that exposure to the Latin rite would turn them into idolaters. Nevertheless, at the appointed time, the Great Cathedral of Granada filled with courtiers, soldiers, even local citizens in their djellabah robes.

Those who knew the Latin intoned the *Kyrie Eleison* in a solemn, melismatic chant. They sang an uplifting *Gloria in Excelsis* as a round. Queen Ysabel, wearing the large, intricate silver cross

Santángel had sent her, sat with her husband, her confessor Torque-mada, and her five children in the front row of worshipers. She felt an exaltation, a presence of the Holy Spirit, which she had rarely experienced in a lifetime of spiritual devotions. God, through this rapture, was speaking to her, thanking her for liberating Andalusia from the tenacious grasp of the Saracens. She knew she would never forget this moment.

Hernando de Talavera launched into an impassioned discourse, an exhortation that tested some of the queen's assumptions about the meaning of victory:

"The Lord said: *Judge not, that you not be judged.* And yet, his contemporaries judged our Lord. Some thought him Elijah, back from the dead, Matthew tells us; others thought him Jeremiah or one of the other prophets. To compare our Lord to a mere prophet was to ignore His majesty. Others, as we sadly know, judged him even more harshly.

"In Luke, we are told, *Love your enemies. Be merciful, as your Father is also merciful.* And again: *Judge not, and you will not be judged; condemn not, and you will not be condemned; forgive, and you will be forgiven.*

"Your Royal Highnesses, and all your faithful servants, and all the children of God gathered here, we have come on this day into a land not our own, and our purpose is to make it our own. We have come into the midst of a people who know not Christ, and we intend to educate them. Let us teach them of God's glory through words and acts of love, as the Lord taught us. But let us not judge them. For if we judge them, and if we condemn them for their errors, we ourselves will be judged and condemned. But if we forgive them, we shall be forgiven."

To Tomás de Torquemada, Talavera's words were arrows aimed at his heart. The Jeronymite monk was brazenly and unmistakably attacking the Inquisition, the arm of the Church concerned with judgment. He was distorting the Word to undermine the authority of the Church. Were we not instructed, in the Epistle of James, *He who turns a sinner from the error of his way will save a soul from death and cover a multitude of sins?* Did such an act not require judgment? Indeed, without judgment, what did righteousness mean?

As Torquemada pondered these questions, it occurred to him that he would have to take an unusual approach, on this particular occasion, to the queen's confession. He prayed that the Lord would guide him in this endeavor, as in all things.

. . .

Hernando de Talavera's sermon moved and challenged the queen. She found herself faced with a powerful dilemma, a question she had been unable, until now, to resolve. To what extent was her desire to purify Castile and Aragon motivated by her love of Jesus, and to what extent by resentment over the Muslim theft of her land, centuries before her birth? If anger more than love fueled this desire to cleanse her nation, was that desire unholy?

She took confession in a vast, intricately tiled room, furnished only with a small table and two chairs, at the heart of the Alhambra castle. She posed this question to one of the men whose sagacity she most trusted. She knew his answer would differ markedly from Talavera's, but cherished their diversity of opinion.

"Where in Scripture," Torquemada replied, "is it written that it is wrong to hate evil?"

The queen, kneeling before him, reflected upon the holy books she had studied. "We can think of no Gospel where that is written."

"Did Saint Paul not say, *if anyone does not love the Lord Jesus Christ, let him be accursed.* And the Jews' own King David, before him, *I have hated the congregation of evildoers, and will not sit with the wicked.*"

The queen raised her gold-flecked eyes.

"Your Highness, by the grace of God," the inquisitor continued, "has been victorious against the infidel. But what is the purpose of this victory? Is it really for revenge?"

"Perhaps not." To Ysabel, this confession seemed centered around receiving guidance rather than exculpation.

"Is it merely so that you and the king will enjoy more land, more castles, more power?"

"Do not insult us, Father."

"Then what is the purpose of this victory?"

"To help accomplish the will of God in this world." She looked up at him, soliciting his approval.

"The will of God? And what might that be?"

"To bring about His kingdom on this earth."

"But allow me, Your Highness, to probe deeper. If God wants His rule to triumph in this world, why do you imagine He doesn't simply will that transformation into being? Certainly, you wouldn't deny He has the power to do so?"

"Because," the queen replied, "we have not yet sufficiently improved this terrestrial dwelling-place of ours. Because we're not yet worthy of such grace. Why should the Lord once again sully his feet on our tainted soil, if we haven't the will to prepare it for Him?"

Torquemada smiled. "Come. Let us sit together."

The queen rose and joined him at the table. She was not sure whether she was still confessing or not. This did not resemble the usual procedure, but she deferred to the monk's spiritual authority.

"Let me ask you something," the inquisitor began again in a more casual manner. "If you invited a great warrior to sup with you in your castle, and if you wanted this hero to have a pleasant time of it and enjoy his meal, would you also invite to the same table that man's avowed enemy? Would you invite to that very dinner one who had openly stated, and called out, all through the village, his intention to murder this gentle knight?"

"Of course not."

"Ah, but what if this knight's enemy were more subtle, more crafty than that. Knowing that you would never place your esteemed friend in harm's way, suppose he hid his murderous intent. And suppose that by rendering great and important services to Your Highness, he ingratiated himself with your court and procured an invitation to this meal?"

"I should hope, Father, that we would not be so foolish as to fall for such a ruse."

"Were this Evil One any ordinary mortal, surely Your Highness would not. But suppose he was exceedingly gifted in the art of deceiving even such perspicacious individuals as yourselves? And suppose further that he managed to trick not only you, but even the pages and squires of the good knight, your guest, so that they became, despite themselves, his accomplices in that man's murder?"

"If we were utterly fooled, Father, I suppose we could do nothing about it, unless someone brought the matter to our attention."

Torquemada paused, his hands folded on the table. "You have been utterly fooled, Your Highness, you and the rest of Christendom. But it is not too late."

"Please, Father, explain to us the meaning of this parable."

"That castle is Your Highness's domain, Castile and Aragon, all of it. Your esteemed guest is our Lord, Jesus Christ."

"And the ignoble creature that would kill Him?"

"That people which has already done so, repeatedly, since the day He walked this earth."

Ysabel knew which people he meant. The Jews' murder of Christ, as Torquemada had previously explained to her, was not an isolated occurrence, but a *pan-historical* event, an occurrence that took place at all times throughout history. In every generation, indeed, at every moment, Christ was dying on the holy cross for the sins of mankind, redeeming those who accepted the validity of His suffering, and condemning those who rejected Him.

Ysabel clutched the silver crucifix Luis de Santángel had offered her, searching Torquemada's eyes.

"I have in my possession a parchment that makes it all clear."

"Makes what clear?" asked the queen.

"How this evil enters our land. Why we've been unable to eliminate it. This parchment was used to provide instruction in secret meetings."

"What sort of secret meetings?"

"They involved a Jew and a highly esteemed *converso* in the court of Aragon."

"And what does this parchment say?"

From under his habit, Torquemada produced the parchment Cristóbal Colón had forced upon Luis de Santángel. Abram Serero had plastered it into the wall of his synagogue before fleeing. He unfurled it on the table and stared down at its twisted, blemished characters.

"It claims to be a lost gospel from the time of Jesus, or a fragment of a lost gospel. But it is not a gospel of the Lord. It is a gospel of the Jews, which they've kept hidden from Christian eyes."

The queen saw magic in those dancing letters, as Luis de Santángel had before her. But this magic was not seductive or alluring. This magic was a dreadful, horrifying demonry.

"What does it say?"

"I dare not even repeat, or give thought to its filthy pretensions, except to say that it makes a mockery of our holy faith and our Lord's mission. But I've taken the liberty of having the translation delivered to your quarters. After you read it, you will know what to do."

"Judica me, Deus," she murmured, *"et discerne causam meam de gente non sancta."* Judge me, O God, and separate my cause from an unholy people.

"Misereatur tui omnipotens Deus," Torquemada answered, *"et dimissis peccatis tuis, perducat te ad vitam aeternam."* May almighty God have mercy on you, and having forgiven your sins, bring you to life everlasting.

"Amen."

The monk's expression softened into a smile. "Amen," he repeated.

  • • •

The queen strode across the stone-paved courtyard, past arabesques in plaster, ornate tile work, a fountain supported by stone lions, and hurried up a narrow staircase to her private rooms. On a table she found Torquemada's papers, sealed with the stamp of the Inquisition. She sat down on a window ledge, covered her lap and legs with a fox blanket, and began reading:

In the year 3671, in the days of King Jannaeus, a great misfortune befell Israel, when there arose a certain disreputable man of the tribe of Judah, whose name was Joseph Pandera. He lived at Bethlehem, in Judah. Near his house dwelt a widow and her lovely and chaste daughter named Miriam. Miriam was promised to Yohanan, of the royal house of David, a man learned in the Torah and God-fearing.

In the border, a monk-translator had scrawled, "Miriam, that is Mary, Mother of God."

At the close of a certain Sabbath, Joseph Pandera, as handsome as a warrior, having gazed lustfully upon Miriam, knocked upon the door of her room and betrayed her by pretending that he was the man to whom she had been promised, Yohanan. She was amazed at this improper conduct and submitted only against her will.

Miriam gave birth to a son and named him Yeshu.

"Yeshu, that is Jesus, Our Lord," the monk-translator had noted.

On the eighth day he was circumcised. When he was old enough, the child was taken by Miriam to the house of study to be instructed in the Jewish tradition.

The queen looked up from the page, attempting to make sense of what she had just read. Jesus, the Lord Incarnate, the bastard issue of the Virgin Mary's rape? Jesus, God Himself, trained in the Jewish tradition? The queen knew that none of the Gospels even entertained the possibility that Jesus had received a Jewish education. On the contrary, the only mention of any event in the Lord's life, between his birth and his baptism at thirty, was found in Luke, who recounted that at the age of twelve, Jesus wandered into the Temple and—far from *receiving* the Jews' corrupt instruction—*offered* instruction to the elders there, who were flabbergasted to discover such depths of learning in a young child.

In the Temple was to be found the Foundation Stone. On it, the letters of God's Ineffable Name were engraved. Whoever learned the secret of the Name and its use would be able to do whatever he wished. However, there were two lions of brass, bound to the pillars at the place of burnt offerings. Should anyone enter and learn the Name, when he left the lions would roar at him. Immediately, the valuable secret would be forgotten.

Yeshu came and learned the letters of the Name. He wrote them upon a parchment that he placed in an open cut on his thigh. Then he drew the flesh over the parchment. As he left, the lions roared and he forgot the secret. But when he came to his house, he reopened the cut in his flesh with a knife and lifted out the writing. Then he remembered and obtained the use of the letters.

Yeshu proclaimed, "I am the Messiah! Concerning me Isaiah prophesied and said, 'Behold, a virgin shall conceive, and bear a son, and shall call him Immanuel.'"

They brought to him a lame man, who had never walked. Yeshu spoke over the man the letters of the Ineffable Name, and the man was healed. Thereupon, they worshipped him as the Messiah, Son of the Highest.

When Yeshu was summoned before the queen, he said, "It is spoken of me, 'He shall ascend into heaven.'" He lifted his arms like the wings of an eagle and flew between heaven and earth, to the amazement of everyone.

The sages of Israel then decided that one of them, Yehuda Iskarioto, should learn the Ineffable Name, so as to rival Yeshu in signs and wonders.

"Iskarioto," read the monk's annotation, "that is, the traitor Judas Iscariot."

Iskarioto flew toward heaven. He attempted to force Yeshu down to earth but neither could prevail against the other, for both had the use of the Ineffable Name. However, Iskarioto defiled Yeshu, so that they both lost their power and fell to earth, and in their condition of defilement the letters of the Ineffable Name escaped from them. On the head of Yeshu, the people set a crown of thorns.

Below her window, dignitaries were gathering in the spacious courtyard of the Alhambra, expecting to meet Ysabel and celebrate her victory. She turned her eyes back to the page in her hands, appalled but also spellbound.

Yeshu was put to death at the sixth hour on the eve of the Passover and of the Sabbath. His bold followers came to Queen Helene with the report that he who was slain was truly the Messiah and that he was not in his grave. He had ascended to heaven as he prophesied. A diligent search was made and he was not found in the grave where he had been buried. A farmer had taken him from the grave, brought him into his field, and buried him there.

The erring followers of Yeshu said, "You have slain the Messiah of the Lord." And the other Israelites answered, "You have believed in a false prophet." There was endless strife and discord for thirty years.

The sages desired to separate from Israel those who continued to claim Yeshu as the Messiah, and they called upon a greatly learned man, Simeon Kepha, for help.

"Simeon Kepha," the monk had scrawled in the margin, "that is, Saint Paul."

Simeon went to Antioch and proclaimed, "I am the disciple of Yeshu. He has sent me to show you the way." He added that Yeshu desired that they separate themselves from the Jews and no longer follow their practices. They were to ignore the ritual of circumcision and the dietary laws.

This text, the queen understood at once, claimed that Saint Paul was nothing but a secret Jew, a *converso* working for the Pharisees, preaching to the Nazarenes to deceive them and separate them from the Jews, so that the faith of the Jews might remain pure and untainted by the deceptions of this "Yeshu."

Further, this monstrous document appeared to claim that Judas Iscariot, the venal, devious apostle who sold the Lord for thirty pieces of silver, was Jesus's equal. She attempted to puzzle through the distortions of history and revelation that this reinvention of Paul and the Gospels represented, until she stopped herself, wondering whether she was being drawn into a devious and perverse path of reasoning.

To give any credence, any thought at all, to the outrageous propositions in this—what was it called again? this *Toledoth Yeshu*—was to expose her mind, her heart, her eternal soul to heresy and blasphemy. She did not know whether to thank Tomás de Torquemada or curse him.

How could anyone, she asked herself, believe such filth? Did not the evidence of history prove beyond a doubt that God hated those who denied His Word? Did not the fate of the Jews speak for itself? Did not her own defeat of the Muslims, hers and her husband's, here and now, on this soil of Andalusia, prove that God was on the side of the Christians?

If this ignominious parody was the secret teaching of the Jews, and she had seen proof of that, in unmistakable Hebrew characters on an ancient parchment—if this was indeed what they taught

New Christians, and possibly old Christians, too, in their secret meetings—then, just as Father Torquemada had predicted, she knew precisely what she had to do.

She stood and, with quivering hands, replaced the translated text in her trunk. Her heart and mind in turmoil, she slowly brought her crucifix to her lips and kissed it. Tears formed at the corners of her eyes. Wiping them, she hurried downstairs to meet her husband and some three hundred courtiers for a sumptuous, celebratory meal. Her thoughts, however, were elsewhere, already planning her next battle, the greatest and holiest battle of her life.

CHAPTER TWENTY-THREE

NAWARE OF THE DISCOVERY of the *Toledoth Yeshu*, Luis de Santángel rode again to Granada to meet with the king and queen. There, he attempted to sleep in one of the numerous homes the Christian victors had seized from their Moorish enemies. A party of noisy, giddy soldiers downstairs, and the knowledge that he lay within blocks of the Jewish quarter and Judith Migdal's home, kept him awake.

He wondered how all this disorder had altered her life. So much had changed since he had first set eyes on her at the Alhambra castle. He remembered the warmth of the vizier whom he had betrayed on Ysabel's orders, the splashing of fountains in the courtyard, the raven-haired silversmith in her gold-embroidered dress, her proud bearing, the softness in her smile.

Now, he reflected, Baba Shlomo was dead, as was his own brother and, in a different sense, his son. Granada now belonged to Ysabel and Fernando, and to Christ. The chancellor's world and Judith's had utterly changed.

Did Judith still reside in Granada? Perhaps she was lying in bed at this moment, similarly wondering about *his* fate. He arose and dressed. With so little left to lose, he found his way to the Jewish quarter.

After wandering through the quarter for some time, he happened upon the synagogue, which he recognized by the menorah and the Hebrew inscription carved in stone over the entrance. From there, he retraced the path to Judith's house, only a few streets away—the heavy wooden gate, the olivewood mezuzah. He stood for a moment at a loss.

It was not Santángel's custom to enter a home unbidden, but if he did not do so tonight, when would he? Now that Granada belonged to the Christians, with Ysabel and Fernando in the city, he would not dare wander into the Jewish quarter in the broad light of day.

He pushed the gate open and entered the courtyard. There was the moss-covered fountain, the jasmine, the door of Judith's dwelling.

He had taken so many risks and lost so much. This small moonlit quadrangle in the midst of a vanquished town felt simultaneously like refuge and perdition. All that had happened to him, to his aide Felipe, to Catalina, to his brother, to his son, to the last shreds of his family, had brought him to this modest home, seeking tenuous consolation.

Inside he found the brass table where he had once dined, the silver goblets, the colorful wool rugs strewn across the tiled floor, the water jar from which he had sipped, that night so long ago. He climbed the narrow staircase to the second story. In her room at the end of the hallway, Judith Migdal lay slumbering on several pillows, her body half covered, molded in a sheet that concealed as much as it revealed. Moonlight streamed over her peaceful features, her graceful neck, her smooth shoulders, her shapely leg entangled in linen. She muttered in her sleep, turning slightly, and the sheet fell away a bit. Luis de Santángel held his breath.

With Judith Migdal lying before him, unaware of his yearnings, the unreality of Santángel's asylum glowed as starkly bright as the moon. He turned to leave, bumping against the door. It creaked loudly. Judith sat up with a start, drawing the sheet around her shoulders.

"Please, forgive me, my lady," the courtier fumbled. "I so wanted to see you again. I meant no disrespect. I realize, now, how rash I've been."

"Chancellor?"

"I shall take my leave."

"No, no. Please." She gestured for him to sit.

Luis de Santángel, the chancellor of Aragon, sat on pillows beside the mattress of Judith Migdal, the Jewish silver merchant.

"What brought you here? Tell me."

He tried not to think of her form under the sheet, so near he could feel its warmth. He spoke of the tragedies and betrayals he had experienced since their last encounter.

• • •

She interrupted from time to time, but mostly listened, more to his distress and confusion than to his words.

She heard something else, too, not in his voice, but in her heart. He had sought refuge in her home. She remembered the brooch he had sent her, their evening together in the king's trysting place, the way he had kissed her hand, when they first met at the Alhambra. She remembered how he had sought her out at her shop, at the synagogue, and then come to her home.

She realized that Luis de Santángel had fallen in love with her and had come to her for comfort when he had lost everything. She had misjudged him. She had thought him a Christian and therefore unworthy of her trust. Tonight he was neither Christian nor Jew but simply a man.

For a moment, she seemed at a loss. Then she made a decision: to trust her instinct, to trust this man, to trust the moment.

She leaned toward him, wrapped her arms around his neck, and kissed him. After hearing the harrowing story of his son's disloyalty and his brother's tragic death, she longed to provide what comfort she could, to herself as well as to him.

They learned that night that even at the center of dismal distress, there beats a heart of hope and comfort, if only one listens for it, if only one allows oneself to feel its affirmation.

• • •

Hours after Judith fell back to sleep, Santángel remained beside her. Finally, telling himself it would be wise to leave the Jewish quarter before dawn, he kissed her gently on the forehead and rose. In drizzling darkness, he marched back through the small, dark streets of

Granada to his temporary lodgings. He tried to imagine how he and Judith could arrange their lives to provide companionship for one another. He could devise only two strategies, both impossible. Either Judith would have to accept baptism, or he, Luis de Santángel, royal chancellor of Aragon, would have to abandon wealth and rank to flee with her.

He would never ask Judith to become Christian. Not only would she refuse, she would also lose respect for him.

He had fought his entire life for acceptance and dignity in a society where neither was his birthright. To abandon that struggle, to walk away from his achievements, would be to hand a victory to those who wished to deny his humanity.

His wealth and eminence had protected him and Gabriel. As much as he wished to spend the rest of his days in the company of Judith Migdal, the cost seemed unbearable. Such a sacrifice would alter his identity itself. A person was not merely a soul or a Platonic abstraction. A person was a web of relationships with social and religious groups, with society as a whole, with God. To change these affiliations was to alter one's being. To sever them was to destroy oneself.

And yet . . . and yet, he had been alone long enough. Having found the answer to his solitude, he could no longer bear the thought of a life without her.

He turned a corner and spotted two soldiers of the Santa Hermandad, stationed before the home where he was staying, oblivious to the rain. Tomás de Torquemada either had shown Felipe de Almazón's confessions to the king and queen and obtained permission to arrest him, or decided to bypass the Crowns entirely.

If they captured him, what would become of Judith? Would she await him the following night, and the night after, and finally conclude he had abandoned her? The thought of her waiting in vain for him was as unbearable as the solitude, interrogation, and judgment that might await him if he were taken.

He looked around, down the street, toward the alleys abutting it. He could still flee, but how far would he get? For how long? What would become of his reputation? To run would amount to suicide. If he allowed the Inquisition to detain him, however, he might negotiate his way back to freedom. The king still owed him a great deal.

One of the soldiers saw him, then consulted with the other. The two men approached. "Your name, sir?"

"Luis de Santángel, royal chancellor of Aragon."

"Sir, we have instructions to take you."

. . .

The Inquisition detained Luis de Santángel in an abandoned private home a few miles outside the city. Hooded Dominicans provided him with bread and broth twice a day. His room afforded a view of wild, unkempt gardens and the Sierra Nevada Mountains.

The monks and their masters forbade him to send word of his arrest, but provided him with a printed Latin Bible, both Old and New Testaments, in two large tomes. Far from the clatter and business of the city, with little to distract him but the soft rustle of wind in olive and oak leaves, the chirping of sparrows nesting under the roof, and his own thoughts, he began reading. The many worlds of the Bible opened their gates as they never had before—the gardens, deserts, and meadows; the mangers and palaces; the past, present, and future.

When he was not reading, he lay on his blanket on the floor, savoring recollections of the night he had spent with Judith Migdal, but anguished to think of the confusion and betrayal she must be feeling as she awaited word from him. He could still hear the bafflement and understanding in her voice when he had unburdened himself. He wondered how the two of them could have allowed themselves to sail into impossible-to-navigate waters.

. . .

When Judith had accepted Santángel into her bed, she had made a decision. She would allow her life to mingle with this man's life. The chancellor was exceptional in so many ways: in the breadth of his intelligence and knowledge of the world, in his refusal to let others define away his own sense of right and wrong, in his ability to sympathize with those less fortunate than himself, in having loved his wife so deeply and not having hurried to replace her.

When Judith held Santángel, she felt she was bathing in warm waters, waters of comfort and certainty in which she had never before immersed herself. She had no doubt his emotions mirrored hers.

When he failed to return the next day, she assumed he had important business elsewhere. Days later, his absence and lack of communication began to trouble her. She worried he had come to harm at the hands of the Inquisition. She set out to find him.

Where, in the former kingdom of Granada, was one to search for the chancellor of Aragon? The only place she could think of was the Alhambra, where the king and queen now resided. As she approached the base of the hill upon which the great castle sat, she found soldiers and other foreigners, thousands of them. They had pitched tents in the streets. Pigs and ducks roasted on spits in the open air. They had converted some of the opulent residences into taverns where they drank and played card games, gambling away their booty. The alleys reeked of beer and wine.

In the heart of her own city, she had entered another realm, a realm free of Jews and Muslims. The only women she met were prostitutes. As she circulated among the soldiers, they whistled, grunted, and made obscene gestures. She quickened her step.

One soldier broke away from his companions. "Do you need something, señorita?"

"Yes," replied Judith in Spanish. "I'm looking for the chancellor of Aragon." She smiled politely.

"The chancellor of Aragon. Is that right?"

"Could he be up there?" She glanced toward the Alhambra castle, at the top of the hill.

"They're all up there. But you and I?" He shook his head.

"And if I tried?"

With his foot, the soldier pointed to a roach scurrying across a cobblestone. "You see that bug?" He squashed the roach. "Can I escort you home, señorita?"

"No, thank you."

As she hurried back toward the Jewish quarter, an opulent carriage clattered up a narrow street. Inside sat an elegant woman in a purple velvet dress with a high, lacy neck. On her chest hung the silver crucifix.

Judith saw Queen Ysabel turn and look at her, smiling icily and fingering her pendant, as if conjuring its talismanic powers to protect her from Judith's stare. The queen's carriage passed and disappeared around a corner.

. . .

The chancellor wondered why Torquemada had placed in his cell not only the Gospels but also the Old Testament. Perhaps the Inquisition was offering him a choice. In which book would he locate his faith?

Santángel would not be coerced into accepting what Torquemada or anyone else wanted him to believe, not after all that had happened to Estefan, Gabriel, Felipe, and so many others. He longed, however, to discover whatever truths he could in the Bible, to arm himself with knowledge.

He began with the story of a man, a woman, a serpent, and the Tree of the Knowledge of Good and Evil. He read and reread this narrative, wondering why it held such power over him and all of mankind.

The serpent of Genesis unexpectedly brought to mind another—a serpent curled into the Latin words of an obscure apothecary's formula. Years before, Santángel had heard mention of *aquae serpentis* not from the king's steward, as Fernando feared, but from the herbalist who had prepared the costly brew. Santángel had not known precisely what the term, or the potion, signified, but it took little prodding to find out. Although he had tried to put it out of his mind years earlier, he was now grateful that he had been unable to do so.

Days and weeks passed in contemplation, longing, and regret. Santángel's cell, isolated and policed, became the only stable point in a world whirling into disorder. His society's moral bearings had eroded under a driving rain of ambition, greed, and misguided piety.

The chancellor clutched at the Bible's promise of a different world, a rehabilitated, renewed world, a world alluded to in the prophecies. At last, he appreciated the yearnings of a Cristóbal Colón.

Three monks, by turns, visited every morning, bringing bread and water and removing the chamber pot. They treated him with cautious deference. One, Brother Donato, seemed gentler, perhaps more respectful than the others. From time to time, he grinned shyly, or placed a morsel of pig's foot in Santángel's broth.

"Brother Donato," the chancellor tried one day as the monk turned to leave.

A short, broad-shouldered man with a misshapen nose and a high forehead, Brother Donato turned back. "Yes?"

"Can you help me with this?" Santángel showed him a passage in Isaiah:

> *Go, swift messengers,*
> *to a nation scattered and torn apart*
> *to a people tall and smooth-skinned—*
> *a trampled tribe, waiting and hoping—*
> *whose land is divided by waters.*
> *All you who dwell in the world, inhabitants of earth,*
> *watch when the standard is hoisted on the mountains*
> *and hear when the trumpet blasts.*

"He's telling us, is he not," asked the chancellor, "to go somewhere. Somewhere in this physical world."

"So it would appear."

"If we want to be present *when the standard is hoisted on the mountains,* to witness God's victory over evil, we're supposed to travel somewhere." He translated another line from the same chapter. "*In vessels on the surface of waters.*"

Looking at the Latin, Brother Donato blinked a few times. "That would seem to be what Isaiah is saying."

"Thank you."

Through the following days and weeks, the chancellor broached the subject again with the monk. He told him that he knew a man who was determined to help fulfill Isaiah's prophecy. He mentioned a generous, secret gift that would be offered to the Dominican monastery at La Rábida, where Colón's son, Diego, resided, if Brother Donato would whisper a word to the Superior there.

. . .

Judith still expected to receive word from Santángel. Every night, she hoped he would once again appear in her bedroom. While waiting, she endeavored to reestablish her trade in a changed society, to enhance her contacts with local and foreign buyers, to find additional markets in the newly accessible lands to the north. In Castile and Aragon, her linguistic abilities would give her an advantage over most of Granada's other merchants.

Today, however, was not a day for work. Today the community was celebrating a bar mitzvah. Judith carried a basket of bread, pastries, and grapes. "Levi, come. Let's celebrate." Although Levi was a man now, Judith still insisted he accompany her whenever she walked to the synagogue. "Enjoy the leavened bread while you can. Passover is coming."

Christian soldiers patrolled the streets in elaborate, tight-fitting clothes, carrying swords. Walking through a city no longer her own, Judith felt displaced. Although she had always taken pride in her Spanish ancestry, she felt that her new monarchs, King Fernando and Queen Ysabel, were the figureheads of a foreign culture.

Rumors swept through the quarter like fire: the Jews would be more strictly confined to their district, they would not be allowed to trade with Christians, they would be required to wear identifying badges. Such measures had already been enforced in Madrid and Toledo.

. . .

A burly town crier holding a lance, his hair gathered at the nape of his neck, shouted the words from a long proclamation. The Jewish community of Granada gathered in the synagogue square to listen.

"From King Fernando and Queen Ysabel, salutations and grace." The crier looked up and nodded to his audience.

"You well know that we have established a New Inquisition in our realms, and that by this means, many guilty persons have been discovered. But we are informed by our inquisitors that great injury still results from contact between Jews and Christians. Jews have found ways to steal faithful Christians from our Holy Faith, and to subvert them to their own wicked beliefs and convictions. This has been proved by statements and confessions, both from these same Jews and from those who have been perverted and enticed by them, which has resulted in the great injury, detriment, and opprobrium of our Holy Faith."

The proclaimer paused, breathed deeply, and resumed. "Therefore, we resolve to order the Jews of our kingdoms and lordships to depart and never return to any of these territories, under pain that if they do not comply with this command, they incur the penalty of death and the confiscation of all their possessions. We secure to them that they may travel and be safe, but they must not export gold, silver, or coined money.

"We command that this our charter be posted in the plazas and places of our cities, towns, and villages as an announcement and as a public document. And no one shall damage it in any manner, under penalty of being at our mercy and the deprivation of their offices and the confiscation of their possessions.

"Given in our city of Granada, the thirty-first day of the month of March, the year of the birth of our Lord Jesus Christ one thousand four hundred and ninety-two years."

The town crier turned and nailed the proclamation to the door of the synagogue. Judith, Levi, and the others stood there long after he left, absorbing and discussing the news. Judith felt as if the land on which she stood had turned to water. No citizenship, not even the deepest-rooted investment in a so-called civilization, was permanent or secure.

Offense, pain, questions of justice and injustice swam through their minds and conversations. They also had to plan their departure. How were they to transport wealth to foreign lands, if they were not permitted to carry gold or silver?

It seemed Ysabel and Fernando cared not a whit if they all

had to begin their lives over in unknown dominions, where as foreigners they would possess no rights. The Christians assumed that Jews should suffer, as foretold in the Hebrews' own writings. The Christians' dark purpose was to assure the fulfillment of such prophecies. This purpose justified the Crowns' wholesale theft of Jewish property—especially after such a costly "holy" war. Judith recalled Ysabel's cold smile, her haughty regard, her necklace. She cursed herself for having fashioned that crucifix.

Isaac Azoulay approached. "This is all foretold, Judith."

"Perhaps," she conceded. "But how does that help?"

"That which we can't control," he philosophized, "we mustn't allow to affect us."

"Why mustn't we? If a bee stings you, you're going to cry out. It hardly matters *why* he harmed you, or whether you can control it."

"Then we must do our best to ensure no more bees sting us."

. . .

Demanding that the bar mitzvah be given a chance to chant his Torah portion, the rabbi asked his congregants not to mention the expulsion. Nevertheless, near the end of the service, a lively debate broke out. Some blamed the moral waywardness of the Jews for their bitter fate. Others lamented the ignorance or barbarity of Ysabel and Fernando. Still others accused the religion of Jesus itself, claiming its founder had been misguided, even though most knew little or nothing about Christianity or its Church. "I should hope you're wrong," observed Isaac Azoulay in a quiet but commanding voice. "How can Christianity, or, for that matter, Islam, be evil, if they grew out of Judaism? Can evil grow out of good?" Isaac's comment engendered even feistier debate. Poisonous mushrooms sprouted from the most generous, fertile soils.

"The coming of our beloved Messiah is, at long last, at hand," sighed a young student.

"We all want a savior," Judith observed from the women's balcony. "Everyone's waiting for that perfect person to rescue us. But so far, our Messiah hasn't come, and all we have is each other."

Below her, in the men's section, Isaac Azoulay looked up at her.

The rabbi asked that this discussion be put aside so that the religious service could resume.

They would all comply with the monarchs' orders, Judith reflected while mumbling the Hebrew words of the liturgy. Their faith taught them to honor the local powers, wherever they resided. Despite their reputation for cunning, industry, wealth, swaggering self-promotion, and exercising a disproportionate influence over important events, the Jews possessed very little power, virtually none.

As she pondered not only her own fate, but also that of all the doctors, scholars, merchants, and traders who would be lost to this land, she could not help feeling pity and, indeed, hatred for its misguided sovereigns. She wondered how Luis de Santángel could serve such monarchs. Once again, she realized, she had chosen the wrong man.

The rabbi recited the *Amidah,* a poem of pious supplication:

Blessed are you, O Lord, who gathers together the dispersed of his people Israel . . . May your compassion be stirred, O Lord our God, toward the righteous, the pious, the elders of your people, the house of Israel, the remnant of their scholars . . .

After the rabbi concluded this prayer, and despite his own warning, he allowed his outrage to overtake him. "Let there be a curse upon this land. For five hundred years, let no Jew dwell here, even if the Christians beg us to return. Amen."

The congregation echoed a heartfelt "amen" and resumed chanting the liturgical texts.

. . .

Brother Donato showed a visitor into Santángel's room, a man in a Dominican habit who gazed at the ground from under an oversized hood. The chancellor had been expecting Torquemada to pay him a visit, but the face that looked into his was not the inquisitor's.

"Señor Colón." Santángel sat up on his blanket.

Colón sat on the floor near Santángel. "The monks at La Rábida are quite excited. They're expecting a generous gift."

"And they will receive it. How is your son faring?"

"Better than any of us." Colón glanced around, taking in the room's barrenness and decency. When his eyes returned to Santángel's, the chancellor saw something in them he had never seen before: pity.

"Have you met again with the queen?"

"I'm still waiting."

Santángel looked out the window. The branches of the pine and olive trees were bending in a strong wind, signifying an approaching storm. "What other news?"

"The king and queen have issued an edict. All the Jews, in all their domains, must leave."

Outside a powerful gust flexed the poplars, then released them like an archer his bow. Santángel rose and walked to the window. "You've seen this edict yourself?"

"It is generally known." The captain joined him at the window.

"If you can find a way to speak with her—the silversmith. Explain what has happened. Tell her how very sorry I am."

"I shall, Chancellor."

"And when you speak with Judith, ask where she intends to go, how she intends to get there. Offer, perhaps, to take her with you. She may have no other options."

"Chancellor, I can't have a woman on board, a beautiful woman like that. She'd be raped by the sailors."

"Her nephew, then, Levi. Perhaps you can find a use for him."

Brother Donato entered and stood near the door, his hands joined behind his back.

"Before you go," the chancellor added to Colón, "I want to show you something."

He opened his cumbersome Bible to Isaiah 33, and translated from the Latin:

> *Your eyes shall behold the land that is far.*
> *Your heart shall meditate terror . . .*
> *You shall not see a fierce people,*
> *A people of a deeper speech than you can perceive—*

Of a stammering tongue, that you cannot understand.
The people that dwell therein shall be forgiven their iniquity.

"It is clear as day," Colón whispered, awed. "Is it not?" He studied the Latin awhile longer, then turned back to Santángel, his eyes glistening. "Can he read the holy tongue? Can he translate it?"

"Who?"

"The boy. The nephew of our silversmith."

"I've heard him pray in Hebrew. He also speaks Arabic. And Spanish."

"Perhaps, then, he can help me."

Santángel turned to the monk. "Brother Donato, may we have another moment?"

With a courteous nod, the monk stepped out.

Santángel lowered his voice. "Please get word to King Fernando."

"And what word would that be?" inquired Colón.

"Two words, actually. *Aquae serpentis.*"

. . .

In the Jewish quarter of Granada the wealthy rapidly discovered that all their possessions amounted to nothing. That was precisely how much silver or gold they would be permitted to take abroad. Creditors, having no other choice, forgave their debtors. The wronged, in many cases, forgave those who had harmed them. Neighbors who previously had little to say to one another now could not stop talking.

Dina Benatar invited Judith for tea. "I saw Sara. The Sultan, in Fez, offered the vizier a great house there. She seemed happy enough."

Judith smiled wistfully. "And you? Where are you going?"

"We want to be near her."

After a few sips, Judith put down her cup.

"Are you feeling well, Judith? You look pale."

"Just a bit queasy."

"Why don't you talk to Isaac Azoulay?"

"I don't need to."

Dina looked at her, puzzled.

"Dina, I may be . . . I believe I am . . ."

Dina's eyes went to Judith's hand on her belly. Judith nodded.

"How did this happen?"

Judith told her friend how the chancellor of Aragon had come into her life, saved her business, called on her a second time in Granada, and never returned.

"And now?" asked Dina.

"I curse the day I met him."

Dina poured herself a second cup. She took some time to absorb the hot beverage along with everything Judith had said. "But if he came back, this chancellor of yours, the two of you would find a way. No?"

"No," said Judith. "That is over." The aching, the anger she still felt, two months after his visit, surprised her.

"You can't bring this child into the world without a father. And you can't leave Granada, and go wherever you go, without a husband."

Judith sipped her tea, her mind and heart far away.

. . .

Another week passed. Another month. Judith packed everything. She and Levi attempted to sell their rugs, tables, and chairs, competing in the public squares for Christians' and Muslims' grudging coins. Of the small profit she made, some she spent on food. Most, she saved to pay for their voyage, even though she had not yet determined where she would go.

On a drizzly late-spring night, she sent Levi on his monthly errand, without any goods to trade, but with a note for Cristóbal Colón. Levi was to entrust this message to Dumitru, but when he arrived at the customary meeting place, he found a man he did not know. The man's thinning hair was drenched. He wore a dark cloak.

"We haven't met, but we have been dealing with each other. I am Cristóbal Colón. There was no need for me to send my courier, since I'm here in Granada."

"We have no silver this time, Señor Colón," said Levi. "We've been busy packing. I'm sure you've heard."

"Yes. Where do you intend to go?"

"We don't yet know. But wherever we land, if you have ships that trade there, perhaps we can resume our dealings."

"I shall no longer be trading in this part of the world."

"Where will you be trading?"

"We intend to set sail, very soon, for regions far more distant. Far more promising. The Indias. Ultimately, Jerusalem."

As water ran down their faces, Levi scrutinized him. "The Indias? Jerusalem?"

"That is what I said. You speak Spanish well."

"Thank you."

"Of course, Arabic is your mother tongue."

"Yes."

"And you read the holy tongue as well. Is that not so?"

"It is. Why?"

"Señor Luis de Santángel asked me to help you."

To this, Levi did not reply. Everyone was gossiping about Judith's belly. Women who passed her on the street whispered to their daughters. In synagogue, men who had once proposed to her wondered aloud who the lucky one was whom she had welcomed into her bed. Prior to services one afternoon, a young man insinuated that Judith was a loose woman. Levi struck him. The rabbi ordered Levi not to attend services for three weeks.

Levi could not bear the isolation. He had questioned his aunt. He had accused her. Finally, Judith had admitted that the child she was carrying was the chancellor's. He resented the man who had seduced and abandoned his aunt, the man who had brought her so much pain.

Colón interrupted his thoughts. "I'll need a translator."

"What sort of translator? On your ships?"

"When we reach the Indias, I'll need a man who speaks Arabic. And when we reach Jerusalem—Hebrew."

The offer seemed preposterous. Colón was obliging the chancellor. Both men knew as much.

"What would I do during the crossing?"

"Over the years," said Colón, "I've collected many texts. Some in Hebrew, some in Arabic. Many of them, I'm sure, contain knowledge that could be useful to me. Will you come?"

"I cannot say, just yet," said Levi.

"Of course not." Colón bowed. "It has been a pleasure, doing business with you and your aunt."

The two men took their leave, both wondering whether their partnership had ended, or was just beginning.

CHAPTER TWENTY-FOUR

TOMÁS DE TORQUEMADA had instructed the soldiers and monks detaining Luis de Santángel to treat him with the dignity his station merited, to leave him alone with his conscience as much as possible, to be prepared for unusual situations. None, however, foresaw a visit from the king himself.

He rode up shortly after dawn one morning, unaccompanied, wearing a floppy cap, a laced-up white blouse, velour trousers, and high boots, demanding to be shown to Santángel's room.

"Sir," explained the guard, "this house belongs to the Holy Office. No visitors allowed, except with special permission."

The king dismounted. "Then give me that permission."

"If you'd like to speak with the rector . . . Whom should I announce?"

"Fernando the Fifth, king of Aragon," replied the king. "And if you refuse to show me at once to the penitent's quarters, I shall personally see to it you never forget your impudence." He held out his hand so the guard could have a good look at his gold ring, which bore the royal seal as well as his etched profile. No one else would have the temerity to possess and display such a signet. To do so, except for its legitimate wearer, was a capital crime.

Stunned as much by the king's imperious manner as by this insignia, the guard fell to his knees and begged pardon. "Had I suspected, Your Highness, I would never have questioned you."

"Get up and show me to the chancellor's lodgings."

. . .

As the king entered, he found Santángel standing at his reading table, studying another passage from Isaiah:

For behold, he creates
new heavens and a new world.
Former things shall no more be remembered
nor shall they be called to mind.

Closing the door, Fernando considered drawing his dagger and killing his chancellor, or perhaps strangling him. Santángel closed his Bible and turned to him.

"Your Highness. I've been expecting you."

Although the king had no qualms about murdering an old friend, he preferred to leave that sort of work to others. "Tell me what you know, Santángel, and how you learned it."

"I know how to keep a secret, Your Highness, as I have proven all these many years."

"Where did you learn it?"

"That is a secret, Your Highness."

The king wrung his hands, a gesture Luis de Santángel had only witnessed once or twice before. Fernando hated the chancellor's words, but admired his courage. "Tell me what you want."

"My release," the chancellor stated calmly. "And I'd like to request that the Jews not pay for the supposed sins of *conversos* like me."

"For that, it's too late." King Fernando looked around for a chair, then contented himself with standing eye-to-eye before his chancellor.

"Too late? Allow me to remind you, Your Highness: you are the king. Your word is law."

"Luis, a certain parchment has got my lady all agitated."

"A parchment?"

"The Gospel of the Jews. *Yeshu* something. I've rarely seen her so troubled."

Santángel crossed his arms.

"The Jews have already received their sentence," continued the king. "It can't be reversed. As for your incarceration here, and loss of liberty, I've had nothing to do with any of it. Indeed, I would have prevented it, had I been consulted. But, Luis, I cannot suffer to be threatened."

"Then, Your Majesty, let us pretend none of this happened."

As the sun rose through the clouds in the east, a ray of light shone on the king's weary face. "And why should I, the king of Aragon, take orders from you, a marrano, a moneylender?"

His viciousness hardly surprised the courtier. "This marrano may be languishing in jail, Your Highness, but he's no fool. He's taken precautions to ensure that if anyone were to murder him, the truth would be known."

"The truth," repeated the king.

Santángel nodded, not daring to repeat the words *aquae serpentis*.

The king thought for a moment. Finally, Fernando extended his hand. "I shall talk with Torquemada," he growled. "Consider yourself free. And let me never hear another word of this."

"Sire, you know what my pledge is worth. And you have it."

The king looked at him long and hard. Without another word, he turned to leave. He felt sure Luis de Santángel would not betray him. The chancellor of Aragon knew better than to test him a second time.

. . .

On a Sunday morning dark with rain clouds, the monks returned Luis de Santángel's purse and the unostentatious clothes he had been wearing on the night of his arrest. He hurried out of his rural prison, toward the main route. He came to a fork in the path, above a wide valley. Looking down, he beheld a sight he would never forget.

Along a small, rural road, little more than a horse trail, thousands of Jews trudged toward the port, spilling over its edges into the surrounding fields. Some in this vast, untidy herd were praying, chanting softly to themselves or in small groups. Some talked with their neighbors. Some fed their children or ran after them. Others plodded forward in silence.

Small children babbled and wailed. Mothers breast-fed their babies. Young Talmudists carried satchels of books. Old men leaned over walking sticks, their wives hobbling beside them. Musicians among them plucked and sawed *Tisha B'av* laments, commemorating the destruction of the Second Temple in Jerusalem, on lutes and violas d'amore. Some chanted along.

Throughout Iberia, uncounted multitudes of human souls, many with their mules, proceeded out of their neighborhoods, out of their beloved cities, to the main highways that would lead them south and east to the coasts, west to Portugal, or north to Provence. The roads swarmed with exiles. Young friends and lovers embraced one last time and parted in tears. Homes that had been occupied by one family for uncounted generations now stood empty.

At night, hordes of city-dwellers camped in forests, in empty fields, on the banks of rivers and streams. Smoky bonfires dotted the broad *vegas*. Strangers shared meals. Men from distant regions prayed together, exchanging information about foreign lands and their rulers. Which kings were good to their Jews? Which languages were easiest to learn? How long was the voyage to Greece? Was one likely to encounter pirates?

Late at night, highwaymen picked through travelers' knapsacks. Fights broke out. Men and women died. And here and there, in villages throughout the land, good innkeepers, feeling pity for the exiles, allowed some to spend the night for whatever small change they could spare.

Luis de Santángel descended into the valley to try to lose himself among the emigrating Jews, hoping against all probability for a glimpse of the woman he loved. In humble garb, with the beard he had grown while in detention, he hardly seemed out of place. He listened to their voices, their melodies, their determination, their resignation.

"Have you ever seen the ocean?" asked a young woman walking beside an older woman.

"No."

"Neither have I."

"It must be wonderful to behold," said the older woman's husband. "Endless and flat, reflecting the sun like a mirror."

"Where are you going? Do you know?" asked a young Talmudist.

"We'll try to make it to the Holy Land," answered a distinguished-looking man.

"And what of the present rulers of that land?"

"We'll have to get along, won't we?"

The student turned to Santángel and eyed him from head to toe. "And you, sir, from which region do you hail?"

"Zaragoza."

"Zaragoza! It must have been an arduous journey."

"Arduous. Yes."

The student looked at him, nodding to himself as they continued along their path.

. . .

Most of the Jewish quarter's residents had already departed. The chancellor ran to the synagogue, which was open, its window shutters splintered. Peasants pillaged the benches and candleholders, pulled out the rugs, removed the intricately carved doors of the ark that had sheltered the community's Torah scrolls. Santángel watched, dejected, his mind contrasting this spectacle with the image of the synagogue as it had looked on that evening, long before, when he had first set foot there looking for the Jewish silversmith.

When at last he reached Judith's home, he found a carpenter and his family moving in. They had accepted baptism three days before. A special commission, set up by the king and queen to oversee the exodus and the transfer of wealth, had awarded this family Judith's residence. A donkey pulled their cart into the courtyard, and as the carpenter and his son unloaded rugs and brass ornaments, he explained to Santángel that the former occupant had left the previous day for the port.

. . .

Salubaña, the port of Granada, was more than a day's walk distant. By horse, Santángel knew he would arrive there at the same time as Judith, if not before. He purchased a dappled Lusitano, found his way out of the city, and kicked it into a canter.

By the time he reached the port, a light drizzle was falling. The wharves teemed with voyagers, vendors of amulets, priests offering Jews a last chance to choose baptism, thieves, border officers whose impossible task was to inspect every emigrant for contraband materials, including coins. Those suspected of exporting gold or silver were taken to nearby homes, ordered to remove their clothes, inspected head to toe, sometimes raped, occasionally murdered.

Scholars, moneylenders, and barbers who had never seen the sea toted heavy trunks up wobbly gangplanks. Parents called to their children. Cousins clasped their cousins, uncles their nephews, brothers their brothers, bidding each other farewell forever. Through this tangle of human distress, Luis de Santángel wandered like a drunkard searching desperately for his home in the wrong town, losing any hope of finding Judith; increasingly prepared, if he found her, to follow her onto any ship, bound for any destination.

Finally he saw her, wandering alone, some distance away, looking fragile and wet. His heart pounding, he pressed further into the throng. In his haste, he bumped into a large man in a fez and almost fell. Scrambling to his feet, he looked where Judith had been.

When he again caught sight of her, she was standing before a three-masted galleon, seeking shelter from the rain, shivering, rubbing her arms. He quickened his pace, almost running.

As he approached, she seemed to see him, but so briefly he could not be certain. He thought he must have been mistaken, for she turned and walked in the opposite direction. The chancellor called her name, but in the hubbub of shouting mothers and children, authorities trying to maintain some semblance of order, sailors rigging the ships, she did not hear him. He hurried along the docks. When he caught up with her, he gently took her arm.

She stopped and turned. Her eyes traveled down his face to his graying beard, his modest clothes, his hand on her arm.

"Why are you here?" Her voice was low, perplexed, cold. "This is no place for the chancellor of Aragon, a Christian, third generation." She removed his hand.

"I came to see you. At my first opportunity."

"Your first opportunity?" she repeated incredulously.

"Señor Colón didn't speak with you?"

"I sent my nephew. They spoke, but . . ."

"I've been in a jail of sorts." Santángel smiled a little nervously. "Now, I'm out."

She observed his sunken cheeks, the beard he had grown, the note of humility in his pleading half-smile—a humility Judith had never seen in him. "In jail? The powerful chancellor of Aragon?"

"Better to have no power, and some security—or at least, an illusion of security."

"What good is an illusion?" asked the fruit merchant's daughter.

Santángel's thirsty eyes drank in her presence: her black, sopping hair, her eyelashes, her lips, her clothes clinging to her body. Then he noticed it—the firm, well-defined roundness of her belly. She placed a hand on it.

His eyes rose to meet hers. He swallowed. Their regard communicated what their mouths could not. *Their* child. Together, half-deliberately, they had tied a knot.

"I've had time to think," explained Santángel. "I've done a great deal of thinking. Praying. Remembering." He glanced at the slate-gray sea. "I spent hours, calling up every detail." He delicately ran his hand along the rim of her ear, down her cheek, under her jaw. "From the first words I heard you pronounce . . ."

She removed his hand from her face, but held his forearm. "What were they?"

"'Allah alone conquers.' The inscription on those beakers you made for the vizier."

"Yes." She nodded with a nostalgic smile. "Allah alone conquers. Even the most powerful of us, we have little control over our destiny."

"Then our only choice is to embrace that destiny."

"Embrace it? Look around, Chancellor. Look around."

Exiles all around them, some emaciated from long travels, many filthy, tried to board ships, pleaded with sailors, appealed to authorities. As he observed all this despair, Luis de Santángel felt more powerless than ever. His mind reviewed his years in the royal court—the perfidy of some, the loyalty of others, the sacrifices, the battles, the triumphs, the fears, the losses. For what good?

"No, Chancellor. Our only choice," said Judith, "is not to embrace our destiny in this world, but to hope for a better world." Her eyes glided to the galleon behind him.

"Then I shall accompany you into that world."

"And leave everything behind?"

He nodded slowly, his eyes boring into hers, expectant, tender, cautious.

"That is not possible." And there was that sweet smile again. Except that now, Judith was weeping, her eyes pressed closed. He took her head to his shoulder until she swallowed and wiped away her tears. He caressed her shivering arms, her drenched back.

"I wish you well, Chancellor." She tried to pull away, but he held tight. She forced herself out of his grip.

He frowned, uncomprehending. He searched her face.

"I'm glad you came here," she finally offered. "I'll feel better about the memory."

"It needn't be only a memory. Why?"

Behind him, Judith saw someone. She smiled.

Santángel turned to see a distinguished man, with a slight stoop and a close beard, emerge from the crowd.

"Ah, my beloved wife, there you are."

She advanced toward the man. He kissed her forehead and stretched an arm around her shoulders to shelter her from the rain. He looked into her eyes. He observed Santángel. "Are we ready?" he asked Judith gently.

"Yes, Isaac. We are ready." She glanced again at Santángel.

"Please," the chancellor pleaded. "Please . . . contact me. At the court of Aragon. From wherever you should land."

She cast her eyes downward to hide her tears. Holding Judith, the man led her toward the gangplank. As they departed, Judith did not turn around for one last look at Luis de Santángel, but Isaac Azoulay did. Neither man smiled, but they saw in each other a certain mutual understanding, a certain compassion. In that moment, when Luis de Santángel's heart broke as he realized he had lost Judith irrevocably, he found reassurance. This dignified man in blue robes, whoever he was, would make a good father to his child. Judith would not have chosen him otherwise.

He stood on the wharf, the rain blinding him. He watched them ascend to the main deck of the galleon, which reminded him of the *Giustizia* and his trip from Rome with Cristóbal Colón, even if this more modest vessel was battered, its paint chipped and fading, its wet sails sagging.

. . .

Long after the talisman vendors, preachers, and guards went home, he stood there. Two longboats, each manned with ten oarsmen, slowly dragged the overcharged galleon to sea. Santángel searched for Judith in the multitude onboard, but could not recognize individual faces through the curtain of weather. He wondered whether she was peering back toward him.

He reflected that for the first time, sadly, he was without obligations or attachments. His son was gone; his staff dead and dispersed. When he had suggested to Judith that he would leave Spain with her, abandoning everything he possessed and everyone he knew, he had passed beyond a precipice he thought he would never approach. Now he stood on the other side, reflecting upon the ethereal threads that wove human souls together.

How far could those threads be stretched without breaking? Across seas and continents? Across the invisible boundary that separated the living from the dead? Could the waters between him and Judith wash away the empathy they had shared, the sense that in some incomprehensible way, despite their differences, they understood each other's sorrows and dreams? Could the fields and mountains that separated him from Gabriel undo all they had lived through—the bedtime stories, the disagreements, the moments of frivolity? Could death obliterate the tower of memories he and Estefan had built, stone by stone, over the course of their lives?

He asked himself whether he was supposed to feel no responsibility for the child Judith carried; whether this world of impermanence, where the condition of an entire people could be reversed in a moment, was all there was; how he could return to the court of Zaragoza, and life as it had been, after all he had endured.

The ship of exiles vanished into the rain. Sea and sky merged into a solid sheet of gray. The gray darkened. Long after all the ships had sailed away, he remained standing on the shore, watching, steeling himself for his return.

CHAPTER TWENTY-FIVE

A WEEK AFTER JUDITH'S DEPARTURE, the chancellor met Cristóbal Colón at the gates of the Alhambra. His intent was to support the mariner's project of exploration, but he secretly feared he no longer possessed the influence necessary to bring about a royal assent.

"Look," burbled Colón, peering out over the city. "The rains, they're ceasing. The clouds, they're clearing. This day could not be more auspicious, Señor de Santángel. At long last, we're about to witness the fulfillment of my destiny."

"Perhaps," said the chancellor. "But the king and queen don't care about your destiny. What they care about is Christianizing millions of pagan souls. This will justify the massive theft they'll authorize you to undertake on their behalf."

Colón smiled. The courtier's bitterness amused and saddened him.

The two waited more than an hour before meeting with the queen and Hernando de Talavera. The king was attending to other business, visibly keeping his distance from his chancellor.

Cristóbal Colón knelt before Queen Ysabel. He reminded her of her promise to reconsider his project following the conclusion of the war against Granada. She turned to the recently installed archbishop of Granada. "Father Talavera, have you had the opportunity to study Señor Colón's proposal?"

"We have, Your Highness. And we have conferred with several of the greatest minds known to us—Diego de Deza, Rodrigo Maldonado, and others."

Both Santángel and Colón knew of these men. They were luminaries of the ecclesiastical and political world the archbishop inhabited, but not the intellectual equals of the greatest living astronomers and cartographers, Abraham Zacuto, Joseph Vizinho, and Paolo Toscanelli—with all of whom Colón had consulted.

"We commend Señor Colón," continued Talavera, "on his diligent work, assembling bits and pieces from sources as diverse as the pseudo-prophet Esdras, the itinerant merchant Marco Polo, whose writings have largely been discredited, and even certain ancient philosophers. What an exhaustive undertaking this must have been for a self-taught sailor."

Luis de Santángel glanced at Colón. The Genoese refused to show any reaction. He was watching the monk's lips, absorbing his every syllable as attentively as a bloodhound stalking its prey.

"However," the archbishop continued, "all of us, without exception, have found Señor Colón's calculations to be wanting in several respects, the most egregious of which concern his estimation of the circumference of our terrestrial globe. In this matter, we have inherited figures from Eratosthenes, Posidonius, and the Arab El-Ma'mun, who agree on a number several times larger than the one put forth in Señor Colón's proposal."

Colón could no longer contain himself. "Father, if I may, Posidonius, according to Strabo, estimates 180,000 *stadia*—70,000 to the east, in the form of land, and 70,000 to the west, mostly water. Such a distance, it would certainly be navigable."

Queen Ysabel held up her hand. "Please, señor, allow the archbishop to finish."

For the first time, Talavera turned to face the captain. "Strabo, Señor Colón, is wrong. And by the way, 70,000 plus 70,000 do not add up to 180,000."

Colón looked down, pursing his lips.

"But these are mere details." Talavera turned back to the queen. "There is also the matter of Señor Colón's compensation. He wishes to be named Admiral of the Ocean Sea and viceroy of all the islands and mainlands he might discover, titles that would make him and his heirs members of the noble class. He wishes to retain one-tenth of all wealth produced in any such lands—again, for him and his heirs, through all future generations. He makes other requests as well that we deem excessive, to say the least."

The duke of Medina-Celi had encouraged Colón to demand these emoluments. "The more outrageous your request," he had insisted, "the more seriously they'll take you." Now, in the light of Talavera's withering critique, Colón wished he could forfeit them.

The queen looked at Talavera for another moment, as if digesting the full weight of his devastating judgment. She was about to turn to Colón, but he spoke first. Behind her shoulder, through a wide entranceway framed by ornate columns, what he saw took his breath away.

"Your Highness, my lady, please." He pronounced these words in such a mellifluous voice, just the opposite of the tone she expected, that she took notice. Clawing the air, his palm facing upward, he waved her toward him.

"What on earth is the matter, Señor Colón?"

"Come."

The queen glanced at Talavera, then at Luis de Santángel, and rose from her throne. She allowed the sailor to lead her out of the room, to a vantage point where they could see the city of Granada, wet with rain, shining in the bright sunlight, which streamed through holes between the dark clouds.

"Look."

As Santángel and Talavera joined them on this portico, the queen's eyes followed Cristóbal Colón's fingertips all the way to the horizon. Rising out of the earth, far to the east, stretched the brightest, most color-saturated rainbow any of them had ever seen—climbing to the clouds, then falling toward the land, to the west.

"The struggles of our Mother Church, in Rome," Colón muttered. "The war against the Jews. The sign of the covenant."

Of those assembled, only Luis de Santángel understood.

"It is lovely," Queen Ysabel replied in an equally calm, low voice. Something at once ingenuous and manic in this sailor's deportment charmed her. "But the most beautiful rainbow in the world wouldn't prove, as far as we can discern, that the Ocean Sea is smaller than Father Talavera says it is."

"It is time." Cristóbal Colón sighed.

Luis de Santángel, no less moved than his Genoese protégé, finally spoke up. He did not know exactly *why* he spoke up, but he knew it had something to do with the last words Colón had uttered, with paradise, with the fate of the Jews, with the destiny of the world, with the Book he had studied while detained. He felt as if a gaping hole had opened in the walls of his office in the royal palace of Zaragoza. He could see beyond the immediate interests of the king and the queen, beyond even his own life. He appreciated the zealous fantasies of a Colón or an Isaiah. The only hope, if there was any hope at all, lay beyond the known world. Its roots stretched deep into the soil of an ancient faith.

"Your Highness," he began, still looking toward the horizon. "All this talk of distances and titles is academic."

The queen turned to him, puzzled. "What on earth are you trying to say, Señor Santángel?"

"Someone will go there, Your Highness."

"Are we deliberately being obscure?"

He continued looking out over the darkening landscape. "If I were to underwrite Señor Colón's voyage, with all the benefits accruing to the Crowns, would you then consider supporting such an expedition?"

The queen's voice betrayed her astonishment. "If you were, in effect, to pay for it, while offering us all profits?"

The chancellor turned to her. "Yes, my lady."

The queen looked at him. This man could not be the ambitious, skeptical, cautious courtier she had known. He had changed. "Why would any man of sound mind contemplate doing such a thing?"

Santángel turned back to the landscape. The rainbow had vanished. So had the rain. The sun was declining. Dusk was falling on Iberia. On the horizon, far to the west, the land shone in hues of gold-streaked ocher.

"Because it is time, Your Highness," muttered the chancellor of Aragon. "Because it must be."

The Scattering

I. The Ocean Sea

Two MONTHS AFTER the *Niña*, the *Pinta*, and the *Santa María* set forth from the port of Palos, two merciless months into a far-fetched maritime adventure he had never envisioned, Judith's nephew Levi Migdal trudged up to the *Santa María*'s main deck to fill his eyes with the endless, dark waters, to ask questions of God, to seek solace in the vastness of the world beyond himself, his people, his time, his home. The moon shone brighter and colder than any fire, casting a tapering ray of light over the sea, a ribbon of hope floating upon an immeasurable pool of sadness. A weak, salt-infused breeze wafted over the still waters. The ship creaked with a soft lament. Although the *Niña* and the *Pinta* stood upright less than a mile behind, they looked as desolate and spindly as skeletons.

What was the likelihood that, beyond the ever-receding horizon, they would discover the Indias, the Garden of Eden, or Jerusalem? No community of scholars had supported Colón's proposition. No one had ever sailed west to the Indias and come back to tell of it.

Levi felt as if he were standing before, or even within, the murky chasm of death itself. As King Solomon had written long before, "Who knows whether the spirit of man goes upward and the spirit of the beast goes down into the earth?" Like the land to the west, if such a place existed, no one had ever returned from Sheol to report of it. All that was said about the boundary of life and what came after, all that the world's theologians had been trying to prove for centuries, was nothing but futility and a striving after wind.

The Ocean Sea: an immeasurable pool of despair, a reservoir of memories, against which Levi had to struggle every moment in order not to drown. The empty houses of Granada's Jewish quarter, which had once been his world, staring at him like the abandoned corpses of relatives and friends. His aunt's face stained with tears as she held him before leaving for the port, and Fez, with Isaac.

Looking out over the endless expanse of water, reflecting on all the change and death he had witnessed, Levi thought of a Hebrew *piyyut*, a meditation on destiny and death, recited on the most holy days of the year, Rosh Hashana and Yom Kippur.

> *Who shall live and who shall die*
> *Who at the measure of days and who before*
> *Who by fire and who by water*
> *Who by the sword and who by wild beasts*
> *Who shall have rest and who shall go wandering*
> *Who shall be brought low and who shall be raised high.*

As these words flowed through Levi's memory, he heard the clack of a boot against the deck boards and turned to see the ship's captain, Cristóbal Colón, standing at the bow, lean and tall, with shoulder-length gray hair and a striking, bulbous nose, looking older than his forty-two years.

Although Levi was a young man and the only hand on this ship who possessed no seafaring skills, Colón treated him with respect, even admiration. Levi was a friend of the chancellor. He also reminded Colón, in some ways, of himself. Like Levi, Colón had once left behind the familiar world of his childhood for a larger world, for the unknown. Like Levi, Colón spoke several languages and had changed his name to match changed circumstances. Like Levi, he possessed a hard-to-place accent and an even harder-to-place identity. Levi kept his faith hidden from the sailors, but alone with the Genoese captain, he translated Hebrew and Aramaic texts with unmistakable reverence.

The captain approached. "Luis de Torres." He used the Christianized form of Levi's name. The *Santa María* was considered Castilian soil; no overt Jews were permitted on board. "Tell me frankly, are you one of those who say we'll never get there, or are you with me?"

Levi looked into his eyes, reflecting the moonlight. "Didn't you predict we'd reach land weeks ago, Captain?"

"So you are with *them*," sighed the captain.

"I'm no soothsayer. Will we find India? Will we die at sea? I have no idea."

Colón nodded and resumed looking over the moony waters.

"And you," asked Levi. "How can you be so sure about things no one has seen?"

"I never claimed I was," Colón admitted in a tone he usually reserved for confession.

Confused, Levi looked at him, but the Genoese continued staring out over the waters. "In my deepest heart," he continued, "I always harbored doubts. So much so, that the outright rejection of my ideas by nearly everyone, it never surprised me."

"In that case," Levi wondered aloud, "why did you persevere? Why did you insist on meeting the queen? Why, after she rejected your ideas, did you insist on trying again?"

"Because," reflected Colón, "I couldn't tolerate life without this enterprise, this hope, this ambition. Working, eating, sleeping, and then repeating the cycle, with nothing awaiting you at the end but death . . ." He shook his head.

Levi wondered whether the captain was not already making excuses for his impending failure. "It wasn't about finding the Indias?"

"It was never just that."

They both stood silently, looking over the waters, wondering what was to become of them.

II. Fez

AFTER STRUGGLING for so many years to provide for a boy not her son and an old man not her father, after sailing to a city she had not chosen, after marrying a man she had not loved, Judith Azoulay found a serene simplicity in the new life thrust upon her by destiny.

She never received word from Levi, nor did she manage to contact Cristóbal Colón to ask for news, but like almost everyone, she learned about the discovery of vast new realms in the west. She heard that Colón left a colony of sailors there. Every night she prayed that wherever Levi was, he was safe.

The fruit of her union with Luis de Santángel, known to all as her child with Isaac Azoulay, was a fine-featured boy with the pale skin, dark hair, and elegant charisma of his Aragonese father. She named him Zion.

In the capital city of Fez, Isaac Azoulay achieved a level of respect that surpassed even his previous reputation in Granada. The sultan, who knew of him through the former vizier of Granada, allotted Azoulay and his family a comfortable residence in the center of town.

Over time, Judith came to love Isaac Azoulay not only for his erudition and wisdom, but also for his gentleness and patience. He never hinted that Zion was not his own son. From the moment he delivered the child, even before he realized he could not father a child of his own, he loved and thanked God for the boy. Nor did he ask who that gentleman was whom he had seen bidding Judith farewell at the harbor.

III. Zaragoza

LITTLE BY LITTLE, Luis de Santángel repopulated his home and office with servants and subordinates. He never came to enjoy, with them, the bond of trust and courage he had developed with Felipe de Almazón. Only with Iancu did he retain a sense of shared tragedy and bitter survival.

He would never again set eyes upon Judith Migdal or hear her voice. He would never meet their child. He did not even know whether they had survived the voyage across the Middle Sea.

Nor would he ever again set foot in a synagogue. Indeed, there were no longer any synagogues in Castile or Aragon. All the synagogues were reconsecrated as churches. Ysabel and Fernando took

to boasting that they had "unified" almost all of the Iberian peninsula. At what cost? Santángel asked himself.

Unification meant all of Spain was to speak one language and
pray to one God. It meant Luis de Santángel would not be buried
with his grandparents, and their parents, and the parents before
them. It meant that one day, the great-great grandchildren of *conversos* would harbor no doubts about the purity of their identities,
their beliefs, their blood. Unification meant no doubt, no dissent,
no debate. It meant forgetting. It meant obliteration.

It also meant that the class of people who posed questions—
scholars, astronomers, cartographers, secret agnostics—would not
return. The advance of knowledge, especially of knowledge anti-
thetical to the teachings of the Church, had ground to a halt.

Santángel inquired about the conditions surrounding the Jews'
exile. He received terrifying reports of pirate attacks, starvation,
Jews sold into slavery, foreign ports refusing entry to ragged boats
packed with exiles. He heard stories of wealthy Jews reduced to
the condition of beggars. Some realms, however—especially, but
not only, in the Islamic world—had welcomed the Jews with open
arms.

. . .

When Cristóbal Colón returned to European soil after discovering vast realms, he wrote first to the chancellor of Aragon. As the
immense success of the voyage resonated through Spain, copies of
his letter were printed throughout Christendom, bringing fame to
both the sender and the recipient:

> *Chancellor:*
> *Believing you will take pleasure in hearing of the great*
> *success that our Lord has granted me in my voyage, I write*
> *you this letter. Thirty-three days beyond the Canary Islands*
> *I reached the Indies and found very many islands thickly*
> *peopled, of all of which I took possession without resistance for*
> *their Highnesses. The lands are high, and there are many lofty*
> *mountains covered with trees of a thousand kinds, of such great*

*height that they seemed to reach the skies. Some were in bloom,
others bearing fruit. The nightingale was singing. There was
one large town of which I took possession, situated in a locality
well adapted for the working of gold mines and for all kinds of
commerce. To that city I gave the name of Villa de la Navidad,
The City of the Birth, and I fortified it with a fortress, which
by now is surely completed. I have established the greatest
friendship with the king of that country, so much so that he took
pride in calling me his brother, and treating me as such. Our
Redeemer has granted this victory to our illustrious king and
queen and their kingdoms, who will acquire great fame by an
event of such high importance, in which all Christendom ought
to rejoice. Done on board the caravel, off the Canary Islands, on
the fifteenth of February, fourteen hundred and ninety-three.*

> *At your orders,*
> *The Admiral*

When he first read Colón's letter, the chancellor of Aragon laughed aloud, amused by the captain's immediate assumption of the title "Admiral." He strode out of his office, waving the missive, shouting the news to others in the royal palace.

That letter made Luis de Santángel a favorite not only of the king, but also of the queen. Tomás de Torquemada was left with no option but to relax his pursuit of the chancellor. King Fernando again behaved toward Santángel as though nothing had changed. He clapped his old friend on the back and confided to him about salacious trysts. He entrusted him with his most important and confidential business—financial, diplomatic, and political.

. . .

Luis de Santángel died in his sleep on a snowy February night, a mere six years after the discovery of the New World. At the moment of his departure, he dreamed he was sitting in the courtyard of Judith Migdal's home in Granada, bathed in scents of jasmine, listening to the splashing of a small fountain, waiting for something or someone.

Many of the most influential men in Aragon and Castile attended his funeral. The celebrated Admiral of the Ocean Sea, Cristóbal Colón, did not restrain his tears. Nor did Luis de la Cerda, the duke of Medina-Celi, standing beside him. But no one bothered to tell Santángel's closest living relative, the pious Brother Gabriel, who dwelled in the new Dominican monastery in Avila, of his father's passing.

THE IDEA FOR *By Fire, By Water* came to me several years ago, when I began to think (as have many others) about the connections between four simultaneous, world-changing events: the establishment of the New Inquisition in Castile and Aragon, the reconquest of Granada, the expulsion of all Jews from Spain, and Cristóbal Colón's so-called discovery of the Western Hemisphere. Taken together, these events amounted to a cataclysm, foreshadowing the collapse of the medieval economic, governmental, and religious systems and the birth of the modern nation-state.

My focus eventually narrowed to the man who stood at the center of it all, Luis de Santángel. Caught between competing faiths, social classes, and loyalties, Santángel seemed to me a prototype of modern man. The character I developed is in some respects an amalgam of several *conversos* close to the king and queen. I have blended into my story elements from the lives of Gabriel Sánchez, royal treasurer of Aragon; Abraham Seneor, tax-farmer-in-chief of Castile; and others. These men faced similar challenges.

Within the scholarly community, a debate rages: Are we to trust the inquisitors' accounts regarding the extent of covert judaizing in King Fernando's court? Some argue that the Inquisition, for political and economic reasons, exaggerated the "problem." However, there is a significant body of evidence, physical and cultural, that covert judaizing did persist in the *converso* population—and continues to do so, here and there, to this day. Defenders of the Inquisition see this as a justification for its methods. The prevailing sentiment in the worldwide Jewish community, however, is one of pride in the fact that so many marranos found meaning in their secret faith, despite enormous risks.

The basic facts of my novel are historically accurate. However, in many ways, I have massaged the facts to fit my dramatic purpose.

- Luis de Santángel's title was "*escribano de ración.*" The iconoclastic historian of medieval Jewish history Norman Roth translates this as "Comptroller of the Treasury." Based on Santángel's function and responsibilities, the historian Cecil Roth refers to him as "Chancellor and Comptroller of the Royal Household."
- The first Inquisitor of Aragon, Pedro de Arbués, was assassinated on September 17, 1485, in prayer at La Seo Cathedral. The assassination was blamed on a cabal of New Christians, including Santángel.
- Luis de Santángel's family was decimated by the Inquisition. King Fernando intervened to preserve Santángel's life. Santángel's son, however, was forced to wear the sanbenito, the smock of shame, and his cousin, also named Luis, was burned at the stake.
- Cristóbal Colón lived for a time with Luis de la Cerda, the duke of Medina-Celi, who was a business associate of Santángel. Various details regarding Colón's relationship with the king and queen have been omitted or simplified. Colón's dramatic final appeal actually took place in Santa Fé, outside Granada.
- Santángel encouraged the queen to sponsor Colón's first voyage and arranged the financing of that voyage, which involved borrowing 1,140,000 maravedis from a variety of sources. Colón's discoveries, of course, ultimately made Spain the wealthiest country in the world.
- The only non-sailor aboard Colón's ships was named Luis de Torres (a literal translation into Spanish of the Hebrew name Levi Migdal). Colón refers to Luis de Torres in his diaries as a Jew, with no discernible animosity. It is known that Luis de Torres (who lived in Murcia, north of Granada, immediately

prior to Columbus's departure) hastily converted to Christianity in order to sail with Colón. His official function aboard Colón's ships was "translator." Along with thirty-eight other sailors, he chose to stay behind in the New World rather than return to Spain. When Colón went back a year later, all the settlers had either fled or died.

- Ysabel and Fernando's war against the kingdom of Granada did take place much as described, though it has been simplified here.

- I invented the *aquae serpentis* subplot, but it does have some basis in history. While Ysabel and Fernando were perhaps blessed in their military career, they were severely disappointed in their progeny. Prince Juan died shortly after marrying Princess Margaret of Austria. Princess Ysabel married Prince Manuel of Portugal, then died in childbirth. Princess Catalina became the first wife of Henry VIII, who eventually divorced her and separated her from their daughter. After Queen Ysabel died, her titles passed on to Juana, who was pronounced mad. The king continued to rule over Castile as her regent.

- I have conflated two popes, Sixtus IV and Innocent VIII. The attitudes of these two popes toward the New Inquisition were neither simple nor consistent. However, it is clear that Rome perceived the New Inquisition as a threat, and that despite their "Catholic Kings" sobriquet, the Crowns of Aragon and Castile well understood how to treat the papacy with contempt.

- Hernando de Talavera and Tomás de Torquemada did hold many of the positions and views attributed to them in this novel. Some thirteen years after the events related in this book, Hernando de Talavera, then archbishop of Granada, was himself tried by the Inquisition.

Regarding the motives of the sovereigns and their associates, historians disagree. Some consider the queen or the king, or both, to have been religious fanatics. Others identify primarily financial reasons for the Inquisition and the expulsion of the Jews. For further insight, I refer the reader to the historical works of Henry Charles

Lea, Cecil Roth, Henry Kamen, and Benzion Netanyahu. For a stimulating, recent overview of the history of Jewish–Catholic relations, I would recommend James Carroll's *Constantine's Sword*. For information on Nasrid Granada, I largely relied upon Rachel Arie's extraordinary and exhaustive *L'espagne musulmane au temps des nasrides*. I have borrowed ideas from all these writers and others, and melted them—sometimes, perhaps, beyond recognition—in the crucible of dramatic narrative.

As for the Hebrew manuscript that lies at the center of my story, the *Toledoth Yeshu*, the following can be said: No one knows when the *Toledoth Yeshu* was written. Fragments of it have been discovered in several ancient *genizahs* (storerooms for damaged texts), and the Church Fathers refer to it as early as the second century. It is true that Colón took a great interest in acquiring—sometimes, perhaps, by dubious means—the works of Jewish (and other) prophecy, apocryphal or not, and in their interpretation. However, there is no evidence that Colón ever possessed this particular text.

The purpose of a historical novel is to locate and reveal the dramatic core of history. While writing *By Fire, By Water* I felt much like a sculptor searching for the statue—the drama, the gist—within the dappled, streaked, sometimes impenetrable marble of chronological events.

MITCHELL JAMES KAPLAN
Mt. Lebanon, Pennsylvania, Columbus Day 2009

ACKNOWLEDGMENTS

FIRST-TIME NOVELISTS constantly hear the refrain, "It's not like it used to be in the days of Max Perkins. Don't expect much from editors."

In my wildest dreams, I could never have imagined receiving the quality of assistance that my publisher, Judith Gurewich, and editor, Katie Henderson, have provided. In discovering my unagented manuscript among so many submissions, in recognizing both its potential and its weaknesses, and in knowing how to address both, Judith Gurewich gave ample proof of her idealism and courage. Katie Henderson deeply and thoroughly understood my intent and provided additional, and no less brilliant, guidance. To them I will be forever indebted, as they taught me a great deal.

Mark Kramer's expert assistance in preparing the manuscript for submission is also very much appreciated. Yvonne Cárdenas, production editor at Other Press, provided expert guidance during the copyediting phase. Valerie Sebastyen kindly drafted the map of Spain that appears on pages x–xi.

My wife, Annie, and two children, Ariel and Ezekiel, put up with a great deal of financial and geographical dislocation over the course of six years so that I could research, write, and rewrite this book. They were patient, encouraging, and endlessly supportive. Annie was far more than my sounding board. At crucial points, she provided insights into my characters' minds and emotions as well as essential research and a limitless passion for getting things right. Without her help, this book would be very different, and far less good.

To all of the above, and to my friends, parents, and relatives who read the manuscript at various times and provided encouragement and help, including Jack Mackey, Chris and Carol Klatman, George and Anna Ganzberg, John Briley, Marc Kramer, Herb Schnall, Susan and Joseph Balistocky, Bob Michel, David Waag, and David McCollum, my heartfelt thanks.